BEDELTH THE ORANGE

BOOK 5 OF THE DRAGONWALL SERIES

MELISSA MITCHELL

To anyone who has felt the sting of conditional love. You are worthy. You deserve all the love no matter the circumstances.

DRAGONWALL
Shadowkeep
Belnesse
Dragonfire Sea
Eagle Lake
Mistport
Redport
Squall's End
Three Horned Man
Scattered Islands
Kastali Dun
Bay of Bandu

Kengr Gate
Northedge
The Gable
Forest
Kaljah
Lincastle
South Sea

PROLOGUE

Kastali Dun

Isabella turned in place, taking in the circular room. Vigilance...*Eymar*...had insisted that an entire tower be used as the royal family's private lodgings. *Royal family*. She took a moment to consider those words. The thought of a family both thrilled and terrified her.

She was well aware of what she'd done. Her final visit with the king tree had confirmed it. In creating the drengr to her own specifications, she'd unknowingly cursed her own future.

The fates loved irony. She had no idea she would be tied to Vigilance when she'd blessed him. No idea they'd be mates. But here she was, days from their bonding ceremony.

If the king tree was to believed—which it was—she would have a daughter some day, but only one, because of the stipulations she'd placed upon the magic that had blessed dragons with humanity.

"Do you like it, Isa?" Eymar's voice held a tentative quality, as if nervous to hear what she thought.

She tensed at the feel of his presence behind her. He must have snuck in without her noticing, or more likely, she'd been absorbed too deeply in her own thoughts.

Isa...not Isabella. No one had ever dared use a nickname on her. She'd already corrected him several times and yet, he did it anyway. She wanted to hate it, but the bond buzzing between them made things like that *endearing*.

"It's perfect," she said, eyes blurring. She clenched her teeth, angry that even her own body rebelled against her. She hadn't chosen this. Hadn't asked to be mated to a drengr, forced to leave her people, forced to mate outside her own race.

She wanted to hate him for it. Oh, how she wanted to hate this male who had declared himself *King of Dragonwall*. But that was another facet of the bond. It gave her all these...feelings. It garnered her control, took it right from her grasp.

She wanted him. She *desired* him. She craved him.

Blinking, she pushed those thoughts from her mind and looked around. This room was entirely for her own, personal use. It was a sitting room, finely decorated, with a roaring fireplace, plush sofas, rugs, and glass doors that glittered along one side, sliding open to reveal a covered terrace balcony to permit the sea breeze.

Eymar had the room decorated in hues of green, as if he'd known how much she would miss the forest. The gesture was thoughtful. Considerate. The kind of thing a mate would do.

He came up behind her. His hands found her shoulders, palms wide and warm. He squeezed gently then lifted a hand to point. "Through there, you'll find a massive wardrobe for all your gowns and things, a mirror to my own. And on the floors below, there are smaller rooms for your ladies and your queen's guard." She almost snorted. There was no queen's guard. Not anymore. They'd abandoned her as part of her banishment. She was no longer a spriten queen. Her belly knotted. Suddenly, her body felt so very heavy.

She was not entirely abandoned, though. Her handmaidens and dearest friends would go to the ends of the world for her. They remained at her side. She had six. They had chosen to stay with her.

"I will have a look at their quarters," she announced, stepping forward, out of his grasp, and taking the stairs that led her to the level beneath. There were indeed two floors of smaller chambers with beds, armoires, tables, and shelves. Everything one would need for a comfortable living space. Each room was decorated and furnished with care. Eymar had been busy while she'd been away.

He trailed after her, silent, observant.

"This will be sufficient," she said at last, returning to the sitting room that was hers. "It's perfect. You thought of everything."

Eymar came to stand before her, his face full of hope. "You will be happy here, then?"

Her chest squeezed but she pushed her aching sadness away. What choice did she have? There was nowhere else for her, even if she tried to reject the bond simmering between them. Even if she tried to run from it, she could never go home. No...it wasn't home anymore. This. *This* was to be her home now.

"Yes," she managed, her throat clogging with emotion, making words more difficult to form.

He stepped forward, his movements slow, calculated.

How much longer could she avoid him? How much longer could she fight the burning attraction simmering between them. How much longer could she keep herself from touching him?

He had been respectful. She'd gone where she pleased, wandered Dragonwall for a time while he poured all his efforts into erecting the greatest city the kingdom had ever seen—or would ever see. She had helped, when she deigned to stay long enough for it, using her magic to pair with his, to construct the great keep that was to be her new home.

He hadn't liked her prolonged absences, though he kept silent about it. He'd been little more than a youth when they first met. Would he always see her as the wiser of them?

Things had changed after he'd become a drengr. He'd been thrust into a role that matured him to near unrecognizable. When they'd met again, all those years ago on the rocky outcropping, when he'd told her what she was to him, what they were to create together, he'd already been different. And now, he was changed again.

The years had caught up with her, too. The time spent away from the forest. The bond tugging at her chest. Was it as painful for him as it was for her?

"Isabella," he whispered. Raw emotion crossed his features, his face turning dark with hunger and desperation. For her—always for her. But it was different from the looks of awe he used to give her, when they'd met all those years ago. When he'd first become human. This was deeper. More desperate. Unstoppable.

"I don't know," she managed, an answer to so many questions he'd posed in that single utterance of her name. She didn't know if she could be what he needed—his mate. She didn't know if she could be Dragonwall's queen, a queen of the race she abhorred, the race she'd tried to sneakily destroy over time. She didn't know if she could be happy here. She didn't know if she could continue to live in exile. She didn't know a lot of things, it seemed.

He lifted a hand, traced the luminescent marking that fringed her jawbone. She shuttered. Fire leapt beneath her skin. Without realizing it, she took a step closer. Kiss me. Her body screamed the words to him, but she couldn't seem to make her mouth work.

"Eymar," she managed to whisper. She'd gotten better about using his preferred name. His drengr name. He'd been so quick to abandon his wild dragon side. She couldn't blame him, after all, with the bad reputation dragons had made for themselves.

"We don't have to do this, love." Her heart burst with unexpected warmth at the endearment. "If you aren't ready, we can push the date back. We can do away with it entirely. I am not forcing you to live here with me. I am not forcing you to become my mate—"

She lifted onto her toes and captured his mouth, silencing him. A small growl of surprise rose from his chest. His arms came around her, pressing her to him. He returned her kiss, his lips moving over hers, turning hungry. Sometimes she forgot how giant he was, how much he towered over her. Even on her tiptoes the top of her head barely reached his chin.

A tingling ache spread through her, pooling in her core. She kissed him harder, opening her mouth when his tongue swept in and met hers. A raw sound split the silence. Hers? His? She didn't know. Couldn't think. His fingers tangled into her hair, pulling her head back to give him a better angle, his movements possessive. She might have been the power between them, but here in this moment he was the reigning force.

It left her aching for him. Aching to hand him everything. Aching to submit.

His kiss said it all. He wanted that. And...she found herself giving in.

There could be no holding back—not now, not anymore. She needed to make a choice. She was either all in, or she needed to leave. Doing things by halves had never been her way.

As if sensing her inner struggle, he pulled away, keeping ahold of her. They stared at each other, breathing hard. "I will have whatever you are willing to give me," he said, his voice a rumble. It was very uncharacteristic of him.

Dragons were a possessive bunch.

"And if I choose to give you everything?" she asked.

His eyes flared like living flames. "Then I will take it all. In return, I will worship you. I will adore you. I will always respect you. Trust you. Lean on you. Love you to the ends of the earth and beyond."

She inhaled. It was so very different from how things were done in Esterpine. Queens ruled, all others submitted. Even the queens who took willing partners to father children never permitted them power. It was a matriarchy. But what Eymar wanted to build, a drengr monarchy...

She swallowed.

"Will you be mine?" he whispered against her lips. "I so very desperately wish to be yours."

Everything in her broke apart. She kissed him again, even deeper this time. "What if I cannot do it?" she said at last, voicing her deepest fear. "What if your people reject me? What if I cannot change what I am? What if I cannot lead beside you, as your queen? What if—"

"Isabella," he said, silencing her with another kiss. "We would be mated. We would be one. Your doubts, your fears, while they are understandable, valid even, they are not something you must bear alone. I will be here. I will always be here."

She inhaled and nodded, letting this small show of weakness, of vulnerability, out in the open.

His hands cupped her face. "I thought you were the most beautiful creature in all the world, that day I beheld you. But you have become something so much more dear to me. I..." His throat bobbed. Something flashed over his expression. She saw then, just for a brief moment, the doubts he carried. "I cannot do this without you," he said at last.

Her eyes darted between his. "I am yours," she said at last, giving him the answer he sought. "Yours completely. And you are mine. We will do this together. We will rule together."

His eyes widened before he pressed his forehead against hers. She felt the heavy sigh that left him, scented the smoke on his breath. For all that he appeared human, there would always be traces that never allowed her to forget what he truly was. But she suspected that once they were mated, even those signs wouldn't bother her anymore.

A tiny, nagging feeling clawed at the back of her mind. She didn't tell him what she'd spoken of with the tree. Didn't tell him of the price she was yet to pay. What was the point? She hadn't a clue what it might be. The time would come when she'd have to say something, but now was not that time.

She brushed her cheek against his, then kissed him again. Her mate. Her future.

Isabella smoothed her hands over the glittering skirts of her gown. It was...obscene, the amount of fabric her handmaidens had insisted she use. It covered nearly every inch of skin. Hardly any of her markings could be seen, as if she were trying to hide who she was—what she was.

"Luth utah aahm luine bei eusil, Ayas Drollaya," Amellee said. *It is what your people will expect.*

She'd gone from ruling an old, proud race, to ruling a people who lived and died in the blink of an eye. Humans were unrefined, unsophisticated, messy, careless. Her lips pressed together.

For a brief moment, her gut tightened into a hard knot. So, this was to be it, then? Her life?

No, she couldn't think like that. She was to be their monarch now. She needed to love them as if they were her children. Instead of seeing the bad, she needed to see the good.

She pushed her pride from her mind. She wasn't just doing this for Dragonwall, she was doing it for Eymar.

"Mi stenn haan nih lit cenvor luth gaanih sin glaha," she complained, failing to hide the whiny tone of her voice. *I still don't see why it cannot be green.*

She wouldn't dare whine like this before anyone but her handmaidens. They were like sisters. Closer, even. She loved them. They'd seen her at her best and her worst, and she'd seen them.

"*Ayas Drollaya,*" Elisyana teased, fussing with her hair. "You complain...much," she said, attempting to speak the common tongue. They'd never had a need before now. Only a fraction of the sprites in her kingdom bothered to learn it.

No, not her kingdom anymore.

Her chest hurt. She pushed the sensation away. She couldn't let herself think of it, of her exile. It was too devastating. Too *humiliating.*

She'd believed her handmaidens would want nothing to do with her once she told them. That they'd see her as a disgrace. But they'd stuck with her.

Her fate was to be theirs, they'd declared, so she'd built a small shrine so that they could continue to honor the king tree in their own way, even if she had no desire to do so.

"But why must it be the color of his scales?" she muttered in Ednuar, still caught up on the color of her gown. It was stunning, truly stunning. The deep blue color of the base layer was covered in a layer of thin crepe fabric, which was covered in shades of dark blue glass beads and crystals. It glittered like dragon scales when it caught the light.

"There was no rule for it, Your Majesty," Amellee explained in *Ednuar*. "But it was suggested, as a way to show you have submitted to your new...mate. That you are willing to forsake your people, to unite with him. United as one."

Again that pang, that tightness in her chest, blossomed. She rubbed a hand over her breast. Elisyana finished with her hair, stepping back. "Is everything...good, Your...Drollaya?"

"Majesty," she corrected, helping Elisyana remember the word.

"Majesty," Elisyana said. Several other handmaidens who stood about also repeated the word. They were all hoping to learn, to fit in.

"It's fine," she answered in the common tongue. "It will all be fine."

An entire ceremony had been planned to celebrate their mate bond. All Eymar's idea, of course. Had it been her choice, she'd have simply sealed the bond. But he felt it important that they set the example.

Ever since King Eymar's new race had discovered the existence of mate bonds with humans, they'd begun to adapt to various behaviors and traditions. Holding a ceremony to honor the bond was becoming common practice, though not every drengr bothered with it. But Eymar thought it might be nice if it was lifted above all else, "Like the humans and their marriage ceremonies," he'd explained.

She had kept from rolling her eyes, humoring his wishes. Now she almost wished she hadn't. She'd be a spectacle. Hundreds would fill the new throne room and she'd be scrutinized, whispered about, as she walked down the central aisle towards the dais where the ceremony would happen.

It was even Eymar's idea to exchange gifts, to speak special words that had been written by a royal bard for the occasion. It was all so...unnecessary.

But, perhaps she only felt that way because these weren't her customs. If they'd been sprite customs, she would never turn her nose up. She needed to remember that. Needed to remember that she was to be Dragonwall's queen now. That meant new customs, new traditions, a new frame of mind, a new way of thinking.

As she made her way from her dressing parlor in the king's tower—another ridiculous notion she scorned, calling the tower for the king instead of both rulers—she could only think about her deepest misgivings. How was she going to survive this new way of life? How was she ever going to be the kind of queen they wanted? The kind of queen she knew was so very different from the one she had always been?

She would simply have to step into the unknown and see what happened. Her time was up. All she could do now was hope for the best.

CHAPTER 1

HEAVY QUESTIONS

Celenore

Claire looked down upon the camp below, unable to make out more than the barest details in the darkness: shadows of white tents with ant-sized bodies and supply wagons. Very few braziers burned. Cook fires were kept to a minimum, all in the hopes of going unnoticed.

They were a mere two days from enacting their plan, ridding the world of wild dragons once and for all. Months of preparations had culminated into a short string of events that could go so, *so* wrong. Everything would be ruined if Kane's dragons spotted them. With each passing day, the pressure mounted. It felt like the lid on the kettle was about to burst free.

King Talon's massive body banked. His right wing pointed towards the ground, sweeping them around and bringing them full circle towards the open field used by the drengr. Her stomach swooped.

They'd made flying a habit since reuniting. With all of Talon's obligations, she got little more than a few minutes with him. Passionate kisses stolen in passing, a few caresses here and there,

11

smoldering looks from across the command tent. This was their way of coming back together.

"*Something is troubling you,*" Talon said, dropping quickly in altitude. "*Would you like to talk about it?*"

"*Would it make a difference?*"

"*It might.*"

She contemplated, then said, "*I don't like what we're about to do. Annihilating an entire race? It feels wrong.*"

While she'd been away, studying spriten magic in the forest, Talon and his inner circle had devised a solution to free Fort Squall. It required poison that would render their dragon enemies power-less, allowing their armies to slaughter them. The dragons would be paralyzed, unable to fight back.

"*Claire, this is war,*" Talon said.

"*I know.*" She tried to disguise her irritation. Of course this was war. She was under no illusions.

"*I did not mean to sound condescending,*" he huffed, a plume of smoke leaving his nostrils.

The ground approached. Talon's body touched down, powerful legs and forearms drumming along at a fast pace before slowing. His claws dug into the field's earth, stopping them entirely. She held still, then exhaled. It was always jarring.

Talon was motionless as she swept over the spires of his mind. There was a profound sadness permeating his thoughts tonight. He hated that his mate would bear witness to the brutal aspects of war. Hated that things weren't easier. But he was also resigned, his mind made up. There would be no changing it.

She let her shoulders drop. Was she truly resigned to hopeless acceptance, left with no choice? Left to accept something that bothered her?

She swung her right leg around and slid down Talon's body, gracefully leaping onto the ground. It was a maneuver she'd perfected. Her contact with Talon broke. He immediately shifted, falling into step beside her as they strode across the field towards camp. Guards nodded to them in passing. Silence fell between them before she said, "What if we give the dragons an ultimatum?"

Talon stopped, taking a gentle hold of her arm, turning her to face him. "Claire, you cannot reason with dragons. They are beasts."

She worried at her lower lip. How could that be true? "Talon..."

"Claire..."

"What about the dragons who forged this kingdom? Vigilance wanted to protect Dragonwall. He wasn't evil."

Talon exhaled, dropping his arms to hang limp at his sides. "I understand what you are saying. It is not the same. These dragons aren't honorable."

"I know that. But, how can we assume they're all bad? This is the last of their race. Once we kill them, all the wild dragons that ever existed will be gone, completely gone—"

"As they should be."

"Talon!"

"Claire!" He was growing agitated. "How will you explain to the families of everyone who lost loved ones that dragons deserve a second chance?"

"I don't... That's not..." She opened and closed her mouth. He was right. Everything had become so very complicated. The people of Dragonwall craved justice. They deserved it. There were monstrous wrongs to right.

"I know that's not what you meant," Talon said, his tone softening, "but that's how our people will see it. Being a ruler is the hardest thing you will ever face. Making decisions like this. Our kingdom comes first. It always will."

She swallowed down the rest of her arguments like stale bread.

These doubts...

Was she failing to be a good ruler? Failing to accept the difficult decisions expected of her? Her stomach dropped straight to her feet, leaving her jittery.

There hadn't been time to prepare. There hadn't been time to learn the role of being queen and what was expected of her. She was already living it. In killing Jade, even though she hadn't wanted to, she was forced into shoes that felt impossible to fill.

Talon hesitated then said, "Come, love. It's getting late and I still need to meet with the dwargs." He placed a hand at the small of her back and nudged her into motion.

Resigned, she meekly allowed him to guide her through camp. Perhaps it was good they weren't yet mated. Her mind was awash with indecision. She wasn't sure she wanted him to hear any of it. She hated this feeling, hated being annoyed with him over this. She refused to believe that all dragons were bad. What if there were dragons in the remaining clan that had felt obligated to act with the majority? What if there were dragons in the clan who hadn't been given a choice? What if this was simply their nature and they couldn't help what they were?

No, that wasn't right either. They weren't rabid animals. They possessed intelligence—a good deal of it. They knew what they were doing, most of them, anyway. All of them? Ugh. Why was she so conflicted?!

You should never feel wrong for trusting your instincts, Cyrus said. *Trust the will of your heart. Your intuition makes you who you are.*

Those words, Cyrus's validation, it felt like she could breathe again.

She and Talon entered the command tent and found it blessedly empty. Talon turned to her, circling her waist with his large hands, pulling her against him. His eyes darted over her face, searching her expression. A frown formed, pulling on some of the scars around his mouth.

"I need to meet with the dwargs," he reiterated, sounding almost reluctant. "But if you need, we can talk about this more?"

"No, it's fine." Talking wouldn't amount to anything, not when his mind was made up. "Will you be out all night? I mean, it's okay, I'm not... I was just wondering." The last thing she wanted was to pressure him, to make him feel obligated to spend time with her. That wasn't at all what she was implying.

"Probably until early morning," he said. "Meetings with the dwargs, then checking on the progress with the armor, ensuring our various wings are ready. Making the rounds—all that. Would you like to join me?"

She should—she knew she should. But she'd been in meetings all day and was utterly exhausted. He must have seen it on her face.

"You don't need to be there, Claire. Get some sleep. I want this to be easy for you. I'm not trying to throw you in the lake before you can swim." He placed a palm over her cheek, running his thumb along her cheekbone. She shuddered, shivers racing down to her toes, heat following.

"Okay," she managed to croak. He had a way of making her forget everything when he looked at her like this, when he *touched* her like this. His hand slid to the back of her neck, wrapping around her, his fingers twisting into the base of her chignon.

An uncontrollable sigh fell from her mouth as his lips molded to hers. His mouth was soft, firm, warm. It roved over hers until she fell into him, all her frustration melting away in an instant. Her lips parted and he swept in, then growled and pulled away, eyes flashing with darkness, with eager want. He followed up with a simple, chaste kiss and stepped away. "Sleep well, love," and then he was gone.

THE FOREST SPREAD out around her, its dim light surrounding her like an old, familiar jacket. A path appeared, not so different from all the other paths she'd once taken, its dirt a sandy brown, bracketed by lush foliage and glowing fauna. She glanced around, then looked down at herself and frowned. "What the...?!"

She was in her nightgown. Why was she in her nightgown?! Had she been sleep-walking from the Crystal Palace? Would Koldis be looking for her?

Come...

A disembodied voice beckoned and her feet moved without her consent. The trees thinned and spread until she saw it. The king tree. She blinked, looking down at herself again.

You carry a troubled mind, Queen. I have witnessed seventeen queens come and go. All of them carried troubles that often felt too great to bear.

She exhaled. Seventeen?

Speak your mind.

"How am I here?" she breathed.

Is that truly your most important question? Amusement colored the tree's words.

"No," she croaked. Far from it. "I don't suppose ruling is as easy as asking you what I should do?"

Perhaps yes. Perhaps no. There was a brief hesitation and then, *I have advised seventeen queens throughout their reign. Only two ever saw fit to completely disregard my advice.*

She snorted. "Is this how things will be? You give me the history of all the other queens?"

Forgive me, but I take pride in the role I've played. Now, ask that which is heaviest.

"Okay..." She swallowed. "What should I do about the dragons?"

*Hmm...*The tree appeared to ponder her question. Time stretched on. It could have been a minute, an hour, more? *What does your heart tell you?* it said at last.

"That it's not right to senselessly kill an entire race? That there might be some worth saving? Maybe? And yet, maybe they're all evil. Maybe my heart is too soft? Too trusting?" She frowned. "Maybe Talon was right. Maybe this is war and I need to accept that some decisions will hurt. But, I can't quite put a finger on it— why I disagree with this. Is it because of the method? Because it's underhanded? Because it's like fighting an unarmed person who sits at a disadvantage? And then—"

She stopped herself.

You have given me many questions, Queen. But I asked for one. The most important.

She opened her mouth, then closed it. This felt like a riddle, one she couldn't fail at. As a newly crowned queen, even if it wasn't a crown she planned to keep, she wanted to succeed. She wanted to be the best queen that she could be.

No, that wasn't quite right either. Deep down, she wanted to be perfect, flawless in her rule. She wanted to prove that despite coming from a human world, despite her meager years of life, she could do this job as well as—or better, even—than those who'd come before her.

"What do I do?" she said at last.

There—that is the question. You have a choice ahead of you. I have lived through the reign of seventeen queens. All of them were given choices. All of them were allowed to choose.

"And some of them didn't always choose correctly," she mused, more to herself than the tree. Queen Isabella, when she played god with the drengr race. And more recently, Queen Jade, when she refused to pass along her mantle well past her time.

"What are my choices?" She asked, lifting her chin.

You may do nothing, let things play out as planned, or you may act.

"And if I act?" she pressed.

Ah. That, then, is a different matter.

She picked at her bottom lip with her teeth. "You once told me that to snuff out an entire race was to eliminate future potential."

Her words elicited a mental snort from the tree before it said, *I believe I worded it more eloquently than that.*

She pressed her lips together to keep from smiling at the tree's sense of humor. "I should try to save them, then? What if most of them aren't worth saving?"

I have found that with most things, the act of making a choice is the only deciding factor needed. There is a place in the Gable Mountains, south of Esterpine, a place once occupied by the Forest Clan. Its hatching grounds are undisturbed. Princess Taylynn knows of it. It would be a place of refuge, a place for a new start. It might be exactly what is needed.

A...what? She opened her mouth to ask for clarity.

Claire...

She blinked and the forest wavered.

Claire! Someone gripped her shoulder. Her heart kicked up, hammering in her chest. She whirled around, looking behind her, but nothing was there. The forest faded. *Claire!*

"Claire!"

She sputtered awake, eyelids fluttering, to find a familiar pair of brown eyes staring down at her. Saffra's face swam in and out of focus. She blinked, adjusting to the dim light of the tent.

Saffra's arm fell away. "There you are, I'm sorry to wake you but..." Saffra bit her bottom lip, indecision written on her face.

"No. No it's... I was having a weird dream. It's okay."

"That's why I'm here, actually. A vision."

Her heart skipped a beat and she scooted across the cot's furs, giving Saffra space to sit. "What did you see?"

Saffra picked at the hem of her tunic, pulling on a loose thread. "I saw the dragons."

"You...the dragons? But is everything okay? The plan?"

"It's all fine." Saffra licked her lips. "What if I made a mistake?"

"What do you mean?"

"I saw... I saw a cave with eggs. Dragon eggs. All different colors. And then I saw the dragons. Claire, there are pregnant mothers among them."

Her stomach dropped uncomfortably. "Babies? Hatchlings?"

"I think so. Some of it was disjointed but what if...what if I've killed them? Babies, Claire. I know in their current state they would grow up to be killing machines. Bloodthirsty beasts. But right now, they're just babies inside of eggs in their mothers' bellies. That blood is on my hands."

"Damn it." She surged to her feet, then began rummaging around in her belongings. "Help me dress."

Saffra didn't argue, helping her slip a gown over her body, the one she'd worn when she first arrived at the battle camp. She then began belting on her weapons. She'd need to look every bit the spriten queen that she was, if this was to work.

"What do you mean to do?" Saffra asked, hesitance clouding her voice.

"I mean to give the dragons an ultimatum."

Saffra took a step back, her warm eyes darting over her, over the cloak she wrapped around her body, the one Taylynn had enchanted.

"But...you can't. If you warn them, our plan could be ruined. I don't want the babies to die, but I also don't think we can afford to fail."

"There isn't much time." Claire stepped forward and took Saffra's hands in hers. Their warm palms melded and she squeezed the woman's fingers, twining them in hers. "Do you trust me?"

Their eyes remained locked. Silence passed before Saffra nodded and said, "I do, Your Majesty, with my life, with all that I am."

Claire's breath stilled in her chest before she exhaled. "Thank you." She dropped Saffra's hands. "I have to go. There isn't a moment to lose."

"But, King Talon? Does he know you're leaving? That you're doing...whatever it is you're about to do?"

She swallowed down the guilty lump in her throat and shook her head. "I don't think he'd allow me to leave. Not that he could stop me. I'd rather have this fight when I return. In the meantime, everything proceeds as planned. If he notices my absence, tell him I will explain when I get back. But *do not* tell him what I'm doing. I'd rather tell him myself." She hesitated and then, "I must go."

Before it was too late.

"But...how?" Saffra stood motionless, a deep furrow marring her brows. "How will you reach the lake before the poisoners do?"

A smile spread across her lips. "Tourmaline, of course. Because I am the queen of the sprites." With that, she left Saffra gaping after her in the tent.

CHAPTER 2
AN ULTIMATUM

Claire stole through the camp, passing within the shadows, unseen. It was the middle of the night. She hadn't slept more than a few hours before Saffra had woken her.

Somewhere near the camp's edge, Talon was meeting with the dwargs. They had only just arrived that morning. He probably wouldn't notice her missing until dawn, perhaps later. Her heart ached when she thought of the pressure he was under.

Her queen's guard was dismissed each night, usually when she went flying with Talon. They would be furious upon discovering her missing. They would simply have to accept that as queen, she would sometimes make decisions they disagreed with.

The paddock housing the unicorns came into view. They were free creatures, the enclosure merely a formality. They could jump the fence and return to the forest if they wanted. It was mostly to keep prying eyes a safe distance away.

Tourmaline offered a quiet snicker and detached from the others when he saw her. All of them had chosen to stay, perhaps because Tourmaline had. "*Queen*," he said by way of greeting, filling her mind with his calm voice. "*Have you need of me?*"

"I need to get to the dragons," she explained. "They're at Lake Plymlet. But I must hurry. Can you take me?"

"*Of course,*" he said. "*I am here to serve, but mostly, I am curious.*"

"Because I'm getting into mischief?"

"*Precisely,*" he concluded.

Holding her staff in one hand, she climbed into the paddock. Tourmaline lowered and she got onto his back, situating herself comfortably, resting her staff across her thighs. For a unicorn like Tourmaline, there were no reins, no saddle. He stood and cantered forward. She frowned and said, "I don't know the way."

"*But I do.*" With that, he vaulted forward, picking up speed before lifting into the air, clearing the barrier with a giant leap. Around them, everything blurred. When she glanced behind her, not a single flame was visible. In a matter of seconds, they were already miles from the camp.

Her stomach lurched. She was doing this! She was *actually* doing this.

A nervous laugh slipped from her lips. It was rather exciting, wasn't it? Doing something she felt strongly about, consequences be damned. She had no intention of giving up the ruse, of spoiling the plot, or risking all the carefully laid plans.

She'd brought nothing with her beyond weapons. Her training had taught her to move through the world singularly. She could grow the food she needed, find water when she thirsted. All those hours in the forest spent wandering, training with Pelwynn, had strengthened her into something *other*.

The darkness pressed in around them, the world nothing more than an indistinguishable blur. One hour slipped into two, and then three, and then four. She was alone with her thoughts. It gave her plenty of time to mull things over.

Wrapping her hand around the spriten staff, she reached out to the king tree and said, "*One thing I don't understand is why you support saving the dragons when you are for the sprites?*"

There was a long silence and then, *"Because I am for all that is good, and just, and fair. I am for Dragonwall."*

Something warm and powerful swelled in her chest. Those words felt so *right*. So many sprite queens of old kept to their forest. Some of them, like Isabella, went further, tried to shift the balance in favor of the sprites. But the king tree had never truly been for the sprites, had it? No, not after all she knew. The king tree was for the world, all the worlds, for balance. There would always be evil, sometimes in the form of people like Kane, and the tree would always be there, a force to fight for balance, to keep evil from spreading, from rooting so deeply it choked out everything else.

That's what the tree meant.

The first vestiges of light pricked the horizon. Tourmaline began to slow. If they passed the operatives who journeyed towards Plymlet lake on foot, she did not know. They'd traveled too far and too fast to see anything.

"Are we here already?" It was a silly question, because a lake stretched before her. She could see its opposite shore. She could also see the dragons swooping about, in every color imaginable. She blinked, not quite prepared for the sight.

"We are, indeed." There was no mistaking the smugness in Tourmaline's tone.

"Wow," she said. "That was fast." Nervous excitement settled over her. She lifted the hood of her cloak, revealing herself, in part.

"All unicorns travel fast," Tourmaline said. *"But I am lord of my race. I travel fastest."*

His statement was drowned out by a bugle, then another, as her presence was announced. Dragons shifted direction midair. Those lounging around the shore took off into the sky, until they swarmed above her. Her throat went dry. She swallowed against the sandpaper feeling of it. "I am queen of the sprites. I will not be afraid," she whispered to herself. Then she let her cloak fall open, revealing her gown and the skin beneath it.

Her hair whipped about her face as a flurry of wings turned the air chaotic. Giant, gem-colored bodies dropped to the ground, forming a tight circle. Warning hisses filled the air. Reptilian tongues flicked out of giant maws, tasting the air, tasting her scent.

Tourmaline did not flinch. He barely moved, save to paw the ground once, then twice, in warning. She admired his bravery.

Tentatively, she opened her mind, winced, then practiced what she'd learned, allowing the storm of dragon voices to wash over her like a wave, to pass through her and break somewhere on the shore behind her. She would not become the rocky outcropping that took the brunt of their conversations. It would break her mind apart.

She'd once suffered from it, from the force of too many voices. When she first came to Dragonwall, discovering her ability to hear other telepathic voices had been a shock. But learning to control that ability had been an entirely different matter. Reyr had worked with her, helped her to close her mind. In time, she'd learned how to handle the voices even with an open mind. It took some effort, but she could do it.

"Who is this—?"

"A female—?"

"A unicorn—?"

"What kind of mischief is this—?"

"Where does she come from—?"

"A Sprite—?"

"Get Wrath—"

"Perhaps the Sprites have come to join us—"

"Where is Wrath—?"

She heard them, and yet, it didn't bother her. Taking a deep breath, she let her eyes traverse the enclosure of their bodies. Then, as loudly as her mind could shout, she made her demand, blasting it through their ranks. *"Where is your leader?! I wish to speak with them?"*

Every voice in her mind fell silent. The world froze. Then it erupted, a hundred voices at once. Heads thrashed. Teeth gnashed the air. A ripple of agitation swept from the inner circle, outwards.

"Silence!" She commanded. Once again, they fell quiet. *"Where*

is your leader?" she repeated, putting a queen's demanding force behind the question.

"I am here," came the response. A male's voice. Bodies parted, forming a channel, and she saw him. A giant red dragon with scales the color of blood. His body reminded her of Verath's, but his movements were less refined. There was something other about him, and she just knew. This was a dragon to fear.

It struck her then. For all the time she'd been around the drengr, seen them in their dragon forms, these were the *true* beasts. It was hard to believe none of them could transform into humans, like their cousins.

The wild dragons parted further and the red beast came to a stop before her. He towered over her, large forearms tipped with lethal talons furrowing the ground where he stepped. His head swung around and then lowered, getting a good look at her with his large, amber eyes. Their eyes were all the same color, she realized, tucking that piece of information away.

"Well, well, well," said the voice, low and syrupy in her mind. Lazy, even. *"What have we here? A sprite queen willing to leave her precious forest?"*

She squared her shoulders, lifting her chin as high as it would go. She did not balk. She did not back down. *"When needs must,"* she answered, ensuring every dragon heard her.

"And what, then, was so necessary to bring you all this way, Your Majesty?" He said her title mockingly. She ignored it, rose above it.

"I have come to treat with you."

A roar of laughter rumbled, vibrating his body, sending tremors through the earth. In response, the laughter was taken up by every dragon present until the ground shook with it. When it abated, he said, *"Have you no idea who I am, Queen? I am Wrath the Red. Wrath of the Bloodied Scale. Wrath of the Old Blood. But lately, I have been Wrath the Victorious. Wrath the Conqueror. I think that is my favorite name. See? See all that I have conquered?"*

She made a point of looking over the dragons gathered around her, made a point of frowning in disgust. *"I see a displaced clan. I see a clan that was punished for the sins of its forefathers. A clan that has been forced to live far from home for far too long. But I also see potential. I see a mighty race that encompasses a huge part of Dragonwall's history. A race that has been manipulated by a delusional sorcerer, one that would use you and discard you at his earliest convenience—"*

"You think we were manipulated? Ignorant queen." She did not appreciate the interruption, but neither would she let him know. *"We chose this bloodshed. Hungered for it. We thrive on it. It is the way of our kind. And here I thought a sprite's memory was long."*

"Is it, though?" She asked. *"The way of your kind? There were other dragons who did not feel the need for bloodshed—"*

"Weak. They were all weak."

"Is that what you tell yourselves? That they were weak? And yet, it was they *who inherited Dragonwall. They who became kings. They who now populate the land and rule, while you scrape and claw your way across the kingdom on false promises."*

Never mind that the drengr were a dying race. That their numbers were decreasing as a result of Isabella's selfish desires. As a result of the one child price she had enacted, and then been cursed with herself. That same curse of loss had come full circle in the form of Claire, who was the long lost descendent of Isabella's daughter, Irelia. Irelia had gone through the gate beneath Kastali Dun's great keep. All of *that* was a problem for another day, one she hoped she could address sooner rather than later.

"Why are you here, Queen?" Wrath asked, getting back to the point.

"Because there has been enough bloodshed in the north. Step out from beneath Kane's hold. Cease your death and destruction at once. The Ice Clan of old felt the need to destroy, and look where it got them. Just because your forefathers set the precedent, doesn't mean you must follow it. There are other ways to exist, or coexist, peacefully."

"Bah! You think to come here in all your queenliness and command us? I well remember what happened the last time our kind treated with the likes of you."

"I am sorry for what Isabella did to the dragon race," she conceded. *"She made many mistakes during her reign. Mistakes that cost her. Mistakes that cost all of us."*

An uncomfortable shifting of bodies rippled through the gathered mass. Several dragons exchanged surprised thoughts, tongues flicking out in confusion. It was unlike a queen to speak badly of her predecessor, or at least, it surprised them that she did. But it was most likely her apology that confused them. What queen openly apologized? This, they struggled to conceive.

"You admit then, to her wrongfulness?" Wrath's smug tone riddled his words.

"I admit that, yes, she was wrong in many ways, but not in every way. Creating the drengr was always a way to bring balance to Dragonwall. But in that, she was underhanded and deceitful."

Wrath fell silent. She held her breath. Her admission must have caught him off guard. He shifted, lifting one strong, muscled forearm, then placing it back onto the dirt. *"Be that as it may, you have wasted your time, Queen. There is no place for us here, and so we must take what is ours. And we will take it, with force. Our foes will pay with blood and flesh."*

"Is that so?"

"We will not submit to the rule of that boy king."

"Is that what this is about? The sprites do not submit to that boy king, as you so eloquently put it. We are a people independent. Your clan would have its own land, be governed by its own rule, as we sprites are."

"And you think to tempt us with such an offer? That you have the authority to offer up a measly spit of land? A mere pittance of what we might have if we do things our way?"

"I believe you should take the offer."

"And if I don't?"

"Then you will all die." Her words fell like a guillotine. *"The least you can do is send your pregnant females away."* An uncomfortable murmur of voices erupted. Good. Her words had left them uneasy. *"Yes, I know you have pregnant females with you. I tell you this now. Cease the bloodshed. Send your pregnant females away. Do not tarnish the young before they have the chance to choose their own path, a choice you should not make for them. If you do not do this, I will ensure that every single one of you is slain, left a bloodied mess on the ground, food for the vultures. Your names will be stricken from history. You will be*

forgotten. You will be nothing." A humming sound filled the air, sending chills over her skin. In her hand, she gripped the spriten queen's staff so tightly, she felt the power of her words turn into something strong and ominous.

A promise.

Foreboding shivers raced through the dragons. They felt it too, felt the power of a sprite queen, the power of the king tree behind her words.

"And what of the rest of us?" Wrath said. *"Do you think that* boy king *will simply let us live after what we've done?"*

At this, she laughed. *"Most of you don't deserve to live, after what you've done. You've destroyed entire settlements, killed countless humans by fire and bloodshed. I do not believe there is any price you can pay to make up for that. Death would be too easy. But neither should you make things worse. There will be a reckoning, believe me. Either on the shores of this lake, or in the days to come. The world will remember you one way, or another, but that is your choice. Save your females and their unborn hatchlings. You have two days, or I will ensure you reap the consequences of your choice."*

An uneasiness eked into the air. Her words had struck a chord. *"And if we decide to leave?"* An unfamiliar, female voice broke into her mind. One of the pregnant females, perhaps? *"What then, Queen? Where then do we go?"*

"Quiet!" hissed Wrath's voice.

Hope burst in her chest. *"If you decide to leave,"* she said to the voice, *"travel south-east, towards the forest. My people will guide you to a safe place, a place given to you, a place once occupied by dragons of old, a place where you can raise your hatchlings when they come."*

"I should kill you now, Queen. I should finish what my forefathers started." Wrath gnashed his teeth, biting at the air.

"Oh?" she said, her voice filled with utter confidence. *"You think that you could? Very well then, I'd like to see you try. Do your worst, Wrath of the Bloodied Scale. Wrath the Conqueror,"* she sneered, exactly like a spriten queen would. *"Conquer me!"*

Wrath's draconic bellow split the air, sending tremors through the earth beneath Tourmaline's hooves. Around him, gem-colored bodies backed up several paces, unnerved. Anger poured off him, a palpable current that seeped through the air like static electricity. She felt it coat her skin. Her taunt didn't go ignored. In the second it took to blink, he opened his maw, took a deep breath and exhaled, engulfing her in a torrent of flame, hot enough to melt rock.

CHAPTER 3
BUILDING TRUST

Celenore

Claire created a protective barrier surrounding her and Tourmaline. It was as easy as breathing. She lifted her staff high, pulling magic from the king tree, an unlimited well of power. The flames bathed her in a fiery glow and she felt the heat of them seeping into her wall of protection, but they did not break through.

Tourmaline pawed the ground. *Dragons and their flexing,* he grumbled. She almost laughed at that. *Almost.*

The flames continued with each dragon, until every last vestige of air left their lungs. A dragon's chest was large, after all, and could hold a great deal. When the fire faded and she remained standing, Wrath said, *"I didn't expect it to work. Begone, Queen. Your welcome here is at an end."*

"I hope you will think about what I've said." This was more for the others, than anything. Just because Wrath was the leader didn't mean they were forced to obey him. If it were a perfect world, they would surrender. Even if they were held accountable, choosing death as punishment for what they'd done, at least they'd die with more honor than they'd lived with. There was no honor in dying

helpless, and that was exactly what would befall them if they stayed. All she could hope was that the pregnant females would leave. And perhaps a few others who weren't like the rest. The hatchlings deserved to be raised by a few of their kind. Perhaps in time, they would turn out different, better.

A path opened behind her and Tourmaline began backing away. She wouldn't risk harming him, so she kept her protective barrier in place as he turned and shot forward, leaving the dragons far, far behind.

"Do you think they will listen?" she asked.

"Have hope, Queen. There is time yet for them to change their minds."

Hope. Yes. Perhaps that was all she had at the moment.

"And if they do?" she wondered. "How will I hold them accountable? Those who decide to forsake the bloodshed of their clan? The king tree said their choice would define them, but Talon was right in that I cannot let them live, when so many have suffered and died by their doing."

"Perhaps the king tree will have an answer for that, as well."

The dawn's rays blanketed the land. If they were lucky, she'd make it back to camp in the early afternoon hours. Her stomach churned. She knew what would come of her actions. Talon would not be happy she'd hidden this from him.

But she'd done what felt right. Her conscience, at least, would be clean. At the end of the day, that was all that mattered.

Hours later, she sensed the camp nearing. She didn't dare open her mind. Mostly because she was acting like a coward. She wasn't ready to hear Talon's angry voice, demanding where she'd gone or what she'd done. That was an answer better given in person.

Sure enough, Tourmaline began to slow. *"We are back, Queen."*

"Thank you, my friend."

He took up a slow trot, giving the guards on duty ample time to spot them. Several near the unicorn paddock shouted news of her return. One of them jumped forward, opening the gate. Tourmaline could have jumped, but they were more graceful and less hurried in their arrival.

Tourmaline pranced right into the paddock.

Keeping her staff firmly in hand, she dismounted. *"You have done well,"* came the distant voice from the king tree. That was all the validation she needed—perhaps all the validation she'd get. She hid her smile and ran her free hand over Tourmaline's sleek coat. "Thank you," she murmured aloud. Tourmaline tossed his head in acknowledgment, then plodded away, leaving her standing.

"Your Majesty," came the authoritative address of a guard nearby. "The king wishes to see you in the command tent."

She inhaled. *Here we go,* she thought to herself. *Any words of advice,* she thought to Cyrus.

There was a beat of silence and then, *You don't need my advice, Claire. Stand your ground. You know your truth. Fate chose you as Talon's mate for many reasons, including your ability to stand firm in what you believe.*

She left the paddock. "I know the way," she told the guard. He swallowed, then nodded. She proceeded at a brisk pace, the guard mere steps behind her. She recognized him as one of the guards that took shifts outside the command tent. Joshua, if she recalled correctly.

"There you are!" Saffra stepped out from an intercepting row of tents. The king's prophetess grabbed her hands again, looking into her eyes. "Well?"

"It is done," she said. "I'd give you the details but..."

"The king is looking for you," Saffra finished for her.

"Desaree and Jocelyn?"

"Attending to their duties."

Claire nodded. "What happened? Will you walk with me?"

Saffra fell into step with her and launched into an explanation of what had happened come dawn when Talon had found her missing. "He was in an uproar," she explained. "Searched the whole camp, but didn't dare let anyone know you'd gone missing."

"Did he ask you what happened?"

"No. You think I want to lie to my king?" Saffra let out a low, humorless laugh. "No, I made myself scarce and avoided his search."

"Well done," she said, chuckling. Avoiding Talon when he wanted to find you was an impressive accomplishment. "On a scale of one to furious, how bad is it?"

"Not terribly bad, I think." Saffra kept her gaze forward as they strode towards the middle of camp. "He doesn't know what you did, exactly—how could he? If I had to bet, his displeasure stems from your disappearance. You left without telling him, took Tourmaline, and kept your mind closed. He couldn't reach you. I think once he realized you were gone, he calmed down and got back to work."

"And you know all this, *how*?"

Her nostrils flared. "Bedelth," she admitted at last.

"Ah. The particular drengr that you keep avoiding."

Saffra clucked. "I'm not avoiding him."

"Right. Don't think I've missed what's going on between you."

"Will you stop?!" Saffra grabbed her arm and rounded on her, eyes flashing, anger lurking. "Just...stop. There's nothing going on between us."

Claire blinked. "Okay. All right. I'm sorry. It's just..." She exhaled. "Never mind. I'll stop."

Saffra's shoulders relaxed. She nodded, dropped her hand, then said, "Forgive me."

"There's nothing to forgive. Don't start treating me like a queen. I wish for you to be my friend first, my subject second. Please don't forget that."

Saffra's lips pressed together but she nodded.

The command tent loomed before them. Her queen's guard stood in formation outside of the tent, probably Talon's doing, so that no one realized she was missing. It was a good ruse.

They shifted, giving her a respectful salute in greeting, their movements coordinated with perfect synchronicity. She let out a relieved breath, glad that not even Feowen stepped forward to question her. Though, she didn't miss the hard set of his jaw, the reproach in his questioning eyes. *"I'll tell you later,"* she mouthed.

He read her lips and nodded. Like the others, he wouldn't dare say a word. None of them would, except, perhaps, Jeanine. Why? Because they were sprites. They were thousands of years older than she. And despite her young age, they knew how to act towards their queen. It was...well, frankly, it was a relief.

"Wish me luck," she said to Saffra.

"You don't need it," Saffra teased. "But I do hope I'll get the full story later."

"You'll be the first I tell," she promised.

Saffra bid her goodbye and melted into the camp, disappearing among the tents. She clutched her staff and glanced down at her gown, smoothing out the wrinkles with her free hand. Setting her jaw, she nodded at Talon's guards then stepped inside.

The murmur of voices ceased, immediately followed by the scrape of chairs as an entire room came to its feet.

She glanced around, letting her eyes adjust to the dim light, a direct contrast to the early afternoon sunshine. Talon's shields were present, including Dallin, who wasn't yet inducted into their ranks. All of them were eyeing her with hard gazes.

Great.

There were also dwargs in attendance, including a few she'd met the day prior. She spotted Byron and Tamara. Tamara offered her a tentative smile.

"We're done for the day." Talon's voice rang out. "Leave us."

Her gaze snapped to him, only to find his eyes glued to her, tracing over her gown, her cloak. He was looking for answers, his face an unreadable stone mask. Her heart gave a heavy thump but she pushed her nerves down.

Everyone quickly filed out, each giving her a respectful bow and greeting. Reyr's eyes flashed with an unspoken question. *Where did you go?* he seemed to say in an accusatory manner, but couldn't, because her mind was closed tight. Her face flushed at all the acknowledgement she was paid as queen. *Will I ever get used to it?* she wondered.

In time you will, came Cyrus's voice, a gentle whisper.

Soon enough, she found herself very much alone with the

hulking form of Dragonwall's king. Talon stalked over to her, his steps heavy, eyes fixed on her face. "Where were you?" he demanded, a hushed calm riddling the whisper of his voice. The quiet demand was made out of worry, even though his expression gave nothing away.

Pulling her shoulders back, standing tall and firm, she said, "I went to treat with the dragons."

Talon's head reared back, composure broken. "You did *what*?!"

"I went to—"

"I heard you the first time," he managed, posture rigid.

She stared at him unapologetically, waiting for him to truly digest her words, to come to terms with what she'd done. His jaw flexed, fists clenching at his sides as he grappled with his anger. It would be confusing for him, she realized. To love her, but be angry with her simultaneously.

His newly budding anger was probably because he believed she'd ruined everything.

So what if she didn't immediately come clean? So what if she didn't immediately divulge the details? It was childish, petty, even, to be upset with him, but she couldn't help it. Emotions were frustrating like that, often uncontrollable.

After how Talon had reacted yesterday, shooting down her misgivings, she was holding a *smidge* of a grudge. But deep down, it was more than that. It was a matter of trust, and she wasn't sure he trusted her. Why *wouldn't* he see her as the girl she'd been months ago, when she'd first come here? Someone to be coddled and protected. Then again, she'd done some reckless things since coming to Dragonwall, making an unbreakable promise ranking highest of all.

"Talon—" she said, keeping her voice calm. A warning, perhaps, or a plea. She wasn't sure.

"How could you undermine me like this?" he growled.

"I did nothing of the sort."

"Then explain." He stepped forward, taking her face in his hands, eyes searching hers. The action—the tenderness despite his anger—caught her off guard. His thumbs stroked over her cheekbones, tilting her face up towards his. Her heart gave several hard thumps. "Help me to understand why you would do something like this, after all that we have worked for? Help me."

She saw it then, the desperation in his gaze. He was trying to understand why she would go against his wishes, go against *him*. Her stomach squirmed uncomfortably.

"I was careful," she said at last, her voice softening. "I would never undermine your rule, Talon. I took precautions. I went to them as the sprite queen. Word hasn't yet reached them about Jade. They didn't know who I was to you, or that your drengr army waits here. I used that to my advantage. I gave them my ultimatum and left. They know nothing of our plans."

"It's your army too, Claire, or are you so quick to forget?"

"I have forgotten nothing," she cried, her emotions getting the better of her. "Believe me, I know exactly what I am, where I stand, the stakes. I am speaking, at this moment, as a sprite queen and nothing else." She reached up for his wrists, wrapping her fingers around them to feel his racing pulse. He hadn't dropped his hands from her face, clutching her. His expression was no longer composed, it was raw and open. "Talon, there were *pregnant females*. Egg-carrying females. *Mothers*. I could not sit back and do nothing. I could not sit back while dragon mothers grew full on poisoned lake water, while they were slaughtered. All those lives snuffed out," she breathed. Her eyes blurred. Tears. She blinked them away, willing, begging, for the icy composure of a queen. Perhaps she'd never have it, never be able to look upon a matter without getting her emotions tied into knots. Perhaps...perhaps she wasn't cut out for this—to be a queen of *any* sort.

"Claire... Love..." Talon's expression softened. His eyes darted between hers. "You're sure? Hatchlings?"

"I'm sure," she said. "We must give them a chance, Talon. *Babies*. Little innocent hatchlings that know nothing of the world. I don't, for a second, believe that dragons are inherently evil. If they were, the drengr monarchy wouldn't exist! And, sure, perhaps they have instincts that make them more dark than light, but they are babies. Gods! I don't even care if they are *evil-little-lake-monster-munchkins*. They're *babies*—"

"All right," he said, his voice low. His thumbs stroked over her cheekbones again, trying to calm her. "All right. I see your point."

She dropped his wrists and placed her hands on his chest, gliding her fingers over his taught muscles. They flexed in response, his eyelids drooping a fraction before he speared her with his gaze. "Tell me exactly what happened."

"Okay," she whispered. She went through every detail, from her initial dreams, to Saffra's vision. She explained how she'd snuck out, the journey through the wilderness upon Tourmaline's back, the sight of the dragons, their leader, Wrath, her conversation with him, and even the way he'd tried to burn her to a crisp.

"And what does Cyrus have to say about this?" Talon arched a brow. "Let me guess, he was encouraging. Did he put you up to this?"

"What do you think?"

"*I think* if he was against it, you would not have gone."

"You're correct in that."

She wouldn't have, but as with most things, she and Cyrus were of one mind. Well, technically, *literally*, they were. A pang of acidic sorrow speared her chest, needling her heart. They would have made the *greatest* friends. She didn't often let herself wonder what it would've been like, coming back with him. Settling into this life with him beside her. A friend for the ages.

But I am your friend, Claire, for the ages.

Talon nodded, oblivious to the emotional turmoil in her mind. "Even still," he was saying, "you should *not* have offered them a safe haven. The pregnant females, yes, but not all of them. As a sprite queen, you would have been upsetting the neutrality agreements in place, stepping in and showing your hand, acting against me. Technically. But..." He trailed off.

"Maybe none of it will matter, in the end," she admitted. "I doubt any but the pregnant females will leave. They seemed pretty dead-set in what they are. But if others do, they will be judged accordingly."

Talon snorted, crossing his arms. "You really think *any* of them are worthy? That even a single one of them deserves to live? Even those mothers did their fair share of burning and slaughtering."

"Well, someone has to raise the babies."

Talon exhaled, finally dropping her face. He began pacing, his arms limp at his sides. "Our cover isn't blown," he said at last, then rubbed the back of his neck. He was calming down, finally.

"I would not have gone, Talon, had I been uncertain," she explained. "They believed I came from the forest, that I was what I claimed to be. I never contradicted them."

He nodded, continuing to pace. "Right."

"Talon..."

He stopped, spun to face her. Her body tensed. She knew, just from his expression alone, what was coming. "What you did, Claire, leaving without telling anyone where you were going, was reckless—"

"No," she held up her hand. "Don't you dare give me the *reckless argument.*"

"You went by yourself! You put yourself in front of a horde of godsdamn wild dragons!"

She inhaled, then spoke with the calmest, coldest voice she could muster. "I am *not* the little girl that left the capital months ago."

He blinked, taken aback by her tone. "No. You're not." His shoulders dropped. At last, he took a deep breath, his barrel sized chest rising, expanding outward, tunic straining. "Sometimes I wish that you were," he admitted.

Her brows knitted together. "Why?"

"I know you are powerful, but it scares me half to death, Claire." He stalked towards her again, his arms going around her waist, pulling her to him. "It scares me *to death*, the thought of losing you. And that fear? I keep projecting it on to you." He lowered his forehead to hers, the gesture wholly intimate. "Damn it. Godsdamn it! I'm so *lost* in you. Out of my mind, lost." He spoke the last as a whisper.

She immediately softened, her heart melting into mush.

"Talon..." Her hands went for his shoulders, wrapping around him, relishing in the feel of his warm skin against her palms before tangling her fingers into the hair at the nape of his neck. "I need you to *trust me*," she whispered. "I know you're scared, but I can't be a good queen if my subjects, if *my mate*, doubts my decisions at every turn."

His nostrils flared and he exhaled. She smelled smoke on his breath, as if despite his human form, the insides of his chest were a raging inferno. "I understand that—understand the feeling all too well. But, Claire, we are a team. We must *lead* as a team. Ruling together means making decisions together. Why didn't you tell me you were doing this?"

Damn it. He was right. Her cheeks washed with heat, with shame and embarrassment.

"Because...because you would have forbidden it."

Up close, with his forehead against hers, she could see his long, dark lashes as he blinked. "I would have *adamantly* advised against it."

"See—?"

"But—" he stopped her, placing a warm finger against her lips. She wanted to lick that finger, but stopped herself, forcing herself to focus. "I would not have forbidden it." His finger fell alway, hand returning to her waist.

Her mouth opened, then closed. She pulled back to look at him. "You...you wouldn't have?"

"Of course not," he cried. "You are the *spriten queen*. Would I have forbidden Queen Jade from acting on her whims and desires, even if I disagreed? Would I have stepped in to stop her? Gotten in her way? Would I have *dared*?"

Her brows drew together. He was right. He wouldn't have. But, wasn't that because Jade was—had been—a powerful queen that no one dared cross? She licked her lips. "And...if I *wasn't* the spriten queen?"

He huffed, his arms tightening around her waist, fingers stroking her back through her gown. "Then our argument would have lasted twice as long, but you would have persuaded me...

eventually. Gods—" he shook his head and snorted, getting a handle on himself. "It wouldn't have taken much. You do realize that, don't you? All you have to do is *kiss me*, Claire, and I'm lost. All you have to do is kiss me, and I'll agree to whatever you want. I'll fall on my godsdamned *knees* for you. Don't you understand, woman? Don't you understand that there isn't anything I wouldn't give you, if you genuinely wanted it?"

"I..." She swallowed against her thick tongue, tears choking her voice. "I guess I probably should have told you, then."

"*Yes*. You really should have. I have an entire kingdom to worry about. Wondering where the hell my mate went distracts me from my work. It shouldn't, but it does, because I care about you. In that, I'm as much at fault as you. I know you can take care of yourself. And this has nothing to do with my trust. I trust you to get yourself out of whatever danger you find yourself in. I might not like it, but I know you're capable. Gods only know you've done it time and again—"

"Except for that time I got kidnapped," she whispered, a small smile tugging at her lips. "And you had to sweep in and rescue me, all *gallant-white-knight-in-shining-armor* sort of thing."

He huffed. "I wasn't wearing armor. I didn't *need* armor for that."

She grinned. "No, you didn't, did you?"

"My point stands. You've gotten yourself out of extreme situations without my help. Kane, the vodar, you name it." His hands slipped down her waist, then hooked around her thighs, hoisting her up until she was forced to wrap her legs around his trim hips, her skirt tangling between them. Heat erupted through her, radiating to the tips of her toes.

He walked them to the nearest chair and sat down with her, holding her close to him. His expression, the love in his gaze mixed with his frustration, made it hard to breathe. But that wasn't the only reason she struggled for air. Everywhere their bodies pressed, her skin hummed, even through the layers of clothes.

"I never expected this to be easy," he mused. "But it will get easier when we are mated."

She sucked in a breath, knowing what he meant. Once their minds were melded, he'd never need to wonder where she was. Never worry that she wasn't off somewhere, elbows deep in trouble, when he might be able to help her. When they'd first come together, she couldn't wait to be mated. Now, she was slightly nervous about it for so, *so* many reasons. Reasons she wasn't sure she had the courage to voice.

He leaned forward and brought their lips together, kissing her, parting her lips to explore her mouth. At last, he pulled away, leaving her head a spinning mess of emotion. "When this is all over, we will return to the keep and plan the ceremony. I cannot wait any longer," he said.

And truthfully, despite how nervous she was, neither could she.

CHAPTER 4

AVOIDING THE TRUTH

Celenore

Saffra wove through camp, attempting to calm her mind. Claire had been successful, though she didn't know the details yet. She could dispense with the growing nausea that plagued her since last night's vision. She wanted the dragons *eradicated*—more so, perhaps, than anyone else. After all, she'd been the first to see what they were capable of. The first to know that they'd come back to Dragonwall. All those months ago— almost a year now—she'd seen them sweep down from the mountains and burn Belnesse to the ground.

The dead couldn't talk. There'd only been one survivor, a man by the name of Mikkin. The rest were slaughtered and charred to a crisp. But she'd seen what their destruction looked like. She'd seen countless deaths, seen the city go up in flames, smelled the sickening scent of charred flesh.

She returned to her tent. It was near the command tent, central to everything. It was nicer than most, but still contained the bare minimum. There were furs and rugs carpeting the ground. A lantern hung from the ceiling in the middle. A crate served as a nightstand and table. There was also a small chest and a single chair beside it. She'd brought very few belongings, now tucked away in the chest with Desaree and Jocelyn's things, as they shared the tent with her.

Currently, they were off seeing to their duties. Desaree had incurred a vast number of responsibilities around camp as punishment for defying the king's wishes, stealing his seal, and forging a letter that would permit them to board a ship and come here. It had been done out of foolishness, Saffra saw that now, but she understood why Desaree had wanted to, understood what it felt like to feel inadequate and useless.

She often felt that way, even though it was silly. As the king's one and only prophetess, she was extremely useful. But the fact that she could do nothing about her visions, other than relay them to someone else, made her feel so helpless. How many times had she seen something, then been forced to watch while everyone else did something about it?

Creating the poison to change the tide of this war, the poison that would allow them to slaughter the dragons, had been the first active thing she'd really done. It felt satisfying in so many ways. Now she wondered if it was the right thing, given her vision. Every action, whether good or bad, had consequences. She gritted her teeth and growled, lashing out, kicking the base of the trunk with her booted foot before plopping down on the chair.

Always so helpless to act against what she saw.

When Cyrus had left before his death, there'd been nothing she could do. When the dragons burned Belnesse? She'd gone to King Talon. He hadn't even believed her at first. When the vodar attacked the keep, at least she'd been able to do *something*. But in the end, she'd still found herself in a helpless situation with Commander Daxton injured beyond repair. She'd been forced to watch as his mind was stolen from him, memories wiped clean. She'd been completely useless.

What good was she, if she couldn't help the ones she loved?

And then there was Bedelth...

No.

No, no, no. She scrubbed her hands over her face, sighing, leaning her elbows on her knees, looking down at the rug beneath her feet. She refused to think about him. Wouldn't even let it cross her mind—

"Saffra? Are you in there?" came a deep voice, as if she'd summoned him.

"Oh, gods," she whispered. Her body went rigid. She surged to her feet, turning towards the tent's entrance. "I do not wish for company," she croaked.

The tent flap opened and Bedelth stuck his head in. He glanced around, then frowned. Bedelth was handsome—gods, he was *so handsome*, with high cheekbones and pointed chin. His rich brown skin was near the same shade of caramel as hers. They'd come from the same territory, after all, in the east. The land of harsh sun and harsher temperatures.

She ignored the heavy weight that settled in her chest. She wanted to hate him for it. "What part of *I do not wish for company* don't you understand, Bedelth?" She immediately regretted the words. Taking a deep breath, she tried and failed to calm her racing heart. It beat faster the longer he stared at her.

At last he stepped in, letting the flap close behind him. In his presence, the tent shrank. It felt small to begin with, but with the hulking form of a drengr—not just any drengr, but a king's shield —there was scarcely room to breathe.

"Saffra..." His eyes searched hers. He didn't chastise her for her snappishness, which made her feel guiltier. "Claire has returned." He waited for her reaction, for which she gave none, so he added, "That was the excuse I used in coming here. Truthfully, I just wanted to see that you were okay."

"Why wouldn't I be?" She crossed her arms.

He let out a loud, resigned breath. "Must you always push me away?"

"I'm not."

"No?" They both knew it was a lie. He ran a hand over his scalp. For as long as she'd known him, he had always kept his hair closely shorn. "Pushing me away is all you do lately. You avoid me. You won't even look at me, unless it's to glare—"

"Fine! What would you have me do?"

He took a step forward, then hesitated. "I would have you *stop fighting it.*"

She scoffed. "As if you don't? Why shouldn't I fight it? Nothing can come of it."

He looked as if he wanted to argue, then said, "You asked me to keep this quiet—no, you *commanded* me to, if I recall—and I have. But I am tired of your punishment. " He lifted his hand and rubbed his chest over his heart, like it ached as much as hers did these days. "I did not *choose* this, Saffra. I did not choose for things to go this way," he said. She tutted, but said nothing. "What happened to us?" he added, forging ahead. "You used to appreciate my company, welcome it, even—"

"That was before," she hissed. "Before I found out what we were—are—whatever."

Before they'd flown together, when he'd taken her to Verath, after Verath had insisted on being the one to trial the poison she'd made. They'd searched frantically for him. After finding him, they'd set up camp until he was well enough to make the journey back to the capital. Bedelth had offered to fly her so that she could be there to take notes about his condition. Everything had changed that day. *Everything.*

"I would have told you, had I known. You know that."

"Right," she huffed. "Except you *did* know. And still, you chose to—"

"I did *not* know!" he all but roared, surging forward, taking her by the shoulders, giving her a little shake, though his hands remained gentle.

She flinched away, afraid to bear his touch. "You *felt* things for me, Bedelth, and you know it. That's how it is with all of you. You feel certain things before you know the truth. Clues. Inclinations. *Things.* You simply chose to keep that to yourself—your feelings, your emotions, all of it."

He made a sound of frustration in the back of his throat. "You would prefer the alternative? Prefer that I had told you? That I admit to having feelings for you, when I knew you were promised to another? When I knew that you loved him? I am not some careless youth, set on selfishly luring someone away from the person they want to be with."

"Of course not. You just sat back," she sputtered. "Sat back and you...and you *let me fall in love with him*." She clutched her stomach, trying to suppress the fresh wave of heartbreak. "You *let* me..."

Maybe if he'd stepped in, told her how he felt, that he felt something for her, she wouldn't have gone and fallen in love with Daxton. Maybe then, she wouldn't have had to bear Daxton's loss, this gut wrenching sadness, knowing that the man she'd spent years loving, didn't even remember a moment of it. Maybe if Bedelth had done *something*, things would have been different.

And yet, she knew that this was unfair. That he was, perhaps, a little to blame, but not entirely. His age made him wiser, certainly. But she couldn't pin everything on him. Knowing that and accepting it were two completely different things. And in her lingering grief, it was far easier to place blame, no matter how undeserved.

"Your life was yours to live, Saffra. I am a *shield*. I told myself that you were better off with him. At the time, my *feelings* for you were not as important as my oath."

"So you just—you let me *go?!*" That hurt, too.

"I didn't know we were mate—!"

"Shut *up!*" she cried, silencing the uproar of his voice, silencing the truth between them. He froze, then pulled his shoulders back, head brushing the top of the tent. "The entire camp will hear you," she snarled, glaring at him.

His throat bobbed and he took a step back. "That's it, then? You want to ignore what we are? Sweep it under the rug?"

She took a deep inhale, closing her eyes. It had been an absolute shock, months ago when she'd discovered it. When everything had changed. The moment she'd touched his scales, her world had fallen apart. It was still falling apart. To say she'd panicked was putting it lightly. But even *he'd* panicked. It took all of two seconds for her to swear him to silence. In his shock, he'd readily given his word, and that was that.

Or...so she'd hoped.

"I'm not ignoring it," she said at last. "I'm choosing to reject it."

"Reject it? *Reject it*, Saffra? That is *not* how this works. You cannot simply reject—"

"We cannot be together!" she cried, her chest heaving. They couldn't! They shouldn't! There were reasons, but the biggest was the most obvious. "You already know this—you said it just a moment ago! Your oath."

His mouth worked, like he wanted to contradict her. Like he wanted to say something. Like he was deciding how best to say it. This was her fault, she realized. When she'd sworn him to silence, she'd also chosen to avoid discussing it. Letting this fester was bound to result in chaos.

"Perhaps this is easier for you, than me," he said at last, his voice a low rumble. "I am a drengr. You are my *mate*. I cannot simply ignore this...this *wanting*. Seeing you and not having you. It's driving me mad." He scrubbed a hand over his face like he could wipe away the feeling. Warmth flooded her chest, followed by more guilt—crippling guilt. Yes, she'd decided to move on from Daxton. Yes, she was putting everything behind her, starting fresh. But those idealistic resolutions were easier said than done, and she hated that she still felt loyal to the love they'd shared.

"Perhaps if I didn't know the truth," Bedelth continued, oblivious to the turmoil in her heart. "Perhaps if your skin had never touched my scales. Perhaps if I could simply *walk away*, never see you again, then I could ignore all of this—reject it as easily as you do. But I cannot do that, can I? I am to see you everywhere. Worse still, you aren't human, which means there will be many long years of suppressing my nature. Many long years of *aching* for you."

Her lips parted.

Aching. He...*ached* for her?

Yes, that's how she felt, too. Was it the bond? Was it...?

No. What did it matter? She squashed her feelings and donned a cloak of anger instead. Anger was easier than pain.

"What are you saying, Bedelth? That you would dishonor your oath? That you would ask the same of me? Dishonor our king by choosing our bond over our duty? Dishonor our kingdom by running away? Fleeing Dragonwall for our own selfish desires?"

She couldn't think about it—couldn't entertain the idea. She wouldn't allow herself to wonder what it would be like, to have him to herself. No, no, no.

"That's not...it would not come to that, Saffra," he managed, his hesitant voice turning hopeful. He licked his lips. "Koldis, he found his mate..."

The tent surged around her. She took a staggering step backwards, ice washing through her veins. "What...*what* did you just say?"

"In the forest with Claire—" Bedelth wrapped his hands around the back of his neck, looked up at the top of the tent, then swore under his breath. "I shouldn't be telling you this. It is not my secret to tell."

Too late for *that*!

She stepped forward. "His *mate*? *Koldis*? But..." A barrage of thoughts stampeded through her mind. "Claire never told me. Does she...does she know?"

"Of course she knows—she knew before the king. She was with Koldis when it happened."

Pain clenched her chest. She tried to ignore the squeezing pressure. Claire was not required to tell her everything. And yet, this hurt.

"She did not tell you because it was not her secret to tell, just as it is not mine."

"But you are telling me anyway!" she snapped.

"Because I am your *mate*, and as such, I do not wish to keep secrets," he whispered loudly. "Because I'm hoping to bring some clarity to this situation."

But she was already beyond the matter of their being mates. Instead, she was stuck on the fact that Claire hadn't said anything.

Bedelth must have felt her turmoil. He groaned. "Gods above. I should not have said anything. Claire and Talon have kept it secret. No one is to know—at least for now. Do not take this as a slight against you, Saffra. Claire did not even tell Talon, she kept it from him."

"She...she did?" Perhaps that made her feel a little better—a lot better, actually.

"She did. She allowed Koldis to reveal the secret on his terms, when he was ready. Our king deserved to hear it from him and no one else."

"Oh..." was all she could say. She moved around his massive body, over to the chair, and sank down onto it. Bedelth was right, it was Koldis's secret to tell. Yet, she couldn't help feeling left out. She took a long, deep breath. Claire was a queen now, and very soon, she'd be *the* queen. Dragonwall's queen. It was time to accept that there would be things as a ruler Claire would be forced to withhold.

"I wish you to be my friend first, subject second," Claire had said earlier. And she hoped it remained true. But Bedelth was right, this had nothing to do with their friendship and everything to do with Claire's loyalty. Claire would do the same for her, keep her secrets and let her be the one to tell them.

Besides, a bigger factor stared her in the face. A glaring one, in fact. She hadn't told Claire about Bedelth. Hadn't said a *word* about discovering her bond with him. She couldn't judge Claire for keeping big secrets when she was keeping the biggest of all. So she dropped it and said, "Who is it? Koldis's mate? Who is it?"

"That is not my secret to tell."

She snorted. "So you'll tell me he has a mate, but not who? She knows what she is to him, then—his mate?"

"She knows."

"Is it another sprite?" But that was a silly question. Of course it was another sprite. How ironic. "Well, isn't that funny?" But no, funny wasn't the right word. It was...*tragic.* Not only did Koldis have his oath, but a sprite and a drengr? In what reality would that possibly work?

"So? He told King Talon, then?" she asked. Bedelth nodded. "And? What did he say?" Bedelth's mouth twitched, no doubt amused by her questions. "Are you going to tell me, or not?"

"He's given his consent."

"His...*what*?" Her voice came out a strangled whisper. "Koldis is being removed as...as his shield? He's abandoning his oath? But... his oath is for life."

"Gods, no." Bedelth huffed. "King Talon wouldn't allow that. He refused, actually. Said that Koldis had to remain his shield. We've had a whole discussion about it, us shields, that is. Talon is rewriting the charter. Says it's outdated anyway, could use sprucing up, to get with the times and all that." He waved a hand.

"But...I don't understand." She opened and closed her hands in her lap, staring at him, struggling to process what this meant, though she was developing a sinking suspicion. After all, why else was he betraying Koldis's trust by telling her, if not to prove a point, to turn the tables?

"It won't be immediate," he explained. "It takes time to change the laws. We are keeping it silent for now. There are more pressing matters."

Like reclaiming the fort, freeing Squall's End from the dragons.

"But..." she said again. "The shields are supposed to serve the king above all else. That's how it's always been, since the founding of the monarchy." It was like the rug had been pulled out from under her. She was stuck in a complicated plot, but all the rules had just changed. Everything was flipped upside down.

"Just because some ancient king—"

"His name was *King Eymar*—"

"I know what his name was, Saffra," he drawled, crossing his arms. His biceps bulged in his tunic. She tore her eyes away from them, looking at his face. "Just because some ancient king did things *his* way doesn't mean we've got to continue doing them that way. It doesn't mean his way was the right way, either. Talon made it very clear that he's plenty capable of protecting himself. That he wouldn't want us to sacrifice our happiness for him."

She snorted. "Of course he said that. Gods, the fool is in love."

It wasn't meant as an insult, and Bedelth didn't take it as such. Instead, he shrugged and said, "With Claire and their future bonding, there's less threat of his bloodline dying out. I'm certain she'll give him a child, in time."

Saffra's mouth dropped open. She snapped it shut. A child? She hadn't even thought that far ahead, but it was valid. If they mated, they would *presumably* try for a child. Warmth flooded her chest at the thought, picturing a little toddler terrorizing the keep, how its existence would send everyone into a flurry of excitement. She'd be an auntie. And the king's shields? They'd be uncles—overprotective uncles at that!

Now she wanted nothing more than to talk to Claire. A fierce burst of longing spread through her. A child!

"Huh," was all she managed to say, mostly struck speechless. It was a lot to consider. A lot to take in. She pulled herself from Claire's future prospects and thought instead about her own. "So then...the oath, us being mates..."

Bedelth shrugged. "I'm not forcing myself upon you, Saffra. I know that you don't want me. I just want to make sure you understand that it's not the oath keeping us apart. Not anymore."

It's you, his words seemed to scream. She didn't allow herself to flinch, but she felt the desire to.

The dejection in his voice made her chest shrivel in on itself. Was it true, then? That she didn't *want* him? She wanted it to be true. Needed it to be, to make things easier. Having the oath certainly simplified the matter, but without it...

"When did all of this happen? How long have you been waiting to tell me this?" she managed at last.

"Two days ago."

"Two days?!" she sputtered. "And you let me...?"

He'd let her go on and on at the start of this conversation, knowing her argument was no longer valid. She surged to her feet. "I'd like you to leave."

Hurt flashed across his face. "Saffra—"

"Leave, *please*," she managed, trying to keep her emotions together.

His shoulders drew back. In that moment, he was every measure the shield. Every measure the proud warrior she knew him to be. "Very well, Lady Saffra. As you wish." With that, he turned on his heel and slipped out of the tent, leaving an oppressive, deafening silence in his wake. Giving into her overwhelming confusion, she collapsed to her knees and burst into tears.

CHAPTER 5
CRAVING UNCONDITIONAL LOVE

Celenore

Bedelth dove towards the stretch of sandy beach, tucking his wings before transforming. Koldis stood some ten steps from the edge of the lapping waves, his hands behind his back, staring out over the water. He didn't turn to face Bedelth as he said, "Still brooding?"

"I don't *brood*."

Koldis gave a suffering sigh. "You're the broodiest godsdamned person I've met—next to Talon, that is."

"And Verath."

"And Verath," Koldis added.

Bedelth mirrored Koldis's stance. The sound of the waves immediately began to calm him, easing the tension strangling his nerves. Koldis was keeping watch.

"Want to talk about it?" Koldis asked.

"Not really."

Koldis paid him a sidelong look. Something in his scrutiny stripped everything away, like his brother could see straight through him. "Something changed while I was gone. Something big."

"Yes, you found your mate. I think we've covered that in great detail," Bedelth snapped.

Koldis's eyes returned to the dark waters. Somewhere across the way was all that remained of Fort Squall. "I was talking about you, Bedelth. *You* changed. Something fundamental—" Bedelth's dismissive snort interrupted Koldis, but the shield ignored it, continuing. "You might think it goes unnoticed, and I am sure those who don't know you as I do, as your brothers do, wouldn't spare it a second thought. The others are merely being too polite to say anything."

"*Or*," Bedelth began, "they are better at minding their own business. Besides, we have more important matters at hand."

"You are important, too. To me, to so many of us."

Something warm spread through Bedelth's chest. He ignored it, pushing it down deep. He was good at that, at controlling his emotions. Ignoring them. Picking logic over the wants and desires of his heart, even if he'd struggled with it lately. His parents had drilled it into him from a young age.

Making *smart* decisions.

At the time, he'd accepted that lesson, taken it at face value. It had cost him more than a hundred years to realize that *smart decisions* merely meant decisions *they* approved of. Now he was two-hundred-and-seventy-nine years old, and despite recognizing this important distinction, he still couldn't seem to break away from the desire to win their approval. Even for the sake of his own happiness.

Silence fell between them, stretching out over a long span. Koldis wasn't one to pry. It's why Bedelth sought his company above the others. Reyr was the most meddlesome, all feelings and openness, always pressing them to share what was on their minds. Jovari was too nonchalant about the world most of the time. Verath was the opposite—too serious. Koldis fell somewhere in the middle and was the closest to Cyrus in personality, even though Cyrus had never been as impulsive.

But he knew—he *knew* Koldis wouldn't let him brood forever. That Koldis cared too much to let it go. Perhaps he shouldn't have come tonight. Perhaps it would have been better to go off some-where alone and let Koldis keep watch without him.

"When I realized what Taylynn was to me—"

"Don't you dare!" he growled, cutting him off before this conversation led where he suspected it would.

"Don't be rude," Koldis drawled. "Let me finish."

His nostrils flared. He sighed, knowing there would be no escaping this. "Fine."

Koldis began again. "When I realized Taylynn was my mate, I was wholly unprepared. It felt like what I imagine falling from the sky and splattering all over the ground might feel like. Not that we will ever know, exactly." Koldis sighed. "We live such long lives, Bedelth, compared to humans. We meet so many people during that time. Hundreds. Thousands. And then you meet *that one*. Your mate. That one single person whom the fates intended. All those people, and not a single one touches you. And then a mere glimpse —that's all it takes. Everything changes. It's like your insides get rearranged and scrambled and suddenly, you're this different person. Yet, you're still the same."

Bedelth exhaled, but didn't say anything.

"I felt so godsdamned helpless," Koldis whispered. And he listened, because when they'd discussed it with everyone in the tent, Koldis hadn't said a word about that. "We're *shields*. People look at us and think we're indestructible. They see us and think that we've got the world at our fingertips. That we can do anything. That there isn't a single obstacle we cannot overcome."

Bedelth's insides twisted. He hated what Koldis described. Hated that it mirrored the way he felt for so many reasons. Hadn't his parents thought the same thing about the *Drengr Fairtheoir*? Hadn't they thought that being a shield was the ultimate honor?

"It wasn't just my oath," Koldis continued. "Yes, that made me feel completely at the mercy of other forces. But really, it was her being a sprite that left me feeling so...weak. So godsdamned powerless."

Damn. Those words struck him in so many ways, straight down to the marrow in his bones. He lifted a hand, cupped his brother's shoulder and squeezed. Koldis paid him a sidelong glance and nodded. They didn't need to say anything. Words could still be passed in a single look.

"What now?" Bedelth managed after a long moment.

Koldis sighed. "Hard to say. She agreed to be my mate so long as my king approved. I left the forest knowing that was enough. That even if I didn't get our king's approval, knowing her choice would be enough—get me through life knowing that someone had picked me, *chosen* me, despite it being...predestined or whatever. She could have refused. That's the important thing."

He nodded, swallowing against his parched throat. He couldn't imagine Taylynn saying no to someone like Koldis. She'd have been out of her mind to refuse him. Which only reminded him of his own situation.

He knew what it felt like to be unwanted. What it felt like when someone didn't choose him. It *hurt*.

"The worst part is," Koldis said, "considering what she is, how she comes and goes, I don't even know when I'll see her again—*if* I will see her again."

Bedelth glanced at him and said, "If she chose you, she won't stay away for long. You'll see her again."

"I want to believe that," Koldis whispered, showing a tender side that the drengr race often kept hidden. "I just hate that she's mine and...and I don't know the *if* and *when* of it. I hate the uncertainty."

"You deserve to be happy," Bedelth said at last. "Talon was right. I'm glad he gave you his blessing."

"You do too," Koldis agreed. "I'm not going to lecture you about her, Bedelth. I see the way you look at her. I know what she is to you. Just know this, if you *do* want to talk about it—*ever*—I'm here."

His chest squeezed, a mix of pain and warmth. He nodded, but said nothing more.

They stood in companionable silence as the minutes ticked on, waiting—

"There!" Koldis pointed.

The glow of a red-orange flame sprouted in the distance, out over the water. They both exhaled, relieved. It was the signal they'd been looking for. The time had come.

Their operatives had been successful. The strategically placed barges—positioned one after another across the bay—began to go up in flames. The small blips of light could easily be explained as lone fishermen. The final signal flared into life closest to them.

"They did it," Bedelth whispered, glancing at Koldis. "I was almost afraid to hope, but they did it." He muttered a few words of power, lighting an orb. He waved it in the air. Message received. Almost instantly, the signal closest to them snuffed out, then the next, and the next, until all was dark once more.

Koldis turned to him. "Let's go and tell our king the good news."

~

After delivering the news, he walked through camp. He did two circuits past Saffra's tent before working up the courage to speak to her. He heard the laughter within and knew what he'd find.

Silence fell when he knocked on the tent pole and popped his head inside. Saffra's face flushed at the sight of him. He held her gaze for just a moment. Then he cleared his throat and offered a dazzling smile to everyone. "Good evening, ladies. The signal has been lit, it worked."

Squeals of delight erupted from Desaree and Jocelyn, who glanced at Saffra with bright, hopeful expressions. If they thought her lack of excitement was strange, they didn't let on. Clearly she wanted him gone, sooner rather than later. He wasn't intentionally trying to make her uncomfortable. He certainly didn't plan to stick around longer than necessary.

"The king has scheduled a meeting for tomorrow afternoon to discuss our final preparations. He wants the three of you there, even though you won't be part of the battle." At this, Desaree's smile widened. Jocelyn glanced between him and Saffra, sensing the undercurrent simmering between them. "Just thought I'd relay the message. Anyway—"

"Would you like to come in for some tea?" Jocelyn blurted.

He stilled. It took a great deal of willpower to avoid looking at Saffra. He kept his eyes on Jocelyn and said, "Tea would be lovely, Joce, but I'm afraid duty calls. I've got a few matters to attend to." The lie easily rolled off his tongue. And so what, he certainly had matters he *could* be attending to, like ensuring that the dwargish armor was in perfect condition for the drengr, ready for when they needed it. "I hope you ladies have a good night."

With that, he retreated, careful to look anywhere but Saffra. He'd had his glimpse, and that was enough. It needed to be. Things were better this way.

Talon's modified charter was one thing, his parents were another. They were as traditional as it came. Even when the king rewrote the law, his father wouldn't agree with it. Why? Because most older drengr didn't like change. His parents wouldn't either. They'd see it as an impulsive move.

Pleasing them was near impossible, but he certainly tried, even after all these years. Deep down, he still craved their scant approval, like his life was meaningless without it. He ground his teeth together and slipped into his tent.

He hated his jealousy towards other mated pairs. Even towards Koldis, despite the male's complications of his newly-found mate-hood. He loved his brothers, but seeing Talon and Koldis with mates who cared for them was a reminder of what he *didn't* have.

His parents had taken his one opportunity to experience unconditional love and snuffed it out, projecting their wants and desires onto his life. Like a starved thing, he'd played right into their hands. Would he ever be strong enough to accept that he'd never gain *their* love?

CHAPTER 6
STORM AT SEA

Dragonfire Sea

Bennett ignored the sight of the Scattered Islands shrinking behind him. He stood at the helm, looking ahead at the opportunity that called them. The deck of the *Lady Faith* was a bustle of activity as the crew rushed about, managing the sails and rigging while they made their way to open water. Still near enough to land, the air was thick with the smell of rotting fish and salt, complemented by the cloudy sky, turning the sun's harsh rays diffuse.

Nearly five days had passed since departing from the drop point, since agreeing to Lord Bedelth's task in exchange for a handsome sum of money. They were headed to Oshea. The country lay across the Dragonfire Sea. It would take two weeks to get there, if they judged the winds correctly and made good time; it was important that they did. According to Lord Bedelth, something was happening there, something that concerned Dragonwall. If the king wanted additional eyes and ears on the matter, then it must have been serious.

He was more anxious than he let on. Oshea was a place he

often avoided. He'd been born there, but felt no ties to the country. Still, money was money.

As planned, he'd stopped off in the Scattered Islands beforehand. One last hurrah for his crew to blow off steam before getting stuck aboard the ship for an extended period. With part of the funds Lord Bedelth provided, they'd loaded the hull to bursting with supplies. Food and water, livestock like chickens and goats, some ale for the harder days, extra supplies to repair the ship should they run into a storm, and other cargo to maintain their ruse. The *Lady Faith* sat low in the water.

And yes, he'd gotten the list of items Cat had requested. He snorted, just thinking about it. Jonah turned to him, his eyes searching. "Everything okay, Captain?"

"Oh, aye. Just splendid," he growled, keeping his eyes on the activity on deck.

He hadn't been happy about the shopping trip, for which Cat had insisted on accompanying him. Turned out, the items on her list were damned expensive. After paying for the third item, he'd thrown her an accusing glare as if to say she'd done it on purpose. She'd merely lifted a brow and shrugged. "It costs what it costs, *Captain*," she'd added. "You *do* want me to take care of your crew, do you not?"

It was her crew too, even if she didn't want to admit it.

She'd left him muttering under his breath, but he'd let it go, used the funds from the king to get what they needed. He hated to admit that she was right. Getting what was needed to help the crew would make things better. A healthy crew was a happy crew. Besides, he prided himself on being a good captain.

Speaking of Cat...

He scanned the bodies on deck. "She's below," Jonah said, reading his mind. "Probably organizing and reorganizing and agonizing over all her new supplies, conjuring up all sorts of wicked concoctions. I'm thinking I might invent some ailment just as an excuse for treatment. Gods know, most of the crew will do exactly that, just to get her hands on them."

He snorted. "I hate to think it, but you might be right."

"Oh, aye, I am," Jonah said, throwing him a knowing grin. Dimples appeared in the man's cheeks.

His damned crew was smitten. He pulled his spyglass from his pocket. Open water stretched out before him, and above it, far along the horizon, a mass of dark clouds. He didn't like the look of the storm they were headed towards. It wasn't the worst thing he'd seen. He'd been caught in some nasty ones, but it would certainly require careful effort. Collapsing the glass, he returned it to his pocket.

"We could try going around," Jonah pointed out, eyeing the distant clouds that would be upon them in half a day.

He contemplated. "It's a far cry from the worst we've seen. Remember that nightmare on the way to Holbeck?"

Jonah's face turned grim. "As if I could ever forget it."

"We endure, as we always do. Going around will cost us days. We'll be okay," he added. Jonah nodded, his eyes tracking the motion of various crewmen. Bennett slapped a hand on his shoulder. "Batten down the hatches, Jonah. Get her ready."

Overhead, the loud caw of a bird echoed over the cry of the gulls. "Ah, right on schedule," he muttered, squinting towards the sky. Beaky soared overhead, nipping at the gulls who flew too close. After circling twice, she alighted on the highest mast, up near the crow's nest, where she settled. She'd be down later to pester him. His bird was an independent sort.

A flare of warmth burst through his chest. He'd never meant to love the little creature. It would be a hard time for him when she grew too old to fly, when he lost her. She'd become a close companion to him over the years, and he wasn't sure what life would look like without her.

~

THE EVENING RUSHED to meet them, the light fading, the storm close at hand. Bennett saw to the crew, ensured they followed their orders, preparing everything as needed, then headed below and sought out the newly named healer's cabin. He rolled his eyes and withheld a snort when he saw the freshly nailed plaque on the door. Literally, *Healer's Cabin*. At least she took her new job seriously. He put his ear to the wood and listened. All was silent, so he rapped his knuckles on the door.

"Enter," came the feminine voice within. He still hadn't gotten used to having a woman aboard.

He swept into the room, his eyes darting over everything, taking note of the newest changes, like the full jars on the shelves, secured in place for obvious reasons. Her back was to him, hunched over the small counter opposite the healer's table. Her stance was wide, to steady herself from the rolling of the ship. His eyes traced over the delicate lines of her neck and shoulders, down to her trim waist and long legs. Her tunic and pants outlined every generous curve of her waist, hips, and thighs. His nostrils flared and he ripped his gaze away.

"Storm's coming," he said.

She whirled, frowning. "Oh. It's you."

He snorted. "Good to see you too, Kitty Cat." A wicked grin split his lips at the sight of her annoyance—a muscle twitch near her temple.

"You're too late. Emmon's already been here to tell me about the storm, so unless you're here for treatment, you can clear off for those who have ailments."

His mouth opened and he quickly snapped it shut. He made a point of checking over his shoulder. "Because you've got a whole godsdamned line waiting at the door?"

The hallway was entirely empty.

"Exactly," she said. He allowed her snarky attitude to pass him by.

"Things could get dicey above," he warned. "Might be good to have your magic for assistance, in case anything goes wrong."

"What are you saying?" Her eyes narrowed.

"What I'm *saying* is, if someone falls overboard, they'll be lost to the sea."

"And you can't fish them out *why*?"

"You ever seen how fast a wave pulls someone away from a

ship, lass? That water's freezing. A human body won't last long with a head above water in a storm."

Never mind that during a storm, it was hard enough managing the ship without trying to go after downed crew members. Losing a man overboard was rare, but it happened. He'd lost a handful over the many long years to various deaths, and yes, a few to their watery graves. Sometimes the sea god was merciful. Most times, he was not.

She planted her hands on her hips. "I'm busy making a concoction for Yerik's joints. After this, I need to mix up something for Zama—"

"I understand you got work aplenty, but if Yerik goes overboard, then that concoction you're mixin' on the counter won't much matter, now will it?"

Her jaw flexed. The desire to argue flashed across her features, there and gone. At last, she nodded. "Fine. How long do I have?"

"Storm'll be here within the hour."

She hesitated. "And what is it, exactly, that you expect me to do? Because for your information, I doubt my magic will be enough to pull a man from the water."

He huffed. "Keep the crew from falling overboard and you won't need to. Keep things from going belly up. This ain't the kind of storm to rip a mast clean off the ship, but, you never know what it'll throw at us."

She rolled her eyes as if to say, *that's your job.* "Right. Okay, let me just pull out my magic wand here—" She made a show of checking in her pockets, patting them down as if searching for something. "While I'm at it, I'll sprinkle some faerie dust in the air—"

"Faeries *do* exist, then?"

"Gods above," she cursed under her breath. "You're insufferable."

"Insufferable's my middle name, lass. Glad you see that." He liked the way her cheeks heated in annoyance. Some of his greatest satisfaction these days came from bringing that kind of color to her skin. Burrowing beneath it, down to her very bones. Scraping around until she was spitting, claws extended.

She made a sound in the back of her throat, turning her back on him momentarily, moving a few items back into their jars, returning them to the shelves.

"Look, I'm just askin' you to do what yeh can," he said, his accent growing thicker by the moment. It always came out in full force when his emotions were heightened. "Help where yeh can— if yeh can. I know you care about the crew. And if not for me— because I know yeh don't want *nothing* to do with me—then for the crew. They're sweet on yeh, the lot of 'em."

She hesitated, her movements stopping. Then her chest rose and fell as she took a deep breath and turned to him, pinning him with her fierce gaze. "I said I'd help, all right? I'll finish up here and come up when the storm starts. Should be finished in a few minutes, anyway."

He nodded, hesitating before he walked out. He wasn't about to say *thank you*. For some reason, she made it seem like everything was such a chore. He only felt the need to say thanks for that reason alone, but had to stop himself from doing it. Frequently.

He dropped by his cabin and sank onto his bed for a few moments of peace—soaking up the calm before the storm. Beaky was on her perch, sleeping. "You'll need to stay down here," he told her. "No use in battering your feathers out there with the winds what they are." She opened a lazy eye, gave a chirp, then closed it. She already knew, and always stayed below during the worst storms. Her intelligence never ceased to amaze him. Spoiled creature. She lived a better life than most.

The waves were growing rougher. The ship rolled violently beneath him, slanting more and more with each. He sighed, stood, and readied himself before making his way above deck. It was a rush of activity as Jonah shouted orders. He kept his stance wide as he made his way. A particularly large wave rose towards them, tall as a two story building. The *Lady Faith* rode it up, up, up, then plummeted headfirst.

His stomach dropped straight to his boots, lost among the planks beneath his feet.

The crew whooped, a few lifting challenging fists into the air, getting their minds amped for the battle ahead. He couldn't help the deranged smile that spread across his lips. Storms were always a battle, not so different from those fought with swords and knives and arrows. But this? This was a battle against the sea, against the salty grave beneath their feet, a fight with dire consequences if things went wrong. Their foe would try to swallow the ship, but they'd make sure that didn't happen. They'd do everything they could. At the end of it, no matter how hard they fought, some things were simply out of his control. She wasn't called *Lady Faith* for nothing.

"Everything's in place," Jonah shouted over the ruthless wind, nodding towards the hurricane force sails they'd hoisted, having swapped the others out, which would be torn to tatters in something like this. They could have reeled them entirely, but they needed the speed. It was important that they keep moving at an angle to the storm; their sails would allow for that. If this *was* a full blown hurricane—and thank the gods it wasn't, or they'd be in real trouble—Bennett would have done things much differently. Plus, that's why he'd requested Cat's presence on deck. He wasn't entirely sure *what* she was capable of, but he hoped she might keep things from going to hell.

Besides that, other precautions had been put in place. They had ample warning, time to run safety lines from fore to aft, giving the crew something to grab onto as they moved about. He'd done this so many times, and yet, his heart still raced. The exhilaration of it never faded.

"This'll be her first storm," Jonah shouted, pointing to the female figure emerging from below deck.

All around them, the wind whipped, slapping his face with icy spring air, mixed with the salty spray as the waves battered the sides of the ship. Cat stumbled for the closest safety line, waited for the ship to steady, between waves, then made a break for the stairs.

"I'm going to secure you so you don't lose your footing," he shouted over the wind once she was beside him. Her throat bobbed as she took a gulp. Her face was white as a sheet. Whatever she might have expected, it wasn't this.

A sudden urge to reassure her washed over him, rising at the same rate as the ship, cresting the next wave. He pushed it down. It wasn't his job to sugarcoat things. He wouldn't tell her everything was fine, because it wasn't. He might, *perhaps*, have underestimated the severity of the weather earlier. Not entirely his fault. It was unpredictable, and while he had plenty of experience with these things, sometimes nature simply turned wild.

Besides, everyone needed to experience one of these storms in their lifetime. It was a valuable lesson. Life was precious. Being reminded of that was important.

Cat nodded. To her credit, she didn't cower or whine. She didn't insist on going back to her cabin. She simply stood her ground. He admired that, was proud, even. He didn't want to feel it—hated thinking anything better of her. But...well, he could still admire things about her and dislike her. There wasn't a rule stating otherwise.

He found an extra spool of rope and secured it around her waist, securing her to the helm. Then he walked her through what to expect, talking about the wind direction, the waves, and the chance for things to go belly up, and what she ought to do if that happened.

"So, basically, you need me to step in if anything goes wrong," she said, brow lifted.

"That's the gist of it."

"You do realize that magic doesn't fix *everything*," she warned.

"Well, it's a lot better than nothing!"

She snorted but said nothing. They stood in silence, side by side, with Jonah at the helm, keeping a steady course at an angle to the storm. The breath before the plunge was always the most intense moment. He could already see the sheets of rain before them, a transparent curtain. He could also see the lightning within, hear the rumbles as they reached the ship. It started as a patter, first, splatters on the planking. Seconds later it turned to a roaring downpour.

He was drenched in seconds. It was cold rain, but not as cold as the winter storms, and for that he was grateful. His crew would stay warm working.

The activity on the deck turned frenzied. Everyone knew what was needed of them, and he watched with pride bursting in his chest. They operated like well-oiled cogs in a clock, each moving about the other, despite the rush of their bodies. *Lady Faith* rose and plunged, rose and plunged. Beside him, Cat's hands clenched her stomach. "Take deep, slow breaths," he shouted at her. He wouldn't dare leave her side, even though he was tempted to, if only to scare the living daylights out of her. She only nodded, eyes wide, darting over each of the crew. To her credit, she kept her gaze watchful.

Lightning forked the sky and he flinched. Thunder followed. He counted the seconds in his mind, using it to judge the distance—a habit, more than anything. Gods, he hated lightning. More lightning forked around them, arcing between clouds and water, until the sky was alight with flashes of blinding white, thunderous rumbles mixing with the rain as the backdrop to their current nightmare.

On and on they plunged, Jonah at the helm, the crew working to keep things in order. An hour passed, and then another, until his feet ached and his mood turned the better side of sour.

"Shouldn't it be over by now?!" Cat screamed.

"Storms like this can last hours, *Kitty Cat*. Days, even." What little color her face had regained faded entirely. Her mouth opened and closed before her jaw clenched.

This one wouldn't last more than a few hours, he was certain, but he decided not to tell her that.

Another series of lightning bolts lit the sky, cracking and rumbling. He flinched again. His heart set off into a gallop. He kept his hands clenched into fists, his blunt nails biting into his palm.

Lady Faith found another wave to crest, riding it up, up, up to the top. There was always a second or two, right at the highest point, where the sea spread out around them and time seemed to stop. It was a beautiful moment in its own right. Glorious and terrifying. Dark, inky waves with little choppy bits of white, large rolling hills, some mountainous in appearance, laid out for them as far as the eye could see. The majesty of the sea. The ship started to tilt, more, then a little more, and then *whoosh*. She flew down the slope straight for the watery valley below.

He saw the edge of the storm in the distance, saw it like a hint of victory. But he wouldn't breathe easier until they were out of danger.

Another burst of lightning lit the world around him, temporarily blinding. The sound of it clenched his stomach. The second the world darkened, the ship had reached the bottom of the wave, righted, and was already riding the next one up. A frightened cry from the crew rose above the din.

His eyes darted over everything until they fell to the new chaos taking place. Peter. He must have slipped, lost his footing when the lightning struck, blinding all of them. His body dangled from the railing, hands like claws holding on, trying to climb back up and over to safety. Bennett's stomach lodged in his throat. For a single inhale, he could only watch as Peter struggled, as the crew attempted to battle the rough seas and high winds. Only two of his men had noticed, with the unfolding frenzy on the deck. Peter tried to lift himself up and over but Bennett could already see what was wrong. The rails were slick with rain. Peter would already be exhausted, with little strength left after battling a storm like this for hours. For a brief moment, the crew who did see him sprinted in his direction. But Peter's fingers were already slipping.

"Cat!" he shouted, as one of Peter's hands completely broke its grip, leaving him to dangle from the other.

"I see him," she cried. "I see him!"

Another second and the other hand—

Cat lifted her arm and shouted something in another language. It was instantaneous. Peter's body rose into the air, was flung back onto the deck, as if someone had wrapped a rope around him and yanked. His body sprawled, going limp, chest heaving, then quickly righted. He took hold of the safety line, head turning in their direction. Bennett's eyes met Peter's and Peter nodded, an indication that he was okay.

They were safe.

He turned to Cat, and this time he didn't stop himself. She was doubled over, hands on her knees, balancing against the rolling deck, as if the effort had cost her a great deal. "Thank you," he said, allowing his genuine relief to seep into his words. She stood. Her throat bobbed, eyes still worried, and nodded.

The break in the storm was approaching. He turned his gaze towards it, spotting the line every time they reached the top of a wave. Closer, closer, closer. Until at last, the rain decreased to a sprinkle, then a dull mist. Activity slowed, then ceased altogether, as tired bodies heaved each breath. A few collapsed to sitting, and even sprawled.

And then a victory cry split the air. Followed by another, and another. Fists lifted into the air. Once again, the sea had tried its damndest to claim them. Tried and failed.

He let his whoops of victory mix with the crew's. Beside him, a feminine voice joined the noise. He glanced over to see Cat's face animated, smiling. His eyes fixed on her mouth, on the way it transformed her features. He lifted his gaze. Their eyes held and his stomach swooped. It had nothing to do with the wave they crested. He quickly looked away, then hefted his fist in the air and pumped it.

They'd live to tell another tale.

CHAPTER 7
AFTERNOON PLANS

Celenore

Claire looked at the faces gathered around the conference table. She sat at the table's head; Talon had insisted upon it, choosing instead to sit on her right. He was hoping to acclimate her to the position.

Talon's Shields were present, as were Byron and Tamara. Desaree, Saffra, and Jocelyn had also been invited. While they wouldn't play any role in battle, they'd become a part of Talon's inner circle. But...what distracted her most were the dwargs.

Dwargs!

It was surreal. She could barely take her eyes off them. The first time she'd seen them, her mouth gaped widely enough to be embarrassing. How many queens turned into a flytrap at the sight of something surprising? Well, she had.

Could anyone blame her? They were *dwargs*! And they were everything she'd expected them to be, exactly like the dwarves she read about growing up. Seeing them was something of a dream, and she'd loved them immediately, especially Berbik, who was her favorite. Not only was he the most sociable of them, he'd plied her with stories about his kind, which she'd eagerly inhaled when time allowed. He sat here at the table today with his comrades. Each time she caught his eye, he gave her a huge grin beneath the beard swallowing up his face, turning his eyes squinty.

"We're relying on the lake, on Saffra's brew, to do the majority of the work for us," Talon was saying. She forced herself to focus on his words. "Given Taylynn's warning, her sending Claire here, we must prepare for the worst."

Taylynn had insisted on sending her here. She often wondered if there was more to it than simply acting as a failsafe—being present in case their plans went awry. Perhaps the princess had anticipated what Claire would do, attempting to save the unborn hatchlings. Perhaps she'd seen the necessity of it.

There was plenty that could go wrong.

"Our forces will be in the sky, ready to neutralize any existing threats," Byron was saying. "We've got the most experience in this sort of combat," he added. "Despite our previous losses, we should be able to handle a few dragons, more even, if Her Majesty is in the city protecting its people."

"I will ensure the city's inhabitants are safe," she promised. "No fire will touch them."

Byron nodded before glancing at Tamara. In the time she'd been away, Byron and Tamara had been voted in as the newest leaders of Fort Squall. She was proud to see Tamara stepping into the role. But she was also devastated, knowing what it had cost, knowing Reyr had lost his twin brother to the dragons.

He'd been so heartbroken.

She glanced at him and felt her cheeks flush. He still wasn't talking to her. He'd been furious over what she'd done—giving the dragons the option to surrender. He didn't care about redemption. Didn't care about their extinction. He wanted to destroy every single one of them. She understood, she really did, but she couldn't slaughter helpless, pregnant mothers. She just couldn't.

The events of the day before still sat heavy in her stomach.

Talon had gathered their inner circle, explaining what she'd done. It had been tense and even embarrassing, but she'd toughed it out with her head held high. She was a queen now, not a cowering church mouse. Their reactions had been mixed. A few had agreed while a larger majority hadn't. She hated that—hated that she wanted *everyone's* approval.

"It's yet another difficult aspect of being a ruler," Talon had explained later that evening. *"You can never please everyone. The best that you can do is make your decision with peace in your heart. Someone will always disagree."*

Knowing he was right didn't make it any easier.

～

SAFFRA LIFTED her cup and said, "This might be our last time all together," then proceeded to drain the contents. Everyone else copied her actions until a chorus of extremely unladylike burps and giggles followed. The eight of them, including Desaree, Jeanine, Jocelyn, Miera, Selphie and Tamara, sat on cushions, a plush rug beneath them, enjoying the empty command tent. The meeting had long since disbanded, everyone going their separate ways.

"That sounds so depressing," Tamara groaned, "but I will be glad to win back the fort and have my home again."

"We're going to miss you," Jocelyn said.

"But you can all come visit," Tamara said, "whenever you wish. You will always be welcome at Fort Squall."

"Easier said than done for some of us," Jocelyn pouted. She'd come out of her shell over the past few months.

"Perhaps you can all take another ship?" Tamara teased, a mischievous glint in her eyes.

Desaree groaned, flinging herself back on her cushion. "Never again," she said to the ceiling.

"Too soon?" Tamara added, giggling.

The rest of them burst into laughter until even Desaree's shoulders were shaking. They leaned on each other, shrieking, gasping, and refilling their drinks. It was good to sit with her friends, soak up their company, because Saffra was right. After they reclaimed the fort, Tamara would return there to lead beside Byron. Those who couldn't fly would return home, like Desaree, Jocelyn, and Saffra. The drengr would fly back to the capital. Claire would be left to return with her queen's guard and spriten handmaidens. Either way, everyone would go their separate ways.

"Just think," Desaree said, changing the topic, "when we return to the capital, we'll have a ceremony to plan!"

A chorus of excited sounds burst from their mouths.

"What goes into planning a royal bonding ceremony?" Selphie asked. Her spriten handmaidens had taken to asking many questions. She loved how curious and eager they were to adapt to life outside the forest.

"Even I don't know *all* the details of it," Desaree said. "But I can guess. I'll need a good deal of help from everyone." She studied Claire's spriten handmaidens, as if a diabolical plan was already hatching. As if she was wondering how she might utilize their strengths for planning everything.

Claire grinned. She'd been nervous at first, that Desaree might feel threatened, or that her handmaidens would act as if they were superior, being inhuman and more experienced. After all, they'd served Queen Jade before she'd come along. None of that had happened. The three of them got along so well that Desaree had already started begging for lessons in *Ednuar,* so that she could share in their side conversations when others were around.

That, alone, left Claire's heart bursting with pride for her friend.

"We are at your service, my lady," Miera said, bowing her head. Selphie bobbed her head, too.

"There will be the gown, obviously," Jocelyn said, to which Desaree nodded. "It must be the most spectacular gown the kingdom has ever seen. There will be nothing to match it."

"The gown to end all gowns?" Jeanine teased, sharing a secret glance with Claire. They both hid their twitching lips.

"Exactly," Desaree said, her voice serious. "Black, of course, as you may or may not know," she explained to Claire's handmaidens. "It's meant to match her mate's scales."

"Ah, yes, we have heard such things," Miera confirmed.

"Claire must also acquire the king's pommel stone," Desaree continued. "It's a tradition. They each exchange an item during the ceremony. He will give her a bow."

"And the ceremony itself? The decorations? The food?" Selphie asked.

"There will be so much to organize," Desaree groaned. "We will work with the keep's staff, but they will handle the vast majority of it. The decorations will fill the throne room, the entry chambers, and the dining hall."

Nervous butterflies took flight in Claire's stomach. She tried not to squirm. For all the time she'd spent eagerly anticipating this event, she hadn't given the event itself much thought. But it wasn't merely the event she was nervous about, it was everything it symbolized. More so, the life changing aspect of it.

"There will be menus to approve," Desaree continued.

"Guest lists?" Selphie asked.

"Oh gods," Desaree said, her eyes widening. "I forgot about the guest lists." She put her head in her hands, momentarily looking overwhelmed. "But we will manage."

"And I will also help where needed," Jocelyn said, "assuming my lady is okay with that."

"Of course." Saffra grinned. "We will all help. We're a team now."

Tamara sighed, long and loud. "I hope Byron and I will be able to attend, but I fear that we will not."

"Why wouldn't you?" Claire's brows pulled together.

"We must ensure the fort is settled. To abandon it during such a trying time..."

Claire reached across the circle and took Tamara's hand. "I want you there," she whispered. "But, I understand what it means to bear the weight of such responsibility. Don't stress if you can't manage it. I know you'll be there in spirit, if not in body."

Tamara's throat bobbed and she nodded.

The rest of their afternoon continued with laughter and conversation as they fired off different ideas. Everyone had an opinion on the types of decorations, the food, the guest list, and all the little details in between. Their ideas got more and more outlandish, from giant chocolate statues that could be broken into pieces and eaten, to transforming the entire throne room into a replica of Esterpine. It helped to distract them from the impending battle.

When night fell, she went in search of Talon for their evening flight. "What's got you smiling?" he asked, snaking an arm around her waist and pulling her along through camp. His body radiated welcome warmth. He'd just come from the field where the drengr's armor was assembled, and though he'd worn a hard expression upon first spotting her, it was already softening. It left her giddy, knowing she could turn his grim mood into something happy.

She'd seen the armor when the dwargs had first arrived. Massive plates that would cover their bodies, keeping them safe from ice metal weapons that might be used. Assuming the poison didn't work on every dragon. Whatever Talon had been doing was stressful, but she intended to make him forget his hardships, even if for a little while.

"*Well*, funny you should ask," she said. "We spent most of the afternoon dreaming up ideas for our bonding ceremony."

"Without me?!" he demanded, eyes already dancing in the fading light.

"Oh? Were you hoping to pick out our flower arrangements?"

"At the *least*. Or something else that might make a statement. Our guests should be condemned to feathered hats, perhaps? Or a few giant ice sculptures, if possible? Maybe acrobats, like those we saw during the tourney?"

She snorted. "Would chocolate sculptures work instead?"

"Chocolate? Why didn't I think of that?" he muttered.

"Because it was Jeanine's idea?"

He barked a laugh, pulling her closer as they walked. "I'm sure whatever you ladies think up will be fine."

She understood why he'd said it. With all his current duties, he was plenty glad to let them handle this. But...it was *their* ceremony. "You're sure you don't want to help with anything?"

He came to a stop, his expression thoughtful. She admired that about him—that he took the time to consider the things he said. "May I assist with the menu selection?"

A grin split her lips. "I'd love that."

He could have declined. She would understand. And yet, he knew how important this was for both of them. Once more, she found herself admiring him, falling even harder for him.

As a king, he'd had time to hone himself. Years to perfect being a ruler. Sure, he was temperamental, and downright frightening to most. But underneath everything, he had a heart of solid gold, and she loved him for it.

"And you know," he continued, "we *can* hire someone to plan everything, if you'd like. You don't have to—"

"Desaree would have an absolute fit!"

The corner of his mouth twitched. "I figured as much. Just thought I'd offer."

They started walking again, this time hand in hand, lacing their fingers together. Her stomach swooped, eyes darting down to their joined palms. They'd held hands a hundred times by now, and yet, she still turned fluttery.

He stopped in the middle of the field, turning to face her. It was full dark now, but she could see his profile, make out the lines of his scars, the glitter in his eyes, the flash of silver whenever they caught the moonlight. He took her waist, pulling her close. They stared at each other, her head tipped back to meet his gaze.

No words were spoken, and yet, so much passed between them.

"Tomorrow will be the start of everything," she whispered, feeling the importance of this moment.

His throat bobbed. "You will be magnificent," he breathed. Her chest expanded, but she didn't answer. He bent forward, dipping to kiss her. The warmth of his breath tickled her lips first, before his mouth found hers. She leaned into him, snaking her arms around his neck, letting their kiss deepen, letting everything unspoken pass between them.

She tugged at his bottom lip gently when he pulled away.

"Ready to fly?" he asked. And somehow, it felt like he was referring to so much more than the simple act of flying. It was like he meant everything else, too. The battle to come, the plan they would enact, all of it.

"I was born ready," she said, squaring her shoulders and stepping away. He gave a single nod, then transformed.

CHAPTER 8

REACHING SQUALL'S END

Squall's End

Claire swallowed against her dry throat, pushing back her nerves. She stood in the command tent, her friends around her. "Everything will be okay, Your Majesty," Selphie said, reaching forward to take her hands. "It is the will of the tree."

"The will of the tree," Miera repeated, nodding. They acted as if what she was about to do was already predestined. But the truth was, so much could still go wrong. Perhaps not with her, but with everything else.

"We'll see you again, once you return," Desaree added, her voice catching. "Just...be careful. Promise you'll be careful."

"She'll be careful," Feowen said. He stood nearby with Jeanine. The rest of her queen's guard remained outside, assembled and waiting.

"I'll be careful, I promise," she whispered, hugging first Selphie and then Miera. Then she stepped up to Des and pulled her tight. "Keep everyone in line while I'm gone."

She moved over to Jocelyn and Saffra, hugging them. "We'll be waiting to trade stories in a couple of days," Saffra said. "In the meantime, be safe."

Next were Talon's shields. She went to each, giving hugs, soaking up their words of encouragement and advice. Koldis lifted her off her feet, as he often did. "Give them hell," he growled, setting her down and winking.

Jovari was a bit more devilish, offering her a charming smile. "They'll rue the day you were born," he said. She couldn't help her grin.

"Trust your instincts, Your Majesty," Verath advised, wrapping her in his arms before kissing the top of her head.

"I will," she croaked, her throat tightening with emotion.

Bedelth stepped forward, pulling her into a tight embrace. "When you get back, we'll do some more sparring. I still haven't had a chance to see what you've learned in Esterpine."

"I look forward to impressing you," she taunted.

Reyr was last. "Are you still mad at me?" she asked, hesitantly eyeing him.

His jaw flexed but he gave a brief shake of his head. "Come here," he said, his voice low. She fell into his arms, sighing with relief. They stayed like that, locked together, just breathing. She felt his apology in the way he held her, but it was more than that. It was acceptance too, for what she'd done; even though he might not agree with her actions, he was forgiving her for them. He inhaled against the top of her hair, as if trying to memorize her scent. "You'll do just fine," he mused, as if sensing her deepest worries. "You are a queen. You were always meant for this. It's who you are inside. Never doubt yourself."

"Thank you," she whispered, her throat thick with unshed tears.

He pulled away, taking her face in his hands to kiss her forehead. Her eyes fell closed.

She saved Talon for last. She stepped up to him, their eyes locked. "Leave us—all of you," he commanded without looking away.

There were no complaints as everyone scrambled to exit the tent.

He leaned against the table with his arms crossed and his feet braced. She pressed in close. He didn't move, just stared down at her looking every bit the grump. "I keep wondering when this will get easier."

"Me being queen? Or me rushing into danger at every possible moment?"

"The latter, obviously."

She shrugged, lifting a hand to trail her fingers over his face, along his scars. His eyelids drooped. "I like to think it will get easier," she mused.

"You are as wild as a raging river," he said, his voice rumbling. "But if there's one thing I can trust, it's that your waters will always flow to the sea."

She bit her lip. "I like that."

He uncrossed his arms and wrapped them around her until their bodies were pressed tight. His warmth and smoky scent enveloped her. Everything always felt safer like this. He rubbed his cheek against her forehead. "All of them were right, you know?"

"Right?"

"About you. That you'll do fine today protecting Squall's End's people. I'll keep an eye out for you when we arrive. Keep your mind open to me, yes?"

"I will. I promise."

"Then I won't need to worry."

"You never need to worry," she said, her voice scolding.

"And yet, I always will. Perhaps it is a product of my scars. Not these—" he added, tapping the dominant one crossing his face. "I speak of the scars that are deeper, borne from the life I have lived. I trust you, but I will always worry. Living alone for so long and finally finding my mate...there will always be this fear in me. Fear of losing you, no matter how capable you are. And you *are*— capable of facing every battle." He hesitated, then frowned. "No, this thing—it is my own burden to carry, my own mountain to climb and conquer. I hope to, in time."

"Talon…" Her body heated. She pulled his face to hers and kissed him, claiming him. He was *her* mate.

Hers.

Her tongue brushed along his. He growled and tightened against her, his arms moving, fingers sinking into her chignon at the base of her neck. She felt every rigid layer of his muscles bulge and flex with each tiny movement. Their kiss was hungry and desperate, a goodbye, a promise for the next time they came together, a messy exchange of everything they felt for each other.

Her chest heaved with gasping breaths as she stepped away. She had to stop herself from fanning her face. Instead, she looked at him, traced every curve and line of his features. There was no part of him that wasn't beautiful. "Come, *my king*, walk with me to the paddock."

"I had planned to," he said, his mouth twitching at the use of his title. He took her hand, wrapping it around his elbow and leading her from the tent. They walked in silence, her queen's guard forming behind her, followed by Talon's shields and their friends. It turned into a procession.

When they reached the unicorns, she gave each of her friends and companions a quick look, a final parting exchange. Then she turned to Talon and kissed him full on in front of everyone. She heard several teasing snickers but didn't care. It was good for their subjects to see the affection they shared. She stretched up on her tiptoes to reach his ear and whispered, "I love you with my whole heart, my king, my friend, my mate, my everything."

He huffed a pleased breath and pulled back to look at her. "And I love you, queen of my heart." He took her hand, kissing her palm, keeping his heated silver eyes on hers. The world around them disappeared. So much passed in that quick exchange. Then she stepped away and went to where the unicorns had assembled.

She climbed on Tourmaline's back. Today, she was dressed in a new gown, one that her spriten handmaidens had constructed with Desaree's input. They'd taken a royal blue number and modified the skirts, using silver fabric from one of her spriten gowns. The shoulders were plated with layers of starlight silver armor that looked like spriten leaves, which came up to form a collar about her neck. The arms were made of a light starlight silver chainmail, paired with the beautiful bracers she'd been gifted. More plates of armor accented each side of her flowing skirt, forming about her hips.

She felt like a warrior. No, she *was* a warrior. Soon, she would prove it.

Feowen stepped forward, handing over Pelwynn's bow and arrows. She secured it in place. Then he handed her the spriten staff. The moment her fingers touched the wood, she felt the world humming through her fingertips. A shiver raced down her spine. She braced it across Tourmaline's back, then looked up. Around her, the rest of her queen's guard climbed atop their respective unicorns.

She pulled her hood low. They would wear the cloaks Taylynn had made for them. The princess had done a magnificent job of imbuing them with magic, allowing the wearer to blend with their surroundings. The unicorns had their own magic, keeping eyes from sticking to them. They'd move fast enough that most things in the world wouldn't even notice them.

Straightening her shoulders, she gave Talon a final look then shouted, "Barihoni vamiaah! Verah riocah!" *Queen's guard! We ride!*

Tourmaline shot forward like a dart. An instant later, the world around her blurred. She heard the pounding of his hooves, beating out a rhythm that matched her heart's. Behind her, the same sound echoed with the accompanying unicorns carrying her guards.

"I am only a thought away," she said, sending the words to Talon and all of his shields.

Their various forms of acknowledgement cascaded through her mind, but Talon's words stood out the strongest. *"Go with my heart."*

~

THE SUN WAS SINKING when the city of Squall's End loomed before them. The blur of their surroundings slowed. Behind the city, water sparkled. Stormy Bay stretched towards the horizon, cast in an orange glow.

She had always wanted to see Squall's End. It was one of Dragonwall's largest cities, but not just that, it was a place rich with history. Reyr had grown up here, his parents serving as fort leaders, and their parents before them. A whole line stretching back for generations. Talon had spent much of his youth here, too.

Goosebumps spread up her arms. The city was old. Something about old things always gave her chills. Perhaps it was the enormity of it—time. To know a thing had existed in the world for so very long.

Where shall I take you? Tourmaline asked.

The front gate, she said. *Our cloaks will keep us disguised.*

There were dragons patrolling the skies, circling overhead. Even from the ground, she could tell that their flight patterns were erratic. She'd been warned about the initial effects of Saffra's brew. Based on the way Verath had acted, the dragons would feel invincible for a few days before they became paralyzed.

If their calculations were correct, the negative effects would set in over the next twelve to twenty-four hours. She wanted to be safely settled within the city before that happened.

Behind her, the other unicorns slowed. The portcullis that served as the city's main entry loomed. Her head fell back, searching the top of its walls. They stood nearly fifty feet in height. With the setting sun, everything on the ground around them was cast into shadow. Despite that, she could see there were city guards on patrol.

She lowered her hood, making herself more visible. Before any fuss was made, she pointed her spriten staff at the portcullis and opened it. She also used her abilities with air to dampen any sound it made.

"Halt! Who goes there?!" A loud voice called. She winced, even though she knew they were protected. She ignored the call. There was no point in a shouting match with the guards watching.

Feowen's unicorn trotted up beside her, motioning with his head towards the entryway. "Well done, Your Majesty."

"We can take no risks," she said.

He nodded.

She urged Tourmaline forward, passing beneath the gaping archway. The sound of scrambling feet met her ears. Darkness briefly swallowed her up. Almost as quickly, she was through, emerging into a massive courtyard.

Guards assembled, weapons in hand. Sensing that the last of her queen's guard was safely through, she released the magic on the portcullis and allowed it to fall closed with a clatter. She kept her other magic in place, ensuring the buffer for sound kept their presence hidden.

Overhead, the dragons continued to circle.

Her queen's guard formed around her and lowered their hoods, to the accompanying sounds of gasps. All around them, city guards stared with open mouths and wide eyes. Had they ever seen a sprite in real life, or a unicorn, for that matter? An urge to grin came over her but she schooled her features.

"Who is the lord of this city?" Feowen called, lifting his voice. He sounded every inch the prince. "Take us to them."

She was content to let him play negotiator. In the meantime, she used this moment to observe.

Beyond the courtyard, houses loomed, multilevel structures with white walls and wooden beams. It looked like something out of a storybook. She'd become more used to the sight of quaint settlements. She found herself blinking, taking it in. The stench was immediately noticeable. A mix of rancid, unwashed bodies, spoiled food, and shit. Like most cities, the poor districts were closest to the outer walls. But not just that. Near the fringes of the courtyard and crowding the streets, tents had been erected.

For all the refugees, she realized. With the dragons burning and pillaging the northern settlements, people had flocked here. They'd filled Squall's End to bursting right before it was taken by Kane's dragons.

A new fear crawled up her spine. Did they have enough food to feed everyone? Would they be forced to starve within its walls until liberated? Were they already starving?

"What is this madness?" a voice barked, a soldier, who pushed his way through the gathered crowd of guards and onlookers. Those who weren't wearing armor had dirtied faces—tired faces. *Hungry* faces.

She studied the newcomer, the markings on his armor depicting his rank. "Who are you?" he demanded of Feowen.

"You are in the presence of Her Majesty, the Queen," Feowen announced. "You will speak with respect. All hail the spriten queen!"

Silence descended. The crowd glanced about, uncertain of *what* to do. Muttering broke the silence, and it grew.

"If you are feeling *particularly* respectful," Feowen drawled, lifting his voice, "now would be the time to bow."

She refrained from rolling her eyes.

Several uncertain soldiers dropped to one knee, only to be nudged, before quickly standing again. The commoners who stood only gawked. No one here was obligated to bow, after all. Only the forest answered to the sprites.

But she had to hand it to Feowen, he was one for trying.

"*Verah callo eah jaanasha aya,*" she said to the gathered crowd, listening to the way her voice carried, the way her words echoed off the buildings.

"We come to liberate you," Feowen translated, throwing her a quick glance. The twinkling in his eyes said he knew what she was doing. The *awe factor*. History books would record this as the time sprites finally left the forest to fight for Dragonwall.

"*Nemaloh mik eah ayas droah!*" she commanded.

"Our queen wishes to speak with the lord of this city." Feowen said, not exactly translating. Still, it got the point across.

The guard who stood before them frowned and glanced at the sky, clearly nervous. Far above, the glittering scales of dragons did not alter their course.

"*Mih franah beinih freja ayas sahale,*" she explained.

"Her Majesty wishes you to know that she is using magic to keep the dragons from sensing our presence."

Again, not quite what she'd said. She glanced at Feowen and

saw the corners of his lips twitch. She refrained from snorting. Good enough, for now.

"Very well," the guard in charge said, hesitating. "This way."

He turned on his heel and the onlookers parted around him. They followed him from the courtyard and into the city. Around them, the houses towered, stacked several stories high. She caught faces peering out, eyes wide with shock when they settled on her before drifting to the horns proudly displayed by their unicorns.

Tourmaline snorted, *also* noticing. His head lifted a little higher, mane fluttering in a nonexistent breeze, using his own magic to draw attention to himself. And if she wasn't mistaken, there was more prance to his step.

Showing off are we? she teased.

It is not every day, Queen, that we are regarded with the respect we are due.

She snickered.

Everywhere she looked, she found evidence of hardship. The deep lines on the faces that stared, in the hard set to their eyes, the press of their lips. This place had seen a great deal of difficulty over the past several months, especially during winter. Her heart ached for them.

Feowen kept pace beside her. "Utah sasit en alscha lerah notasth ana Ednuar?" *Is there a reason for using the spriten language?*

"Ninneem," she returned, giving him a knowing look, an arch of her eyebrow. *Of course.*

"Ain, cilhar, Alas Drollaya." *Very wise, Your Majesty.*

They fell quiet.

The streets were narrow in some places and wider in others. The buildings towered over her and grew more lavish the further they went, with white-washed walls and large windows. There were fewer refugees, too. The oppressive stench diminished, transforming into something just as eye-watering.

She knew it before she saw it. Still, her stomach dropped straight to her boots. They were led along a detour, passing around a large, blackened section of Squall's End. An expanse of emptied space, void of all life. The heavy silence spoke of death, but it was the evidence of dragon fire, of the brutality of it, that froze the breath in her lungs, turning it to shards of ice.

Nothing. There was *nothing* left. Just ash—heaps of it.

"Luth cardah mik challa," she gasped, not bothering to look at Feowen. *It makes me sick.* She couldn't tear her gaze away. "Mayr faldu fradin edah fraste. Stahka, gendiah." *So much damage and destruction. All of it, needless.*

He hummed his agreement.

"Ah, yes, horrifying, is it not?" the guard said, glancing back and noticing her expression. His voice was solemn. She didn't answer him, but her blink was enough to confirm her shock.

Her stomach squirmed at the sight—at the thought of people burning alive. How many had lost their homes? Their lives? There was no coming back from this sort of devastation, even for those lucky enough to survive.

The dragons would pay for this. Seeing their destruction with her own eyes left her reeling. She felt far less guilty about the way they planned to destroy them. It didn't change her mind about the pregnant mothers, though.

The demolished portions of the city faded away and they came upon a wide, cobbled lane, dotted with elegant townhouses. These were the richest of all. *This* was where their lord lived—the jewel of the city.

"We have arrived in Squall's End," she said, sending the thought to Talon and his shields. *"All appears as expected. The city is heavily damaged in places where it succumbed to dragon fire."* She included projections with her thoughts, despite knowing it would upset Reyr to see this. *"I have yet to assess the extent of the damage. The city is overrun. They will need a great deal of assistance when this is all over. I will report back with what I find."*

Talon's answering thoughts followed her.

The guard came to a halt before the city's keep. More guards stood at the ready. Their escort spoke to them in a hushed voice, and then they were being motioned through.

She caught sight of servants rushing ahead—a result of quickly muttered words from the guards on duty. She glanced at Feowen, whose eyes darted about, always assessing, ensuring there were no threats.

He took his role with the utmost seriousness.

They passed through the keep's gate and came to a stop in the large courtyard beyond. She rubbed Tourmaline's neck, her way of thanking him, then dismounted, keeping a tight hold of her staff.

I will see that you are tended to, she told him. *But it could take time. We must meet with the lord of this keep and determine what is to be done.*

I will wait, Queen.

With her feet on the ground, she inhaled. Her nose felt stained with the putrid scent of dragon fire. Her eyes darted around the courtyard, lingering on the shadows beyond arches. There was a fountain in the center. A ship was deftly carved out of rock, sprouting water from various windows cut from its hull. The sounds of trickling broke the silence.

A man rushed forward. He was elegantly dressed, with an air of authority. "Forgive me, Your...*Your Majesty?*" he said with uncertainty, eyes wide as they swept over her. "We were not expecting you."

She blinked at him.

Feowen was already beside her, her queen's guard fanned out behind them. "Are you the lord of this city?" Feowen asked.

"Me? Oh." The man's brows drew in confusion. "I...I daresay... no, sir. I am its...its steward. But if you will follow me, I will take you to...to Lord Rhal. If that is favorable?" The steward's eyes darted between her and Feowen, as if trying to figure them out. He'd never seen a sprite before, nor a unicorn. She was surprised that he managed to speak at all, given his clear show of shock.

"Aik bunoh gethlah aik mek lagyu," Feowen said. *He looks like he might faint.* He seemed to find this amusing. Of course he did. He probably liked all the attention. After a day or two in camp, it had worn off. Now he was getting the satisfaction of surprise all over again.

She withheld her snort. Instead, she nodded in agreement. Feowen turned back to the steward, as if he'd just translated the man's words to his queen. "Yes, that would be favorable. Thank you."

"Right. Very good, then. Very good. This way."

Feowen's eyes lifted, rising up to the tops of the castle. A frown pulled at his lips. "Haan luine sahla yaat ynn kehv modah geth-luth?" *Do people really live in stone buildings like this?*

The rest of her guard smartly held their tongues, though she could feel the curiosity, and even excitement, radiating from them. This was the first time they'd entered any kind of structure that wasn't made from things in their forest. The camp had only tents.

She stifled a snicker. In *Ednuar*, she said, "They do. I once thought them quite romantic. Magical, even. Someone once told me they were oppressive, and now I'd have to agree."

"I think I'd go mad," Feowen also said in *Ednuar*.

"And what did you plan to do when we reached the capital?" she asked, lifting a brow.

He frowned. "I suppose I hoped it wouldn't be this… oppressive."

She snorted. This time, she didn't hold back. The steward glanced over his shoulder as they made their way down a corridor, up a flight of stairs, then down another. She wondered what he thought of her language, if he found it peculiar.

"Perhaps the king will allow you to sleep up on the top of his tower, in the queen's garden," she teased. "Out under the stars."

"If you care for me, dear cousin, you will convince him to agree."

She grinned. She'd only been joking, but clearly he liked the idea. All too soon, there was no more time to joke. They'd come to a large, wooden door.

The steward knocked, then entered. She heard his voice as he said, "Forgive me, my lord, but the queen of the sprites has come, and she requests an audience."

With a final glance at Feowen, she stepped through the doorway without any further invitation.

CHAPTER 9

TRANSLATIONS

Squall's End

Claire's eyes darted around the large meeting chamber dominated by a table of dark wood. It was only filled with three people, presumably one of them being Lord Rhal. It was easy to pick out nobility once you knew what to look for. Mostly, it was their fine clothes and their air of superiority.

Lord Rhal sat at the head, two others sat beside him on his right. Advisors, most likely. Chairs scraped the floor and the three occupants shot to their feet. Her eyes lingered over Lord Rhal. He was handsome. Younger than she expected. A brief flicker of realization made her falter. *This* was the lord Tamara had told her about. The one her parents had tried to marry her off to.

"Your Majesty," he said, his wide eyes darting over her, lingering on the places her sprite markings were visible. "This is an unexpected surprise!"

"She doesn't speak our tongue," the steward warned, his haughty tone lingering in the air, as if her inability to speak their language was an inconvenience. She tried not to bristle. Even if that were the case, it didn't make her any *less* because of it. There

90

would always be people like him, people who carried underlying prejudices.

"Gods above. Is that so?" Lord Rhal asked, taken aback. "Do any of them?"

"That one there," the steward said, pointing at Feowen. He'd made an assumption based on how they looked and it stoked her ire. "Forgive me, sir," he added, looking at Feowen. "I don't believe I caught your name."

"Ah," said Feowen, smiling his most charming smile. Beneath it, there was a subtle threat. Feowen was a powerful being, thousands upon thousands of years old. Older, even, than the drengr who lived today. He took a single step forward. "I am Prince Feowen. This is my cousin, the spriten queen. You may address her as *Your Majesty* and nothing less. You may address *me* as *Your Highness*, or Prince Feowen. I am also the captain of her guard. Behind us, the rest of her guard."

Lord Rhal's eyes darted over them, mouth hanging slightly agape. "And..." His throat bobbed. His tongue darted out to wet his lips. "You really *are* sprites?"

Feowen's gaze darted to hers, a single brow lifting. "Utah aik amdah? Gaanih lit outah lamenahi?" he asked. *Is he blind? Can he not see our markings?* She didn't miss the scorn in his voice.

"Sincid, Feowen. Canmah sasam sasa jiasin," she scolded, shooting him a look. *Hush, Feowen. Allow them their surprise.*

"We are indeed sprites, my lord," Feowen said, his voice turning sugary sweet with politeness. "My queen says she is pleased to meet you."

Lord Rhal bobbed his head, his eyes darting between them like he wasn't sure *who* to address. "Not that I'm not pleased—honored even—by your visit, Your Majesty, but things are dire here. I fear this could be dangerous for everyone, having you in our city. May I..." He hesitated, clearing his throat. "May I inquire as to the reason for your visit?"

Feowen turned to her, arms casually clasped behind his back. "Ynim mi eanish eah malioh eah trighah stahka, uen aeth aya laail taventa?" he asked, his expression serious. *Am I meant to pretend to translate all of that, or did you catch everything?*

She almost snorted. Behind her, one of her guards actually did.

She sighed and stepped forward. "We are here to protect you."

Lord Rhal's eyes bulged and he took a step back. His face turned red. He threw a nasty glare at his steward. "I thought you said she couldn't understand us?!" he hissed.

The steward sputtered in shock, embarrassment even. Good. Perhaps he'd think twice next time before making rash assumptions about other people.

"It is quite all right, my lord," she cut in smoothly. "It was a simple mistake. I merely did not wish to address you until now." As was her right, as queen. "As I said, we are here for your protection. The drengr plan to reclaim the fort in the coming days. We are here to ensure your city does not succumb to fire as it did before."

Lord Rhal's brows knitted. "And...and you can do that?"

"Of course. Between myself and my guards, I am certain. We will weave enough protective magic over the city to keep everyone safe. Not even a single ember will pass through our wards."

Lord Rhal grappled with this news then said, "We would be most appreciative, Your Majesty."

"Good. Then let us begin. There are many things to discuss." With that, she strode across the room, stopping behind the chair opposite Lord Rhal's. Feowen rushed forward, pulling it out for her. She would have done it herself but it wouldn't have appeared queenly. She took a seat, propping her staff against the table beside her. She invited her guards forward to join them.

Lord Rhal glanced about, looking between his two advisors, whom he hadn't yet introduced, then took his seat while they followed suit. As if sensing this blunder, he rushed to say, "This is Kevin Pendra and Yusuf Adel, my advisors. And you've already met my steward, Nigel Mitchum. Is there something we can get you? Refreshments, perhaps? I assume you've been on the road, traveling for a good deal of time?"

Not as long as he probably assumed.

"Thank you. *Shalaya.* And yes, we have," she answered.

"Refreshments would be most welcome." She considered simply using magic to summon goblets and water, as a show of her abilities, but decided there was no need to flex. Her abilities would be known soon enough.

Lord Rhal gave the steward a look and he rushed off. She used this opportunity to launch into their plan, explaining what Dragonwall's king had done, and where the sprites played into everything. She left a good deal out, only giving him the necessary basics. He'd find out the rest from Talon.

Servants entered carrying trays laden with pitchers of water, wine, and an assortment of pastries. She was starving, so she helped herself to a goblet of water and a few fancy rolls. Her guards politely waited, holding back until she finished before also taking part. It left her uneasy, this level of formality. Something she should probably be used to, but struggled with.

A good queen adapted, but she had trouble doing that. The attention, being treated differently, everyone putting her before themselves, it was all so...foreign. Reyr said she was meant for this, but if he was right, why was it such a struggle?

With the majority of their plans discussed, she turned to other matters. "Tell me of the fire and your losses," she said to Lord Rhal. "We passed through that section of the city on our way to your keep. It was...unsettling."

His face paled. "We lost nearly everyone in that area," he said, his voice pained. "By the time the fire was upon us, there was no way for them to evacuate. Dragonfire burns hot and it burns fast."

"There were no survivors?"

"A mere twenty seven out of nearly a thousand. Their burns were significant. Our healers have done what they can, but their scarring will be unfortunate."

"My people might be able to help," she said, trying to ignore her churning stomach.

"We would be most grateful for any aid. Thank you."

"And you will assist the survivors beyond healing?" she inquired. "Replace lost belongings, ensure they have a home, et cetera?"

"Of course. We have city funds from taxes to cover such things." He waved a hand.

She hesitated, then nodded, letting it go for now. When this was over, she'd have Talon speak with him on the matter, ensuring those who had suffered were taken care of and properly compensated. For now—

"Our queen will require adequate lodgings for the night," Feowen interrupted, "while we wait for King Talon's arrival. Your best room, if you have it."

Her head whipped around. "Bih sassih gendlla, Feowen?" *Was that necessary, Feowen?*

He offered a casual shrug and replied in *Ednuar*, "We've been traveling half the day. I intend to make sure you're taken care of, Cousin."

She sighed, turning back to Lord Rhal. "What my cousin means to say is, we would be most grateful if you have a place for us to pass the night."

The plan was to wait until dawn the following day. Talon would give her the signal when he approached with their army. Until then, they'd wait here.

"Of course, Your Majesty. We have several guest suites available. Nigel will show you to your rooms."

Everyone rose. Nigel motioned them forward, leading her from the meeting chamber. Feowen offered to see to the unicorns, and the rest of them left to settle in.

It was full dark by the time they were settled. She was given a modest suite with adjoining rooms for her guards. There weren't enough for all of them, so they paired up, assuring her they were plenty fine with the accommodations.

Lord Rhal invited them to the evening meal in the dining hall. Knowing him, he'd do as any lord would. He'd make an event out of it, celebrating her arrival. She hadn't brought more than the clothes on her back and the cloak used to disguise herself during their journey. They'd opted to travel light.

As they traversed the corridors, heading to the lowest floor of the keep, her queen's guard surrounded her, four in front and four in behind, walking in sets of two. She'd selected eight back in Esterpine, when Feowen thought it would be a grand show of spriten strength to one-up Talon with his six. She hadn't much cared. It was a formality, more than anything. But she was glad to have them. She looked forward to the day when she could count every one of them as a dear friend.

Already, she was getting to know their personalities better.

She got along best with Jeanine. Probably because she could relate to her. They'd bonded over their shared humanity, even if she wasn't technically human anymore.

Rahlif Dorvyre was a quiet sort who rarely spoke or smiled. At first, she thought it was because he was too proud. But she caught him wearing small, secret smiles when the others said or did anything worth laughing over, when he thought no one was looking.

Elyon Marquin was a fierce fighter, besting even the males. She hadn't known what to expect of Aolis Marquin's daughter. Elyon had a hard exterior, always wore a stern expression, and was quite serious at any given moment. But she had a soft voice and liked the color purple. She wore every shade of it imaginable when she wasn't wearing her guard attire.

Filvro Holowyn was a direct opposite to Elyon. She was always smiling, always cracking jokes, sometimes to solicit smiles from Rahlif, since they all knew he was the quietest of the bunch. Of her spriten guards, Filyro was the one she felt most comfortable around. The woman just had a way about her, like she wanted everyone to be as comfortable as possible.

Gorded Cawyn was too smart for his own good. He knew far too much about everything, and was a walking brainiac. She could count on him to offer random useless facts about everything when she wanted, and even when she didn't. It was often Feowen who silenced him when it was clear the others couldn't stand another minute of his prattling. But she appreciated his mind.

Aithlin Naeris was the most stunning woman she'd ever laid eyes on. Even more beautiful than Jade, with dark hair and pale skin covered in numerous markings, dainty features, crystal blue eyes, and a lush set of lips. But there was no disguising the ferocious way she fought with a blade. She gave even Eylon a good fight when the two of them sparred. And yet, she dressed less feminine than the other females, and didn't mind getting her hands dirty for the tasks that required it. She appreciated that about her. So did some of the other males back at camp, whom she'd caught gazing at her, enraptured.

And then there was Jassin Orythra, who spent most of his time pining after Rahlif. She hadn't realized it until she continuously caught him staring at the other male when he didn't think anyone was looking. Jassin loved singing. She loved listening to him hum tunes when they walked through camp. Whenever he opened his mouth to sing something in *Ednuar*, she got chills. His voice was ethereal and haunting. She couldn't wait to make him sing something in the great throne room of Kastali Dun, couldn't wait to hear the way his voice echoed through the cavernous room.

Together, they descended the final flight of stairs bringing them into the keep's dining hall. Feowen led the procession from his place in the front. He paused in the entryway, forcing all of them to stop. "All hail the spriten queen!" he cried, his voice echoing through the space.

"Mi ynim haruin eah themadar aik rayih gethek haanik sassih," she muttered to Elyon, who stood on her front right. *I'm starting to think he really enjoys doing that.*

Eylon laughed and said, "Mi ynim haruin eah thermandar aya kunyn sahwyr," which earned a snort from Filvro, behind her. *I'm starting to think you are correct.*

Filvro said, "Aik gethlahi ana juhlah nin aiklan eigah rohmme. Uen kansylla aik utah sighir lerah einha." *He likes the sound of his own voice. Or perhaps he is merely showing off for someone.*

Several snickers rippled through her guards. So it was common knowledge then, the way Feowen felt about Jeanine? It shouldn't have surprised her. Sprites were astute beings.

Feowen heard the exchange. Sprite ears and all. He glanced over his shoulder, lifting a brow. Then he turned and led them into the dining hall. Jeanine hadn't yet picked up enough *Ednuar* to know what had been said, but if she got the chance, she'd tell her later.

She'd asked Jeanine several days ago if it bothered her that they sometimes spoke a language she didn't understand. Jeanine had shrugged and admitted that it motivated her to learn, but that it didn't upset her. "As long as you're not whispering bad things about me," she teased, but Claire had assured her they would never do such a thing. Plus, Feowen would never allow it.

The hall's nobility were on their feet as her procession made its way to the dais. Lord Rhal stood beaming. His arms spread wide. "Welcome, welcome," he said. "Our table isn't large enough for everyone, so we've placed seating at the front for those who do not fit here."

She nodded. The lord's table wasn't nearly as large as the one in the great keep, seating only five. Lord Rhal hadn't yet found a wife to sit beside him. She took the seat on his right, with Feowen on his left. Jeanine sat to her right, and that left one open place at Feowen's left, taken by Filvro. The others took seats at the front of the hall.

Platters were brought forth, but it wasn't the kind of feast she was used to in Kastali Dun. Root vegetables, apples, and warm bread. "We have rationed everything," he explained, noticing the way she looked over the food. "I understand that sprites do not eat meat."

"You are most thoughtful, Lord Rhal," she said, confirming.

"Most of what we have left in the city are foodstuffs that can be stored for long periods. Things have grown rather...dire."

"Then it is good we have come," she said, dishing food onto her plate. "How much do you have left?"

Feowen kept his hands busy too, but she could tell he was listening intently.

"Enough for two more weeks, unless we further cut rations." He lifted his gaze, glancing about the hall at the nobles sitting within. "It has been a challenge. I do my best to ensure that everyone in the city has enough. As you can imagine, those of nobility make the matter difficult for me."

"You mean, they believe they should have more," she answered, to which he nodded.

"I am sure you can understand the difficulty, being a queen. It is no easy feat, making everyone happy."

"Impossible, yes."

"Indeed." He offered her a small smile, eyes lingering over her face. He found her attractive, she realized. She almost snorted. He didn't yet know she was promised to another. Being young, handsome, and opportunistic, he would likely throw himself at her if he felt inclined.

"Will the leftovers go to those in need?" she asked, keeping the conversation moving.

"Yes. Nothing in my city is wasted. Especially not now. If this experience has taught me anything, it's to be overly cognizant of how food is allocated."

"I can imagine," she mused. "Tomorrow, at first light, I will see that you have an abundance of fruit trees in your courtyard garden."

"Forgive me," he said, brow furrowing. "But I do not understand."

"I will grow the trees and ensure they are heavy with fruit. Liberating your city will not fix your food problems overnight. I do not wish for your city to starve."

"But the king—"

"—will have many matters occupying his time once your city is freed. I can help in this way. I will also see to those who were scarred by the fire, but that must wait until after the dragons are gone, as I wish to have adequate time to work with them."

Lord Rhal's throat bobbed. Again, his eyes darted over her face, lingering. "You are too kind, Your Majesty. I do not know how to... That is to say, thank you. I am grateful."

"Varsik, Ayas Drollaya. Aik bei sin hallah klah ayas codah veh danah," Feowen said. *Careful, Your Majesty. He'll be falling at your feet by tomorrow.* He lifted an eyebrow.

She huffed and said to Lord Rhal, "My cousin has just informed me that he will likewise help in this matter."

Feowen snorted, but returned to his food.

Lord Rhal's eyes danced. "Is that really what he said?"

She bit her lower lip to suppress a smile. "More or less—less, perhaps,"

Lord Rhal didn't believe her but he grinned anyway.

Dinner passed quickly after that, followed by a dessert of warm, spiced wine and sweet custard. They talked about inconsequential things. Mostly, Lord Rhal plied her with questions about the forest. She was all too happy to indulge him. Even Feowen chipped in.

She was glad when it was time to retire. Being queen was exhausting. She had no idea how she'd do it day in and day out, once she returned to Kastali Dun. But that was a problem for another day. For now, her only concern was the people of Squall's End. Tomorrow morning would come soon enough.

CHAPTER 10

DRAGONS AND BLOODSHED

Squall's End

Bedelth waited as the remaining plates of armor were fastened into place along his body. The metal was strong but it was the sleek craftsmanship that truly impressed him. Ice metal was near indestructible. It was the base metal for every drengr's sverak. Mined by the dwargs, and found only in the Northern Barrier Range, it was one of the most valuable resources in the world. He'd never worn anything like it.

Plates interlocked down the back of his neck, splitting around his spikes, down over his back, around the joints of his wings, down the muscled parts of his legs and forearms, and around the front of his chest, where the softer scales on his body resided. A number of people were assigned to the task, fastening each segment into place. Riders helped their mates, but...he had no rider to assist.

He had no mate...

He wasn't hurt by Saffra's rejection, knowing that she didn't want him. Things were better this way. They *were*. If he repeated it enough, it would get easier. He'd tell himself whatever he needed to, to get past this. Yes, that was it. He needed to get used to the notion that he didn't have a mate. The sooner he accepted it, the sooner he could move on—

A deep, challenging bellow split the air. He turned towards the source. Talon. His king was antsy to get going, to reunite with his queen. A soft snort escaped his chest. Talon was anxious whenever they were separated, even if by a mere scrap of distance. Claire had only been gone for a single span of a day.

The field around him was packed, groups of drengr already assembled into their respective wing formations. The kingdom's soldiers were long since on their way to Squall's End, accompanied by a select group of dwargs. They had boarded several transport barges in the middle of the night and would be landing on the opposite shore in the next couple of hours. Claire was assembled with her guards in the city, weaving her magic to ensure that no one came to harm. Every step of the plan was falling into place.

King Talon's shields were already in formation. They were allowing Dallin to fly with them; Talon had all but adopted him into their ranks at this point. If he wasn't mistaken, the king would give Dallin the opportunity to swear his oath when they returned home.

His gums peeled away from his razor sharp teeth. It wasn't a smile, exactly, but perhaps the closest thing to one. Dallin had melded into their ranks. While the young male was still naive to so much of the world, he fit in well. If this was truly what Dallin wanted, then he was glad to have him. All of them were.

Their attendants finished, stepping away. He shifted, anxious to get this over with. His sharp talons gouged deep furrows into the soil—

A soft scent filled the air.

Shivers raced down his spine, straight to the tip of his tail. He froze. She smelled like warm vanilla and eucalyptus. But there was more to it than just those worldly components. There was something deeper, something only *he* could discern. His mind knew it for what it was, and it had only taken *years*. The scent of a *mate*. A reaction in his brain that made her smell different than anyone else.

He'd never realized it before, after all their time together. Now he couldn't get enough. Wanted to breathe her in, hold the scent of her inside him forever.

He whipped his head around, eyes zeroing in on her. She stood off to the side of the field, watching him. No, she was watching the entire king's wing. After all, he was not so lucky as to earn her entire focus. Wishful thinking—too wishful.

Her hands were clasped in front of her, fingers twisting together out of nervousness. She looked so small, so fragile, dwarfed by hundreds of draconic bodies. A fierce urge to race over, to wrap his powerful body around her and shield her from everyone else, erupted through his chest. He pushed it down.

Her hair was pulled back into a tight chignon, with a few loose strands framing her beautiful cheekbones. Black pants and a yellow tunic molded to her frame, accentuating her feminine curves. It was trimmed with green embroidery. The colors enlivened her caramel skin, leaving her radiant. To him, she was bright sunshine on a cold and dreary day. A starburst of life. Everything his heart *craved*.

Her soft, brown eyes locked on his. His breath caught, chest pulling tight. He held still, so very still, as if a single hairsbreadth of movement would frighten her away.

But she didn't flee. Her gaze was on him, lingering over the armor he wore. Even from across the field, he could see her swallow.

She stepped forward. His chest heaved outward, sucking in a deep breath. When she came to stand before him, he let out an exhale. It came out as a plume of smoke.

He wished they could speak, craved the ability to say something, anything, to her at this moment. If only she would reach out —touch his scales. She appeared to struggle before saying, "Be safe, Bedelth."

He gave an answering hum, deep in his throat. He tried not to show how pleased he sounded, at her having come to wish him luck. Perhaps all was not lost?

She stepped past him, moving on to the others, wishing them

luck, too. He hid his jealousy. It was within her right to wish them well. *But she came to you first*, he tried to tell himself, practically snorting at how pathetic the reassurance sounded.

After she finished, he watched her every step as she made her way through the assembled drengr, back towards camp. As the distance increased, he felt her pull a part of him with her, like a string stretched tight. He'd heard of this—heard Talon talk about the string that linked mates and what it felt like. He should have taken it more seriously.

This wasn't goodbye. He'd see her when he returned, even if she didn't want anything to do with him. He'd be the one to tell her how everything went. He'd do it before anyone else had the chance.

Talon reared back and roared. *"We fly!"* He sent the telepathic thought to every drengr in the vicinity. The resounding bellows blasted into the air around him, deafening.

Thoughts of his mate were pushed from his mind. A new frenzy took hold. The beast in him was waking up. The drengr were cousins to the dragon, after all. There was still a wild side lurking beneath their scales.

Nearly two hundred draconic bodies vaulted into the sky. A vast sea of colors spread out around him. The time to reclaim Fort Squall was upon them.

~

THE OPPOSITE SHORE MATERIALIZED. Squall's End was a massive expanse along the coast, one of the largest cities in Dragonwall. Beside it, Fort Squall sat empty and desecrated, ruined by the dragons who'd claimed it. They passed overhead, continuing on.

Beneath them, he spotted their reinforcements moving in an organized formation. Half would split to stay at Squall's End, the other half would head towards the lake. Field units weren't entirely necessary. The drengr were the only logical match for wild dragons. But it was expected of Talon to include soldiers. He'd kept their numbers low, since transporting them was a tedious task.

Besides, it was better to be prepared. If things went wrong, they might be glad of the extra blades. That's why the king had allowed several units of dwargs, too.

"I can see you." Claire's words broke into his mind. Words intended for Talon, though she included his shields. She'd been keeping them updated. It was still miraculous—and he hadn't yet gotten used to it—having her voice in his mind. *"Be careful,"* she added to all of them. The city shrank behind them.

Whatever Talon said in response, his king kept between the two of them.

Bedelth sucked in a sharp breath. The lake materialized, but that wasn't what caught his gaze. It was the glittering clusters of bodies littering the landscape. Like they were merely napping. Except...they weren't.

"The poison worked," Talon said.

A weight lifted from his chest. He hadn't realized how anxious he'd been, nervous that their plan wouldn't work. Glittering clusters of color were gathered around the shores of Plymlet lake. As they neared, the clusters grew more distinct, the colors more identifiable. Kane's wild dragons had succumbed to the paralysis that overcame them when the poison's effects kicked in.

A roar split the air.

"Incoming," Talon warned. Several bodies separated from those on the ground, springing into the air.

"It was too much to hope they would all succumb," Reyr said, unamused.

"There aren't that many," Koldis pointed out. There couldn't be more than ten heading for them.

The various wings around them began splitting away according to plan. The dragons on the ground required their attention. They would be dispensed with as quickly and painlessly as possible.

King Talon stayed true to their flight path, aiming straight for the wild dragons. They were flanked by Byron's wing and two others, on hand if necessary.

Seconds ticked by. The dragons came close enough that he

could count them easily. His heart hammered loudly in his chest, eager with anticipation.

A piercing draconic scream split the air, filled with fury. For a moment, he didn't question it, and then—

"I am Fright the White, and I have come to seek revenge for your betrayal," a voice roared, bursting into the mind of every drengr and dragon alike.

Those words were followed by a string of swearing from Koldis. *"It would seem my mate has decided to join the foray,"* Koldis said, his tone dry.

Bedelth's head snapped around. He spotted the giant, ancient beast. A white dragon that looked oddly familiar.

"The marble dragon," Talon said, not sounding surprised.

Upon its back, sitting as if she owned the entire world, was the spriten princess. She flew like a goddess upon the wings of vengeance.

"I will rip and tear and maim. You will remember me as you breathe your last, dying breath, remember what your clan did. You will remember your betrayal," Fright continued, flying in a straight path to intercept the wild dragons headed straight for Talon.

Taylynn's head turned, her gaze locking on Koldis.

"Do not harm my mate," Koldis warned. *"Or there will be hell to pay."*

"Like any of us wish to suffer your wrath?" came Talon's sardonic reply. That was all they had time for.

Fright barreled through the formation of wild dragons, scattering them. A second later, the king's wing smashed into the chaos. Bedelth's talons were out, ready to rip gouges through scale and hide and muscle and sinew.

He snapped his teeth, latching onto the leg of a red beast, redirecting its flight pattern. It twisted off course, wings flapping to regain control. He gave chase, grappling with it until he had a good hold. Hot pain seared his flank, needle-sharp talons dragging down his body as they found purchase between his plates of armor. The rest of the beast's talons merely scraped over metal. A burst of flame hit him square in the face. He was careful not to inhale. *"I am*

Wrath the Red. I will destroy you," it hissed. *"You will be nothing but fodder for worms."*

He didn't waste time arguing. Besides, he didn't need to make threats. Didn't need big words to do his talking.

The red dragon was closely matched in size. It didn't matter. He was gripped with a fury unmatched. These beasts had caused enough bloodshed. Their time was at an end.

Growling, he released a torrent of flames, distracting it long enough to rip its wing clean from its body. Wrath screamed, the piercing sound too much for his sensitive ears. He shuddered. A moment later, his teeth found Wrath's neck. He clamped down. Hot liquid pooled into his mouth, down his jaws, as he ripped its throat clean out. A resultant screech laced with fury and pain was the only answer before the limp body dropped from the sky.

He didn't bother watching long enough to see it strike the ground.

His brothers grappled with their own opponents. The world was a chaotic blur of colors and roars, the snapping of teeth, flashing of talons. There were more dragons in the sky now, more than they'd anticipated. Still, far fewer than there would have been. Saffra's poison had done its work. Her creative thinking had saved them from a great deal of bloodshed.

His lungs expanded with pride. She was fierce and smart and beautiful—*no*, he couldn't think of her now, couldn't think of her *at all*. That would make everything more painful.

A flash of red orange caught his gaze. Before he could find a new opponent, he turned on his wingtip and caught sight of Squall's End. Three dragons had split away, perhaps having come from the west. Plumes of fire blossomed from their maws.

A ball of cold, hard dread settled in the pit of his stomach. A single dragon's fire—that is all it would take to decimate an entire city. He thought of Kastali Dun, of what it would be like if a single dragon set fire to the entire city. His stomach churned.

"Claire?" Talon's question burst through his mind. His heart skipped. Somewhere beneath the flame and smoke was his queen. He watched as flames hot enough to melt rock bore down on the

city, watched as each of the three dragons swept over the tops of the buildings.

"I've got it," came Claire's confident reply.

The flames broke over an invisible barrier. They didn't spread. They didn't destroy a single thing. They merely snuffed out. The dragons tried again and again. Several tense minutes passed. Still nothing.

Projections filled his mind. Claire stood on the ramparts facing the city, watching the dragons fly above. Her spriten guards fanned out around her, each wearing a fierce look of concentration. Jeanine was there too, on Claire's right, sword in hand. She watched Claire's back so that the spriten queen could focus entirely on her magic. In one hand, Claire gripped the strange spriten staff. The other was outstretched, as if holding her magic in place. He saw the hand before him as if it were his own, viewing each of the flashes from her vantage point.

Dragon maws opened wide, belting tongues of flame. The city was eerily quiet, its inhabitants hunkered down. If he looked close enough, he could see faces pressed against windows, trying to watch.

Kane's threat to destroy the city was rendered useless, all because a spriten queen had chosen to fight for Dragonwall. No, not just *any* spriten queen. *His* queen.

"Well done, my love. Well done." King Talon's rumbling voice oozed with pride. Bedelth pulled out of Claire's projections. He glanced over to find Talon had broken away from the fighting. Several dragons from Fort Squall had taken his place, slaughtering the remaining beasts.

Below, pools of blood spilled from the now lifeless bodies that littered the landscape. His stomach roiled. He'd been one of Claire's proponents, arguing against the slaughter of pregnant females. What she'd done had been risky, warning the wild dragons to surrender, but he trusted his queen. Killing helpless dragons was a ruthless way to kill—ending an opponent that couldn't fight back. He'd had no qualms in supporting her decision to give them a choice, to save their pregnant females, at the least. He glanced around, but didn't see any bulging bellies. Perhaps those females had made the right choice in the end, to save their unborn hatchlings.

When he fell into formation with the king's wing, Talon did a final sweep of the area, observing the activity below. Seconds later, the only sound was that of their beating wings. The seven of them, a complete wing, circled in a wide path, then descended.

"*No sign of Kane,*" Talon said. "*I am not sure how I feel about that.*"

"*Be grateful,*" Verath answered. "*He's licking his wounds in private after his encounter with Claire in the forest. I would imagine that distracted him enough, he didn't see this coming.*"

"*Except, this feels almost...anticlimactic,*" Koldis mused. Bedelth had to agree. It was too easy. That's what they had wanted—what they had hoped for—but when was life ever straightforward?

"*I think we know what it means,*" Jovari said, giving voice to their fears. "*Something else is coming, something bigger. Nothing is ever this easy, planning or no.*"

"*What could be bigger than reclaiming a fort?*" Dallin asked, speaking up for the first time.

"*Orchestrating another attack?*" Bedelth said. "*Hitting us somewhere else. Somewhere it hurts. Somewhere it would crush us. A killing blow. Hopefully Captain Bennett's work in Oshea will be fruitful.*"

"*The capital?*" Dallin dared to ask. "*You think Kane would try to hit the capital?*"

"*I think he's capable,*" Talon said, bringing the conversation to an end by adding, "*For now, let us be happy with our success.*"

The king was right. It was done. After months of planning, headaches, and heartache, the jewel that was Fort Squall was theirs once more. And yet, he still felt hollow. The silence that met his ears was the loudest form of quiet he'd ever heard. It spoke of awful things. Of death. Of bloodshed. But...whispering on the currents of the breeze, it also spoke of victory. Kane needed to try a lot harder if he wished to take their kingdom.

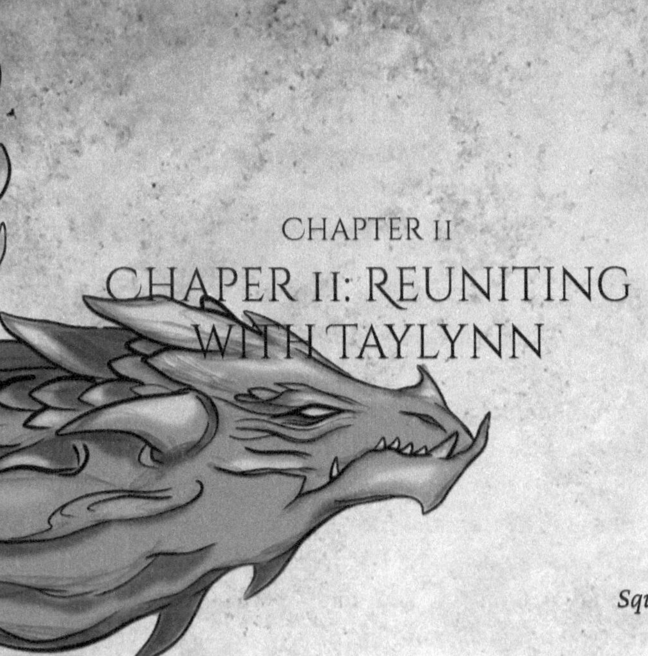

CHAPTER 11

CHAPER 11: REUNITING WITH TAYLYNN

Squall's End

Koldis found a place to land. The air was drenched with the metallic stench of blood. Draconic bodies littered the ground. They hadn't yet discussed what to do with them, they hadn't gotten that far.

"I must check on the city," King Talon announced. *"But I will return shortly."* Anyone who knew him knew his words translated to one thing. He was checking on Claire. Talon was a king first and foremost, so that was his diplomatic way of putting it. Jovari and Reyr split away to accompany him.

Byron sent out several wings to ensure there were no survivors. It was unlikely, but it did not hurt to be certain.

He shifted into human form, landing near the shores of Plymlet Lake. His remaining shield brothers came to stand beside him. Above them, there was a flash of white. His shoulders tensed.

Taylynn was on the back of a dragon that *wasn't* him. It felt like a betrayal. He ground his teeth, forcing his mind to calm. It wasn't as if she had much choice. Taylynn was a fly caught in a web of the tree's doing. He couldn't take it personally, even though he wanted to.

"*So...*" Verath said. "I wasn't expecting to see your *mate*."

"If you're asking whether I knew she'd be here, the answer is no." The words came out as a growl. "Her coming and going is her business."

The king tree's business, really.

"Shouldn't it be *your* business as her mate?" Dallin piped up, curious.

Verath put a hand on Dallin's shoulder and squeezed. "Careful, young one. The sprite princess is a fickle creature."

Bedelth scoffed as he said, "I think you mean all women."

"No—not really. *Your* mate, perhaps," Verath said, shrugging.

Bedelth stilled, his expression turning stricken. "Don't you dare. We may be brothers, but don't you dare go there..."

Verath hesitated. He must have seen the warning in Bedelth's gaze, the pain. He lifted a shoulder and said, "As you wish."

The truth was, none of them had any idea what the hell was going on between Bedelth and his new mate. Whatever it was, it was not good. Bedelth should have been brimming with happiness, overflowing with it, but instead he was brooding.

Most paths between mates were straightforward. But for a select few, like himself, like King Talon, and clearly like Bedelth, there was a lot more to it. It wasn't going to be an easy road, even if Talon had agreed—much to his shock—to amend the laws.

Still, if Bedelth thought they were simply going to ignore the fact that Saffra was *clearly* his mate, he was wildly mistaken. They all knew—even Talon. Though, their king was being respectful of Bedelth's privacy and ignoring the matter. They were attempting to give him his space, tiptoeing around the glaringly obvious.

The air whipped around them as several wings shot by overhead, finding places to land. The drengr maintained form so their riders could dismount. He glanced up again, just in time to see the white dragon circle once, twice, then dive towards them.

It was a frightening sight, one that would send most humans running. As it was, he stood motionless, watching as the dragon landed a hairsbreadth from him, as if taunting him. Fine.

"Is there a reason there's still a living, breathing wild dragon on this battlefield?" he said to no one in particular.

Taylynn's soft snort was followed by a distinctly draconic grumble.

His chest buckled at the sight of her. Nearly two weeks had passed since their parting. To say he ached was an understatement. Did she feel the same pain in his absence?

He assessed her, from the tiara resting on her brow, her hair littered with forest debris, to the tips of her booted toes. He drank her in like he was stranded in the desert and she was the water he needed to survive. She was stunning in a gauzy, light pink gown that didn't cover much. Her body was littered in markings; there was more luminescence than actual skin. A small growl rose in his throat, making his irrational jealousy obvious. He wanted her to himself, wanted every measure of those beautiful markings for *his* eyes only. Instead, she was proudly displayed for all to see. Not atop *his* back, but the back of a godsdamned wild dragon.

Their eyes locked. A pink flush rose on her cheeks. Was she remembering how deeply he'd kissed her? How he'd claimed her mouth when they'd last parted? Was she thinking about what was next in store for her?

Her throat bobbed. A span of silence stretched between them and for a moment, he forgot there were others in the vicinity. At last, Fright snorted and furrowed the ground with his talons.

She blinked and the spell was broken. Swinging a leg over the beast, she dismounted. Koldis forgot how to move. He stood stock still as she walked over to him, stopping before him. She was *here* —right here!

They stood face to face, their eyes locked. A heavy flutter dropped into his belly. He inhaled, and her scent washed over him. She smelled like *home* and something distinctly *his*. There was no other way to describe it. Something in his brain snapped. He didn't think, he acted. His arms reached for her and he pulled her against him, burying his face in her hair before inhaling deeply.

Immediate calm settled over his muscles.

Her arms came around him, tentative at first. "Koldis..." she said, keeping her voice low. His chest began to rise and fall in rapid gasps. She stroked the hair at the nape of his neck. "Koldis," she said again, her voice soothing. She was comforting him. Comforting him like a beloved thing.

He didn't care. Didn't care what his brothers thought of it. Didn't care if it made him look weak.

When she pulled back, he framed her face with his hands, their noses nearly touching. He didn't know what to say, how to voice the myriad of emotions coursing through him. All he knew was that he wished they could share minds so that he wouldn't have to explain anything, so that she might already know everything.

"Will you stay with me?" were the words that came from him.

A tentative smile pulled at her lips. "It was a tedious flight. I am not eager to turn around and leave."

Everything in him lightened, like he was floating. He pulled her to him and kissed her. The warmth of her mouth was instant comfort—

A throat cleared.

"Godsdamn it," he muttered.

Her laugh made his insides drip with liquid fire. "Are you going to introduce me to your...brothers?" The last was a question as her eyes darted over his companions. "Lord Bedelth, good to see you again."

"Indeed, Princess," came Bedelth's rumbling reply.

"This is Verath and Dallin," he said, trying not to sound irritated.

Taylynn's face lit up. "Ah. The young drengr who wishes to become a shield."

Dallin's swallow was audible. Koldis hid the grin pulling at his lips, knowing what sort of effect Taylynn had on others. "Pleasure, Your Highness," Dallin managed to say.

"Put Koldis out of his misery, will you?" Verath said, more of a command than anything. "I'm tired of his pining."

"I don't pine," he scoffed, giving Verath a glare. To Taylynn he added, "I don't."

"Of course not," she cooed, placating, *teasing*.

He grumbled, his irritation mixing with the happiness of having her close. What was this? Pick on Koldis day? He wasn't having it. "The rest of you can certainly manage things without me. I'd like some time with my—"

"Actually," Taylynn said, cutting him off, "I was hoping to have a few words with my queen first."

He exhaled, pushing down his disappointment. "Of course."

Taylynn saw it anyway. She never missed a thing. It reminded him of how much younger he was.

"She's just there," Taylynn said, motioning with her head. He glanced up sharply. Claire was indeed approaching on the back of Tourmaline. Her queen's guard followed behind. Overhead, Talon flew, keeping an eye on his mate. "I'll only be a few moments," Taylynn added, her voice softening. She took his hand. At the sudden pounding of his heart, he could do little but nod in acquiescence.

Claire came to a stop.

The first thing Koldis noticed was her pale face and the way her eyes darted to the dragon carcasses. A moment later, Talon was on the ground, transformed. "Princess Taylynn," he drawled, eyeing her. Dragonwall's king had always been careful around the female.

"Your Majesty," Taylynn said, attempting to drop Koldis's hand like they'd been caught doing something naughty. He kept a firm grasp on it. Her eyes darted down, a question in her expression. He gave nothing away.

Claire hopped down from Tourmaline's back. "Taylynn," she breathed, as if seeing a dear friend. She rushed forward and threw her arms around the princess's neck. Taylynn was forced to hug Claire with only one arm. Claire stepped away, keeping a hold of Taylynn's shoulders. "It's good to see you. I didn't realize you'd come for this."

"I didn't want her out here," Talon said by way of explanation.

"I can handle it," she snapped at Talon. Something in the way she said it told him enough. They'd probably argued before this. Talon was likely being overprotective, *yet again*, and trying to shield her from the harshest realities of the world. That was their own business.

"I promised Fright revenge," Taylynn explained, her eyes darting to the white dragon waiting patiently. "He'll have to be happy with the two deaths he caused." A loud snort meant Fright was absolutely *not* satisfied. "And anyway, he has agreed to help raise their young."

Claire gasped. "So, the mothers?"

"Mostly safe," Taylynn said. "I was sent by the tree to intercept those who chose to live. I led them to the forest's edge, where several spriten attendants are escorting them through to the Gable Mountains. There is a cave there, once used by the Forest Clan, with warm sands ideal for—"

"Your Majesty!" A voice called. "Your Majesty."

A rider appeared beside them, out of breath. "Your Majesty," she said to King Talon. "There... We found... There is a pregnant female, incapacitated. I wouldn't let our wing slaughter her. Not without your command. It didn't feel...it didn't feel right." The rider's hand went to her belly, and Koldis realized it was rounded. She was carrying a child.

Claire's body went rigid. "What did you say?" she managed, pinning the rider with her green gaze. "A pregnant dragon?"

The rider nodded, hand still resting on the slight swell of her abdomen.

"There were only four," Taylynn said, by way of explanation. The tone of her voice said what her words didn't—that she knew something more.

"Four females?" Claire's gaze landed on Taylynn. Her eyes narrowed. "But, in my dream, in Saffra's dream, there were five."

"They were given a choice," Taylynn explained.

"But..." Claire's brows drew together. "Well, we can't kill her."

The rider stood there, awaiting the king's orders.

Taylynn's hand tightened in his. "In life, there is nothing more defining than the choices we make. Every being is free to make their own. She made hers."

"*Ni!*" The authority in Claire's voice was followed by a powerful silence.

Ni meant *no*. He'd been in the forest long enough to pick up a few simple words.

The two women stared at each other, unblinking. Behind her, Claire's queen's guard stood at the ready. He noticed Feowen's gaze, darting between his queen and his sister.

"*Aahm ella aya saphi mik haan, Ayas Drollaya,*" Taylynn said, her tone respectful.

Claire's eyes closed. In her hand, her fingers turned white around the staff she clenched. Behind her lids, her eyes danced. He wondered what she was doing, what she was thinking. When her eyes opened, her expression was resolute.

"I would have you spare her," Claire said. "That is *my* choice. If I must bear the consequences, so be it. She cannot make this decision for her unborn hatchlings. If I must kill her myself once the eggs are laid, so be it. But I will not slaughter a pregnant female."

Talon's exhale was audible.

"Ain nuah," Taylynn said. "Fright and I will escort her to the forest when she regains her body and mind. She will be kept under careful watch. But..."

"It will be I who must kill her," Claire said, nodding. "Yes, the tree made that clear."

Talon shot a glance at his mate, his lips pressed into a tight line.

Fright trumpeted some form of a response, then shot into the air. "He will guard her," Taylynn explained.

IT WAS DECIDED they would burn the carcasses. While fire didn't harm dragons when they were alive, it was not so when they were dead. With the help of the drengr and their riders, it took less than an hour before the shores surrounding Plymlet Lake were dotted with small, magically controlled fires.

"Fly with me," Koldis said, taking Taylynn by the hand. "You've never flown with me. I had to see you on the back of another—" He stopped himself, trying not to scoff. "Come, fly with me."

Taylynn's eyes darted over his face before she nodded.

He sent a quick word to King Talon, letting him know, then led her away from the others. They went far enough to find some semblance of privacy. His muscles twitched as he made the change from his human form to his drengr form. She was going to touch him, here and now, for the first time. They hadn't attempted it in the forest—hadn't needed to because she'd known.

What if you discover that you were wrong? a dark voice said, bleeding into his mind. *What if* she *was wrong?*

He hated the thought that they might not be mates. After all their assumptions, they had never done the *one thing* that would confirm it. Skin to scale—a practice as old as his race.

This was an irrational fear. Of course it was. He knew with absolute certainty. It was the way his heart beat faster in her presence, the way breathing became difficult when she was away, the pain at being separated, the way she smelled, the way her mere existence rearranged all the particles of his being, scrambling them and rebuilding them into something *more*.

She stoically watched his transformation, waiting. When he settled, he eyed her. She looked so small compared to his hulking green form. Every fiber of his being wanted to curl around her, to drape his wings over her and cocoon her in safety. It was a ridiculous thought. She was more powerful than him, perhaps not in physical form, but magically.

She rolled her lips between her teeth. Perhaps she was thinking the same thing . She took him in, from the tip of his forked tongue as it tasted the air, to the end of his tail, nervously lashing about.

"I..." She trailed off. It was a rare occurrence, seeing *Esterpine's princess* at a loss. Her eyes shone with something that made warmth spread through his body. "You are the most beautiful thing I have ever seen."

His breath caught.

"The fates could have chosen any color for me, but they chose green."

His chest rumbled with a deep, affirmative growl; the reverberations vibrated into the earth beneath him. Green. He'd never considered it. His emerald scales were perfect for her, loving the forest as she did.

His belly swooped. This was meant to be—them, together, even if many things stood in their way. Her being a sprite, him being a drengr, it was all inconsequential where fate was concerned.

A tremor ran through him as she approached, her steps slow. The moment she lifted her hand, time stretched to infinity. A single heartbeat became a thousand. A single breath, a million inhales. And then the warmth of her palm connected with him.

The world tilted on its axis. He was thrust into her mind as quickly as she was thrust into his. They were in a forest. For the first time, he didn't balk at the towering trees or the scent of pine or the rustling leaves. A deep love blossomed for the world she held so dear.

This was the place where they were joined. The place they came together. The inbetween of their minds.

He felt her all around him. She was the sunshine filtering through the foliage, the cool breeze on his skin, the soft mossy earth beneath his feet. A shiver raced over him.

"It's magnificent," he whispered, feeling her agreement.

A laugh split the silence, more beautiful than the sound from any instrument he'd heard. And then the realization hit him—every thought in her mind was a tree. He went to one and placed his hand atop it. Memories rushed in. The moment she'd first laid eyes on him, when he'd traversed the forest with Claire, Jovari, and Reyr. She'd watched him from afar. The monumental realization she'd reached, knowing even then, what he was to her. His stomach swooped, tingles spreading through him.

"Sasyia kunyn stahka mih hukohnai," she said. *They are all my memories.*

"I can understand you," he realized, thrilled. *"I can understand Ednuar."*

"Of course. Your thoughts are my thoughts. Your mind is my mind."

"What do you see?" he asked, eager.

"The same as you, only, the trees in your mind are fewer, but they carry memories nonetheless."

He looked out over the sea of densely packed trees. There were hundreds, thousands, more. He couldn't hope to count them, even if he'd wanted to. He took a step back, his throat squeezing tight.

"I have lived a very long time, Koldis."

There were moments when he was very aware of her long life span, and then there were moments when he completely forgot. When she was just a female—a beautiful, vibrant, female, but a female nonetheless. As he beheld the forest that tied their minds together, a deep chasm of wanting filled him. Even knowing that he might never visit every single tree, he wanted her more than he'd ever wanted anything.

"The king has given his permission," she realized, having plucked the knowledge right from his mind. He didn't mind—wasn't bothered that she'd discovered the truth before he had the chance to tell her. *"He will rewrite the charter,"* she added, her tone soft. She was taken aback that Talon had agreed so readily. A soft laugh sounded. It made him feel warm and so very alive. He wanted to hear the sound more—much more.

"Will you be mine, then?" he asked, not wanting to betray his hopefulness. She saw it anyway—saw everything—especially how desperately he wanted her. He wanted to claim her here and now, spirit her away into the wilderness and seal the bond. They both knew he wouldn't. A king's permission was one thing, but the charter had not yet been changed. Taking her as his mate right now would still be a breach of his oath, as much as he wanted to step around the technicality.

It would be better to wait. Besides, she deserved more than a rough claiming in the middle of nowhere. He would make it special for her, take her in the forest, or somewhere that held meaning for her. She saw his thoughts on this, too, and offered a pleased, mental smile. She admired his honor.

"I am yours as much as I can be," she said. Because they both

knew that first and foremost, she belonged to the world, to the king tree, to her purpose.

But those words were enough for him.

The world around him faded, replaced by his surroundings once more, the field, the lake beyond, the buzz of drengr and riders in the distance as they finished their work. His heart didn't slow, didn't stop hammering in his chest.

Taylynn climbed atop his back. Their minds remained connected, thoughts buzzing between them with no need for speech. He knew what she knew, and she knew what he knew. It was...nearly indescribable. No wonder mates revered this aspect of their bond.

"Let us fly, then," he said, lightness seeping into every part of him.

He felt every place her body aligned with his, from where she sat, nestled in the nook where his neck met his back. Rising up, he took several steps forward, getting a feel for her on his back. She felt good there. She felt *right*. Sinking low, only briefly, he shot up into the sky. The sound of her excited laughter wrapped around him, filling him to the brim. This. *This* would make every struggle, every obstacle standing in their way, completely worth it.

CHAPTER 12
WICKED THOUGHTS

Claire vaulted onto Talon's back. He sprang from the ground, taking them into the sky. Far below, her queen's guard set off on their unicorns, escorted by Tourmaline. They would return to the city without her.

This was the first time in months that she'd flown with Talon in broad daylight. She smiled, closing her eyes and tilting her face to collect the sun's warm rays. *"Take me away from here."*

"As you wish, my queen." He changed direction, not towards the city but away.

She was still reeling after seeing so many slaughtered dragons, after discovering only four of the five mothers had accepted her offer and none of the others. Her throat was clogged with smoke and grief. It hurt.

Talon was tense beneath her. He felt what she felt. Felt her anguish as if it were his own.

"I'm sorry," he said, his voice sincere. *"If I could have spared you this, I would have."*

"There is brutality everywhere, Talon." She blinked her eyes open. *"My world—my old world, I mean—isn't perfect, either. We might have*

technological marvels that far surpass Dragonwall's, but that hasn't made humanity any kinder. You can't shield me from the harsh realities of life. You know it, and so do I."

"If there had been another way—"

"You would have taken it. I know."

She was beginning to understand—better than most—the difficulties of ruling. She'd barely scraped the surface. She swallowed against the ache in her throat. *"I thought* all *the mothers would choose their hatchlings over war,"* she admitted. *"I thought I was doing the right thing, but look where it landed me? None of the other dragons even made the correct choice in the end, and I made Reyr so angry with me."*

Reyr's expression of betrayal would stay with her for a long time.

She had only tried to do the right thing. To be a good queen. To put personal feelings aside and act for the greater good of a kingdom. All those dragons who might have surrendered could have changed the world's perspective.

Would she always be forced to walk a tightrope? Disappointing some just to make others happy? How many more times would she receive this sort of reaction for her decisions?

"Many more times." Talon's admission soured her stomach. *"It is not easy. I never said it would be."*

"I...I know."

"This is why I wanted to give you time, plenty of time, to think about becoming my mate. Time to consider what it meant."

A prickle of misgiving formed in the back of her mind—a thought from a dark place. Had she made a mistake? Had she been too hasty in her decision? Had she allowed her love and their mate bond to make the decision for her?

"Only you can answer that, love. But I am here for you. There is still time to change your mind if you wish?" He disguised his desperate fear, but she felt it there anyway, buried deep. He would break if she rejected him.

"No," she said. *"I stand by my decision. For all the hardship that ruling brings, you make every minute worth it."*

Warmth burned through her—through *him*—at her admission. He gave a pleased warble, the sound entirely draconic in nature. He radiated with love for her and that would make every challenge worth it.

Talon's iridescent black wings flapped, strong downward thrusts, taking them north. She was becoming much better at judging distance, and she only had to drop a little deeper into his mind to simply *know*.

She leaned forward, resting her face against his glassy scales, closing her eyes. Beneath her cheek, she felt his powerful corded muscle bunch with each movement. He had chosen to fly into battle without armor. There hadn't been enough to outfit the hundreds of drengr with them.

Letting her shoulders relax, she exhaled, her mind melding deeper with his. The steady beat of his wings lulled her into a trance. Before she realized it, she was lost to their shared thoughts. She wandered the lava fields, pausing on the memories that intrigued her. This stasis was nearly as restful as sleep.

The afternoon slipped away. They didn't talk. Talon simply gave her what she needed—what *he* needed, too—peace, if only for a short while. Eventually, they returned to Squall's End. There was still much to be done.

"*You deceived Lord Rhal,*" Talon pointed out. Their descent was gradual. The city took form below, Stormy Bay glittering behind it.

"*Mayr?*" she said. *So?*

"*Mayr,*" he repeated. "*Anoa mi cathalla laryara sassih aya kunyn nih baracha ana andmalla barihon, achen mih barihon, frelikah.*" ... *Now I must explain that you are not merely a spriten queen, but my queen, too.*

"*You're speaking the spriten language.*"

"*Of course.*"

"*You plucked the words right out of my mind.*"

"*I did.*"

A laugh burst from her chest. She was delighted. A pleased draconic rumble vibrated against her legs. He loved when she laughed.

"Perhaps when we are mated and I have access to Ednuar all the time," he said, *"I'll use the fancy trick you pulled on Lord Rhal to exclude people from our conversations."*

She snorted, rolling her eyes—

"Did you just roll your eyes at me, Ayas Drollaya?" he drawled.

"Ni," she lied. But the single word turned into a screech as he plummeted towards the ground. Her stomach lifted into her throat before he leveled out. Punishment, a mild one, for giving him sass.

"And besides," she shot back, gasping through her laughter. *"If we wanted to exclude others from our conversations, you do realize that we can just converse with our minds telepathically—Ahhhhh!"* She broke off in a screech as he did another nosedive.

She clutched him, her hysterics turning into full-bellied laughter as Talon swept so low to the ground that his talons grazed the long grasses. It was magnificent. Utterly magnificent.

The city's walls loomed before them. They could have landed inside the walls, in one of the many large courtyards, but this would allow Talon to walk the streets with her. It meant more time in his company.

"I am always thinking of you, Ayas Drollaya. We can walk as slowly as you wish, for I know you are not eager to tell Lord Rhal who you really are."

"Me?!" she squawked.

"You," he confirmed. With that, he came to a cantering stop.

"You...you mean to tell Lord Rhal that I'm to be your queen?" she all but gasped, seeing the knowledge clearly in his mind.

"You, Ayas Drollaya, not me, since you saw fit to establish your identity so firmly."

"Then...you wish to make it public? That we are mates?" Her heart began to pound, wildly flapping in her chest.

"Not quite, we will continue to keep that knowledge limited. But the announcement will be made publicly soon. Sooner, rather than later."

Because when they returned to Kastali Dun, they would begin planning their bonding ceremony. So, of course the secret would be revealed. She hadn't even realized what that meant—

"Open for the king!" several voices called from the city walls. The portcullis began to lift immediately.

She could feel multiple sets of eyes on them as the guards above watched their arrival. Would there be gossip about her flying with him? Did she even care?

"You will get used to it," Talon said. It was the last thought she heard from his mind before dismounting and severing their connection.

"I must get used to many things," she said, continuing their telepathic conversation, this time glad for the ability. Glad they weren't entirely cut off from one another. *"But I stand by my decision. You are worth it, Talon. You are worth everything."*

He transformed, coming up beside her. His expression was a mask but the warmth in his eyes sent flutters racing through her stomach.

"Ayas Drollaya," she said, gazing up at him. *"My king."* She didn't miss his slight shiver at her claiming him. He was hers, completely hers, and she wouldn't let him forget it.

They walked through the city together. Her hand gripped Talon's arm, feeling the bunch of muscles in his bicep. Her cheeks flushed. She knew exactly what those arms looked like uncovered. Exactly how magnificent they were—how magnificent *he* was, scars and all.

Her chest expanded. They would be mated soon. Then she would finally know every part of him. What would that be like? To know a king so intimately? To know him as well as she knew herself? Better, perhaps?

She'd been with other men, but certainly not a *drengr*, not *this* drengr.

Heat raced over her skin. Something told her that despite Talon's *extremely long* dry spell, he would make an excellent lover. Something of that knowledge made her suddenly shy. That was saying a lot because she was *not* one to be shy about these kinds of things.

"What are you thinking about?"

"Nothing!" She bit her lip to keep from nervously smiling.

Talon made a humming sound.

"Fine, if you must know," she said, keeping her voice low. They passed from the city into the keep's portcullis. "I was thinking about what an excellent lover you'll make—how good you'll be in bed."

Talon made a choking sound and his steps faltered. "You—"

"Welcome back, Your Majesties," a guard interrupted, greeting both of them in the keep's courtyard.

Talon's gaze was a blazing inferno even if his face remained effortlessly emotionless. She glanced down, finding evidence of the way her words had affected him. He caught her looking and a low growl sounded in his chest—a warning, one she was tempted to explore.

A wicked smile formed and she shrugged. "You asked."

The guard nervously cleared his throat. "I was...I was told that Lord Rhal is expecting you."

Talon held her eyes a moment longer, then he turned to the guard and said, "Fine."

The guard paled, nervously fidgeting. "Excellent. If... If you'll follow me, I'll take you there."

"Thank you," she said sweetly, pulling on Talon's arm. The guard escorted them inside. She felt the king's attention like a hot brand, searing every inch of her skin. She didn't dare look at him or she'd lose her composure.

The keep was a rush of activity but she hardly noticed. Talon certainly didn't. He hadn't stopped staring at her.

"*Steely* for your thoughts, Majesty?" She bit her lip to keep from laughing as a low, draconic rumble filled the corridor in answer. The guard gave a little yelp and nervously glanced over his shoulder.

"Oh, don't mind him," she said, trying to put the guard at ease. "He gets a little testy from time to time."

Talon's growl only grew louder. "You do not wish to know what I am thinking, Ayas Drollaya. It is not a suitable conversation for public audiences."

Heat dropped straight into her belly. She risked a sideways

glance and had to look away immediately. The way he watched her said enough. Like she was a tasty meal he couldn't wait to eat.

"What's the matter?" he taunted. "Wraith got your tongue?"

"Oh. Not at all," she managed. "I'm just using my imagination to dream up scenarios of what you might be thinking. And I do have a *vivid* imagination."

His steps faltered. Again. Gods, she loved her effect on him.

Her voice was all low seduction as she said, "*Mi irjalla aya ah ayas taynai, raklende mihroi, liadahik mih jhaam.*"

His composure briefly cracked. "That's hardly fair," he warned. "*What does it mean?*"

"*Perhaps I should make you beg for the translation?*" she replied. "*Since it already has something to do with you on your knees, worshiping me?*"

His breaths grew heavier. "*I will gladly get on my knees for you, Claire. Right now, I'm thinking of how delectable you will taste on my tongue. I'm going to sample every measure of your skin, until I sup from the juncture of your thighs—*"

She sucked in a breath just as the guard interrupted to say, "If you'll just wait here, Majesties, I'll inform Lord Rhal that you have arrived."

"We'll continue this conversation later," Talon said, his voice rough.

"I certainly hope so," she managed, her heart pounding like it wanted to free itself from her chest.

The guard disappeared, only to reappear seconds later. "This way, if you please."

They entered Lord Rhal's study. "Your Majesty," Lord Rhal blurted, bowing deeply to Talon. "It is an honor to meet you."

He seemed to have forgotten her entirely as his eyes nervously took in the king. She didn't take it personally. Talon had that effect on people.

"There are important matters we must discuss before I return to the capital."

"Of course, yes." Lord Rhal's eyes darted around the room,

uncertain. He wasn't used to hosting royalty. "I see you have met the sprite queen."

"Yes. Claire and I have known each other for quite some time, ever since she stole into my kingdom. What was it, love? Nearly a year ago? Has it truly been that long?"

Her lips parted but her ability to speak failed.

"Lady... Lady Claire?" Lord Rhal blinked in confusion. "But, I don't understand."

She blew out a breath. "I owe you an explanation, my lord. Perhaps we should sit?" She gestured to his desk and the two chairs before it.

"Oh. Yes. Right." He rushed over to claim one for her, gesturing for her to sit.

"No need, Rhal." Talon strode forward. "I will take care of her."

Lord Rhal took a step back. "Of course, Your Majesty. Apologies." He strode around his desk and sat, eyes on them.

Talon insisted on settling her before taking the other chair. "There now. You may continue. I believe you were about to explain the situation?"

"Right." She cleared her throat. "Um. So...nearly a year ago, Lord Cyrus escaped a band of wraiths only to land in my cornfield. He died on my watch. It's a story you've probably heard?"

Lord Rhal's throat bobbed. "I...yes. I heard it from Lord Davi—may the gods keep him. But you are a sprite. You can't..." He trailed off.

"I am." She took the next several minutes to give him the abridged version of all that had happened to her.

"It is a lot to take in," Lord Rhal admitted when she finished. "So, you really are the spriten queen?"

"Indeed."

"And...and they accepted you?"

"They had no choice," Talon said, speaking for the first time. During her retelling, he'd only gotten more comfortable. He was leaning back, his legs comfortably splayed in front of him. Casual but collected.

After a few additional questions, Lord Rhal was willing to accept what and who she was. When Talon revealed their mate bond, he was shocked all over again. His face flushed with embarrassment. Probably remembering how he'd flirted with her during dinner. Talon was especially smug to see it, having seen the lord's flirtations in her mind.

"You're enjoying this, aren't you?" she shot at him. The corner of Talon's mouth twitched but he said nothing.

Talon moved on to other matters more political in nature. She allowed him to lead, sitting back, letting her shoulders relax as she observed him. There was so much to admire. The way he spoke with such authority, the manner in which he articulated his thoughts, and even his methods of handling things.

She observed and memorized, hoping that some day she'd be as good a ruler. He'd had centuries to perfect it. Sometimes it was difficult to remember that little tidbit, when she was beating herself up for not being better.

"I'm also to understand that Claire has agreed to heal your injured and ensure you've enough food to tide you over until trade resumes," Talon was saying.

Her shoulders straightened.

"Indeed," Lord Rhal confirmed. "We are most grateful. I will ensure that your secret is kept, until such time as you deem wise to announce it publicly. I like that history will remember these days as I have. Sprites are a part of Dragonwall, too. I am honored that your people are here to help," he added, looking at her with sincerity etched into his features.

"Thank you."

"You are every bit the queen, Your Majesty," he added. His words made her throat tighten. "Now, if we're done here, I will happily introduce you to those survivors you wished to meet."

"Yes," she managed before rising to her feet. Lord Rhal and Talon did the same. He led them from his study, with Talon at her back. The comforting hand her mate placed against her as she walked sent warmth radiating through her.

Perhaps she needed to be less harsh on herself. Lord Rhal thought she was a good queen. That counted for something, didn't it? Lifting her chin, she followed him through the keep, determined to show his people exactly what a queen ought to be.

CHAPTER 13
JAMIE'S FAMILY

Mikkin followed Jamie into Squall's End, both Berbik and Unka on their heels. The archway beneath the portcullis plunged them into brief darkness before spilling out into a large courtyard. It was a rush of activity as the city's guards darted about. The smell of dirty, cramped bodies hit him with full force.

"She was there on the walls. I saw her—I did," came a child's voice. Mikkin glanced over. He caught sight of a band of bedraggled children huddled together. His chest tightened, but he didn't glance away. "A real sprite! All of them. They was all in armor that shined like stars, with marks that glowed. Then the dragon fire came, big plumes of it. She lifted her arms"—the little boy mimicked the motion—"and *bam*! Swallowed it right up. She *saved* us."

A young girl snorted. "Naw she didn't. The *king* saved us. His shields flew with him. I saw 'em overhead."

Mikken had slowed his pace, stopping to observe the exchange; his mouth twitched into a smile.

"No you didn't!" another child scoffed. "You only heard rumors, and now you're repeating it like truths…"

He turned, hurrying forward to catch up with Jamie and the others. Everywhere he looked, tents were crammed against more tents. A refugee camp, for all those who had fled their towns and villages hoping to avoid the chaos that swept Vestur's territory.

Jamie made the realization about the same time he did. The lad stopped, spinning in place, taking everything in. "How the hell am I supposed to find my parents here—in this mess?"

Mikkin put a hand on Jamie's shoulder. "We'll figure it out, lad."

They'd begun to attract attention. Well, Berbik and Unka. He caught sight of a middle aged woman rushing by with a basket of supplies. "You there, Miss—" She stopped, looking at him over her shoulder, a downward twist to her mouth. "We're looking for a group of people from the north, refugees."

"We're all refugees here," she said with a snort before taking a wary step away from them. Mikkin produced a coin and held it forward. She rolled her eyes and did not take it. "Your money can't do much in a city that ain't got food."

Jamie jumped into action, pulling a cloth bundle from his pack of rations. "Please," he said, holding it out. "It would be a small group from Landow, south of Belnesse."

She eyed Jamie's offering, then snatched it, depositing it into her basket. "I ain't heard naught—most of us is from the north. Can't expect us to remember names at this point. But the city guards has a manifest, documenting all that come through. My name's in it. Reckon those you're searching for are too. You'd need to check with the gate guards."

Jamie's shoulders rose and fell. He nodded, shouldering his pack again. He thanked the woman and turned. "Right, then. I guess we can check with the guards at the gates."

They turned back the way they'd come. Mikkin caught a flash of gold in his periphery. He spun. Now, *that* was a head of hair he'd recognize anywhere. It was burned into his memory since the day they first met. "Lord Reyr!" he called. The hulking drengr was strolling towards a group of guards, but froze, then spun on his heel. Reyr's searching gaze landed on Mikkin and then the others. His expression morphed into one of recognition.

There was something haunted dwelling deep in Reyr's eyes, but it cleared a little as he strode over. "Mikkin. Good to see you." He reached forward and grasped Mikkin's forearm, giving him a warm greeting, nodding at the others. "Didn't expect to see any of you here—"

"We're looking for my parents—my village," Jamie blurted.

Reyr's brows pulled together. "They're here? I thought..."

"We don't know for certain," Mikkin cut in, trying not to dash the lad's hopes. "A while back, we saw smoke over Landow. We were hoping that perhaps Tynen got some of their people out. Right, lad?" He glanced over at Jamie, who nodded.

"Of course," Reyr said. "Tynen seemed like the knowledgeable sort, and practical, too." The king's shield had been to Landow once, when they'd first met, investigating what might have happened in Belnesse. He'd met Jamie's parents along with some of the other town's folk.

"A woman said there might be a manifest," Berbik added, his eyes flicking towards the city guardhouse near the portcullis.

"Yes. I do believe so. Most cities keep track of those who pass through, for legal reasons and such. Let's go and see, shall we?" Reyr offered Jamie a reassuring smile, placing a hand on the lad's shoulder, steering him across the courtyard.

Every pair of eyes that fell on Reyr's hulking form widened. Polite bows followed. The shields were as close to royalty as one could be, excusing the king and king's kin.

"You've come a long way since I last visited Landow," he could hear Reyr saying to Jamie, distracting him no doubt, from nerves. There hadn't been much time to catch up with the shield after they'd arrived at camp. Too many preparations, but they'd greeted each other a few times in passing, during meetings and such.

"I...yes, my lord. It's been quite the adventure." Jamie's eyes darted over his shoulder, hitting Mikkin before bouncing away.

"Call me Reyr, please. No need for formalities. I've never been one for them."

"Right. Reyr."

"It was no easy endeavor, convincing the dwargs to side with King Talon. I'm still impressed you managed it," Reyr continued, speaking to Jamie in a low voice.

"Oh..." Jamie trailed off, but his shoulders straightened slightly. "Yes, well, they were smart to heed us."

Mikkin hid a small smile. Reyr had a way of making Jamie feel more comfortable in his presence. He supposed most of the king's closest were skilled tacticians as well as warriors. Always knew the perfect thing to say in each situation.

"There now, here we are." Reyr came to a stop. The guards outside the guardhouse jumped to attention. "At ease, gentlemen," Reyr commanded. "We're looking for a manifest, documentation on the refugees. I assume you've been keeping track of those who enter the city?" His words rang with authority. It would have taken Mikkin and Jamie twice as long to get what they needed, but with a king's shield...

"The captain keeps a log book documenting everyone," one of the guards piped up.

"Good, show me." The five of them were led into the guardhouse. Suspicious looks were thrown at Berbik and Unka. Unka merely regarded everyone as if he didn't see their expressions. Or, as if those hostile expressions didn't bother him.

Mikkin frowned, wondering if they did. Was Unka simply good at hiding his reactions?

"Don't mind him, lads," Berbik said to a pair of guards that stood gaping at Unka, their mouths wide enough to catch flies. "The goblin is harmless enough."

"Never *harmless*, Master Dwarg," Unka said, turning to the guards and smiling. Both guards took a step back at the chilling sight of teeth on display.

"*Unka*," Mikkin warned. "No need to frighten them."

Unka merely shrugged and turned away.

Reyr stood with Jamie, the two of them scanning a log book

that rested on a tall stand. It looked like an intake station. If he had to guess, each new city visitor checked in here before continuing into the city. He took a moment to glance around the rest of the chamber. It was sparsely furnished, utilitarian in nature. The stone walls created an oppressive feel, helped little by the small windows and dim lights from the candelabras. Off to one side there were three desks, each occupied by guards who sat gazing at them in curiosity. A plain, empty table sat in the middle, surrounded by six chairs. Not a place to linger, merely a means to an end.

"I think we'll wait outside," Mikkin decided, giving Berbik and Unka a knowing look before leading them out. There wasn't enough air in here for all of them. They stood silently, just outside the door, observing the courtyard's activity.

"Will you come to the capital with us, Master Mikkin?" Berbik asked.

He hesitated. "I suppose it depends on what we find here. It would be another adventure, to be sure."

Berbik nodded. "And you, Unka? The king's offer was generous."

"Unka accept," Unka said, his shoulders drawing back, his short, green head lifting higher. "This king offers jewels."

"And we *all* know how much you covet jewels," Mikkin muttered, chuckling. "Never mind the honored position."

King Talon had offered Unka a unique opportunity, to act as emissary between Pavv and Dragonwall. It would be dangerous for the goblin. He might be completely ostracized by his people, perhaps his family, too, but it would give Unka a position akin to a nobleman at court. He'd have fine lodgings within the capital's keep, if he wished for it. There had never been an alliance between Dragonwall and Pavv. But perhaps by creating a new position, a goblin emissary might be the bridge that allowed both countries to traverse their treacherous past and travel beyond it.

"So long I live through job," Unka said, navigating the common tongue with his broken speech.

"I'm sure you will live through it just fine," Mikkin mused.

"You're plenty capable of protecting yourself. And despite Pavv's ruthlessness, it honors a white flag the same as most kingdoms."

"You so certain, Master Mikkin?" Unka lifted both eyebrows. A challenge.

"I suppose I'm not. Just hearsay."

"Goblin people like killing. Unka has family protect."

"Will you bring them here, then?"

Unka snorted. "They never come."

"No?"

"Too different," Unka mused, his intelligent eyes dancing over the activity in the courtyard. "But...different-good, perhaps."

"*Perhaps*," Mikkin corrected. He'd been helping the little urchin, much to his own surprise. Berbik had been, too.

"Perhaps," Unka repeated, and Berbik chuckled.

An excited cry interrupted them. Jamie strolled out a moment later, a wide smile on his face. Reyr followed, steering the lad with a hand on his shoulder. "I think we found what we're looking for," Reyr said.

THERE CAME A FEMININE SHOUT, followed by a wave of sobs. Mikkin heard it clear down the street. "Sounds like Jamie found them," he told Berbik, stepping back from the cluster of tents he was about to search. They'd split up, Jamie with Reyr, while Mikkin kept with Berbik and Unka, searching the general area of tents where they believed Landow's refugees had set up camp. It had taken some hours of inquiry.

They strolled down the street and Mikkin hesitated, watching as Mary and Tynen came into view, wrapping themselves around Jamie. Mary sobbed hysterically enough that he couldn't make out much beyond, "thought...were...dead."

He strolled up and Tynen broke away, turning to him. He clasped Mikkin's shoulder and nodded. "You kept him safe. Thank you." Then Tynen's eyes darted to Berbik and Unka and he took a step back.

"No need to worry about them. They're harmless," Mikkin reassured Jamie's father.

"That…that's a goblin."

"Aye. And you needn't worry," he repeated.

Tynen looked as if he wanted to argue before shutting his mouth. He turned back to his son.

A deep throat cleared and Reyr said, "I don't know about the lot of you, but I haven't had a bite to eat all day. Why don't we head up to the lord's manor and have some food? We can catch up over a meal, yes? I'm sure there's plenty to be shared."

Mikkin turned a thankful smile upon Reyr, who knew exactly what was needed at a moment like this. "That…that would be most welcome, Lord Reyr," Tynen said, stepping forward.

"Just *Reyr*," the shield assured him, taking the man's forearm and shaking it.

Other villagers from Landow had come forward. Jamie laughed and hugged each of them. It took several minutes before they could break away and make their way towards Lord Rahl's keep. Jamie kept close to his parents as they walked. Reyr fell into step beside Mikkin, Berbik and Unka, chatting amiably.

"Now then, what are your plans, Mikkin? Will you be heading for the capital with the dwargs?"

"To be honest, I hadn't thought that far ahead. I only ever wanted vengeance for my family. The dragons—?

"We slaughtered them," Reyr assured him.

Mikkin nodded, swallowing the hard lump in his throat. He'd known they'd been successful after word had reached camp. But he hadn't seen it with his own eyes. That left him more disappointed than he cared to admit. "I had hoped to kill one myself, but…"

"But your strength was better suited elsewhere, in negotiating with the dwargs," Reyr stated. His voice softened. "That didn't make your contribution any *less important*. Closure comes in many forms. It goes beyond the swing of a sword or the scratch of a claw. While those forms might be visible, they are no more powerful than the quieter acts. Acts that are just as impactful."

Mikkin faltered, struck by the powerful notion. Reyr's words meant a great deal. An ache built in his throat but he managed a humble, "Thank you."

When they reached the lord's keep, they were taken straight inside. Having a shield present offered many perks. Every person in the keep was eager to please. Because there was so much activity taking place in the city, Lord Rhal was out and about. They were taken to the cookery and settled at a large wooden table. The cook jumped into action, whipping up a meal for them.

Mikkin half expected Reyr to rush off as soon as they ate—surely the shield had plenty of important matters—but he didn't. He sat with them, listening to Jamie recount their adventures. "So, you met Fort Edge's fort leader, did you?" Reyr was especially interested in that.

"Aye. Good man—drengr," Mikkin corrected.

Reyr looked thoughtful. "Good. That's good. Might come in handy—that. Having someone from our forts familiar with the bowels of Shadowkeep."

Mikkin snorted. "I'd hardly say *familiar*."

Reyr lifted a brow. "More familiar than anyone else in the king's circle."

"You plan to move against Kane, then? Are you thinking of sneaking into the fortress?"

"If it comes to that," Reyr said. "It probably won't be that simple. But..." The shield hesitated. "It might be a good idea to keep you close."

"You want me in the capital, then?"

Jamie's voice cut off, his head whipping in Mikkin's direction. "You... You're going to the capital?"

Mikkin shrugged. "Suppose it's as good a place as any to lay down new roots. I grew up on the outskirts of a large city. Could take some getting used to."

"But..." Jamie's mouth opened and closed. "I thought you might return to Landow with us."

"Son..." Tynen reached for his son's arm and squeezed. "There isn't anything left. Landow's gone."

"But," Jamie's brows drew together. "We will rebuild."

"Aye." His father nodded. "But it will be a long time afore we get to where we were. Let the man choose his own path."

Mikkin exhaled, looking at Tynen and Mary. "You'll be heading back up north, then?"

"That's the plan, now that we're safe. Soon as possible, if we can manage. I don't think I can stand another day in this city. But..." Tynen's eyes softened, falling on Jamie. "Lad, you're a man grown now. You have been for a couple of years, much as I hate to admit it. You're free to make your own way. Your mother and I...we can manage. You aren't obligated to follow us home, if you'd like to spend your life on other pursuits. Travel some more. Settle elsewhere. What have you."

Indecision crossed Jamie's features. He leaned back, his brow furrowed. "But...I've only just found you."

"Aye. And a joyous relief that is. Whatever you decide, we will always be your parents and you will always be welcome. We'd be glad to have your help rebuilding, but we can certainly manage it without you. Hell, I built our home afore you were even born, boy."

Jamie's throat bobbed and his eyes darted towards Mikkin, who kept his expression neutral. Somehow, he knew what Jamie was going to choose before the words were out of his mouth, but he didn't want to be responsible for influencing those words. "I... I've always wanted to see the king's great keep."

A small smile tugged at Reyr's lips but the shield said nothing beyond, "You would be most welcome, if you decided to venture there."

"*Yes*. Unka get whole chamber lodgings in great keep," Unka said, breaking the tense moment. "And jewels—from king."

Berbik snorted, disguising his laugh behind his hand. "What the goblin is *trying* to say is, he'll be there too, if you should decide to journey there with us, Master Jamie. A merry band we will make."

Jamie hesitated and then, "If Mikkin goes, I go."

Mikkin's throat thickened and he found it hard to swallow. Over the past several months, Jamie had become close to a son, or, what he pictured his own sons might have become in time. Sure, they were only separated by a decade—fine, perhaps a little more. But it was clear that Jamie had grown attached to him.

"I'll be going, then," Mikkin decided to say, giving Reyr an affirmative nod.

"Excellent." Reyr's eyes glowed. "That's settled then. I'll make sure you have a place on board one of our ships when it comes time to depart."

Mary reached out and grabbed her son's hands from across the table, holding them in hers. She offered a warm smile. "I'm so proud of you, Jamie," she whispered.

"Well," Reyr came to his feet, glancing across the cookery. "A fine meal, Master Cook." Then, looking back at them, he said, "I've got some things to take care of. Feel free to stay as long as you like, and find me if you need anything else. I'll be near the gate keep."

With that, Reyr gave them all a final bow of his head and strode from the room.

CHAPTER 14

ACTING A COWARD

Celenore

Saffra heard the commotion. She went to collect Desaree and Jocelyn. "They're back," she gasped, bursting into the tent. Together, they raced to the command tent where they found Miera and Selphie. "They're back," they all blurted together. Both sprite handmaidens froze, eyes going wide, then dropped the gown they were working on. The five of them rushed to the edge of camp.

She had to admit, wearing pants made life much easier, especially here in camp. Where before she'd have to fuss with skirt hikes, this eliminated the need. Sure, it was less feminine, perhaps, but it also made it easier to run, to move, to breathe. Besides, there was still something entirely feminine about displaying more curves.

They weren't the only ones gathering on the edge of camp.

Her stomach filled with flutters as she searched the sky. Wing formations of drengr descended. She spotted several orange dragons, but none of them were the correct coloring. The vibrant hues that only he possessed. He'd always been beautiful to her. Perhaps because she'd grown up in the arid east, where deserts spanned to the horizon and beyond.

Orange was warmth and positivity, it was the rising and setting sun, it was a bright smile, a fierce exclamation, a thing to be noticed. "It's my favorite color," she muttered, only just now realizing. She kept her voice low so the others didn't hear. She'd always loved bright colors. Yellow had been a favorite for a long time, paired with pastel pink. But people changed, she had changed.

When...when had that happened?! *How* had it happened? How had Bedelth's scales become the most beautiful and precious color imaginable?

"Godsdamn it all to hell," she muttered under her breath.

"Are you okay?" Jocelyn asked, taking her hand. Jocelyn's fingers massaged hers, soft and soothing. Her handmaiden always knew when something was wrong. She was perceptive—*too* perceptive.

"I...I'm fine, Joce."

Jocelyn's eyes lingered, but she accepted the answer.

"Look," Selphie cried, "there is Lord Bedelth."

Saffra's pulse kicked up. "Where?!" But even before anyone could answer, she saw him already transformed, striding towards them. His long legs ate up the distance with each step. Her breath caught. Somehow, he was *always* bigger than she remembered. Whenever he was near, regardless of form, he towered over her with bunched muscles and broad shoulders.

Daxton had been taller than her, with nice firm lines. She'd always enjoyed looking at his arms, his chest, all of him, really. But as she allowed herself to do the same with Bedelth, she felt the fiery rush of heat on her cheeks. And yet, she couldn't stop herself, couldn't stop the way her eyes traced the lines of his body, the way his black tunic fit snugly over him, ending at his trim hips, pants clinging to his every muscle. His sverak was lashed to his back. Bandoliers crossed his rigid chest, a shorter blade in each.

There was nothing wrong with looking, was there? Just because she appreciated his body, didn't mean she was required to accept their mate bond—

Someone's shoulder nudged her. She blinked, turning. Jocelyn stared at her, eyes prompting.

"What? Oh…" An unpleasant tingling spread up the back of her neck, sending waves of embarrassment with it. "Forgive me, did you say something?"

Bedelth, because he was standing square in front of her, clearly waiting for an answer. The corner of his lips twitched, but he didn't smile. Was he…amused? "I just asked if you would walk with me, Saffra. A few minutes, if you can spare it?"

"Oh…" She glanced around. "Claire?"

"Still with the king in Squall's End. They will stay for the night." He offered his arm as an invitation.

"All right. I'll see you back at camp," she said to the others before he led her away.

Why did he want to get her *alone*? Was he trying to push the mate bond again? Did she *want* him to? Perhaps a small part of her. A small part liked knowing that someone *wanted* her. Especially if that someone was a powerful drengr—no, not just any drengr, a shield.

"I thought you would want to know what happened out there today," he said. "Don't worry, I will make it quick. I know you do not wish to be in my company longer than necessary."

She grimaced. "Bedelth…"

"No, it's quite all right. I understand."

But did he? She tried to answer. Tried to say *something*. Her words got stuck in her throat.

"Everything went smoothly. Your poison did the trick, though it didn't work on all of them for whatever reason. Likely, they didn't all drink from the lake water. But a vast majority did."

"Casualties?"

"None. Well, I took a bad scratch—"

She sucked in a breath, whirling to face him. "Are you all right?" Her eyes darted over him, searching. There was no sign of harm.

His brows pulled together. He watched her assessment, though he didn't say anything. His lips pressed into a hard line. "I'm fine."

She exhaled.

They resumed their walk, dodging around the drengr bodies in the field as their riders dismounted. If she had to guess, the armor they wore was much like their clothing. If they transformed with it on, it would stay in place when they changed back. It was a rush of activity and noise, so no one paid them any mind.

"The pregnant females took Claire's offer," Bedelth continued.

"They did?" she breathed. Muscles she hadn't realized were clenched, unknotted in her shoulders.

"All but one."

She missed a step. "All but...but one? Did she—?"

"She's still alive. Claire would not allow anyone to harm her. She will be permitted to lay her eggs and raise her young, but who can say after that."

He filled in the remaining details, talking about how quickly everything ended, with no sign of Kane. Claire would remain in Squall's End with Talon to handle political matters. After that, they would return and Camp would be disassembled. Then everyone would go their separate ways.

"Will you be returning by ship?" Bedelth asked. "Unless you would rather—" He stopped himself.

Something hot dropped into her belly. Was he suggesting they fly together? Even as a young girl, she had harbored a bit of jealousy towards riders. Who didn't? The idea of coming and going, flying wherever one pleased, was enticing.

"Are you asking if I wish to fly home with you—?"

"No," Bedelth answered too quickly. Her skin warmed. It stung, even if it was a lie. He was only trying to protect himself. She swallowed, pushing down her embarrassment. It shouldn't have bothered her. So, why did it?

Gathering what little courage remained, she said, "Was that all you wished to tell me?" Her cold voice made him flinch, but he nodded. "Very well, then. I'll take my leave."

He didn't move, didn't respond. She took a step back, then stopped herself. "Bedelth?" Something like hope exploded across his features. "I am glad you are safe—that you are okay."

His throat bobbed. He gave her a single nod, then turned and strode off in the opposite direction. She watched him go, frozen in place.

~

"He did *what*?!" Jocelyn gasped. "You... How could you keep this from me?" Hurt passed over Jocelyn's features, there and gone. Saffra didn't say anything. What was the point in making excuses?

Jocelyn sighed. "Does anyone else know?"

"No."

"Not even Claire?"

"Not even Claire." A dull ache filled the back of her throat. "I need to tell her. It's just... There hasn't been a convenient moment. Claire has—well, she has a lot on her plate."

"Those are excuses, and you know it."

"I know it," she repeated, feeling worse by the moment. "I'm being a horrible friend."

"No. We all struggle on occasion. You have *always* carried a great deal of responsibility—since the day you started working for the king. You're allowed some privacy to think. You're not obligated to tell your friends everything important the moment it happens. But for the sake of the gods, don't let it bottle up inside you until you're crushed under the weight of it. Let us share some of the weight. I am willing to share *all* of it." Jocelyn reached for her hand and squeezed.

Saffra's eyes blurred. Before she realized it, tears were falling down her cheeks. "Thank you," she managed. "You're a better friend than I deserve."

"Hardly," Jocelyn said, then pulled Saffra into an embrace until they were hugging and laughing. Well, she was cry-laughing. A hiccup escaped, then another, and then they were laughing even harder. "Now, tell me exactly what happened?"

She explained everything, from the moment she touched Bedelth's scales to their final conversation. She constructed a wall, filling in the holes with mortar as she elaborated over her feelings and Bedelth's reactions. With every word, her chest and shoulders felt lighter. It was a weight lifted, sharing this secret with someone who knew and understood her.

"Are you going to accept his offer? To fly back to Kastali Dun?"

Saffra made a choking sound. "Are you serious? No. I'm traveling back by ship with you and Desaree."

"You don't have to, though. Des and I will be fine. Verath is coming to make sure we are okay. He'll look after us, not that we need looking after, but you know how these drengr males are. So protective."

She bit her lip and said, "I don't think I can fly with him."

Jocelyn snorted. "I've heard your reasoning and it's nonsense. Most of it, anyway. Yes, you feel guilty about falling for someone else so soon after Commander Daxton. Yes, you understand that Bedelth is a shield, that he will have plenty of duties for the king, even though he's made it clear the king plans to change the charter. Yes, he failed to act on his feelings when you were courting Daxton. But to be fair, you were younger then, Saffra, much younger. He's old—relatively speaking." Jocelyn shook her head. "We both know none of those are good enough."

"They're plenty good enough. Gods, everyone in the king's circle has turned into lovesick fools—you included."

"You're being such a coward."

"Excuse me?" Saffra's skin turned cold.

"I said it, and you heard me. You're being a coward. You had nothing against love when it was you and Dax. But the second things change? Bedelth is a good person, one of the best. I know you don't want to hear it, and if you were anyone else, you'd accuse me of overstepping. I'm not saying this as your handmaiden, I'm saying it as your friend. You're scared to get hurt again, after Dax. Rightfully so! No one can blame you. But...in keeping yourself guarded, you're hurting him in the process. You should tell him the truth. He probably thinks you don't want him, that he's not good enough—"

"I don't," she managed, her voice wobbling. "Want him, that is."

"Yes! But it's because you're *scared*. You owe him that truth. If you refuse to fly home with him, it will only further hurt him. You can't hide from this. You can't run from this." Jocelyn sighed. "If you *really* aren't interested, that would be one thing. But I've seen how you are around him—how he is around you. You could cut the tension with a knife. Truly."

Saffra shrank in on herself, her shoulders slumping. "I don't want to go through it again, Joce. He... He's a shield. We're at war. All it would take is...is..." She couldn't even *say* it. One wrong move, and Kane would deal them a heavy blow. There was no guarantee they'd make it out alive. Cyrus hadn't.

"Fine. What if he dies tomorrow?"

"What?!" she hissed. "Don't talk like that."

"I'm serious, Saffra. What if he dies tomorrow?"

Saffra gazed at her handmaiden, her lips parted and eyes wide. She let the question sink in. What *if*? No, she didn't want to think about it. She clenched her fists, squeezing tightly. It did little to calm her heartbeat.

If Bedelth died tomorrow...

"He would die believing I didn't want him," she managed. It was a punch to the gut, awful and sad.

Did she want him? Could she admit it? Did she have the courage to face this? To allow her heart to open up after such horrible heartbreak?

"There," Jocelyn said, wiping her hands and climbing to her feet. "I need to find Desaree. But I think you have your answer."

Saffra's mouth opened, eyes widening in alarm. "Answer to *what*?!"

"To whether you should fly home with him, silly. Duh." Jocelyn only grinned before slipping out of the tent.

Bedelth was in the command tent. He stared at her, caught off guard by her sudden entry. Her hands balled into fists as she froze. Coming here had been so...so stupid.

"Lady Saffra."

"I..." The word came out like a frog's croak. "Never mind. I shouldn't have come." She turned to flee.

Gentle hands closed around her waist, pulling her against a firm chest. She sucked in a breath. Bedelth released her almost immediately, but the damage was done.

She rounded on him, swallowing. She'd never admit to how she was feeling. Never admit how quickly her heart raced at his touch. The sensations that erupted because of it.

She *hated* it. Hated herself for it. Hated the guilt still clawing at the back of her throat. Hated the fear. Hated how even the *thought* of getting close to someone sent her cowering, clawing at wounds that hadn't yet closed.

"What did you come to say?" Bedelth asked. She also hated the hope lining his face, that he so carelessly let it show.

"There's... I owe you the truth," she admitted, still searching for her voice. Taking a deep breath, she charged on. "I'm not ready for this, Bedelth. That's why I pushed you away, made you think I didn't want you. It was wrong of me."

His eyes widened, lips parting. "Oh."

"Do *not* mistake my words for acceptance," she clarified. "I'm not accepting this thing...this...bond. I have a lot on my mind. Everything is so fresh, that I feel guilty for even letting myself entertain the possibility."

His mouth opened—

"No, let me finish. This decision has nothing to do with you —you must understand. You're..." She sighed. It sounded a lot like surrender. "You're handsome—no, that doesn't do you justice. Handsome is too mundane. You're the most beautiful creature I've ever seen. When I look at you, my blood hums, my heart races, my skin burns. But I can't let myself go through any of it again, the heartbreak, the hurt. I'm trying to move on from Dax, but that doesn't mean I need to move straight into your arms."

Heavy silence fell between them. She waited for him to process her words. Waited until the tension was palpable.

He huffed and said, "You think I'm the most beautiful creature you've ever seen?"

A choked laugh burst from her chest. "*That's* what you're fixating on?! Out of everything I just said?"

He took a step closer. Their chests were nearly touching. She had to tilt her head back to see his face. She could smell the smoke wafting off him, mixed with a hint of male musk. It took a great deal not to close the distance between them, but her fear was good at keeping her rooted in place.

"I'm fixating on the part I liked best. But that was a very pretty speech. I admit, your words are eloquent and logical and all I hear is your fear talking. You're scared." He arched a brow in challenge, daring her to refute it.

She groaned, stalking away to pace the tent. "Of course I'm scared, Bedelth. That's why we're not doing this. That's why I can't."

He scoffed. "Let me get this straight. You're scared, so you choose not to accept this thing between us? You? The great and powerful Lady Saffra? The king's prophetess? The woman who changed the course of not one, but two wars? *You're* scared?"

"Stop!"

"No, no, I don't think I will." He stalked over to her. His brisk pace had her scrambling backwards until her thighs struck the table and she leaned back into it, grappling for purchase. He towered over her. Her eyes were level with his clavicle, so nicely on display.

"Being scared of heartbreak is a valid excuse," he growled. "But I don't think that's what you're *really* scared of, is it?"

Her throat dried up. She swallowed, to no avail.

"You're scared of how happy I'll make you if you accept the bond. You're scared that I'll love you so godsdamned fiercely, it will shatter everything you ever had with *him*. Pulverize it into dust. You're scared that you'll regret your choices with him. Scared that —" He stopped himself, breathing hard. "Shall I go on?"

"No," she half gasped, half whispered, her eyes wide. *Yes. Gods,* yes. She wanted him to keep going—needed him to stop. Her breaths came faster and faster. "Please, stop."

"All right." He stood a little straighter, crossing his arms. They were so close, she could feel the heat rolling off him. "So, are you going to fly home with me tomorrow or not?"

"What?!"

"That's why you came here, was it not?"

"I...no, it's not," she snapped.

"Oh?" He lifted both brows. Damn him. Finally, he took a breath. "Look, I'm not asking you to rush into anything, Saffra. You were hurt. I understand. None of this has played out cleanly. We have a long time to consider our options. All I ask is that you don't continue to shut me out. Fly home with me tomorrow. You might find that you actually enjoy it."

"That's what I'm afraid of," she managed. Because he'd been right. She feared what she might feel if she got close to him. Feared how much she'd like it.

"Yes, I know." He uncrossed his arms and lifted a hand. Warm fingertips brushed along her jawline, the gesture tender. Shivers raced over her skin. "Fly home with me tomorrow," he said again. There was so much in his voice. Hope, longing, excitement. Jocelyn had already given her blessing. But if she flew with him—

"Do the others know?" she asked, realizing what the other shields would think, seeing them together.

"That we're mates? Yes. I haven't said a word, but they gleaned the information well enough. Koldis was first to pick up on it, I think."

She exhaled.

"Flying with me tomorrow won't tell them anything they don't already know, Saffra."

"What about my mind? My thoughts? I'm not ready to share any of that." *With you.* She left that part out.

"I'm not asking you to."

Her heart raced faster and faster, taking off into a full blown gallop. Was she really doing this? "And, if I agree? I have your word that you won't continue to press me on the mates matter? That you won't take this as my acceptance?"

"You have my word. There does not need to be strings attached. You're flying home with me, nothing more, nothing less."

"And if I don't change my mind? If I never want to...to complete the bond?"

His throat bobbed. "Then I accept your decision."

She nodded, tucking her trembling hands behind her back. It felt a lot like relief. Despite everything he'd said, most of which was correct, it didn't change anything. She wasn't planning to take him as her mate. Wasn't planning to surrender and allow the fates to use her as a punching bag. She was in control of her own choices, and she refused to let anyone, even fate, change that.

"All right," she said, lifting her chin. "I'll fly home with you."

The corners of Bedelth's lips twitched before pulling into a genuine smile. He nodded, then stepped back. "Excellent. I look forward to your company." His gaze lingered on her a moment longer, dropping briefly to her lips, then he turned and left the tent, leaving her very much alone. Very much subjected to her own self conscience, to question if she'd just made the most rash decision of her life.

CHAPTER 15
SAYING GOODBYE

Fort Squall

Claire slid from Talon's scaly back, dismounting with the grace of a queen. Fort Squall's courtyard lay in ruins. Even the central fountain was smashed. She blinked back tears at the destruction Kane's dragons had wrought. Purposeful destruction meant to send a message.

She almost regretted giving them a choice. In the end, they were irredeemable. It was silly to feel sorrowful about that.

"Will you be able to fix it?" she asked Tamara, who stood silently regarding the space.

"Yes, in time." Tamara's gloomy expression brightened somewhat. "They were not able to fit into the smaller spaces, so those remain undamaged, including the fort leader's chambers."

"Good," Talon said, his deep voice drawing near. "Let's see it, shall we?"

A hand landed at the base of Claire's spine. The press of it paired with the heat of his palm, seeped through her meager layer of fabric. She loved the way his height and bulk made her feel safe as he crowded in behind her.

Last night was the first they'd spent together in nearly a week.

Too exhausted to do much, they cuddled. In the depths of his silver gaze she'd seen her entire future. They'd kissed, then stared at one another, then kissed some more. He'd whispered things that made her blush, even now. Like the way he counted the days. His eagerness to make love to her. To claim her. What he intended when that night came.

She thought of those things as they moved through the fort, letting it distract her from the obvious destruction. Dragons weren't made for small spaces, but their message was clear enough. *If we can't have it, no one can.*

They stopped before a large, ornate door. Tamara hesitated before opening it. They found Byron with several wing leaders and wing seconds; he quickly dismissed them. Turning to Talon, he said, "It's not as bad as we first thought. Much of the structural damage is confined to the larger spaces, as Tam told you. But the majority of smaller rooms are all right, thank the gods."

Claire looked around. "This is the fort leaders' chambers?"

"Aye." Pain flashed across his face. She regretted the question almost immediately. This room had been Davi and Emmy's.

Byron gave them a tour and brought them into the study, inviting them to take seats around the giant desk piled with papers —papers that had probably been left behind by Davi. Another pang of sadness constricted her chest. She'd never met Reyr's twin, but she'd heard enough about him. She could almost picture him, a perfect replica of Reyr, sitting right here. She cleared the image away, swallowing against the building ache in her throat. Life was so precious. Davi and Emmy had died together. It's how Reyr wished he'd gone when his mate died. No doubt Cyrus felt the same.

I did. For a very, very long time, Cyrus said.

What changed? she asked.

You. Discovering my purpose in this grand scheme. And time.

She was filled with gratefulness, glad that he'd seen something in her, chosen her to harbor his soul. It was a selfless sacrifice.

Talon and Byron discussed business. Mostly the work needed to restore the fort to its former glory and necessary repairs for

Squall's End. It was a long meeting that stretched for hours. She was tempted to let her mind wander—her exhaustion ran bone-deep—but she forced her attention to remain fixed on the conversation. It's what a good queen would do.

"Well, I think that covers it," Bryon said. "Thank you for everything."

"It is the least I can do," Talon said, standing. She exhaled in relief. "Is there anything else you need before we go?"

"All set for now. Uncle Reyr will be a great help in the days to come."

"Good. We'll miss him, but you need him more." Talon and Byron grasped forearms. She sighed. It was selfish to wish Reyr was coming home with them, but Talon was right.

Byron and Tamara escorted them through the fort's remains. All too soon, she was hugging Tamara goodbye while trying to withhold tears. Her voice was choked as they made plans to see each other in the future. It would be difficult for a while with all the new duties Tamara inherited. "I will do my best to make it for your bonding ceremony," Tamara assured her. "I would hate to miss it."

"I would love to have you there. But don't stress if you can't make it. I know you've got a lot on your plate." They shared a final hug. She squeezed Tamara tight, relishing in this moment. "I'm glad to have met you, Tam," she added.

"Me too," Tamara said, offering a shy smile as they broke apart.

"Ready, love?" Talon stood watching the exchange. As usual, his expression was unreadable, but his eyes held warmth.

"Ready," she said.

He held out his hand. "Good, then let's go."

THE CAMP WAS a flurry of activity. Tents and cooking fires were dismantled, packed onto carts that would travel the short distance to the coast. Whatever hadn't yet been loaded was stacked in piles.

Claire dismounted and Talon fell into step beside her. They

found Bedelth, Jovari, Koldis, and Reyr at the heart of the activity. Talon greeted them warmly, grasping forearms and clapping each of them on the back.

"Koldis," he said. "Everything all right with your mate?"

A burst of warmth filled Claire's chest. That Talon thought to ask after Taylynn was sweet. She had to agree with the others. Matehood looked good on him. There had been changes in him, each subtle in its own right, but as a whole, more noticeable. He didn't seem as broody or temperamental, not like when they first met.

"Everything is well, Your Majesty," Koldis answered, his eyes glowing with pleasure. It was the happiest she'd ever seen him. But there was something more to his expression. Contentment. "We went flying yesterday after the battle, she stayed with me in my tent last night." He rubbed the back of his neck.

She sucked in a loud breath.

Koldis shot her a wicked grin. "Never fear, my queen, nothing happened."

Her mouth dropped open. "Why would I...? I wouldn't care if... I mean, I care if something *happens*. I just mean that you guys aren't... You're not children! You can do whatever you want. I... just...you..."

"What my queen *means* to say,"—amusement colored Talon's voice—"is that she is happy for you, and wasn't expecting you to share something so private. And while it's none of my business, I am surprised you didn't seal your bond."

"We're waiting—I'm waiting," Koldis said, crossing his arms.

"For the charter?" Talon lifted a brow.

"Correct. Your blessing is one thing, but breaking the law is another."

While Jovari snorted, Bedelth grunted, clear approval in the sound. Koldis shrugged and offered them a sly grin. "We're shields. If we're not honorable, our name will be tarnished."

Talon grunted, but clearly approved. "We could have kept things quiet, but I understand." He clapped a hand on Koldis's shoulder, a rare smile stretching across his lips. "And to think, you and I can suffer through this painful drought together."

She choked. "Okay, I'm standing *right here*! Take your man-speak-whatever elsewhere, please."

Truthfully, she didn't mean it. It was cute to see this bonding moment.

Verath strode up and cleared his throat. "Looks like I missed... whatever is going on here. Ships are at the coast. As soon as we get the rest of the supplies loaded, they can depart. I sent the first group of pairs back to the capital. They left hours ago. The rest will depart as soon as the ships are loaded."

Her queen's guard appeared, filing through the mass of swarming bodies just as Talon and his shields broke into traveling logistics. She turned to face them, unable to help her smile. They fanned out around her and gave their customary salute before standing at attention. Taylynn appeared a moment later. In the background of noise, she heard Koldis's speech falter before continuing.

"*Ayas Drollaya*," Taylynn greeted, bowing deeply.

"You know I hate it when you do that, right? We're cousins." She stepped forward to gather the princess in a tight hug. "You won't be going home with us, will you?"

A heavy sigh fell from Taylynn's chest. "No. Your wily shield, the green one there, has already tried. My answer remains the same. There is much work to be done."

She said in a teasing voice, "By *green one*, you mean your mate?"

Taylynn's eyes danced. "Yes, I suppose everyone was going to find out one way or another."

"Gods," she hissed, flooded with guilt. "I'm sorry." She glanced over to find several surprised expressions. Most of her queen's guard hadn't known. "That wasn't my secret to tell."

"Think nothing of it, *Ayas Drollaya*," Taylynn said, taking her by the shoulders. A forgiving smile stretched across her lips. "As I said, Koldis and I have decided to accept the bond. It is only a matter of time before the rest of the world knows."

A smile made her cheeks ache. Maybe it was the hopeless

romantic in her, but she loved a good, happy ending. If she could see all her friends properly fixed up with someone they loved as much as she was growing to love Talon, well...life would be even better. But that was a selfish thought, and not everyone wanted what she did. There were others who didn't crave intimacy, and there wasn't anything wrong with that.

"Now, I have come to say goodbye, but before that, you and I must speak," Taylynn said, breaking into her thoughts. "Fright and I will escort the remaining pregnant female dragon to the caves. The other mothers should arrive any day now. Their gestation periods are slow, but eventually, they will begin to lay."

Her pulse increased and she swallowed back her excitement. Hatchlings! "Will I...do you think I'll be able to visit the eggs? I want to see the baby dragons." Her voice breathless. Just the thought had her body vibrating. Taylynn's eyes softened. Behind Taylynn, there came a soft snort. She threw a glare in Feowen's direction and heard him mutter something about the *soft hearts of women*.

"You are the spriten queen, Your Majesty. You may do as you wish. But I should dearly love to see them too. Perhaps we will witness the moment together. In the meantime, there are things that must be considered." Taylynn took her hand and pulled her away from prying ears, lacing their fingers together in a firm hold. "Come, walk with me."

Sprites often held hands; it was part of their culture. She was finding the custom had grown on her. It felt nice to walk with Taylynn like this. She kept her staff in the other, using it as a walking stick. Her guards moved to follow them.

"*Ni*, thank you." The princess stopped them. "Our queen will be quite safe in my company."

They halted.

Once they were out of earshot, Taylynn said, "Have you given any thought to reclaiming Kane's three dragonstones?"

She grimaced. "I admit, I haven't had much time to dwell on it."

"As suspected. But surely you know how important it is to find them?"

"I've had dreams about them," she admitted. "When I first came here, I dreamt of Kane a lot—more than I do now."

"Did you dream of him while you were in the forest?"

"I...no." Her brows drew together.

"That is good," Taylynn said. "I wouldn't expect it. The barrier, remember?"

"Oh, that's right. I think my last serious dream was before the attack on Fort Squall," she explained. Taylynn made a humming sound. "Long before that, he haunted my dreams more frequently. I saw him hiding each stone. Saw the places he hid them—but how could I ever know where exactly they are? It's not like I'm familiar with the terrain. I can guess at it. I can describe it to you."

Taylynn made another thoughtful humming noise. "The stones must be found. Now that this business with the fort is over, it's time to shift our attention. There are two tasks at hand, finding the stones, and defeating Kane."

"And since Kane is entirely my responsibility," Claire mused, "then you'll help with the stones?"

"Uncertain. I have other matters, other responsibilities."

"What about the tree? Does it know where they are?"

"Unfortunately, no."

"Damn," she muttered, scowling.

"I must assist with the dragon hatchlings. After that, I will visit Kastali Dun. You and I will spend some time pouring over maps, seeing if we can't determine the locations of each. Whatever work you can do beforehand would speed us along."

"That..." She hesitated. "Actually, I'd like that. I'd love for you to visit the capital. Have you ever been?"

Something mischievous sparked in Taylynn's gaze. "Once or twice."

Their short walk brought them back to the others. "Now then. We will see each other again soon." Taylynn sighed. "I suppose I ought to say goodbye to my mate? That's something mates do, *ni*?"

"Neem, luth utah," Claire said, fighting a smile. For all her wisdom, Taylynn was in over her head with this whole mates thing.

The sprite princess offered a gentle smile. "Neem, nua sasian, sladaeah, Ayas Drollaya." *Yes, well then, fairwell, Your Majesty.*

They hugged again before Taylynn made her way over to Koldis, whose face instantly brightened. If she wasn't mistaken, Koldis had discreetly tracked their entire walk. Perhaps Talon had done the same. The drengr were a protective bunch. They didn't like letting their mates out of sight.

That thought brought a soft smile to her lips right as she caught Talon's knowing gaze.

The rest of the afternoon passed in a blur as the remainder of camp disappeared. Supplies were loaded onto ships, overseen by Talon and his shields. She found herself standing on the beach, saying goodbye to her friends. They wouldn't be apart for long, but she was growing tired of saying it so often. She longed for the day when she was surrounded by the people she loved without coming and going, without having to separate so frequently.

Her handmaidens and queen's guard stood a safe distance away, giving them privacy. She was aware of Talon and his shields, speaking with a few of the ship captains. Verath was set to travel with Desaree, Jocelyn, and Saffra, even though they could take care of themselves.

"We'll see each other soon," she said. "I'll have everything ready for your return." Her gaze snagged on Saffra. The prophetess chewed on her lower lip as if this goodbye was leaving her uncertain.

Desaree was the first to rush forward, throwing her arms around Claire. "Your handmaidens will take good care of you in my absence. I've already given them plenty of instructions."

"I'm sure you did!"

They would be returning to the capital by unicorn. Talon and his shields—with the exception of Reyr and Verath— would accompany them by sky. There was also a massive force of drengr-rider pairs coming along. The unicorns would travel faster, but she didn't intend to arrive before the king, so they'd camp together in the evenings, stopping early to allow the drengr to catch up. She was already trembling with nervous excitement.

Jocelyn stepped forward, glancing between her and Saffra. They hugged. "Take care of them, Joce. I know you're the wise one of the bunch these days. Don't let Des do anything reckless."

Des made a scoffing sound that left her smiling.

"Actually, Your Majesty..." Jocelyn's words died and she stepped back, throwing another glance at Saffra.

Claire frowned. "Okay," she said, suddenly suspicious, "*what* is going on?" Saffra's throat bobbed. "You're both being weird and I want to know why."

Desaree frowned.

Jocelyn cleared her throat and said, "You had better just tell them."

"Tell us what?" Claire demanded.

Saffra stepped forward, uncertain. When she finally opened her mouth to speak, Claire's eyes went round. The ground surged beneath her. She blinked, then blinked again, gaping at Saffra. It was the last thing she'd ever expected to hear—*the absolute last*. A moment passed, then another, and then she burst into hysterical laughter.

CHAPTER 16

FLYING WITH BEDELTH

Celenore

Saffra gaped at Claire, doubled over and clutching her stomach, laughing so hard she could barely breathe. It wasn't the sort of reaction she'd expected. Far from it.

"Claire?" She chewed on her bottom lip. "Perhaps you didn't hear me? He's my mate," she said, throwing a nervous glance in Bedelth's direction, just in case he was close enough to hear them. He wasn't. But Claire's laughter was so loud that heads were already turning.

"I'm...sorry..." Claire gasped, finally righting herself, wiping tears from her eyes. Desaree's reaction was the opposite of Claire's. She merely stood gaping like a fish. "I just... Wait, you... Are you serious?"

"Dead serious."

"Oh, *Saffra!*" The smile slipped from Claire's face and her eyes widened. She shot forward, launching herself into the air. Saffra had just a moment to catch her, staggering backwards, before they both tumbled to the sand. A strangled laugh burst from her chest. She gave into her own hysterics, collapsing in Claire's arms. Laughing felt good. It felt *freeing.* So they lay there and laughed.

Sadly, she wasn't laughing because she was *happy*. Even Claire's laughter wasn't exactly happy. They were laughing because this was so impossible to believe.

"This is *crazy*!" Claire gasped. "Just crazy. First Koldis and now Bedelth? Gods above. And you're sure?"

"Absolutely positive," Saffra managed.

They finally got up, brushing sand from their clothes, only to find the king and his shields gaping at them. Claire's eyes went unfocused and then she smiled. "Talon says he's missing all the fun."

Saffra scoffed. Fun. *Right.* There was nothing *fun* about her circumstances with Bedelth. Nothing fun about the road she must navigate.

"All right ladies, wrap it up," Koldis shouted towards them. Row boats had disappeared. Nearly everything was loaded into the waiting ships.

Saffra's stomach fluttered with nerves. "So, uhm, Bedelth requested that I fly home with him—with the king's shields, I mean. I have decided to accept—" A chorus of squeals cut her off. "I am *not* accepting him as my mate! Stop it. You are *all* being ridiculous. This is just...an experiment. An opportunity to see what it's like to travel by flight. I don't intend to... Oh my Gods! Will you all just..." She finally gave up, arms going limp at her sides, giving in to the heated flush that coated her skin.

Claire was clutching Desaree, laughing with glee—acting like a gossiping hen at court who'd just found out the juiciest tidbit and couldn't contain herself. Jocelyn was giggling, her hands pressed firmly over her mouth. Desaree supported Claire, taking deep breaths and trying not to squeal like her counterpart.

Saffra's teeth ground together. She *wanted* to be angry—furious, really—that they were behaving like children. But as she looked at their expressions of mirth, she saw something much deeper. Her heart lifted. They looked at her with overflowing love and happiness, their eyes glittering with eager anticipation. They felt all of this *for her*?

She cleared her throat, pushing away her frustration. "Anyway,

Des, you and Joce are sailing back with Verath. I'll be with Bedelth —" She faltered, realizing exactly how that sounded. "And Claire will be with King Talon...I presume?"

"*Uh-huh*," Claire answered, wagging her eyebrows. "You'll be with Bedelth, all right." Saffra attempted her best glare and Claire held up her hands. "Fine. I'll stop. But it's going to be a lot of evenings spent resting around the campfire, and don't think for a *second* I won't get all the details from you."

Saffra couldn't stop her eye roll.

"Did you just *roll your eyes* at a queen?!"

Saffra crossed her arms. "That's exactly what I did, *Your Majesty*."

"Thought so," Claire grinned. Then she turned to Desaree and hugged her again, following it with another for Jocelyn. "Take care of each other," she said. "I'll see you soon."

"And take care of my lady," Jocelyn said in return.

"Oh, I plan to." Claire threw Saffra a wicked smirk that had her wanting to roll her eyes all over again.

THE SHIPS HAD LIFTED anchor by the time Saffra watched Claire gather with her guards. Aside from their small party, everyone else was gone. There was no sign that a war camp had blanketed the land. It's like it had never been there.

Nearly twenty ships sailed towards the mouth of Stormy Bay. Most carried supplies, but some carried soldiers and others carried dwargs. King Talon had invited them to the capital. He'd offered to warmly host them within the keep for several weeks. Approximately half had accepted. She couldn't imagine what their arrival would be like. They were a rambunctious lot. She had enjoyed her time in their company, moments stolen during rushed mealtimes or quick chats. She looked forward to truly getting to know them.

Dragonwall was finally uniting. She took this as a good sign. Together, at full strength, Kane couldn't hope to bring them down. They would stand firm until Claire was ready to defeat him.

"Having second thoughts?" A deep, honeyed voice said. "The ships are close enough. We can flag one down, get you on board before it's too late." His voice had become so familiar that her body hummed in joyous recognition. Gods, how unfair was that?!

"No second thoughts," she said, sounding far more confident than she felt.

"Good." There was a long hesitation before he handed her a pair of gloves.

"What are these for?" She took them and winced. What a stupid question—

"To keep your mind protected."

She jolted, staring at them. They were made from a soft animal hide, dyed a deep, forest green, delicately embroidered with gold thread. The insides were lined with white fleece. She slipped them on, immediately comforted by the softness.

"What do you mean, my mind?" she asked, already guessing.

"I would never dream of prying into your deepest thoughts, Saffra, but those at the forefront are fair game. I know how you feel about this. This will allow you privacy." He motioned towards the gloves, now wrapping her hands in the softest warmth.

Guilt hardened her stomach. She tried to ignore it. This was for the best.

Bedelth rested a hand on his sverak. "It means we cannot communicate while in the sky, but there won't be a need for it. Unless..." He cleared his throat. "Unless you wish to." There was a sliver of hope in his voice.

She hated it—hated how awful it made her feel. *She* was the monster for allowing fear to come between them. Her soul felt stretched in two directions. Part of her wanted to be *more* monstrous, to push him away so he'd stop wanting her. The other part wanted to throw her arms around him, to embrace the things he made her feel.

"Anyway, this will be good for you. Shed the rigid cloak of expectation you keep so tightly wrapped about your shoulders. Embrace the sky, the enjoyment flying brings. I have no plans beyond that." With that, he strode away.

No plans to push the mate bond, he meant.

She flexed her fingers. The gloves were a nice touch—brand new, too. They fit her small hands perfectly. Warmth exploded in her chest at the thought of him having them specially made. He didn't want to push her. This was his way of easing her into things.

A relieved exhale left her lungs. Things would be easier once they were home. She'd return to her normal life. Avoiding Bedelth wouldn't be so difficult.

"All right, let's go," King Talon's voice called. She moved closer, as did everyone else. "Claire will return to the capital with her queen's guard. We will follow in the sky. Drengr can't match the pace of unicorns, so they will make camp early and wait for us each evening. We fly by day and rest by night. There's no need for haste, although I am eager to begin planning our bonding ceremony." He threw his mate an affectionate look and everyone chuckled. "Let's get going."

Claire and Talon stole a few minutes together, saying goodbye. Tourmaline waited patiently with the other unicorns and sprites. Saffra's cheeks heated at the sight of Claire and Talon's passionate kiss. A burst of jealousy took her. She knew what it meant to have someone, to kiss them like that.

"She makes him very happy," Bedelth mused. She was startled. Where had he come from? "I never thought I'd see the day, but he deserves it."

"He does," she agreed, continuing to watch their monarchs. "It's hard to believe the way everything turned out."

"It certainly is." His sidelong gaze made her shift nervously. She flexed her fingers and glanced down. "Thank you for the gloves, Bedelth. They're beautiful."

"Of course. My pleasure." He attempted to make his response casual, but she could hear something deeper. "My parents would disown me, you know. If I took a mate—took you as my mate, I mean. Even knowing the king will change the law. Even knowing who you are, and how important you are to this kingdom."

Her stomach dropped. "What? What do you mean?"

He scoffed, staring straight ahead. A line had formed between his brows, marring his otherwise flawless brown skin. "They've always been...strict. They won't approve. I am a *shield*. Shields do not take mates. It would dishonor me in their eyes."

Her mouth opened as she struggled to find the right words. *Why* was he telling her this? She swallowed down the tightness forming in her throat. "I...I didn't know your parents were still alive."

In fact, she didn't know anything about them. He'd never mentioned them. They'd been friends, spent time together, and he'd never once mentioned his parents. Was he...did they have a bad relationship?

He gave a brief nod, as if he'd read her mind. His gaze remained fixed on the king. His arms were clasped behind his back, looking casual as could be, but she felt his tension. "They were young when they had me. Younger than most. My father is over eight hundred now..."

"Oh..." She fidgeted with her gloves. "But...shouldn't they be happy for you? Happy that you found someone to spend your life with—hypothetically speaking, I mean."

He snorted.

The dismissive sound made her insides twist with anger. What parent *wouldn't* be proud of a son like Bedelth? She opened her mouth, almost ready to say that, then snapped it closed. The pain she felt—pain for *him*—was something she didn't want to feel. "I suppose there won't be much need to worry, since we don't plan to acknowledge our mate bond."

She hated the words the moment they left her mouth. Wrapping her arms around her middle, she hunched inward. Regardless of what she'd said, she suddenly disliked his parents very, very much.

"Right." He lifted a dismissive shoulder. "Exactly. It's for the best."

His agreement made her chest feel heavy.

He turned towards her. "It's nearly time. When I transform, we won't be able to converse unless you touch my scales. If you need something, you can speak aloud and I will hear you."

"Okay."

"Your cloak should be sufficient, but if you get cold, let me know. My scales will keep you fairly warm. Right, well then. Whenever you're ready." He gave her one last look, then walked away. The others began assembling around King Talon.

Claire came over and briefly squeezed her hand. "I'll see you when we make camp tonight?"

"Yes," Saffra managed.

"If you want, we can talk about it?" Claire added, throwing a glance in Bedelth's direction as he transformed into a hulking orange dragon. His scales shifted from his spine down his belly, taking on various shades of a sunset orange. There was even a bit of yellow and pink.

"I might need that," she managed, nodding.

"Good. Well then." A grin spread across Claire's features. "Enjoy yourself."

"Thanks," she croaked, her throat parched.

Claire reached over and pulled her into a tight hug. She was too ruffled to do much more than lift her arms and squeeze her friend back. Claire walked off and found her guards, already waiting with their unicorns. Claire climbed upon Tourmaline's back. The spriten queen gave a final wave, then bounded away. A blink later, they were gone.

She made her way to Bedelth. Her head fell back, taking him in up close. She gazed up and up and up. Most of the shields had transformed already. Heat rushed across her skin. This was going to be *so* embarrassing—

"Need a hand?"

"Oh," she said, placing her hand over her heart.

Jovari grinned down at her. He laced his fingers together. "It will get easier, but here, you can step into my hands, and then up onto his foreleg. You'll have to jump to grab his neck spike there, but you should reach it okay. Then you'll have to pull your body up and over. It's not like riding a horse. Or so I'm told. Wouldn't know, really." He winked.

"Yes, I found that to be the case once before." This would be her second time flying with him, after all.

"Well then, let's give it a try."

She was vaguely aware of everyone watching her. Gods! This was the worst. She didn't *dare* glance over her shoulder.

Stepping into Jovari's laced fingers, she began to climb. When she managed to grab the correct neck spike, she pulled herself up. Her first attempt was appalling. She huffed, tried again, then got it on the second try.

"Nicely done!" Jovari called up to her. A pleased smile stretched across her lips. She'd do better next time. There'd be...how many days to practice? Perhaps she ought to have asked.

She caught Talon's eye, noticed his draconic smirk—how had she never noticed that dragons could smirk?—and quickly looked away. She felt a jolt and tightened her legs, smothering a squeal that threatened to break free. Bedelth stood, moving into position.

Moments later, Talon took up the pinnacle and Jovari got into position. She couldn't hear what was happening, whatever they said to each other. She closed her eyes, taking in a deep breath, ignoring the heaviness in her heart, ignoring the temptation to remove her glove and touch Bedelth's glassy scales.

In the end, she convinced herself that it was better this way.

King Talon lifted his giant head to the sky, releasing a deafening roar. His shields took up the call. A moment later, they sprang from the ground. Her stomach dropped out beneath her as they lifted into the air. There was that startling sense of heaviness, something pressing her into the dip at the base of his neck. She remembered this from the first time. It only lasted a second. Then Bedelth's wings stretched out and swept downward. They climbed into the air, higher and higher. Glancing below, she watched the ground fall away. A gasp fell from her lips. A fully fledged laugh crawled up her throat, until she didn't care that she was giggling.

They rose higher and higher. Then, as a single unit, they turned south. It was time to go home.

CHAPTER 17

IMPOSTER SYNDROME

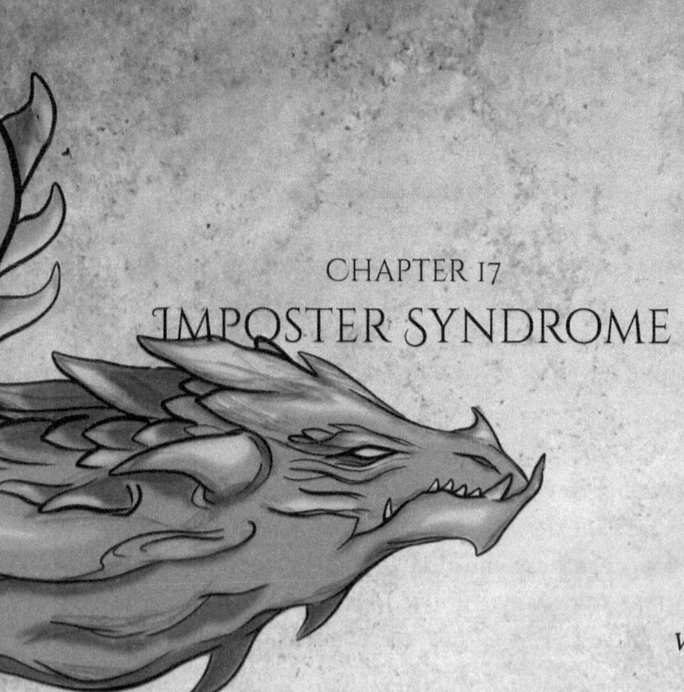

Wilderness

Jeanine swung a leg over, gracefully dismounting from her unicorn before giving the beautiful creature an affectionate pat. "Thank you, my friend," she whispered. Opal swung her head around and nudged her in *Feowen's* direction. She chuckled but ignored the creature's obvious attempt at matchmaking.

Her fellow guards dismounted from their own unicorns. Their tall, lithe forms moved with grace, outfitted in beautiful suits of starlight silver armor. Her armor was the same, yet, she couldn't help but feel like an imposter in it. She wasn't a sprite and yet, Claire had accepted her pledge. Heat washed her cheeks. She looked away from the gathering who fussed about their queen.

Claire wouldn't have accepted her pledge if she believed her unworthy...right? Her stomach squirmed uncomfortably. She pushed the thought aside.

"*Ahhh.*" A deep male groan distracted her. "*Aahm seamih.* It feels good to be on my own two feet and see the world standing still. Am I right?" Feowen came to stand beside her, nudging her with an elbow. "What's the matter?"

"Nothing," she muttered, plastering on a bright smile.

"*Gadhaah.*"

She sputtered. "Did you just call me a *liar*?"

"Fine. But I will gladly lend an ear, if you wish to discuss it. I need to speak with my cousin. I'll find you afterward. Let's go for a walk. My legs are positively screaming at me." The last he muttered darkly.

"Fine."

"*Fight it if you must, but his heart is set upon you,*" Opal said, interrupting her brooding.

"So much for not sticking your horn where it doesn't belong," she hissed, teasing the unicorn.

"*I shall stick my horn—*"

"Don't finish that thought," she sputtered. Opal gave a loud snicker and plodded away to graze. She watched the unicorn affectionately. The friendship that had formed between her and Opal ran deep. She felt as if she had some claim over the creature. Opal felt the same, surely.

Tears clouded her eyes. She'd had very few deep friendships in her lifetime. She blinked, clearing her vision. What would she do when it was time to say goodbye? Would they see each other again? She rubbed a hand over her stomach, absently. The thought made her uncomfortable. She'd already had to say goodbye to another friend.

A part of her heart had shattered when Jahl had left the forest, accepting the king's offer to journey to the capital and take up a position with the city watch. She couldn't blame him. He'd always wanted to live a soldier's life, had talked about it when they'd spent time together growing up in Kaljah.

An ache formed in her throat, for the past, for what she'd lost. Her village, her father, her previous life. It all felt like a lifetime ago. It was said that time moved differently in the forest and she believed it did. Things felt drawn out and stretched when one lived within the trees.

Jahl had been a constant part of her life since her mother had uprooted her from Lincastle, moving them to the far reaches of nowhere to be with her crippled father. Jahl had always been there for her. Then he'd left and she'd felt betrayed, even though she couldn't force him to stay. Couldn't force him to linger somewhere he didn't feel he belonged.

Now she was traveling to the capital, his new home. Might they run into each other? If they did, would he regard her coldly for her attachment to Prince Feowen? Or would they meet as friends?

Part of her didn't *want* to know the answer and hoped they wouldn't cross paths. Kastali Dun was a huge city, after all. Besides, she'd be serving the queen while he manned the city walls. What were the odds?

She saw to her own business then walked about the landscape, keeping close to their party. The fields were open and dotted with trees. They were on the fourth day of their journey, traveling much slower than they would have had they not needed to wait for the king and his shields. Each day they set out at dawn and stopped midafternoon, setting up camp. It usually took the drengr until nightfall, sometimes much later, to catch up with them—

"There you are." Feowen appeared beside her, stopping to gaze at the cluster of trees in the distance. "Shall we walk there?"

"Sure," she said, glancing at him. His uncanny gaze was fixed on her, his blue hair braided tightly down his back. Her cheeks flushed, recalling the softness of his hair when he'd asked her to braid it for him. The intimacy of the act had been surprising.

He took her hand, lacing their fingers together. Her breaths quickened, but she forced them to slow. If he noticed, he made no indication. It was always like this around him, ever since they'd kissed, which they'd done plenty more since the first. Each time was just as delicious, just as fiery, turning her insides to liquid heat. But he hadn't pushed her further than that, and she'd been grateful.

Perhaps it was cowardly, but she was afraid to get closer to him. Did he feel the same? Was that why he hadn't taken things further?

No, you dolt, said a voice in her head. *It's because you've been fighting a war. There are more important things than tumbling into bed together.* She cleared her throat, trying not to be shocked by her own rogue monologue.

"Anything in particular you'd like to see when we reach the capital?"

"Oh." Her thoughts scattered and she focused on his question. "The keep, of course, with its sparring grounds and royal garden. The Bay of Bandu, obviously. The city's market—I've heard it's spectacular." He hummed in agreement. "The arena, where events are held. The shopping districts." He began to chuckle. "Yes, I guess everything, if I'm being honest."

"Then that's what we will do."

"You think there will be time?" Hope rang heavy in her voice. She wasn't sure what their duties would entail once they arrived. Back at camp, they'd kept close to their queen to serve and protect. But in the keep? Claire would be surrounded by the king's people, his shields close at hand. Perhaps there'd be more time to herself, to explore the city and hopefully *not* run into Jahl.

"*Sasit bei likah.* There will be time," he translated. She committed the words to memory while repeating them aloud. He corrected her pronunciation several times, then smiled, satisfied. "You're learning quickly."

She snorted. "Right."

"You are," he assured her, squeezing her hand.

"Claire was in the forest half as long as me and she's already fluent."

"*Claire,*" he emphasized, "is part sprite. My cousin by blood. She isn't human, even if she may look it, or did look it, before she got all those markings." He sighed, the sound heavy, laced with something she couldn't quite read. Frustration? Sadness? "Do not compare yourself to an impossible ideal, Jeanie. It is unfair and unrealistic. It will only bring you displeasure."

Heat prickled to her skin. He wasn't scolding her, per se, but it still embarrassed her. Why in the name of the gods *was* she being so hard on herself?

Oh. Right. Because she was surrounded by sprites. Sprites craved perfection with their tall forms and their perfect manner of speaking and their perfectly beautiful faces and their perfect fighting form and...perfect everything. Feowen had even teased her for less in the past, but that seemed to have largely abated now that he'd accepted her human ways.

He stopped, abruptly, turning to face her. His expression said he'd read her thoughts well enough. He took her face in his hands. "*Jeanine*," he said. A shiver raced down her spine. "I like you how you are. I hope you understand that. If I wanted a sprite for a companion, can you not see that I have my pick of them? I shall never forget the sight of you on that hill, bow in hand. It's imprinted in my mind. I knew then, as I know now." He hesitated. "*Aya kunyn mirsaah edah alskedirahil. Aya kunyn javkain eah mik.*"

Her insides turned to liquid warmth. The passion in his voice, the declaration, felt like the kind of words lovers whispered to each other. "What does that mean?" she managed. She didn't recognize enough to make sense of them.

He placed his forehead against hers, leaning down to do so. "You are fearsome and unapologetic. You are beautiful to me."

"Oh..." she breathed. Her stomach somersaulted. "You think that of me?"

"Of course I do." He rubbed his nose against hers, the gesture so affectionate it made her throat ache. The warmth left behind was enough to stave off the spring chill. He could have made some joking remark about his thoughts being obvious, but he must have sensed her moment of weakness, that she needed his sincerity. He gave it freely. "Come on, let's explore this little grove."

He pulled her along, dragging her through the trees, a look of wonder on his face. Like other sprites, he hadn't left the forest much. She couldn't help the flutter of her heart as her mood lifted, seeing his joy.

Birds chirped, flitting between branches. The grass didn't grow as tall here in the shade of the trees. It was littered with fallen leaves, leftover from autumn before being frozen in winter. Shrubs were sparse, unlike in the forest. They could easily walk wherever they wished. Every so often, Feowen lifted a hand to run it down the bark of a tree.

"Here. This one will do." In a flash, Feowen snagged her waist and pressed her against it, meeting her mouth with his and pressing a knee between her legs, melding his body against hers. She gasped as his kiss overcame her, falling into it, letting the warmth crowd out every unwanted thought.

She didn't think about what their future might hold. Didn't think about how he could have *anyone*, but seemed to only want her. Didn't think about how inadequate she felt around the other spriten guards.

There was only his curious fingers, his hot mouth, and the new rush of thoughts that left her skin flushed. His hips rocked against hers, the motion erotic, their bodies hard everywhere they met. New feelings awoke in her, and she began to wonder if perhaps she might be willing to forget her fears in lieu of satisfying her desires. But in the end, Feowen didn't push anything forward, and she was plenty content to kiss him for all eternity as the afternoon light waned into a gloaming evening.

∼

"You and Feowen seem happy," Claire said, making Jeanine choke on her dinner. Abrupt as it was, she should have been prepared for it. Even though she and Feowen didn't make public displays, they snuck away frequently enough.

She and Claire sat slightly away from the others, but still close enough that sprite hearing would pick up their words. Case in point, she noticed the way Feowen's conversation with Rahlif faltered, then picked up again.

"I...yes, we are. And he can hear you, by the way."

"Oh." Claire glanced over towards the prince. "I keep forgetting things like that. You'd think I'd be used to it by now."

Jeanine snorted. "I suppose we haven't been all that covert about things."

"And why should you be?" Claire asked, picking at the bread and cheese laid out on a cloth before them.

"I guess I don't know."

"Sprites seem pretty open-minded when it comes to public displays, from what I've gathered. Not like the prim and proper behavior I've witnessed in the capital. Everything *there* is secretive, kept behind closed doors." Claire chuckled. "I think if Dragonwall saw the way sprites hold hands so naturally, our healers would have an epidemic of aneurysms on their hands."

"Aneur-*what*?"

Claire laughed. "It's a very serious medical condition that can occur in someone's brain. I shouldn't joke about it so lightly. That was in poor taste."

"Hmm..." was all Jeanine could manage. Any other time, she might be more curious about things from Claire's world.

"Something's on your mind," Claire observed.

She snorted. "First Feowen, then you."

"I'm guessing you didn't talk about it with him?" Claire asked. Jeanine shook her head. "Would you like to talk about it with me? I'm a good listener. Here—" Claire wrapped up their dinner and stood, grabbing Jeanine's hand and pulling her up. When they stood, Claire didn't relinquish her hold. Jeanine wasn't sure how to take that, but in the end, allowed herself to be flattered. Knowing sprites held hands with their good friends meant Claire regarded her as such. "Let's find a new place to picnic."

Feowen turned, taking several steps towards them. Claire added, "*Ni*, Feowen. We will be fine. I've got a guard with me, see? And we'll still be visible." To Jeanine she rolled her eyes and said, "Obviously we wouldn't be moving away if we didn't want privacy."

Jeanine's eyes locked with Feowen. He clearly wanted to tag along for more than Claire's protection. Likely, he wanted to know why she was brooding. Her gaze narrowed in warning. He nodded and turned back to Rahlif.

Claire kept a tight hold on her, pulling her along. Once they were out of earshot she said, "Okay, spill."

Jeanine sighed. "I guess I've just been feeling...inadequate."

Her words were met with a loud sigh. "Now *that* is something I can relate to."

"You...you can?"

"Uhm. Duh. Newly appointed sprite queen here."

"Yes, but, you...you're..."

"I'm what?" Claire turned to her, dropping her hand.

"You just seem like you always have everything together." At this, Claire's eyebrows knitted. "It's true," she argued. "You're strong and unruffled. Like, no matter the situation, you are its equal. Everyone tells me I'm brave and courageous for what I did in Kaljah. That I'm unapologetic for not conforming to the behaviors expected of most women. But then I look at the other spriten females and I feel so *inadequate*. Like, how could I ever measure up? And you...you don't just bear the title of queen. You *look* like a queen. You...you *speak* like a queen. Act like a queen. I just find it hard to believe that you..." She exhaled. "I'm doing a poor job of explaining this. What I really mean is, you do well at hiding how you feel. No one would ever look at you and think you were struggling with feelings of inadequacy. I wouldn't have known."

"We call it imposter syndrome where I'm from."

Imposter syndrome. "That makes sense, actually."

They found a spot to sit and Claire opened the cloth, unveiling their unfinished dinner. Jeanine grabbed a hunk of cheese and bread and took a small bite. "I know it's ridiculous to feel this way," she said after chewing. "They're sprites. I'm not. At least you have a good reason. Being a queen...that's...that makes my worries feel small. Makes me feel silly."

"Jeanine." Claire placed a hand on her arm. "No worry is ever small or unimportant. Certainly not *silly*. Especially if it's something heavy on your heart. You have every right to feel exactly the way you do."

"I...I do?" She frowned.

"Of course!"

She opened and closed her mouth. "But, I'm being ridiculous for comparing myself to an impossible ideal. That's what Feowen said."

Claire scoffed. "What a male thing to say—of course he'd say it. In some respects he *is* right. Logical, really. Males love logic. They are creatures of problem solving and calculation. Females, we are creatures of the heart, of feeling. I read this book once—well, never mind. That's beside the point. What I mean is, we females don't always want a *solution* to our struggles. Sometimes we just want someone to *hear* us. We want to feel understood and supported. We want to feel like we aren't alone. You know?"

Jeanine blinked, processing this revelation. Night was falling, but there was still enough glow to the sky. The roaring fire in the distance gave off shadows as various people in their party moved around it.

"But anyway," Claire went on to say. "Feowen was right in that comparison is dangerous. And comparing yourself to a sprite is like comparing an apple to an orange. What he should have *also* said was that regardless of the comparison, your feelings are no less valid. You feel how you feel, and that's not wrong. It is simply what it is. Don't *ever* feel ridiculous for feeling how you feel." Suddenly, a surprised laugh burst from Claire's lips. Musical and light. "Now, if only I could take my *own* advice to heart."

Jeanine's eyes blurred a little, but she blinked and cleared them.

Claire scoffed. "I hate that feelings can be irrational. That they can make so little sense, and yet we feel them acutely. That doesn't make it wrong, though. I just wish I wasn't always so worried about being perfect. It's like, I know how I *should* feel, and that I'm not seeing things the way I ought to, but I can't seem to avoid it." Claire opened her mouth again, as if she wanted to say more, then snapped it shut. She picked at a stalk of grass, her dinner forgotten, shredding it before tossing it away. Then she looked up, giving Jeanine a hesitant grin. "I didn't mean to take over this conversation with my own troubles."

"No—no. Actually." Jeanine hesitated. "That's exactly what I needed to hear."

Claire's head tilted. "Was it? Perhaps I'm better at this than I realized. I should open a practice."

Laughter burst from Jeanine's lips. She wasn't sure what *a practice* was, but Claire was definitely good at this. To know she also struggled with similar feelings... Well, it made a huge difference. Knowing she wasn't alone, that she wasn't the only one feeling this way, lifted something from her chest. Something heavy that felt entirely too suffocating at times.

"I do agree with you, though," Jeanine found herself saying. "Knowing isn't the same as putting into practice *what* you know. But at least I don't feel stupid about it now."

"Good." Claire smiled. Then her eyes went blurry. Her smile widened, face transforming into beatific grace. It was miraculous to watch how she went from happy to joyous and radiant. A true queen. "That was Talon," she breathed. "They're almost here."

They quickly finished their dinner, chatting about inconsequential things after that. She would always appreciate that Claire could appear queenly in one moment and perfectly normal the next. That she wanted to talk about males and romance. That she avoided political matters and things that were too serious when the occasion didn't warrant serious conversation. That she could give sage advice, but still admit her own flaws.

Claire made an excellent queen, even if she didn't see herself that way. Perhaps in time, she would. As for her own struggles, Jeanine was determined to worry less about how she compared to others, and more about how she compared to herself. Determined to recognize her feelings for what they were, and keep from beating herself up about it.

As shadows passed overhead, churning up the air, they stood and walked back to camp. Again, Claire took her hand, swinging their arms back and forth as they walked, all smiles and excitement. And in that moment, Jeanine realized there would always be difficulties to face, but having someone face them with you made them a thousand times easier.

CHAPTER 18

STOLEN MOMENTS

Celenore Wilderness

Talon soared overhead, picking out Claire's form beside Jeanine. His chest heaved with a pleased rumble as the threads knitting them together loosened. It was always difficult putting distance between them. He'd gotten more used to it, but that did not mean he *liked* it. In truth, he was a little jealous of Tourmaline. It was selfish. Claire was aware of how he felt, but she never commented on it, never faulted him for it.

"I missed you." Claire's voice brushed against his thoughts.

"I missed you too," came his hearty reply.

His wings pumped a little harder at her declaration, then tucked tightly to his body. His shields did the same as they landed. He hit the ground on two feet. The only one in their wing who didn't transform was Bedelth, so that Saffra could dismount.

Bedelth and Saffra. He hadn't seen that coming. He and Koldis had joked about who might be next, but it had been exactly that, a joke. Now he was starting to wonder how much fate was involved.

Two shields with mates. It was a sign. It *had* to be. Things were changing. At this rate, Jovari would be next. He almost snorted at the thought. Jovari had slept his way through half the female nobility. Seeing him leashed, now *that* would be something.

Claire's Spriten delegation greeted him with bows of respect. "Ayas Drollaya."

By now, they knew a mate bond existed between them—

He caught a blur of movement from the corner of his eye. "Oof!" he cried, gathering a laughing Claire into his arms. He lifted and spun her, ignoring the resultant snickers. They'd been apart for the better part of a day. Yet, it was as if they hadn't seen each other in weeks.

He exhaled, letting go of his tension.

Her body felt perfect in his arms; this was exactly where she belonged. He tightened his hold, molding her to him, breathing her in. He dragged a hand down the back of her head, pressing her face into the crook of his neck. She wore her hair braided back in something she'd called a *French braid*, or some sort. A name from her world—her *old* world. This was her world now. She'd chosen *him*, his scars, his faults, his kingdom, his responsibility, forsaking her family, her past, *everything*.

All for him.

Most days, he still couldn't believe it. Some days, when his crown was especially heavy, a dark voice whispered that she'd eventually change her mind. That she'd come to him and admit it was too much. Admit that ruling wasn't what she'd expected—was more than she could handle.

Except...when had she ever shied away from anything?

Even still, he was terrified of the possibility of losing her. And so he tried to make this as easy as possible. A gradual transition into the role, exactly the opposite of what had happened in Esterpine, which infuriated him to the core. Those damned sprites never should have thrust a crown upon her.

Her nose nuzzled him, cold against his hot skin, pushing his dark thoughts away. Her lips brushed his pulse, making his breath hitch. When he set her on her feet, he dipped his head and kissed her, letting his mouth linger over hers, letting his tongue dart out for a taste, caring little for watchful eyes. They were surrounded by their inner circle. There was nothing to hide from these people.

Koldis's smug chuckle had him breaking away, but not before he brushed his nose along hers.

"Shall we walk?" Claire asked.

He hesitated. "You'd rather walk than fly?"

"Talon," she laughed. "You've been flying all day."

"That hasn't stopped us before." The corner of his mouth twitched. He knew how much she adored flying. With him, especially. Gods, he felt exactly the same.

They were four days into their journey, with nearly that many left to go before reaching the capital. He didn't mind spending extra time in the sky, as long as it was with her, but he refused to admit that it made him fatigued after a day of intense flying. He'd never say it, but she saw it plainly enough when their minds were melded.

"Let's walk tonight," she decided, taking his hand and weaving their fingers together.

"*Ayas Drollaya! Fian verah baejah?*" Elyon Marquin stepped forward, her hand on the pommel of her sword. The fire cast Elyon in an orange glow, making her armor shine in the darkness. The effect was ethereal, out of this world.

"*Ni,* Elyon. I will be fine. And the common tongue, if you please, when we are around our own."

Elyon nodded. "*Ninneem.* Of course, Your Majesty."

Elyon fell back and they began their walk. He said, "I look forward to the day I understand the language, but until then, I do not mind if they converse with you in their native tongue."

The camp faded behind them. "It doesn't bother you that you cannot understand them?"

He lifted a shoulder. "I suppose a little. But I trust that if it's important, you'd translate. At any rate, I do not wish for them to be closed off from their heritage."

Claire sucked her bottom lip between her teeth, thoughtful. "I would prefer they include everyone when there are others around. Others that we trust, I mean, like our shields. It is a sign of respect. More so, it's simply courteous. I want there to be no animosity."

"Our shields," he teased. "I love hearing you say that."

Her eyes darted up to meet his, and she smiled. "I'm trying to get better about it."

"And I appreciate the effort." They fell silent, letting the darkness surround them. Soon the days would lengthen enough that it would still be daylight. He loved the longer days. His mood did too. He needed all the help he could get on that front.

"I know we are coming off a battle high," he said, "but I think it's time to start considering our next move."

"I was wondering when you'd bring that up." Her hand squeezed his. "What are your thoughts?"

"I wanted to hear yours, first."

She made a humming sound in the back of her throat. "That's hardly fair. You're the one who brought it up." He lifted a brow. "Oh, all right." She fell into silent contemplation. "We should focus on the stones. Taylynn and I discussed it."

"Yes, I saw that." Call him selfish, but he made it a point to sift through her mind at every opportunity. He'd always loved flying, but having her there, having access to her mind, made him love the experience infinitely more. Being able to know her better, understand her, simply by traversing the paths of her memories. He'd seen so much of her world, its strangeness, its curiosities, its evils. Admittedly, it fascinated him, and he found himself tumbling into various memories more than once, simply to see some of the *technological advancements*. Metal airplanes that carried hundreds, giant cruise ships, telephones that fit in a pocket, allowing the speaker to talk with someone across the world. He wondered what Dragonwall would be like with some of these inventions. Would it help them, or destroy them?

"I'm thinking I'll write out what I saw in my dreams," Claire was saying. He snapped his mind back to the present. "That way, perhaps we can narrow the landscape down to several locations. Like, in one of them, I saw a place that looks like a cave. So maybe we can look at the map and find places where caves are located?"

"I can take a deeper look as well. See if I recognize any of it. But, it sounds like finding a needle in a haystack," he mused.

She frowned, her brow furrowing. "Maybe if we just get rid of Kane, there won't be any need to find the stones. Leave them hidden under whatever protection he's given them—"

"No." He hadn't meant to cut her off. "I will not risk another Kane rising to power ten thousand years from now. We do this right, so that Dragonwall never goes through it again."

She blew out a breath. "Yes, you're right."

"Besides the stones, we still need to take care of Kane. Your magic has grown significantly. Are you ready to take him on?" His stomach turned rock hard. He *hated* the idea. Hated that she'd made this promise, taken on this responsibility.

"I..." She slowed to a stop, turning to him. Her lip caught between her teeth, a nervous habit. "I wasn't able to do it before, in the forest."

"You didn't have the staff."

"True. Maybe that will change things."

"It gives you access to a well of power, the tree's power."

"Yes." She hesitated and then, "Perhaps I will speak to the tree about it. I'm certain there is a time and place for everything, and the tree orchestrates it. I won't face Kane until the tree is ready for it."

He snorted. "Gods. I really want to say something snide— about you sounding like a sprite."

Her face split into a grin. "Except you can't, because I *am* a sprite."

"But you are also born of drengr ancestry. Irelia was both."

"True. And I have not yet found a way to be comfortable with both of my magics. I find myself resorting to my spriten magic almost exclusively. I still need them to make peace with both, before I'm powerful enough for Kane."

"Can Cyrus help with that?" he wondered. Her eyes took on a far away look. A look he'd come to know. "What is it? What is he saying?"

"That he *can* help, but that it is a task I must learn for myself, must conquer on my own." She snorted and her eyes sharpened. "He's being stubborn." There was a level of fondness in her voice that made his heart swell.

"I miss him," he admitted, showing his vulnerability. "Even having him closer, feeling the touches of him in your mind, I wish... I wish he were here. I wish he'd held on a little longer, for Reyr. I..."

"Talon..." Claire's eyes softened in the gloaming. She reached up and took his scarred face in her hands, caressing his jaw with her thumbs. His skin warmed everywhere she touched. "I wish it too, so much. But everything happened exactly as it was supposed to. The tree has made that much clear. I wouldn't have come here if he'd lived. You know that. I know that."

He sighed, hating it.

"I was the key—I *am* the key—to defeating Kane. Promise or not, Queen Isabella paid a price, and I was the result of that price. I'm the one who's supposed to bring balance back to Dragonwall." A strangled laugh burst from her chest. "That sounds rather ridiculous, doesn't it? Like, I'm the *chosen one* blah, blah, blah. But I guess I am. I needed to come here, Talon. If Cyrus hadn't died, I wouldn't have."

"That's not true." He said the words, even if he didn't believe them, didn't *want* to believe them.

"No. It is. If Cyrus had lived, he would have left with Reyr and the others. Talon...they never would have flouted the laws to bring me to Dragonwall. Cyrus *knew* that. No, they would have left immediately to get him the help he needed in Dragonwall." She sighed, her expression turning unreadable. Her voice lowered as she said, "You would still be alone, none the wiser of my existence, and I'd still be—"

"Stuck in your world, applying for jobs and fending off attempts from your ex to get back together."

"Oh, please. Don't remind me." Amusement crept into her voice. She lifted onto her tiptoes and kissed the corner of his mouth. He dropped his forehead to hers and inhaled, letting the moment wrap around them. His eyes fluttered closed.

Eventually, they continued their walk. The final vestiges of the sunset faded until the darkness lay heavy like a blanket, shrouding them. The sky was overcast, clouds glowing bright where the moon was hidden. Humidity signaled approaching rain, but he wasn't worried. It had rained two days past, overnight, and he'd been thrilled to witness spriten magic as several of Claire's guards wove a protective bubble around their encampment, allowing the others to sleep without concern.

"Will things change much, when I return?" she asked.

"You know they will, once I make the announcement." He hesitated and then said, "Claire, I would like you to move into the tower with me. I know our ceremony has yet to happen but—"

"All right."

He blinked. "All right?"

"Yes. All right. I'll move into the tower." Her face gave nothing away, until a tiny twitch at the corner of her lips made him chuckle.

"You're toying with me." She lifted a shoulder. "You are not going to fight me, then?"

"Talon, when was the last time I fought you on something?"

He opened his mouth—

"Never mind! Don't answer that. But no, I am not going to fight you on this. I have my queen's guard to think of now. The *Hall of Kings* will be rather crowded, trying to find accommodations for all of them, don't you think?"

He hummed in agreement. It was one of the reasons he'd made the suggestion. No, that was a lie. He'd made it to have her closer. He said, "I know the queen has her own floor in the tower, and below that, more chambers for her entourage, but I want you sleeping in *my* bed—my room. Give the other to Desaree, or your spriten handmaidens."

And then he held his breath.

Her smile was slow and soft. "You're just dying inside right now, aren't you?"

"I'm not," he lied.

"Yes you are. I can feel the anticipation rolling off you in waves."

"Claire…"

"I *almost* want to stretch this out. Won't that drive you mad?"

"Claire!" he growled, dragging her into his arms. She squealed. "Gods, woman. You delight in vexing me. Give me your answer."

She threw her head back and laughed. "In *my* world, many married couples share beds. Even unmarried couples. It is not as inappropriate as it seems. Gods. Dragonwall is archaic. Don't think I haven't noticed the way Desaree's been sneaking off to Verath's tent back at camp, or that she was sneaking into his chambers at night before that, hoping to avoid notice. Are people really such prudes?"

"You'd be surprised," he chuckled. "Servants love their gossip, remember?"

She groaned.

He couldn't stop looking at her, soaking in the mirth in her expression. He loved her like this, unguarded and happy. Perhaps he'd be able to make her happy enough that she'd never regret her decision to rule beside him. He pushed the thought away and said, "Your answer?"

She gave him a chaste kiss. "I'll gladly share your bed, but—"

He groaned.

"—only on one condition."

"What is it?"

"You are not allowed to stay up all hours of the night, leaving me alone. I'm serious, Talon. You could benefit from more sleep. Most nights, you don't sleep at all. Don't think I haven't noticed the shadows under your eyes. You might be a drengr, but you need sleep just like everyone else."

"If it means holding you in my arms, then you have a deal."

He kissed her, letting his hunger show. When they came up for air, her smile faltered.

"What is it?" She was looking at his scars, *really* looking at them. It made him squirm uncomfortably.

"I love you, Talon. *So freaking* much."

He blew out a breath, dropping his forehead to hers. Their next kiss was tender and slow, exploratory. He loved the taste of her on his lips, the warmth of her mouth. The fire in his chest exploded until his center clenched with desire.

He pulled away, their heavy breaths mingling, and said, "I want to let my talons free, to shred your clothes to ribbons and feast on your body."

"Talon!" she breathed.

"And just so you know, I love you too. More than I can put into words."

"That's okay, dragons aren't much for words. Besides, who needs words when you could just growl at me like you usually do."

"I do not," he growled, which made a burst of laughter break free of her chest. "I do not!

"You do too—*ooo*!"

Her words cut off as he threw her over his shoulder. He swatted her bottom hard enough to make his palm sting, earning a furious screech. "You think I'm some beast?!" he growled, this time *really* growled. "Fine. I'll return you to camp like one."

"Talon!"

He quickened his stride heading straight for the glowing orange light in the distance. Claire beat her fists against his back, squealing and laughing, positively incoherent as she begged him to put her down. He could hear it in her voice; her request was half-hearted. All he could do was smile, withholding a chuckle as he savored the remains of this moment alone together. For all too soon, getting even a few minutes from his duties at court would be a battle.

CHAPTER 19

RENDERED SPEECHLESS

Notna Bay, Oshea

Bennett stood with his hands clasped behind his back, surveyeing the unexpected sight. Notna Bay was packed with military vessels anchored in formation, swaying and bobbing. After first spotting the mass of ships, he'd nearly demanded they turn around, but they'd cautiously made their way into the bay, dropping anchor and sending a small party to speak with the master of the docks.

Jonah had returned with proper permitting. His first mate had weaseled very little information out of the dock master. Training exercise, apparently. He didn't believe it for one second. "There's only one reason a country musters a navy like this," he muttered.

Jonah stood beside him, mirroring his stance. "You sure you don't want to go with us?"

"Tempting, but no. Not with all these ships about. Makes my skin crawl."

They'd arrived yesterday after making good time. Traveling through the storm had been a calculated risk, but they'd benefited from it. Dragonwall's king wanted to know what was going on in Oshea, and judging from what he saw, it wasn't good.

Aside from sending a few crew members ashore, he'd refused to allow the rest to disembark. It didn't feel safe, what with the Oshean navy mustered. He wouldn't risk anyone. Not until they had answers. *That* was where Cat came in.

A few appreciative whistles distracted him. He turned, looking across the ship. Cat had emerged from below wearing a pinched expression. Annoyed, no doubt. But that wasn't what stole his attention. Her gown—an Oshean harlot's gown, brightly colored with a dirtied hem and a few snags in the fabric—had the entire crew gaping. He didn't blame them, especially not when his own eyes remained fixed on her chest. *Gods above*, but she was well endowed. Jonah elbowed him. He growled, prying his eyes away and snapping his mouth shut.

When Jonah snickered, he growled and said, "Not a word," knocking the grin right off his first mate's face.

Cat marched over to them. A saccharine smile stretched across her lips. "What's the matter, never seen a lady in a gown before? I should have thought you'd be well acquainted."

"Oh, aye," Bennett said. "But I'm more used to seeing them discarded on the floor. Almost forgot what they look like otherwise."

She rolled her eyes. "I'm sure."

He awkwardly cleared his throat. "Jonah will take you ashore. Are you ready?"

A flash of uncertainty crossed her features, there and gone. He frowned. Had she been hoping *he* would be the one? No. He pushed that thought aside. She picked an invisible speck of lint off her lacy sleeve. "I'm ready."

"Good. Then get going."

She nodded before turning away for one of the row boats already waiting. Jonah followed. Several crew stood by to accompany them. He had to hand it to her, she did an *admirable* job looking unbothered and confident. Beneath it all, something softer lurked, something she rarely let anyone see. Except she'd let *him* see it, once, back in Ice Port when she'd shared her story.

He was glad he'd secured her for his crew. Glad of her healing abilities and magic, even if it was questionably obtained. He'd never been more glad after the storm. If there'd been any question before, there was none now.

He watched her climb into the row boat, watched as it was lowered into the bay, he knew her usefulness would continue. She was getting under his skin in a completely different way. He hated that his feelings towards her were changing. Bringing her aboard had been the right thing to do, but he hadn't expected to soften towards her, especially when he knew that getting tangled up with her was a bad idea.

The ropes were detached. The crew's shouts and whistles wished her luck. A couple of his men made lewd comments, ensuring that she'd hear them. They all knew what the plan was. While they probably didn't care much about the mechanics of it, he did.

It clawed at his chest and aroused his ire to know what she was going to do. As he watched the little boat draw towards the docks, he gave a final sigh, then shouted at the others to get back to work before disappearing below deck.

A KNOCK at his cabin door roused him from a fretful sleep. He jolted upright and leaned over, lighting the bedside lamp. "Enter," he called, his voice scratchy. He scrubbed a hand over his face, trying to rub the sleep from his eyes.

Jonah stormed in, followed by Cat.

Bennett blinked. How many hours had passed? How long had they been gone? It must have been close to dawn, at least.

Jonah's face was pale, even in the dim light. Cat's was blank, but her eyes were shards of ice. There was a blotch on her cheekbone. The sight of it sent fire roaring through his veins.

He surged to his feet—didn't bother looking for his shirt. "What happened?" he demanded.

"What happened?!" she seethed. "What *happened* was that I had everything under control." She glared daggers at Jonah as she spoke.

Ah. So *that's* why she was angry.

Jonah glanced between them and said, "We'd better sit," then dropped into one of Bennett's desk chairs.

Bennett stalked over to Cat. She regarded him, but didn't move. He took her chin in his fingers and lifted her face, getting a better look at the bruise. "Who did this?" he snarled. Blood roared through his ears. He brushed his thumb over the darkening skin and she flinched away. He dropped his hand.

"It's nothing," she snapped. "Your first mate forgot that I'm perfectly capable of taking care of myself." Jonah scoffed, crossing his arms.

Bennett scrubbed a hand over his ropes of hair, then walked to his desk chair and sank into it. "Sit, Cat," he said, keeping his voice low and even. Her chest deflated, but she did as he commanded. "Now, tell me what happened."

"She was—"

"No." He cut Jonah off, giving him a warning glare. "Cat."

Cat seemed to like this. "Everything was going fine. I found the other...sex workers right where I knew they'd be." He didn't miss the way she hesitated, avoiding the word *harlots*, *whores*, or other variations. He respected that. "I started with *them* first, maintaining my ruse, giving my story. They..." Her throat bobbed. "They were nice, actually. Took pity on me. But, there was no sugarcoating it. They were frank about what they did, about what to expect. I played my part adequately—the demure, shy new girl. It was easy to hide deeper in the alleyways as they worked, so I was able to befriend a few of them while the others were picked for..." Her cheeks washed red.

"Sex?" He leaned forward in his chair. He'd never taken her for a *prude*, couldn't help but enjoy it.

"*Services*," she amended. "The women spoke plenty about the increased presence of navy and military men in Notna. Apparently their earnings have never been better. That's probably why they didn't see me as competition when I showed up. 'Plenty to go around,' one of them said."

"Did you find out why?"

"They didn't know much," she admitted. "When I grew bold enough to ask, one of them said, 'We're paid to fuck, not talk.'" Cat rubbed the back of her neck. "A few *did* mention that the military was mustered for some far-off war, but they didn't know anything. I took matters into my own hands."

Jonah's scoff sounded more like a snort.

She glared at him before continuing. "When a smartly dressed navy man appeared—oh, there had been a steady stream of them—I knew he was someone of rank and titles, judging by his uniform. He was even a little handsome." A growl rose in Bennett's throat. He suppressed it, pushing his anger away. "I shed some of my shyness and slipped into better light. He spotted me, singled me out almost immediately. We went off together."

Bennett's palms were beginning to sweat.

"I made small-talk, telling him this was my first time in my new...role. He got excited about that." She snorted, disgusted. He felt the sudden urge to break something. "I did what I could to flatter him, talking about how distinguished and smart he looked in his uniform. I think he liked hearing it. He let me keep going. I even managed to get him to admit that the mustering navy had been gathered by the Oshean emperor for war. When I told him how dangerous that sounded, he got excited, let slip that they had a long voyage ahead, that they'd be traveling *over* the Dragonfire sea."

Bennett's heart kicked up, both at the implication of her words and at wherever this story was ultimately going.

"Anyway, we found a secluded place off the streets, another deserted alley. I grew bold, asked how many men were under his command, because surely it *must* have been a lot. He...he hit me. Told me he was tired of listening to my smart mouth and that he'd rather see it wrapped around his..." Her words trailed off.

Bennett swore. The idea of someone hurting her like that. Gods above. He was ready to row ashore and find this rat-bag. Make him pay.

"Anyway, I had everything under control. I was perfectly capable of—"

"It certainly didn't *look* that way," Jonah cut in. "Forgive me, Captain," he added. "After that piece of filth hit her, he took her wrists and pinned her to the wall, started groping under her skirts. She was struggling against him. She told him to *stop*, to *wait*. Far as I'm concerned, a woman says *stop*, you stop. I might be a scalawag and a seaman, but even I got morals."

Cat jumped to her feet. "That's *enough*," she spat. "Did it ever occur to you that I was *acting*? That I could have used my magic to stop him?!"

"Then why didn't you?" Jonah cried. "Captain Bennett sent me to protect you. That was *my* job."

"I was trying to *excite* him. I needed to stay in character. Needed him to enjoy himself enough to come back the next time around. Tomorrow, the next day. I needed to win his confidence. He might have told a helpless woman his secrets. Military numbers, plans, et cetera. He certainly won't now," she scoffed, glaring down at Jonah. "I'll have to start all over again, with someone else."

"Sex was never part of the plan," Bennett said before he could stop himself. He stood, his chair sliding out behind him. "Seduction, not sex."

"Forgive me, *Captain*, but generally, you can't have one without the other in that line of work."

"It's too dangerous." Never mind that he didn't want to think about the implications of this conversation. "The last thing I want is you picking up some sort of disease."

She snorted. "There's plenty of mage medicine for that. And I can assure you, being a mage means I have a certain...immunity from that sort of thing."

He clenched his jaw. "No sex."

Her lips parted. "Forgive me, but my body is mine to do with as—"

"That is *not* what I'm saying," he growled. "You're on the job.

Therefore, you're under my command. Have sex on your own time."

She crossed her arms and made a scoffing noise. "I have nothing else to report."

"Fine. You may go." His voice softened. "And Cat? Let me know if you need anything for that bruise." It was a stupid statement. She was a mage and a healer. Still, he couldn't help himself.

Cat hesitated, then turned on her heel and left. Once she was out of earshot he turned to Jonah and said, "You did the right thing."

"She doesn't think so."

"You did."

"You're only saying that because you don't like the idea of her with anyone but you."

He made a choking noise. "Don't go there, Jonah. I'm not in the mood."

"Why not? I've seen how you look at her. Something's changed. I'm not blind to it, Bennett. And for what it's worth, I don't think anyone in the crew would mind—"

"Enough! What else do you have to report?"

Jonah hesitated, then shrugged. "While I was tailing Cat, the others slipped into a few pubs. They got similar information. Oshea is gathering for an attack in a foreign land. Dragonwall was never mentioned but...they aren't interested in any other country on this continent. Didn't get numbers, nothin' like that. But...they *did* report some strange rumors, too. Seemed a bit far-fetched."

He sat back down, bracing his forearms on the desk.

"There's talk of some strange creatures, birds, or something of the sort, been spotted flying overhead. Rumor is, the Oshean emperor has some kind of new weapon of war."

He sighed, leaning back. "Birds..."

"Big ones, from what's being said. But...seems outlandish, like I said. Doubt it has anything to do with the navy."

"All right." He scrubbed a hand over his chin, grazing the stubble that needed his attention. "Cat reported they'd be departing in a few days."

"Aye. Not the best news."

"They'll travel slower as a contingent."

"Aye."

"That gives us one, perhaps two more days. We cannot afford to linger. We need this information, then we must set sail for Kastali Dun."

Jonah rubbed the back of his neck. "I was thinking the same."

"We'll give her two more days at most, send her out into the city tomorrow afternoon." Jonah nodded. "I'd rather have something substantial to report. Military numbers, where their forces plan to attack, et cetera. Won't be much help to the king otherwise. Can't offer someone like that smoke and mirrors."

"They could be planning *anywhere* along the coast."

"Could be," Bennett mused. "Or...it could be the most obvious place."

"Kastali Dun?" Jonah's brow furrowed. "You really think so?"

Bennett shrugged, letting his eyes dart around his cabin. Beaky was still snoozing on her perch. Hadn't done more than open an eye when he'd been pulled from sleep. Lazy bird.

"Very well. I'll hand select another group for tomorrow, those who'll be the most discreet. We'll send them into every establishment across the docks."

"Give 'em money for the women, too," Bennett mused. It was a double standard—he was well aware. Letting his men pay for sex but forbidding Cat from engaging in it. Well, he was who he was.

"Oh, they'll like that, they will."

He snorted. "Make sure they understand that just because they're dropping trow doesn't mean they aren't working."

"Aye, I'll make sure of it." A long silence stretched before them. "Will that be all, Captain?"

He nodded. "Get some sleep, Jonah. We'll talk at dawn."

Jonah left and Bennett stood, stalking over to the secret compartment in the wall, pulling out one of his most expensive bottles of whiskey. He poured a glass and tossed it back.

There'd be no sleep for a while, not when every time he thought of another man's hands on Cat, his blood raged. He set the glass on the desk and strode from the room, pausing at Cat's door, ear to the wood, listening. No sound came from within.

He made his way to the deck, took note of those on duty, nodded in greeting, and went to stand watch along the prow, looking out over the water. Even in the middle of the night, the sounds from land, the blazing glow of windows along the docks, drifted out to him. He listened, smiling faintly at the music and laughter.

"Couldn't sleep?" Cat's voice startled him and his head whipped around.

"Something like that." He turned back towards the water.

She came beside him, mirroring his posture, looking out over the water. She had already changed into a tunic and trousers. He opened his mouth, then closed it and scowled. There were a thousand things he might have said, and yet, he didn't. She didn't speak either, content to stand in silence. So that's exactly what they did. As the minutes ticked by, one into the next, the tension from her appearance eased.

"I never thought I'd see a country like Oshea in my lifetime," she admitted. He grunted. "I suppose this is what you meant, when you said I might see the world, sailing with you." He grunted again. "A person can't really appreciate how big it is until you spend weeks traversing the ocean, one continent to another. Seeing foreign cities, cultures, people."

"Most will never know," he mused, keeping his voice low. "Never understand."

"You're right. I suppose I should thank you for opening my eyes." He went completely still, blinking to clear the spots from his vision. Had hell frozen over? A near silent huff fell from her lips. He glanced at her. She was assessing him.

"What?"

She lifted a shoulder before turning back towards the water. "I guess I never realized how handsome you were until I really started looking." His mouth fell open. He blinked. "Good night, Captain."

He spun towards her, but she was already walking back to the hatch.

Him? Handsome?

Had she really just... His mouth snapped shut. *Gods above.* She certainly knew exactly how to render him speechless. He made a sound of annoyance in the back of his throat, then turned back towards the city, pushing the infuriating woman as far as possible from his thoughts.

CHAPTER 20
A SMALL VICTORY

Wilderness, Celenore

Bedelth spotted their camp as he descended. King Talon flew at the front of their wing. Today, he'd opted for second position. It was more strenuous than other positions, but he didn't mind. It gave his wings the challenge he craved, building muscle.

Saffra leaned forward. The press of her against his scales was sweet torture. Such an intimate thing, flying with one's mate. Everyone knew the drengr didn't fly with anyone else, and he wasn't sure she understood what it did to him, the severity of it.

The first day of their journey, it had been impossible to calm his heart. It had raced, tiring him more quickly. He'd been glad for his position in the back, knowing it was all he could do to keep his wings going and his breathing controlled.

The second day had been easier, even if it still started with a thrill. He'd hardly slept, counting down the moments before they could return to the sky. Counting down the moments when he could *feel* her against him. Each day thereafter had been a gift. It was a precious thing, to have her here with him, even if they weren't bonded.

They didn't share minds, and yet his was still lost. Lost in thoughts of her, thoughts of what it might be like if they *were* mated. He even allowed himself to pretend that they were. That this was their life, flying together, *being* together. He imagined what he'd find in her mind, the thoughts they'd share.

It was a dangerous pastime.

They were two days out from the capital. A new panic rose, piercing and painful. What if this was *it*? What if this small gift was all he'd ever get? What if she put space between them again?

His throat closed up as the ground rose to meet him. The others were already transforming. He landed, his sharp talons digging deep furrows into the earth. There came a sharp intake of breath from Saffra, a physical reaction. He'd grown attuned to those little tells without the ability to see into her mind.

He waited until she dismounted. The moment her feet hit the ground, he transformed. It was a quick process, shedding his scales for skin. His eyes darted over her, assessing. She watched him, lips parted. He'd never grow tired of that expression, but he didn't call attention to it.

"Are you all right?" he asked, taking several steps towards her.

Her mouth closed and she nodded. "Yes... I... Thank you. Just getting my feet beneath me, is all."

"Good. I'll track down some food."

"Bedelth..." She sighed. "You don't have to fuss over me. I am capable—"

"I'm aware, Lady Saffra. You are capable in every sense of the word. But you are also flying with me, as *my* guest, at *my* invitation. There comes a certain level of pride in seeing you cared for. Let me do this, *yes*?"

An internal battle played out over her features until she said, "Of course. All right. I'll just..."

"I'll come and find you once you've settled."

"Thank you."

He gathered with the others. "Aha! Just the male I wanted to see." A firm hand landed on his shoulder. He spun to face the spriten prince. "Care for some sparring? I'm stiff as a tree, and

Jeanine is off...gossiping somewhere with Elyon and Filvro, gods save me."

Bedelth chuckled. "You're asking if I want my pride handed to me on a silver platter?"

"As always," Feowen said, raising his brows in challenge.

"You're on. I need to track down some food first, and then I'll join you."

"Ah, yes, of course." Something knowing burned in Feowen's eyes.

He gathered a bundle of rations and went looking for Saffra. He found her sitting alone. "Here you are," he said, dropping into a crouch beside her.

Her soft expression melted to guarded indifference. "Thank you, Bedelth. Would you...do you want to join me?"

His heart skipped; it was the first time she'd asked. "Actually, I promised Feowen we'd spar. Would you care for some entertainment while you eat?"

"Entertainment?"

"Oh, yes." He stood. "Prince Feowen is about to grind me into a pulp. What could be more enjoyable?"

A small, unguarded laugh burst from her lips. The sound sent wings fluttering in his stomach. She stood, dusting off her pants. "Yes, all right. Lead the way."

Without meaning to, he placed a hand at the small of her back, guiding her forward. His chest flapped when she didn't move out of reach. He wanted to count it as a small victory, but he knew better.

"Ah! An audience." Feowen grinned. "Not that it will lend you any added skill against me."

"No, certainly not," he growled, moving away from Saffra.

"Let's make it fun, shall we?" Feowen removed his blade and used a bit of magic to smooth the grass around them before creating a large circle. "We stay within the bounds, or we lose. Think of it as a way to get one up on me, if you can manage to press me outside. Best three out of five wins?"

"All right." He removed his own blade. The sverak sat heavy in his grip. It wasn't the first time he found his eyes darting to the empty place where a pommel stone ought to be. He didn't let his mind linger.

They got into position. He steadied his breathing. Feeling Saffra's gaze upon him, knowing she was here by choice, raised the stakes.

They circled. Feowen was the first to lunge, cutting through the air. He dodged. It was a move meant to intimidate, to goad him into attacking. He opted for patience. Feowen tried again and again, always taking an offensive approach. The sprite was skilled enough to get away with it. Bedelth had learned *that* the first time they'd sparred.

Still, when Feowen dropped his arm and his guard—a feigned movement, naturally—he accepted the invitation. Feowen met his blade, the sound of the spriten weapon singing. And then they began to move in earnest, spinning and darting, feet nimbly moving back and forth across the circle as their blades clashed.

He managed a punch to Feowen's side as their blades caught—

"Yes! Get him!" Saffra cried.

His movements faltered. Feowen used the distraction to sweep his blade around. An explosion of pain lit up his side. He grunted, out of range. "That's one," Feowen taunted.

He growled a warning.

Saffra's cry had completely disarmed him. That she would cheer for him sent warmth exploding in his sternum. He didn't care that he'd suffered a blow on account of it. *She was cheering for him.*

A newfound determination burst through him. He jumped forward, taking the offensive. Feowen met him with a downward blow. Again, they fell into sparring, blades singing. Theirs wasn't the only song. Several others did the same. A couple of the queen's guards were enjoying the same activity.

He pressed Feowen back, landing blow after blow against his upturned spriten blade, until the prince came dangerously close to the line. A low, feral laugh bubbled up Feowen's chest. "I see what you're doing, *Drengr*," the male growled. "Don't think for a minute you'll trick—" Feowen hissed, eyes darting downward.

Bedelth had used the boundary line as a distraction, to swipe his blade along the prince's leg. "Yes!" Saffra cried. He grinned, unable to help it.

A surprised laugh burst from Feowen's chest. "Well, well, well. Impressive. Well played. Who knew you simply needed a pretty female watching?"

That brought a low chuckle. Feowen's words were meant as a taunt, but his use of the word *pretty*, the way he'd said it, gave the intended effect.

They burst into action, falling into round three. He felt Saffra's eyes like a hot brand. Feowen managed to disarm him. The fourth round lasted much longer, but in the end, he earned a blow to the face and a stab to the hip. By the fifth, he was panting, sweat beading his forehead. "I'm already three in," Feowen pointed out, smug. "Even if you get this one, I win."

He snorted.

When he next lifted his arm to block, it felt heavier. Against a human, he could have gone hours and hours. All day even. But against a forest sprite? A *true* immortal? He couldn't even last a single one.

His arm shook from the effort of holding Feowen's blade at bay. The last thing he saw was a wicked grin on the Prince's lips. Feowen landed a heavy punch to his chin before planting a foot in his stomach. He went flying, grunting as his back struck the ground. "And that's four, my friend," came the prince's arrogant reply.

"You couldn't even give me my dignity?" he huffed, staring up at the stars.

"Bedelth?" Saffra crawled over to him, until her face filled his vision. Her lip pulled between her teeth. "Are you okay?"

"I'm not so sure, my lady," came Feowen's wicked response. "He looks rather injured. You should tend to him, make sure I didn't do anything...*permanent*." At this, Feowen threw him a wink and sauntered off. Bedelth could only snort.

"He can't do anything permanent. You're a Drengr." It was a statement. Yet, he heard a measure of question in her voice.

"Oh, I assure you, he can. But only to my pride."

"Right." Saffra sat back, her muscles relaxing.

"But by all means, do follow his advice. I wouldn't mind your fussing. Your hands, in particular." It was a brave move, one that paid off. Even in the darkness, there was no mistaking the flush spreading across Saffra's cheeks.

"I'm only teasing, Saff." He sighed, sitting upright and nudging her foot. He lifted his sverak, regarding it. Saffra's eyes darted to it as well. He didn't miss the way she lingered over the missing pommel stone. He steeled himself and rose to his feet, sheathing it. Then he held out a hand. "Walk with me, my lady?"

Saffra's brow furrowed. "Walk...with you?"

"Sure, why not?" He did his best to sound casual.

"Okay..." Her voice squeaked, but she lifted her bare hand. The feel of her skin—only briefly—sent longing through him. He dropped it immediately.

They moved away from the camp. He tucked his hands behind his back, adopting a casual air. He'd thought long and hard about his next move, what he'd do in the coming days, coming weeks, to keep her from pulling away. It was a calculated, tactical approach, one that would take time.

"So," he said. "What do you think of flying thus far?"

"Oh..."

He dared a glance. The question had caught her off guard. Good.

"Well, it's rather wonderful, actually."

"I think so, too. It's freeing."

"Yes. Exactly."

"The sky is the only place I don't feel constrained," he admitted.

A small huff fell from her lips. "I can see that, yes."

He kept his face forward. "I was fourteen when my form came. Drengr children don't gain the ability to transform until puberty, you know."

"Yes, I'm aware." Her eyes were on him, even if he didn't dare meet them.

"It was...gods, it felt *good.* My parents—well, I've told you a little about them. Perhaps you can imagine how stifling it was having overprotective parents. Suddenly gaining the ability to sprout wings and fly was...incredible."

"You must have felt so free."

"I did," he managed. He didn't hide the small smile playing on his lips. "Whenever I felt trapped or frustrated or angry, I could simply sprout wings and fly away. Leave the world behind."

"What of the actual process? Learning to fly? You didn't just grow wings and jump into the sky, did you?"

He huffed, almost a laugh. It felt like a tiny victory, her question.

"No, indeed. I'm embarrassed to tell you what happened."

While they'd known each other a decade, they'd never discussed anything serious. A long silence stretched between them. Those moments from his childhood felt so long ago, now. The years had slipped away. One century into the next, bringing him to this moment.

"Well?" she said. "You can tell me. I promise not to judge you."

Another victory.

"All right, then. The day I gained my form, my parents were beside themselves with pride. My father insisted I learn to fly *immediately.* I wasn't one to argue. I'd yearned for this moment for years. But as you say, you don't simply sprout wings and jump into the air. You must *learn.* Or rather, be taught.

"Every drengr feels they are the sole authority on first flights. One of my father's friends, Tahan, joined my father and I out on the field. Everything went well, initially. A fledgling's wings are weak, to start. The muscles must be strengthened. That first after-noon, I couldn't get more than a few flaps of altitude. Tahan decided that gliding would be easier. My father was easily convinced.

"He was always pushing me to be the best—my father. I was one of the youngest to fledge, you see? Fourteen is on the younger side."

Saffra made a humming noise, but she listened intently.

"Anyway, we went to the battlements. I was to glide off the wall and onto the grass below. I did it, perfectly, of course."

She scoffed. "How is that embarrassing?"

"Oh, but just wait. Intent on proving that I could master flight, I struck out on my own later that night. Since gliding was the fastest way to get into the sky, I figured starting from the tallest tower would give me a good start. Admittedly, I really wanted to fly. At that age, a person can be impatient.

"The tallest tower also happens to be just across the way from the fort leaders' chambers. As soon as I took off—mind you, I'd been practicing with my father for hours that day, thoroughly exhausted—my wing got a godsdamned cramp. A spasm, really. My whole body seized up and stopped working. I slammed right into a large glass window, shattering it. I went right through. Fledgelings aren't as big as fully mature dragons and it *was* a rather large window."

Saffra sucked in a sharp breath, hands coming up to cover her cheeks. "The fort leaders' chambers?"

"Horrible, isn't it? Right into their sleeping chamber. While they were—not sleeping."

"Oh, my gods!"

He squeezed his eyes shut, letting his head fall back. A huff of laughter fell from his lips. "I was fourteen. I had little experience with such things, but I knew *enough* about what they were doing. Gods, the shame of it. I'll never forget the screech of shock that followed my intrusion."

"But...your parents?"

"My father was furious. So ashamed. My mother just walked around with her lips pressed into a firm line. It was barbed remarks for weeks. Not just from my parents. Gods, the whole fort. 'Careful, Bedelth, wouldn't want you flying through another window.'"

"But..." Her expression changed. "Didn't that bother you?"

He took note of her expression. It wasn't one of mirth, but of anger. For him? His chest lurched.

"I pretended it didn't." He sighed. "It's funny now, as a mature male. It wasn't, then. I didn't tell this story to garner your anger or sympathy, Saffra. But to make you laugh. It really is funny, thinking back to the way I smashed through the window, their expressions."

She huffed, her gaze lingering on his face for a few moments more before she resumed their lazy walk. "I take it you were extra motivated to master flying after that?"

"Oh, yes. And look at me now. Excellent in the air. Excellent with a blade. A *king's shield*." He didn't mean to say it with a scoff. He loved his brothers and his king. But there were times...times he hated that his father's expectations had forced him down a path he might otherwise not have taken.

"You're..." Saffra trailed off. "You've always been forced to prove yourself, haven't you?"

He shrugged. "Most of us are at some point or another. Anyway, it's nothing."

She hummed.

He struggled to regain control of the conversation. He'd meant it to be fun, to put her at ease, to make her more comfortable around him. And it seemed to do the opposite—

A laugh burst up from her chest. "Gods, the more I think about it..." She shook her head. "How many fledglings smash through their fort leaders' window while they're...you know? Gods."

His shoulders relaxed. "You can't tell anyone..." he said, not because he cared if she did, but because he liked having secrets with her. "It would be utterly humiliating. Very few people know that story. I'd like to keep it that way. It would shatter my image. Ruin me. The king might even have to force my resignation. Send me away in shame."

She bit her lip. He could see the laughter she struggled with. Her expression was worth all his efforts in planning. It sent warmth, hope even, radiating straight from his chest to his extrem-ities. Even his fingertips tingled.

"Your secret is safe with me." She forced her expression into one of seriousness. "My lips are sealed. I won't even tell our queen."

"You are most considerate, lady."

"But now you are forever at my mercy," she teased, lifting an eyebrow.

This. *This* was what he'd hoped to bring out in her. This playful side. The way she used to be around him.

"Indeed. I had better be on my best behavior from now on." Lording this mundane secret over him was nothing. It changed nothing. The truth was, he'd always been at her mercy, even if he hadn't realized it.

CHAPTER 21

SETTLING IN

Kastali Dun

Claire blinked, her vision blurring with tears. *"Something in your eye, love?"* Talon's amusement was impossible to miss.

"I think dust or something," she managed, pawing at her eyes.

The sight of Kastali Dun twisted her emotions into knots. She spread her fingers across Talon's glassy scales, grasping as much of his neck as possible, feeling his muscles shift.

Home...

That single word carried so much. She'd been in Dragonwall for nearly a year. Somewhere along the way it had gone from a detour to a destination. A place she wanted to lay down roots. She had never felt such a profound sense of belonging. Not until *this*.

With that desire came guilt. Guilt for the ones she'd left behind.

"You are exactly where you need to be," Talon said, his voice filled with pride.

She'd decided to make the final leg of the journey on Talon's back. She may have been a spriten queen, but Dragonwall was her heart and soul, and this place, this city, was to be the lifeblood of her very existence. This is where she'd rule, where she'd build a life, where she'd forge new memories and new experiences. She wanted to see it from the sky with the person who would rule beside her.

A pleased rumble came from Talon's chest.

Her contingent of guards and handmaidens rode beneath them. They'd slowed to a lazy canter. This way, everyone would arrive together.

The capital city was a vast expanse beside the sea. The keep towered over everything. The ruling seat of Dragonwall. It held the promise of a hot bath and soft bed. She couldn't wait.

The king's wing landed just outside the city's gates. She dismounted, breaking contact with her mate, already feeling emptier for it. The unicorns came to a stop beside them. Her chest expanded at the sight of such magnificent beasts. Her guards and handmaidens dismounted, carrying their belongings in packs across their backs. Their armor shone like starlight, bright even in the daytime.

Tourmaline made his way through the contingent, stopping before her. *"This is where I leave you, Queen."*

"Must you go?" she whispered, knowing the answer.

"A city is no place for a unicorn. We are free creatures, unbound by walls of stone."

"I know," she managed, stepping close to him, wrapping her arms around his neck, rubbing her face against his sleek coat. His response? A patient snort. But he let her fuss, even as tears filled her eyes. "We had some good adventures you and I, didn't we?" Her words came out choked.

"The very best. I shall miss you, Queen Claire." He stepped back, then lowered his head in deference. She gaped at him, at the silvery liquid pooling in his dark eyes. He blinked and a droplet fell like a tear, forming into a beautiful pearl.

She gasped, lowering to pick it up from the hard earth. "It's…"

"A unicorn tear, freely given. Carry it with you and I shall know if you need me."

Her throat tightened. "You… Thank you." She clutched it to her chest, then stepped back, colliding with a warm body. Talon's hands came up, squeezing her shoulders, keeping them pressed together.

"You have my thanks, Tourmaline," he said, his voice low, "for helping my queen."

Tourmaline's head bobbed. Whatever he said, if anything, was for Talon's ears only. Her abilities to hear everything, it seemed, only encompassed the dragons.

She watched as Tourmaline turned and walked away. Only then did she notice the rest of her contingent bidding similar good-byes to their unicorns. Talon lowered his lips to the side of her head, kissing her ear. They watched the other unicorns form up around Tourmaline. The beautiful creature lifted his head, horn pointing towards the sky, and neighed. A final goodbye. The others followed. They bound away, racing back towards their forest. A blink later, they were gone.

A heavy sigh fell from her lips. She stared at the place they'd disappeared. Some day—some day she'd see him again.

"Shall we, my queen?" Talon squeezed her shoulders. She nodded, slipping her arm through his while holding her staff in the other hand. They would return to the keep on foot, walking through its streets. He led her to the front of their procession. His shields, her guards, her handmaidens, and Saffra got in formation behind them.

"All hail the king!" came a shout from one of the city's guards manning the walls.

"The king has returned!" came another.

The gates were already open for the day. Those passing through had long since stopped to stare. They bowed as she and Talon strode forward. Guards jumped to attention, offering their king a formal salute as he passed.

"It's good to be home," Talon mused as they moved beneath the portcullis and through the city's walls.

They made their way through the city's streets. She took every-thing in with fresh eyes. When she'd left for Esterpine, ruling from Kastali Dun had been a mere possibility. A duty she'd yet to accept. The city hadn't changed, but she had.

Citizens stopped to gasp and point before bowing. She caught faint exclamations of surprise. "The king! The king has returned!"

Talon's eyes were often upon her. She felt the familiar brand each time he glanced down, each time he studied her. What was he searching for, and did he find it?

Nearly an hour later, the walls of the keep came into view. A slow smile stretched across her lips. She stopped to gaze up at it. Once, the sight had brought a deep sense of fear, symbolizing a step into the unknown. She'd come here as an outsider, an accused criminal, scorned by an entire kingdom. Now there was a new fear, a different fear, but still, a step into the unknown. She was no longer an outsider but a spriten queen, her veins thick with two kinds of blood. Two contrasting facets in constant struggle. Order with disorder.

Now she knew the truth. She had as much claim to Dragonwall's throne through Irelia as she did to rule Esterpine. She was *meant* to be here.

A gentle hand squeezed her arm. Talon, reminding her that he was beside her. She exhaled and squared her shoulders, offering a single nod, then stepped forward into her new life.

THE QUEEN'S quarters transformed around her, white sheets pulled from furniture, sending dust motes into the dazzling sunlight. It streamed through the tower's windows creating patterns on the floor, across the plush rugs beneath their feet. Servants in tower livery rushed about. The keep had an entire host of them on hand, however, those who worked in the king's tower were distinguished. They wore white and gold as a symbol of their position—one of the highest caliber, and compensated as such.

Feowen stood beside her, frowning. "Well, I suppose it's not the crystal palace, but it will do."

She barked a laugh. "Thank the gods. That place makes me uneasy."

"Come now, *Ayas Drollaya. It* wasn't so bad."

"We'll have to agree to disagree."

It wasn't just the servants buzzing about. Her handmaidens took stock of her wardrobe and oversaw the transport of her belongings from her old suite to here. On the lower levels of the tower, her queen's guard had already scampered off to inspect their new accommodations, rooms that had once been prepared for a *different* queen's delegation.

She could just picture Isabella here in this very spot, studying her new accommodations that King Eymar had constructed especially for her. There were spriten touches everywhere, from the forest colors to the shape of the furniture. She could even smell it in the wood. It was calming.

The queen's portion of the tower occupied its lowest levels, even grander than those above. Two thirds of the tower held everything Isabella had needed to keep her companions happy. She had her own dining room, sitting room, study, wardrobe—which Claire was already intimately acquainted with—bathing chamber, and more. Like the other levels, a large covered balcony spanned the length of each floor, and the glass doors were already thrown open to accommodate the sea breeze.

She walked towards them, giving the tower's servants more room to work. Her lungs expanded, breathing deep as she emerged into the fresh air. Feowen stayed close, just a step behind. She studied the large balcony. A staircase on one side connected it to the levels above and below.

A tiny smile pulled at her lips. She was tempted to go upstairs, to find the one leading to Talon's study. That's where she'd find him, brooding over paperwork.

He'd brought her down here, given her a chaste kiss and said, "This is yours, my queen, to do with as you see fit." Then his eyes flicked towards the bedroom. "And find some use for that sleeping chamber, because it's my bed you'll be occupying henceforth."

"Henceforth?!" she'd taunted.

"Forever more." He'd tugged on her braid, then left.

A wistful sigh fell from her lips. She braced her forearms on the balcony, leaning out over the cliffs, to look upon the sea.

"Gods, you're besotted." Feowen adopted the same stance.

"As if you don't get all dewy-eyed whenever Jeanine's around."

"Hardly. I'm more dignified."

"Oh?" He didn't rise to her taunt. She nudged him with her shoulder. "What do you think?"

His face remained passive. "It's so...grand."

"Wait, my tower? Or the sea?"

"The sea, you idiot." He nudged her back.

"Did you just call your queen an *idiot*?!"

"Only the best, greatest, wisest, most beautiful idiot."

They burst into laughter. She looped her arm through his, leaning against him as they stared out into the vast beyond. When their mirth settled, they fell into comfortable silence.

Ships dotted the water, arriving and departing, going about their day. She watched them come and go. Wondered about the people on board. About what their lives were like. Soon, a ship would come bearing Desaree and Jocelyn, and they would all be together again. She'd gone from having one person to having an entire mob of them.

"Do you think they'll be happy here?" she asked.

"Your queen's guard?" He kept his face forward, eyes gazing off into the distance. She made a humming sound. "I don't see why not. They will miss the forest, yes. But you are their queen. Serving you is their purpose. Besides, you have given them permission to return home, if and when they wish. This is a new experience for *all* of us, a time of self discovery."

"A...quest?"

"Exactly. Sprites are no strangers to it."

"And you? A mighty prince of the forest, will *you* be happy here?"

"I'll be happy wherever my queen wishes me to serve."

She snorted. "That's bullshit, Feowen. Be truthful."

He sighed, eyes still on the horizon. "*Mi haan nih veraf*," he said at last.

"You don't know?" She frowned. "Well...I did ask for honesty."

"You did indeed—"

"*Ayas Drollaya? Haan aya yasklle en balaam?*" Selphie appeared in the dooway, a stack of plush towels in hand.

Claire stood, taking an eager step towards her, then paused.

Feowen placed a hand over his heart. "Go and have your bath, *Ayas Drollaya*. I'll see that everything is managed." She opened her mouth to protest. "You are allowed to indulge. You need not wait until the rest of us are settled."

Still, she hesitated.

"Gods, Claire. Go! Wash the stench of travel off. I'll manage the rest."

"Okay," she finally said, turning away from him. She followed Selphie into the tower. "I would prefer to use Talon's bathing chamber," she said, when it was clear Selphie was leading her towards the queen's. "This one can be used by my contingent."

Selphie faltered. "*Aya kunyn cinaha?*"

"*Neem.* I am sure."

Selphie nodded, motioning to Miera to follow. The three of them took the stairs, leading up into Talon's main floor to the bathing chambers. Both of her handmaidens looked mildly uncomfortable. "You should bathe in your own chambers, Ayas Drollaya," Miera said, speaking in *Ednuar*. They'd done it heavily since coming to the capital. It was nerves.

"*Ni.* He will be my mate. We will share a bedroom and bathing chamber. The queen's levels will be for the rest of you."

Selphie and Miera shared a look.

"*Neem.*" She sighed, switching to the common tongue. "I know it will be less convenient for you to drag my gowns up here."

"*Ni, Ayas Drollaya,*" Selphie said. "*Aya kunyn outah barihon.*"

"I may be your *queen*, but that doesn't mean I'm going to take advantage of it. I care about the things that inconvenience you. However, this is my one ask. Talon wishes to share my bed, and I his. I do not want to exist apart from him. These floors will remain his, and those below will be mine. But our bed and our bathing chamber will be shared. You may move some of my things, whatever you'll need to ready me for each day, into his chamber. He won't mind."

"*Aya...aya kunyn cinaha?*"

She laughed. "*Neem!* I am sure."

At last, they nodded, accepting her request. The tower's servants threw them glances but said nothing as they closed themselves into the king's bathing chamber. A rush of memories came back as her eyes fell on the giant pool. It felt so long ago, that day Talon had rescued her and brought her here, bathed her with the gentleness of a caregiver.

Her cheeks flushed.

She began removing her clothes and made her way to the tub, climbing the stairs before sinking into its depths. Selphie and Miera rushed into action, gathering soaps and loofahs to wash her hair and body. They chatted easily in *Ednuar,* mostly about the things they'd seen upon entering the city.

Claire was content to remain silent, listening to their excited words.

It was better this way. While the lower levels housing her guards had shared bathrooms between them, none were as lavish as the queen's bathing chamber. And none had a pool quite like it. She wanted them to have it. There was no need to keep it for herself. And the same with the other rooms.

She'd share most of Talon's space. Except for her study. She was eager for that little slice of paradise. It had its own set of bookcases and a desk where she'd keep her important papers. A frown pulled her eyebrows together.

What important papers?

What sorts of duties would she inherit now that she was falling into this role? In the forest, most of her duties had been overseen by advisors. She'd merely made final decisions as the matriarch. Up till now, Talon had managed everything himself, with the help of his steward and lower council. She'd seen the evidence of his work strewn across his desk. Would he pass some of it off to her?

A door closed. She peeled an eyelid open. Talon swept into the room, his shrewd gaze quickly analyzing the scene. "Leave us," he commanded.

Both Miera and Selphie shared a glance. They'd long since

finished with her hair and sat off to the side, still quietly chatting as she enjoyed the hot water. At the sight of his massive, towering body, they jumped to their feet. "I am perfectly capable of seeing to my queen's needs," he assured them.

They scuttled from the room.

She sighed, letting her head fall back against the tub, letting her eyes close. "You make them nervous," she said.

A gentle chuckle turned her insides warm. His boots clicked across the tile, stopping at the tub. He crouched beside her, his mouth whispering against the shell of her ear. "How are you settling in, Claire?"

She opened her eyes, a smile tugging at her mouth. "Better, now that I'm in the bath."

He hummed, then stepped away, going to the door to lock it. Something curled deep in her center. He stayed in her line of sight, shedding first his sword and baldric, his weapons clunking to the tiled floor, then his tunic, boots, and pants, all in a heap, until he was naked before her.

Her mouth went dry, tongue stuck to the roof. Shameless. She was so shameless as she took him in, especially the places that left her cheeks heated. He noticed her blatant perusal. His lips twitched with smug male satisfaction. He moved to the tub's stairs and climbed in. When he sank onto the ledge opposite her, a low groan filled the chamber.

She squeezed her thighs together, suddenly *far* too hot. A sheen of sweat kissed the parts of her skin above water. His head tilted back, eyes growing hooded. His massive chest and broad shoulders remained above water, on full display. She watched as every worry line disappeared from his features, leaving only his scars behind. "Come here, love," he rumbled, as if sensing her stare.

She was moving before her brain realized it. He opened his eyes and pulled her against him, settling her onto his lap. Her skin was an inferno. Talon's acknowledging chuckle only made it worse. "You're burning up," he cooed, fingers trailing down her spine, sending shivers over her skin. "Hot as dragon fire."

His lips found her shoulder, placing tender kisses against her skin. Her heart pounded and she blurted, "Did you finish all your work?"

He huffed, pulling away. "Hardly. There were hundreds of missives. My steward sorted out the most important things. A few highly pressing matters. That was all I could stomach before the stench of travel got the better of me."

This time, he laid a soft kiss on her cheek, eyes focused entirely on her face.

He was always doing that, little tender gestures. But there was nothing tender about the arm that *wasn't* hooked around her waist. That one moved down her chest, possessively cupping her left breast. Kneading and squeezing, almost painfully. A mewing cry fell from her lips.

"Soon, love," he whispered against her temple. And then, "Have they already washed you?"

She managed a nod.

He sighed in clear disappointment. "Well then, would you like to wash *me*?"

"Yes," she cried, squirming free of his lap. Anything to put a little distance between them. Distance, before she lost complete control of her senses. One second more, and she'd have thrown caution to the wind. Waiting for the bonding ceremony? Too bad. She would have pinned him down and wrapped herself around him. She'd have claimed him the way a queen *ought* to claim her king.

Instead, she grabbed the soap and led him to the center of the pool.

"Hold still," she ordered, her voice low. A command, because if he let his hands wander, she wouldn't fare well.

He clicked his tongue. "So bossy. Is this how you're going to behave in bed, too?" She froze, then continued her motions. "Because if so, it won't go over well."

The low threat sent shivers racing through her. "Is that a threat, *Your Majesty*?"

"It is."

She paused, looking him in the eye. He was serious. His voice was a low warning as he said, "You may boss me around all you wish, but in the bedroom, I'll leash that smart mouth of yours and enjoy every moment you try to defy me. We'll see just how far a queen's boldness gets you."

Her breath caught as her brain short-circuited. She couldn't form a single word. It wasn't the first time he had murmured wicked, *wicked* things to her.

"Are you planning to finish washing me sometime *today*, my love? Or have I shocked you senseless?"

She made a choking noise, only to realize she'd been standing there, staring at his erection beneath the water for at *least* ten seconds. Oh, gods! With more force than she intended, she continued with her motions.

Eventually, the trickling water helped to calm her down.

There was something so familiar about the act of washing her mate, as if she'd done it a thousand times already. She lingered over certain scars, sometimes kissing them. When her lips found the underside of his jaw, he hummed and his arms strained, fists clenched to keep from reaching for her. It was hard for him—hard to resist her pull. A small smile spread across her lips, knowing the power she had over him, glad that she wasn't alone in what she felt.

Each time she rinsed the loofah, the sound of trickling water was cathartic. She was cleansing more than just travel grime from his body. She was washing away the things he'd done to free Squall's End. Putting the memories to bed—letting them trickle away. She was giving him a fresh start, a new beginning, one that had *her* in it. And when the two of them emerged from the bath and Talon wrapped her in a fluffy white towel, she was eager to face whatever challenges that new beginning was sure to bring.

Kastali Dun

Claire entered the dining hall with her arm linked through Talon's. Voices faltered and chairs scraped the flagstones as everyone surged to their feet. Talon's steps did not slow. His posture remained proud as he led her past the threshold and down the central aisle.

Every pair of eyes felt like a weight. She placed a hand over her stomach, then dropped it. A queen *did not* show her nerves, even if tonight was a good reason to be nervous. Her gown swished, brushing against her bare legs. Miera and Selphie had taken yet another and modified it to look more spriten. This one had come from the vast supply in the queen's wardrobe. It was a vibrant, royal blue, a color reserved for royalty alone, with heavy skirts. Her handmaidens had removed a large portion of the corset bodice, replacing it with a matching tulle, over which they'd sewn swirling patterns of glass beads. They'd also removed the sleeves, usually attached with ties and laces, and swapped them for tulle sleeves of the same color, also covered in glass beads.

It showed her spriten markings without being obnoxious. She glanced down the length of herself. Like the others, the dress was exquisite. How they'd managed in such a short time while settling into their new life in the capital was a mystery.

She caught Saffra's gaze and bowed her head. Saffra offered her an encouraging smile. She returned it.

The head table loomed before her. Talon led her up the steps and around the back. He'd insisted she sit beside him. It had been a point of contention but he'd won the argument. After all, the head table was a place for royalty.

He pulled out her chair, settling her in. This was where Reyr usually sat. Talon had already commissioned a new table, one that would seat his shields *and* her guards. The massive piece was due to be finished in a few days.

"*My queen*. Looking ravishing, as ever." Sitting on her right, Koldis nudged her. Talon took his seat and Koldis said, "Doesn't she look ravishing, Your Majesty?"

"Always."

She watched her queen's guard take their seats closest to the head table. She caught Feowen's eye. He grinned, wagging his eyebrows. If it was meant to be reassuring, the gesture failed.

Her stomach erupted into a fresh wave of butterflies.

Clink. Clink. Clink. She jolted as the ringing chime filled the air. Talon's cutlery clinked against his goblet. The hall fell silent.

Talon stood. She swallowed down the nervous lump in her throat. She was half tempted to slide out of her chair under the table, disappearing. Instead, her wide eyes turned towards Koldis, as if he could save her from this. "Relax," he hissed, then reached for her hand under the table, lacing their fingers together and squeezing.

How the hell was she supposed to *relax*?!

"Good evening," Talon said, his calm, eloquent voice carrying. He'd done this a thousand times, made announcements, proclamations, speeches, you name it. But he'd *never once* said what he was about to.

"I think I'm going to vomit," she muttered.

Koldis snorted, squeezing her hand tighter. "You're overreacting. They're going to love you."

"Would you both be quiet?!" Talon's silent command speared their minds.

She pressed her lips together and shared a knowing glance with Koldis, like they were two errant children.

"Tonight is special," Talon continued, looking upon the crowd. Most of them fidgeted, glancing anywhere but their king, too afraid to make eye contact. Only her guards held his gaze. "Our success with Squall's End has given us much to celebrate. But tonight..."

And here, Talon fell silent. His eyes turned upon her, his throat bobbing once, then twice. Like he was also nervous. Perhaps just as nervous as her. Though, he was better at hiding it.

"Oh, gods! He's getting choked up," Koldis said.

"Yes, thank you. I think I can see that." She kicked him under the table.

"Ow!" Koldis hissed.

"It's okay, Talon," she said. *"Keep going."*

He nodded, steeling his nerves and turning his gaze back to the crowd. "Tonight, I wish to announce something very important. Something life changing. As you know, I have been mateless for a very long time. I once promised you that I would rule just as well, if not better, than any who had come before me, all without the help of a mate. It seems fate had other plans. I have found something I never believed existed—*someone* I never knew I needed. My mate." Her eyes began to fill with tears, her heart racing. "This is not merely a love match, but a *true matching*, a mateship, the recognition of my other half, my soul."

Muttering broke out, racing around the hall like falling dominos. "Is it Claire?!" a voice shouted, laced with excitement. "The spriten queen?!" another clarified.

All at once, the entire hall erupted into speculation. She couldn't help the smile spreading across her lips. Her nerves began to fizzle and she relaxed. There wasn't an ounce of disdain in their voices. Instead, there was hope.

Koldis squeezed her hand as if to say, *I told you so!*

They already love you, Cyrus said, clogging her throat with emotion.

"Yes, yes." Talon lifted a hand to quiet the room. "It came as a shock. But Claire is my mate. We have touched skin to scale. A bond was realized. Now, all that's left is to—"

"Seal the bond!!" several raucous voices shouted. Talon opened his mouth. It did little good. Whatever he might have said was drowned out. The sudden pounding of fists and cups, feet stomping, loud cheers, and whistles, exploded into the air. Beside her, Koldis drained his goblet, then began pounding it against the table. A chant rose, lifting into the air. It took several seconds to make out the words. "*Kiss, kiss, kiss, kiss—*"

She opened her mouth, her eyes darting up to Talon who looked as shocked as she felt. He stood frozen, his lips parted, blinking at the rambunctious audience, taking in their acceptance. She surged to her feet, her chair scraping behind her. She was grinning as she grabbed Talon's scarred face and pulled him in for a kiss.

The hall erupted, the noise lifting to unimaginable heights as catcalls joined the din. Talon barely responded to her lips, his eyes still wide open, wide with surprise. Had his people ever acted so excited over something like this?

When she broke away, she couldn't help her laughter. Talon was *stunned*. What had he expected? Rejection? Then again, that's partly why *she'd* been so nervous.

With her king struggling to recover, she turned towards the crowd. "Do you accept me?!" she shouted, smiling wide. "Will you take me as your queen?"

"Yes!" came the cry, mixed with more pounding fists and feet. Someone else took up the kissing chant again. Just for the hell of it, she turned back to Talon and pulled him in again. This time, he was ready. A slight laugh burst from his lips before he wrapped her in his arms, lifting her off her feet.

The noise faded to whispers before it was replaced with wistful sighs and breathy declarations.

When she reclaimed her seat, she felt ten times lighter. "See?" Koldis nudged her again. "Told you you'd be fine."

"I am not so sure Talon is." She smirked. The king still looked gobsmacked.

"Now," said Talon, shaking himself. "The date for the ceremony has yet to be finalized, but it will be announced in the coming days. In the meantime, let us feast."

Another excited cheer went up, this one not nearly as hearty as the others, but still reassuring. Servants rushed forward with platters laden with delicious food. She'd missed the keep's cooking after spending so long in the forest. Thinking of the cookery reminded her of Tess. She made a mental note to visit the head woman as soon as she could.

"Sarah!" She waved at Desaree's friend who was depositing a tray at their table.

"Congratulations, Your Majesty!" Sarah said, beaming.

"Thank you. Are you well?"

"Aye. I'll be better when Desaree returns, though." They shared a knowing grin.

"Me too," she agreed.

"Enjoy your meal." Sarah bobbed her head, then rushed off.

"Skittish, that one," Koldis observed.

"They usually are," she pointed out as they began dishing up plates of food. For a short while, silence fell as they ate.

Koldis said, "Has the king shown you your surprise yet?"

"Koldis," Talon growled, a hint of warning in his voice.

"What?" he scoffed. "I was merely curious."

Next to Koldis, Jovari chuckled. "He loves making trouble, this one."

"One more word," Talon said, "and you'll be the next one I send out for those unfavorable duties you all despise. Or perhaps I'll make something up and send you up north, to Mesdon or some sort."

Koldis groaned, sinking low in his chair.

"What's in Mesdon?" Claire asked.

"Nothing," Koldis snapped as Jovari said, "An ex-lover he spurned a few years back."

"Oh?" She sat forward.

When they refused to tell her more, she was forced to draw her own conclusions, and with someone like Koldis, those conclusions were creative.

As dinner came to a close, Talon waited until most of the hall's patrons had left before turning to her. "Koldis was right, I *do* have a surprise for you. I wanted to wait until after the announcement." Talon's eyes shot towards Koldis and they exchanged some silent, unspoken communication. Her stomach leapt. When she next blinked, Koldis was racing away.

"Is it a good surprise?" They were up to something.

"I certainly hope so. Come." Talon held out his hand and led her down the central aisle, through the keep, and back to their tower.

The tower guards saluted them and then opened the door. Talon led her into the main room. Servants stood about, blending into the background. Talon quickly dismissed them for the night and they rushed off to enjoy dinner. Her eyes found Koldis, standing with a large box in his arms. It was topped with a bow.

Her gaze narrowed. The box made a sound and she gasped, heart leaping in her chest. Her head whipped around towards Talon. "Is that...?"

He dropped her hand, a grin transforming his scarred features. "Why don't you go and see."

She rushed over to Koldis and removed the lid, looking down into its depths. *Meowwwww.*

"Oh my gods!" She backed up a step, placing both hands over her mouth, eyes darting between Koldis and Talon.

"It was Talon's idea. I merely helped him track the thing down before dinner."

She gaped. "I thought you... I thought you were attending to obligations?"

Talon appeared beside her and said, "Well, we were, sort of. You said you wanted a kitten, did you not?"

"I... I..."

"I think you've positively shocked her," Jovari drawled. Bedelth chuckled.

Meow! The little black kitten rose on its hind legs and reached up the box for her. She burst into tears, racing into action, snatching it from the box and cradling it to her chest. "Come here, you darling thing," she cooed before turning to Talon. "It's... It's precious!" She detached its claws to hold it up. "A little gentlemen," she announced, looking him over. *Meow!* "Oh, I'm sorry. I'm sorry. Here—" She cradled it again, then began rocking it like a baby.

A deep rumble of a laugh sounded from Koldis. "Look at that, she already knows what to do. Just think of how doting of a mother she'll be with your child—"

"Don't you *dare!*" she screeched, whirling around to face the unruly drengr. "We haven't even, we're not even *mated* yet. Gods, Koldis!"

Koldis merely grinned.

The kitten settled against her, beginning to purr. Her heart cracked open. It was barely old enough to be without its mother. She glanced about. "Did you get supplies for it?"

The drengr standing in the room—Bedelth, Dallin, Jovari, Koldis, and Talon—exchanged questioning looks. She glanced over to where her guards stood, taking up a vantage point along the wall. Feowen looked immensely entertained, his mouth twitching. Jeanine looked bewitched, her eyes locked on the fury black bundle cradled in her arms.

"What..." Talon cleared his throat. "What sort of supplies?"

Her eyes narrowed. "*Cat* supplies, silly."

"You never said I needed supplies." Talon snapped at Koldis. Koldis just shrugged.

"You don't want it pooping and peeing all over the tower," she said.

Talon's eyes bulged. "Wouldn't it just...?"

"Just...*what?*"

Talon ran a hand through his hair, forgetting about his crown as he knocked it off. He reached out with an inhuman reflex, and caught it before it dropped to the ground. "Wouldn't it just go outside?"

She barked a laugh, clicking her tongue. "You hear that, darling? He wants you to treck all the way through the keep, through all those confusing corridors, to find some courtyard where you can bury your poo. Silly, *silly* male. He has no idea what it takes to have a kitty. But that's okay. Your mommy knows just what you need."

"Gods above," Koldis muttered. "She doesn't even coo that tenderly for you, Your Majesty. You're already being replaced by a cat!"

She speared Koldis with a glare.

He lifted his hands. "All right, all right. Tell us what you need and we'll go collect it." Her eyes narrowed. "Directly, my queen. Immediately."

She suppressed a laugh. "I'll need a litter box, at the least." They stared at her. "You know, a cat toilet?"

"A cat toilet?" Talon's brows rose. He turned to Koldis and whispered, "What in the gods' names is a cat toilet? Do you know?"

"It's a box with litter, well, probably dirt since I don't think they make such things here."

Koldis squared his shoulders. "There, you see, my king? They don't make such things here. How were we to know?"

A laugh burst from her chest. Once she started, she couldn't stop. Soon, everyone in the room was grinning.

"A box with dirt then, something intuitive so our handsome guy can bury his poo. It will have to be cleaned daily—"

"The servants will love that," Jovari said, smirking.

"I will manage it," Claire said, paying him a scolding look.

"That's rather undignified, don't you think?" Feowen drawled, breaking away from the wall, coming over to run a hand over the kitten. "Aya kunyn en calinah shaah." *You are a pretty thing.*

"He sure is!" she confirmed. "And as for *dignified*, I am a queen, but that does not mean I am above the lowest."

"My, my," Koldis said. "Rulers around the world could learn a thing or two from her."

She looked up and grinned, welcoming the burst of warmth that his words brought.

"What else do you need, love?" Talon asked, voice softening as he took in her protective stance, cradling the kitten.

"He'll need bowls for food and water—and something to eat, obviously. Some cat toys—"

"Cat toys?" Bedelth's nose wrinkled.

"Honestly, have you never had any pets? Any of you?"

The drengr in the room exchanged dumbstruck looks. "My queen," Koldis said. "We are predators. We eat things like that for breakfast—metaphorically speaking."

She sucked in a shocked gasp, arms tightening around her precious bundle. "Keep your sharp teeth away from him."

"Well, I take that back," Koldis amended. "He's not quite big enough to satisfy the appetites of a dragon."

"Hardly enough meat or fat," Talon added, nodding with a serious expression, studying the little thing like he was appraising prey.

"Gods! You're all *awful*. Don't listen to the mean males," she cooed, rubbing her hand over the purring kitten. "They won't harm a single hair on your soft furs. They're just trying to be ominous and frightening. That's what dragons do. But really, they'll be cuddling you in no time."

A snort sounded, but she wasn't sure who.

After a few more explicit instructions, the tower emptied of both shields and guards, sent on errands to collect all the things she'd need. It was just her and Talon, sitting side by side on the sofa before the fire.

Meow!

The kitten began crawling all over her, stretching its little kitten arms. "It looks kind of like a little bat, don't you think?"

Talon made a humming noise. His arm was wrapped around her shoulders as he leaned in close, observing the kitten's movements. "It's so small," he mused. "I'm afraid to touch it, for fear I might crush the thing."

She huffed a laugh, petting it as it nestled into the groove where her thighs met, purring loudly. "It does that when it's happy," she explained. "You won't hurt him."

Hesitantly, he reached out and stroked his pointer finger down the kitten's back. The kitten arched into Talon's touch, purring louder. "There, see?" She glanced up to find a soft expression on the king's marred face. "He likes you already."

"Of course he does," Talon huffed.

"You know what is wonderful about pets?" she asked, quietly.

"Hmm?"

"They don't see scars, Talon. They don't care for such things." He blinked at her, taken aback. "They only see a person for who they are on the inside, for how they take care of them. Pets make the best companions."

He blinked again, then seemed to regain his composure. "Are you saying I should replace all the people in my life with cats?"

She burst into laughter. "Oh, come on. You know I care nothing for your scars. I just mean to say, that is what's so pure about animals, pets like dogs and cats , horses, all that."

"I like my horse," he mused. "Though I've gone through too many of them to let myself get close."

She nodded. "That makes sense. Human lives are short, animal lives, even shorter."

"What are you going to name him?"

She sucked her bottom lip between her teeth, contemplating. "He really does look like a bat."

"So, Bat?"

"For a name? Hmm. How about Batty?" As soon as she said it, a laugh burst from her chest. But...as she looked down at the little thing. "That's perfect. Batty."

Talon snorted. "I was only teasing."

"Well, too bad. It's official. Little Batty."

"Sounds like Bratty."

"Perfect, because I can already tell he's going to be a little brat."

Talon huffed. "Gods, what did I get myself into?"

She snickered, then turned and planted a kiss on his cheek. Talon froze, then a small smile spread over his lips. He took her chin in his fingers and tilted her head up, crushing his mouth to hers.

When her tongue parted his lips, he groaned, holding her tighter—

Meow!

She pulled away, snickering. "Look at that, my little gentleman is already jealous. Okay, darling. Here's your pets, little thing."

Talon's arms tightened around her shoulders. He nudged her hair with his nose, inhaling her scent. She was vaguely aware of the others returning at some point, to deposit all the cat supplies they'd acquired. Jeanine, thank the gods, directed them in setting everything up. Then they crept away.

She and Talon remained on the couch long into the night, cuddling with the little black bundle between them. For now, there was only this. No talk of plots threatening to destroy their kingdom, no nerves about planning their ceremony, no fear over what the future held. Just this.

CHAPTER 23
A CLOSE CALL

Notna Bay, Oshea

Bennett reached for his pocket watch, checking the time. It wasn't unheard of to set sail in the middle of the night. Merchant ships had tight schedules to keep, after all.

It was all hands on deck as they prepared *Lady Faith* to depart Notna Bay. Working in the dark was tricky, but the crew could do it blindfolded. Lanterns swung on posts, casting moving orbs of orange light. Between the mass of bodies and the shadows, a dance was struck. All that was missing were the instruments.

"Faster, you lazy louts!" Jonah demanded, his voice a subdued growl.

Even Cat was out to help, dressed like one of the crew, holding some of the rigging for one of the men. She wore gloves, as he'd insisted. Her hands were not roughened like theirs. And she needed them to work.

He'd tried to send her below after her return. Gods only knew she'd done plenty for them already. But she'd insisted, and rightfully so. With the information they now carried, and the manner in which she'd left the city, they were in a hurry to retreat.

Even still, they might be in trouble.

The anchor was pulled next, and with it, the sails unfurled, catching the wind. *Lady Faith* began to move, cutting through the water as wind whipped across the deck. His gaze darted towards the collection of navy vessels in formation. They sat waiting, but soon they'd also depart. He only hoped there'd be enough time to warn the king.

"Think we'll get out okay?" Jonah asked, coming up beside him. They watched the crew work, legs braced wide for balance.

"Pray to the gods we do," he growled, his eyes flicking towards Cat. She'd shed her gown, dropped it overboard right after her return. "Takes a lot to rile her."

"Aye," Jonah agreed. "And you believe the numbers?"

"Not got much choice," he mused. "Look at the galleons there. Each one'll carry near a thousand. I can't even count them all. Must be near a hundred."

"A hundred thousand men..." Jonah mused.

"I'm more worried about the bats." A shudder worked through him. "Hard to say how many of those ships carry them."

"But the king has the drengr."

"And thank the gods for that. Even still. A surprise attack like this?"

"How many drengr you suppose are in Fort Kastali?"

"Damned if I know," Bennett barked, running a hand over his ropes of hair, eyes darting back to Cat. She stood observing the others now that the work had slowed. Her eyes swiveled in his direction. He didn't turn away from that gaze, instead giving her a brief nod. She was the one to turn, to head towards the deck below.

Lady Faith picked up speed, passing by the mass of navy ships. In the distance a horn blew, the sound sent chills over his skin. He and Jonah looked at each other, their eyes meeting and holding. Somehow, they both knew what the sound meant. Still, they continued on.

The mouth of the bay crept closer. He shut his eyes, taking a deep breath. They just needed to make it to open ocean. Then, they were free.

Cat had returned less than two hours ago, her breaths labored and eyes wide. She'd returned with the rest of the crew that he'd sent. They'd all looked just as fearful.

When he'd seen the blood spattering her gown, he'd nearly exploded with rage. Only a quickly uttered explanation from Jonah kept him from blaming the crew. She'd been their responsibility, after all. Didn't matter that she could take care of herself. None of his rational thinking had worked properly in those moments.

She had delivered her story in rushed gasps. "We need to go *now*, Captain," she'd insisted. It wasn't often that he heard fear in her voice—not fear like that. Still, he'd wasted valuable minutes drilling her for an abridged explanation.

The long, mournful call of a horn sounded again, and Bennett's stomach twisted.

"Godsdamn it," Jonah muttered. The wind was only so strong. "Look, there," Jonah said, pointing to a smaller navy ship that had broken away from the others.

"A coincidence, perhaps."

"No, I don't think so. Look—"

A growl rose in Bennett's throat at the sight of the flag they hoisted. He might not have spent much time in Oshea, but he knew what that flag meant. It was a beacon and it carried a message.

"Think we can outrun it?" Jonah asked.

"Not with the cargo we carry." He ground his teeth.

"We prepared for something like this, Captain. We just stick to the story and we're fine."

"You better damn hope so," he muttered, as if any of this was Jonah's fault.

His first mate gave the order and the crew exchanged nervous glances before jumping back into action. After all, that's what a merchant ship would do, was it not?

The anchor was dropped.

The navy vessel approached. Rigging was used. He braced himself as several of the emperor's Oshean navy climbed aboard. One of the men separated from the others. "Who is the captain here?" he demanded, a sneer on his lips.

"That would be me," Bennett said, walking over to the man, looking over his fancy uniform. He withheld a sneer of his own.

"What is the manner of your cargo? The reason for your departure at this hour?"

There was only one reason they'd be asking this sort of information. "Jonah, retrieve the documents," he called before turning back to the man. "And you are?"

"Captain Fenworth. Received some troubling news, looking for a person of interest."

"Oh? And you thought to come aboard *my* ship for that person?" He curled his thumbs through his belt loops. "I've got a tight schedule to keep, Captain Fenworth. We need to be in Aplia by midday tomorrow. Jonah will bring you the documents. Got a hull full of goods to deliver."

"Yes...well..." The captain's eyes were already darting over his crew.

"Who exactly are you looking for?"

"A woman, a harlot. Someone killed one of the emperor's captains. Got a description of her, and a sketch. We're not letting anyone out of the harbor without a thorough search."

He snorted. "No harlots aboard my ship, Captain Fenworth. And you're welcome to search below. You'll find naught but cargo. All the crew is here on deck, making sure we adhere to our timetables."

"Right." Captain Fenworth didn't look like he bought the lie. "Line 'em up."

"You heard the navy captain," he called to the crew. "Get in line for a search!"

There came a series of low grumbles, but everyone got in line, Cat included. His stomach lurched. A series of thoughts crashed through his mind. He needed to be ready in an instant, if needs be.

The man beside Captain Fenworth produced a sketch. He exhaled, but still didn't relax. "Never seen that woman in my life," he said. "And for the sake of bein' obvious, we don't keep women on our crew."

"Then you are not hiding one aboard?" The captain lifted an eyebrow.

"You have reason to think I might?"

"The woman in question was seen rushing from the *Exotic Cup* earlier, right after one of our officers found her leaving Captain Alden's rented room. They found his throat cut."

"That's awful, truly, but it ain't my problem."

"Interesting, since the only vessel rushing to leave the harbor is yours."

"We informed the dock master we'd be leaving at this hour, earlier this afternoon," Jonah said, appearing beside him, holding out their papers. Captain Fenworth's expression was hard. He snatched them from Jonah's hand, looking them over, before shoving them back at him.

"A lucky coincidence. The whore could have known you were leaving, and paid her earnings to be snuck aboard."

Bennett refrained from an exaggerated snort. "Fine—you seem set on the matter. Search the crew then. You want them to drop trow too, show you their baggage? That'll be the surest way, won't it. Whatever you decide, hurry up. I got a schedule to keep."

"Mind your tongue, swine. You might be a merchant captain, but you are speaking to a navy captain," said the man beside Captain Fenworth.

Bennett's jaw ached. His nostrils flared but he nodded. With a great deal of restraint, he stepped backward, indicating that Captain Fenworth could begin his perusal of the crew.

The captain moved from one to the next, with his assistant's help holding the sketch in front of each person. So...the navy captain had reason to believe that the whore was masquerading as a crew. The only relief he felt was that the sketch was gods-awful. Cat's hair was let down in the recreation, and that was perhaps the only thing they'd gotten right. Perhaps the only thing that might save them.

His breath caught as Captain Fenworth hesitated. Cat stared at the captain, a look of defiance on her features. The captain held the sketch closer. "Take off your hat," he demanded. Bennett's fist clenched. Beside him, Jonah took a step closer.

Cat hesitated, then removed her cap.

Bennett's stomach lurched at the sight. It had been a precaution, one she'd taken after returning. She'd been smart to do it. Even still, his chest wrenched at the sight of her shorn hair, no longer than half a finger's length.

Captain Fenworth's gaze lingered on it. Then he nodded, glanced once more at the sketch, then moved on. Cat replaced her hat, shot him a wide-eyed look of relief, then turned her face forward. They'd been lucky she hadn't been asked to drop her pants. That would have blown the whole thing out of the water.

But the real luck came when he caught sight of another vessel moving through the harbor. One of Captain Fenworth's crew spotted it, too. They shouted something to the captain. Captain Fenworth took a quick glance at the sketch, looking down the remaining line of crew. He said something quiet to his first mate, then the two of them turned and headed back in Bennett's direction.

"We've got another ship to search," he bit out.

Bennett nodded. "Good luck with that, Captain. Hope you find what you're looking for."

The captain eyed him a moment longer, then strode across the deck and returned to his own ship.

"That was godsdamned close," Jonah muttered. Then his first mate gave the call to their crew, and everyone seemed to expel a pent up breath before jumping into action. They needed to get out of here now, while luck was on their side.

"Take a seat, lass," Bennett said, shutting his cabin door behind him.

"Don't call me lass," Cat said as she settled in.

"No? Why, because you look like a boy?"

"I don't—" She made a scoffing sound of annoyance in the back of her throat. He was only baiting her. An attempt to quell his anger. But it wasn't *only* anger he felt.

"You didn't have to go and cut it off," he said, rounding the desk, taking a seat on the other side.

"If I hadn't, we would be in deep shit, Captain. We both know that. I spent years growing my hair to that length." And within a few minutes, it had been shorn clean off, tossed overboard, to remove all trace of its existence. "You should be thanking me."

"I—" He blew out a breath. "Thank you, Cat." A frown pulled her eyebrows together. She hadn't been expecting his gratitude. "We can have Monty take his shears to it. He does a pretty good job with the others."

She snorted at that. "Not a single person on this ship has nice hair, Captain—"

He jerked in his seat, affronted.

"—except, perhaps, you."

"Ah, so you like my hair, then." He patted it, offering her a wicked grin.

She scowled, but he knew it was an act to hide whatever she was feeling. "How do you even get it like that, anyway?".

If he didn't know her better now, he'd think she was only asking to sass him. But he knew better. So he said, "With a good deal of effort and care," because he knew it would irk her.

She huffed. "Whatever." Her arms crossed and she eyed him. "You didn't call me down here to talk about my hair. Or did you?"

Gods, she was still beautiful. Even without the long tresses. They'd grow back, but if anything, the loss of her hair left her face on full display. "You are far too beautiful," he mused, then realized he'd said it aloud.

"Yes, and?"

He snorted. "We both know why I called you down here. Tell me what happened. You failed to tell me you murdered a navy captain earlier."

"As if there was time. I told you I—"

"You said you did something bad. Not something stupid."

She sputtered.

"Forgive me, that was rash. I don't know the circumstances, so I will refrain from judgement until you give me your story. Tell me why it was necessary to kill your informant. The whole story, if you please."

She sighed. "I met him outside the *Exotic Cup*. Knew by his uniform that he was important—knew that I hadn't much chance for more information since we were leaving tonight."

"Uh-huh. So, you resorted to drastic measures?"

"Well..." The grin she offered sent chills over his skin. He wasn't sure if he liked it or feared it. "Not initially. I invited him to have a drink with me, several, in fact, then suggested we get a room."

"Despite me telling you I didn't want you spreading your legs on the job."

She snorted. "I wasn't going to take it that far."

"Course not, cause you were just going to kill him, eh?"

"Will you let me finish? Or have you already worked it all out for yourself."

"Fine, fine." He waved a hand.

"We went upstairs, and I used magic to—"

"You did what?!"

She shrugged. "Desperate times call for desperate measures, Captain. I had it all worked out. I'd already slipped him a dose of *sanidi*—truth serum," she added, when he gave her a look. "I was going to follow it up with something to make him pass out afterward, so that he'd be out cold for a solid half day before he realized he'd given away valuable information. We'd be long gone at that point. Turns out, cutting his throat was a better option."

His mouth worked. "So you just decided—"

"No I didn't *just* decide," she scoffed. "He broke free of his bindings and I didn't realize it until his hand was wrapped around my throat. He tried strangling me and I panicked." She pulled down the collar of her tunic and his blood turned cold. He saw the obvious bruising there, not quite healed yet. It would heal faster with her mage blood, but it wasn't instant.

"I didn't think to use my magic. I grabbed the knife on his belt and slit his throat. Wasn't until I was covered in his blood, and he was laying on the floor, that I realized what I'd done. By then, I'd already gotten all the information I needed. So I slipped out the back, but there was a group of his friends out there, smoking. They...they saw me. They called me back but I ignored them. Didn't have the fortitude to hold a conversation without giving myself away. They no doubt saw the blood on my gown."

"So you raced to find Jonah and the crew, and got back to the ship as quickly as possible." She nodded. He swore under his breath. No wonder she'd been so frantic.

"And the numbers you gave earlier? A hundred thousand men?"

"That's what the navy captain gave me. Along with the blood bats."

"Did he say anything about the blood bat capabilities?"

She shuttered. "He said they've been trained to eat people and beasts alike. That they swarm in formation and attack whatever's in their path. That they will be the destruction of the drengr."

"Godsdamn it," he muttered. "All right, anything else?"

Her throat bobbed and she shook her head. "That about covers it," she managed, her voice low.

He stood and poured them both a drink, passing one over to her. He downed his in a single swig, then eyed her. At last, she picked hers up and did the same. He refilled their glasses.

"Think they'll have enough warning?" she asked. She didn't bother hiding the worried tone of her voice.

"I'm going to get us there as quickly as possible."

A bark of laughter fell from her lips. "I hated them all so much —still hate them. And yet, I'm worried for them."

He lifted a shoulder. "You are allowed to feel both emotions simultaneously. For example, right now, I'm godsdamned furious with you. So angry I want to push you against the wall there and punish you for being so careless. And yet, I'm terrified and afraid because you could have gotten hurt, could have gotten hauled back by the navy for your crimes."

She snorted, but he saw it for what it was, a way to hide her surprise at his words. "Don't lie to me, Captain. You were just worried I'd put your crew in danger."

"You are my crew, Caterina." Her eyes widened. It was the first time he'd bothered to use her full name.

"So, you care because I'm crew."

"No..." He let the quiet admission sit in the air. "I care for more than that..." But he didn't elaborate. She probably didn't want him to.

He poured a third refill and they drank in silence, until at last he said, "Go and get some rest. You did well tonight."

"So you're not going to scold me any further. Punish me? Discipline me?" A brow raised in challenge.

He felt his insides curl. Instead of ignoring it, he said, "Is that what you want, kitty cat? You want me to spank you for being so carelessly naughty?"

Her mouth opened and closed, then she stood. "Good night, Captain."

He nodded, letting her go. "Sweet dreams, little kitty," he muttered as she shut the door behind herself, looking down into his empty glass with a frown. He was playing with fire and he knew it. A dangerous thing aboard a ship. And yet, like a moth, he knew it was bad and still flew directly into the flames. If he wasn't careful, she was going to incinerate him. The only problem was, he was starting to *want* her to.

CHAPTER 24
BEDELTH'S PARENTS

Kastali Dun

Bedelth knocked and waited but he was ignored. "I know you're in there," he called. His draconic ears picked up a long sigh. A smile twitched at the corners of his lips.

Saffra had made it a point to avoid him since their return, locking herself away with the mages, Marcel in particular. He had a feeling Mage Marcel was trying to tempt her into teaching. She would make an excellent teacher with her knowledge and kind heart.

He hadn't had much time to allow her avoidance to bother him. The king kept them busy. After being gone from court for so long, hours were spent in the throne room, working through negotiations on various trade and industry, and seeing to the fort as it settled back in.

Then there'd been the correspondence from his parents. A letter that had soured his mood days after returning to the capital. His stomach lifted into his throat. He swallowed against the acidic taste. He was a grown male. Yet, he still hadn't conquered this.

The door opened. Saffra's beautiful face popped out into the hallway. Jocelyn hadn't yet returned. She was due back later this afternoon. Saffra looked him over and said, "I'm in the middle of writing up a document for Marcel."

His eyes narrowed. "You're not very good at lying, are you?" Her cheeks flushed. "I wanted to see if you'd go flying with me." She blinked. "My parents have decided they'd like to visit. It's put me in a right mood. If I don't get out of this city and clear my head, I might go mad."

"Your parents are coming? *Here*?" There was a quick flash of anger but it cleared from her expression.

"Indeed. Will you join me?" The words came out sounding slightly vulnerable.

Her face softened. "Yes. Let me—here, come in. Let me just..." She trailed off, striding across the room. She was dressed in a plain, homespun gown for comfort. He'd grown used to seeing her in pants when they'd traveled. She grabbed a couple of skirt hikes and secured them at the front of her dress, revealing a pair of leggings beneath.

Interesting.

He took a few moments to glance around. There was indeed a scroll and writing supplies scattered across her desk. But the ink was capped. Terrible liar indeed. He almost chuckled. Especially when he saw the book on the sofa, opened face down, and could almost smell her faint, lingering scent from that direction. The lilac she used in her soap.

He casually strolled in that direction, as if interested in the mantle. His gaze flicked to the spine, *The Smith and his Maiden*. He forced his lips together in a flat line to keep from chuckling. He'd caught her in the middle of a romance. No wonder she'd been hesitant to answer the door, to tell him what she'd been doing.

He casually moved away.

She turned toward him, slipping a pair of gloves into place. He ignored the gloves—didn't think about what it meant. She'd agreed to fly with him, hadn't she? That was good enough. "There. Ready."

"Very good. Come."

He led her to the king's tower. Talon had already given him

permission to use the garden atop it, which really was the only secret space large enough to take off with a rider. If they used any of the open courtyards, they'd attract attention.

An ache formed in his chest.

"Let me transform and then we can go," he said, sparing her a glance before morphing into his form. Dragons were lumbering creatures, but they were also agile and careful. He didn't trample a single flower, stayed on the cobbles to ensure no harm was done.

He swung his head in time to watch Saffra spring onto his back. She'd grown skilled at the task. He refused to let his lungs expand with pride.

He leapt from the ground, taking them high above. Her breathless laugh made his chest rumble. He circled the keep and trumpeted a greeting to the other drengr out flying, then took them out over the sea. It took an hour before he spotted the contingent of ships returning from Celenore, Desaree and Jocelyn aboard one of them.

Verath's greeting filled his mind. *"Well, well, well. Did you miss me?"*

"You wish. I couldn't take another minute in that city." With his keen eyes, he spotted his shield-brother on deck. He gave a playful roar. Saffra squealed at the surprising rumble.

"Hmm. Is that your mate I see?"

"So what if it is?"

"You convinced her to fly with you? Impressive."

"Hardly a difficult task. I mean, look at me. Who wouldn't want to fly with all this?" A telepathic grumble of a laugh filled his mind. Changing the subject, he said, *"Enjoying your final hours of freedom?"* He circled the ships. While it had only taken an hour to reach them, it would take the ships hours more to reach the Bay of Bandu.

"You always were extra pissy over courtly duties. I certainly won't mind returning to them."

He didn't point out that Verath had likely chosen to be a shield for different reasons than he had. But he wouldn't dare voice that.

"You might not say that when you discover the newest addition to our inner circle."

"And what's that supposed to mean?"

"You'll see soon enough." Verath had no idea of the little ball of fur now terrorizing the king's tower.

"Look!" came Saffra's excited cry. "I can see Desaree and Jocelyn, just there!"

He wished he could answer with his words. Instead, he gave a muted roar of confirmation.

"Hello!" Saffra called down to them. He swept lower, just low enough that they saw each other wave, but not too low as to catch any of the tall masts with his wing-tips. Desaree and Jocelyn grinned, all but jumping up and down with excitement.

He made one final circuit then said, *"Enjoy the remainder of your voyage. We'll catch up later."*

Verath's mental snort was his only response.

He flew them back towards the coast, then spotted a deserted beach and landed. He gave a huff, the only way to indicate that Saffra should dismount. She did, and he shifted, then peeled off his boots, discarding them. "Care for a walk?"

She opened her mouth, hesitated, then shrugged. Her boots were discarded beside his, her leggings beneath her hiked skirts pulled up to her knees. He took in her delicate calves, then turned away.

They set off along the surf line in silence. He didn't care to talk, even if he could have filled the silence with questions. He focused his gaze out at sea, his mind thoughtful.

The wet sand squished between his toes. Such a wondrous feeling. He'd been raised at Fort Lin, so he'd always had the luxury of a nearby beach. He didn't know how the northerners did it, up at Fort Edge. To be closed in by the land, never seeing the vast ocean. The thought felt claustrophobic.

"How often do your parents come to visit?" Saffra asked.

His mood darkened. "Every decade or so. When it suits them. When they wish to gloat over my accomplishments." He ground his teeth. "Or when they wish to come and make themselves useful, by analyzing every aspect of my life and critiquing it down to the smallest detail."

"Which they assuredly do every time they come?"

"Assuredly." He deflected, saying, "What are your parents like?"

A soft smile parted her lips. "Supportive. Kind. Humble." She shrugged. "I only got to spend that first decade of my life with them before coming here. But we exchange letters frequently, and visit when we can. They're proud of me, but I know they miss me. And I, them."

"They should be proud—very proud. You are an amazing woman, Saffra."

She was young, so young, he reminded himself. It was easy to forget, surrounded by long-lived drengr. That only made him feel guilty. His frustration over their situation, that she hadn't outright accepted their mate bond, lacked insight on his part. That was his fault.

What she grappled with, her position, her situation, had all been thrust upon her without a choice. She'd been forced to grow up quickly, unfairly. In a way, he could relate.

He needed to remember this, when his frustrations grew. He'd been alive centuries while she'd been alive a mere two decades. His hurt over her rejection was selfish.

She deserved space. Room to discover herself. To understand herself. To grow and mature, especially after what she'd been through with Daxton.

He ought to say this to her, to apologize, but he didn't want to bring up uncomfortable topics. Instead, he steered their conversation to safety. Books they'd enjoyed. Speculation over Claire and Talon's bonding ceremony. Places they wanted to visit. Foods they'd enjoyed since returning to the capital.

Simple topics.

When he returned to the skies with her, his chest felt lighter than it had in days. He took the long way back to the keep, soaring high over fields and pastures. He thought of the other places they might fly together. Irelia Island was at the top of that list. But there were other secluded spots he wanted to show her, too.

Maybe this thing between them was fine as was. Perhaps he could be content with her company and friendship—nothing more. He'd take whatever she was willing to give. Anything was better than being shut out.

JUST BEFORE THE EVENING MEAL, the contingent of ships reached the Bay of Bandu, dropping anchor. Many happy reunions took place. The dwargs were introduced to the city, given accommodations within the keep and several inns. Mikkin and Jamie were also given their own accommodations while they remained here. Even the little wretch of a goblin was given a suite befitting of his new position. The first goblin diplomat Dragonwall had seen.

It was a blur of activity that bled into the evening meal, and then into the night, as Bedelth met with the king and his shields, like they did every night. Over the years, it had become a ritual. By the time he collapsed into bed, he didn't have the capacity to think.

It was a blessing.

He woke the next morning to rocks tumbling in his stomach. He may as well have been a nervous youth. His parents were set to arrive that afternoon. He talked Koldis into sparring with him before court, just to blow off some steam. He envied Reyr and wished he'd begged King Talon to stay in Fort Squall to assist. Talon would have said no, but it might have been worth the try.

If anyone suspected his growing anxiety, they didn't let on. He'd always done well to hide it. It wasn't until the end of the midday meal, as he was striding from the dining hall and news of Kadeen and Seishi's impending arrival swept through the keep, that Saffra sought him out. He didn't allow himself to think too deeply on that.

"Would you like me to stand beside you when we welcome our honored guests?"

He almost declined. *Almost*. "That would be... I would appreciate it, if it is not too much to ask."

Her lips rolled between her teeth. "If it will help, yes."

"Thank you," he said, his voice quiet.

They assembled in the lowest courtyard, where guests were generally greeted. While it wasn't formal, like when the king returned from his long journeys and the entire keep was required to be present, there were still a number of courtiers, as well as Talon, Claire, and their respective guards. Saffra was a steady presence beside him while Koldis stood on his right.

He caught sight of his father's glittering body, glinting in the sun, flanked by an entire wing of drengr. His father's scales were darker than his, nearly red, but not quite the blood red of Verath's. He circled and landed. His mother, with her deep brown skin, sat with her shoulders back, chin up, proud and regal.

She dismounted, detaching a pack that carried their belongings. The other drengr circled above. His father gave them a signal and they departed for the fort. While they could have stayed within the keep as guests, they'd be more comfortable there.

"My son," Seishi said, her voice smooth and honeyed. She strode for him, his father transforming and falling into step beside her.

Saffra's fingers brushed the back of his hand. He hid his surprise before stepping forward to greet them. "Mother, Father, welcome." He and his father grasped forearms, earning him a clap on the back. He turned to his mother and folded her delicate frame into his arms, hugging her.

For all he detested them, he still loved them.

"You look well," she said, holding his shoulders, peering up at him. He was a whole head and a half taller. She was a small thing, but only in physical size. The rest she made up for in her presence. "Such a force to be reckoned with."

A movement in his peripherals showed the king and his future queen approaching. His parents swept into a deep bow. "Kadeen, Seishi, please rise. It is a pleasure to see you again." Talon and Kadeen grasped forearms. His father's skin was a shade lighter than his mother's, his face angular and firm. Unyielding. But in his old age, his dark hair was now streaked with white. Even his mother, regal as ever, had streaks running through hers.

A pang of guilt had his gaze shifting downward. For all their flaws, they were still his parents. They were aging. Even now, he could see the change the last decade had wrought.

"This is my mate, Claire," Talon was saying. Their gasps followed his introduction as they took her in. "She straddles both races, descended directly from King Eymar and Queen Isabella," he explained.

"It cannot be," Seishi said, breathless. "What a pleasure, my lady. An honor, truly." Seishi bowed, and Kadeen quickly followed as he added, "The rumors are true then? A new spriten queen?"

"Indeed," Talon said. He didn't tell them it was only temporary. That information remained within their inner circle.

"Such a union as has not been seen since the first drengr," Kadeen murmured. "What times we live in. To witness such history in the making. My son is honored to be a part of it."

Bedelth tightened his fist, then quickly released it to hide his annoyance. If he was indeed honored—which he was, of course he was—then that was *his* honor to claim, not his father's on his behalf. He refrained from pinching the bridge of his nose. It was going to be a long visit.

"Mother, Father, let me introduce you to the others," he said, speeding things along. They nodded. He went through Claire's entourage first, including Desaree and Jocelyn, who looked exhausted from their journey. "And this is Lady Saffra, our prophetess."

Seishi preened, bowing low. "It is such an honor to hail from the same lands as the esteemed *Prophetess of Dragonwall*," she said. "You are beauty and power. There are none who haven't heard of the things you've done to help our kingdom over the years. Especially during the Goblin Wars."

"Thank you, Lady Seishi."

"I do hope you and I might have tea together while we are here? I suspect my son will be busy most of the time, attending to his duties. I'll be in need of a companion."

He almost protested, then stopped himself. Yes, he would be as busy as he possibly could be. Especially if it would limit their time together. But not at the sake of forcing Saffra to take his place with them.

"I would be honored, Lady Seishi," Saffra said, giving a small bow of her head.

"Come, I will show you to your rooms," Bedelth said. "I am certain you are tired from your journey. Lady Saffra, would you care to accompany us? I'm sure my mother would love to get to know you better."

He half expected Saffra to throw him a glare, to call him out for it. She didn't. She merely murmured her acceptance. It was selfish, yes, but he wanted her here with him. Needed her.

He walked beside his father, Saffra and his mother trailing behind. His father launched into a myriad of questions about the recent battle. How many wild dragons did he *personally* slay? How much of a role did he play? How much honor did he win? He gritted his teeth through each response, relieved when their door finally came into view.

"I must return to my duties, so I will leave you here," he said, opening the door and motioning them through. "I hope to see you at the evening meal."

"Of course," they both said, his mother going so far as to lean in and kiss him on the cheek.

"It was a pleasure making your acquaintance," Saffra added.

They said their goodbyes and walked down the corridor side by side. It wasn't until he rounded the corner that a breath burst from his lungs. He could breathe freely again. Holy gods.

A soft hand closed around his forearm, stopping him. "Bedelth?" He turned to Saffra. "Will you be all right?"

He half snorted. "I'll live through it. I always do."

She sighed. "I see what you meant about them. How they are." Her mouth pressed into a firm line. "Your mother just peppered me with endless questions about you. She wanted to know all about how Dragonwall's people view you. How the court views you. As if their opinions are the most important thing."

"As if my status, reputation, and deeds are the only thing they care about," he said. She nodded. "It has always been that way." His throat tightened and he shrugged, slipping his hands into his pockets. "Thank you for being here. I... After a decade away from them, I'd forgotten how trying they can be."

"If you need me to help during their stay, just ask."

His chest swelled. He searched her face and said, "I couldn't."

"Why not? We are mates, after all," she said. His world tilted on its axis. "You're allowed to ask these sorts of things of me. Even if we weren't, we are still friends, no? Or, trying to be?"

His thoughts scattered. He wanted to turn back time, to hear those words again. *We are mates.* He wanted to request that she clarify what she'd meant by acknowledging the bond. Was she aware of what those words meant to him?

He hid his surprise and said, "We are friends. And if you can help me get through the next few weeks alive, I would be forever grateful."

A small grin pulled at her lips. "I'm sure that together we can successfully conspire against them to ensure your survival."

His lips twitched. "With your cunning? I have no doubt on the matter. Thank you."

"I should return to my work," she said. "I'll see you later, Bedelth."

"Good day, Lady Saffra." She turned and disappeared down the corridor and around the corner. He simply stood there and watched her go.

His heart thumped, swelling against the inside of his chest. Was it too much to hope that things were changing between them? If they did, would he have the courage to suffer his parent's disapproval in claiming her, regardless of how the laws were amended?

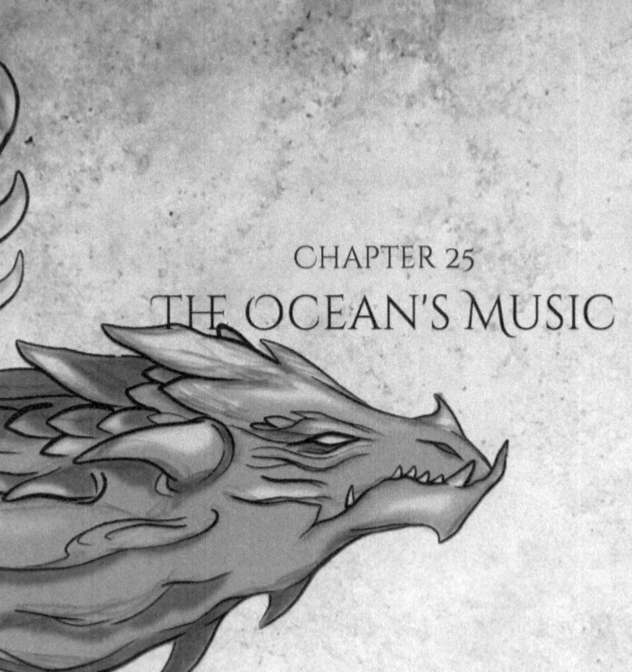

CHAPTER 25

THE OCEAN'S MUSIC

Kastali Dun

Claire sighed, rubbing her temples. Her desk was a mess, scattered with parchment. Just the sight of it made her temples throb. "Ugh," she muttered, eyes snagging on a particularly lengthy missive she'd set aside this morning to procrastinate reading it.

The days had blurred together after Talon's announcement of their mate bond. Her kitten was a handful, but a joyous one. Not like this new task. The day after their announcement, a contingent of spriten emissaries had arrived. She'd expected them, but had hoped it wouldn't be so soon. They'd handed her a tall stack of documents, sealing her fate. At least, for a while.

In the days after taking the spriten throne, she'd worked with Taylynn and her nobility to ensure the kingdom would thrive in her absence. Decisions were to be made on her behalf by those who had her people's best interests at heart. Every matter was to be documented by the scribes and sent to her. She would then have a set time period of two months to review and refute any decision she disagreed with. It was a failsafe, so that they couldn't do whatever they wanted.

249

She'd gotten a head start on the stack of documents the day it had arrived, eager to feel useful. But as the days passed, that enthusiasm had dimmed. Especially when Desaree and Jocelyn had returned.

It had been a joyous reunion. She'd stayed up late into the evening in her queen's sitting room, sharing stories. Their time at sea had been entirely uneventful. But they wanted to hear all about her journey back to the capital and the announcement that had everyone gossiping—

A knock came. She all but groaned in relief. "Come in," she called.

Desaree poked her head in. "Can you step away?"she said. "Madame Rosanne is here."

"Thank the gods," she muttered, massaging the crease between her eyebrows.

"Hard day of work?" Desaree grinned.

"I shouldn't complain." She stood, following Des from her study and into the main room. Her other handmaidens were already there. "*Ayas Drollaya*," they greeted, offering her a small bow of respect.

"Madame Rosanne," she all but squealed, throwing herself at the familiar face. Rosanne beamed, taking her by the shoulders, kissing one cheek and then the other.

"Darling girl," she breathed. "What a beauty you are, and queen now, too? I always knew you would take this kingdom by storm. My, but it is good to see you."

"You too! Des has all sorts of grand ideas for my bonding ceremony gown. I hope you are up for the task."

Rosanne chuckled. "I would never turn down the honor. This will be even more stunning than your ball gown."

"And it must reflect both of my bloodlines," she warned.

"Indeed," Rosanne beamed, eyes darting over her markings before returning to her face. "You would not believe the requests coming in for translucent gowns. Half the ladies are grumbling over the *indecency* of it, the other half are applauding. And yet, *all* of them are rushing to my door for new creations."

"Then business is good?"

"Dear girl, I have a backlog that will take me three years to finish! I've had to expand, buy out my neighbor's building, and set to work enlarging the store front. I've hired six—six!—new apprentices."

Claire's cheeks hurt from grinning so hard. "That's amazing."

"Come, come," Rosanne motioned, urging her over to the table where a large sketchbook waited. They sat, flipping through dress designs while her handmaidens set out tea, offering their opinions here and there. Rosanne admitted that she'd seen this day coming, had anticipated it, and had already started several creations. Each sketch was stunning. They came to life when the page was touched. The models swirled and turned, showing off tulle and lace, satin and silks, beads and sequins. Each one left her breathless.

"We can substitute lace for this portion to show off your marks," Rosanne said. "And this ought to be tulle."

An entire afternoon passed in a blink. They enjoyed tea and finger foods. Batty crept into the room and curled up in Desaree's lap. By the time Rosanne said goodbye, they'd decided on a preliminary design.

Her gown wasn't the only preparation underway. Her little army of planners had already completed the guest list, invitations (which had gone out days ago), centerpiece designs for the banquet tables, and flower choices. They worked from sunrise to sunset, overseen by Desaree, splitting the tasks while still seeing to their other duties.

Desaree was a blessing. She organized their schedules expertly. She would have made a good head woman in Tess's place some day. Speaking of, Claire had managed to pay the woman a visit, finally. She'd been in the cookery as expected, and had treated her to tea and frosted buns while they sat catching up.

Tess wasn't the only person she'd visited. She had also gone to visit Mage Marcel and her other teachers. Marcel had taken the opportunity to remind her of the importance of a good education. She'd felt a little guilty for declining, but promised that once the ceremony was over, she'd resume some of her private lessons.

Marcel hadn't liked the answer, but he'd sent her away with a whole stack of books to study. She had tried to read them in the evenings. It was too difficult to come back to the tower after dinner and tuck in to tedious topics when there was a kitten and a king vying for her attention. Talon insisted she attend his nightly meetings. She declined half of them, wanting him to have time alone with his shields. But she did pop in every so often, sometimes when they were least expecting it.

Dinner was little more than an hour away when Talon descended into her sitting room. Rosanne had just left. Desaree and her handmaidens fell quiet. "You weren't talking about me, I hope?" he teased.

"Never, *Ayas Drollaya*," Selphie gasped, blushing.

"He's only teasing," Claire said, going over to greet him.

"Should we..." Miera trailed off.

"Oh, do not mind me," Talon said. "I am stealing my queen until dinner."

Her heart skipped. They'd spent so little time together. So very little.

She might have shared his bed, but he still tumbled in close to dawn most nights, despite her insistence he get a good night's sleep. The few times he came to bed with her, they were both too exhausted to do little more than kiss before falling into a deep slumber.

Talon had nightmares, she'd discovered. It had shocked her at first, to hear him crying out in his sleep, thrashing in the sheets. But it went a long way to explain why he was inclined to sleep so little. It made her heart weep. She knew—or had a good idea—of his dreams and fears. The moment that had changed everything, the battle that had taken his parents from him, had given him both surface scars and scars that went much deeper, had turned him from a prince into a king. That fateful day still haunted him.

In those moments, when his distress was obvious, she'd reach for him, drape her body over his, and he'd stir. He'd wrap himself around her, sigh, and fall back to sleep.

Her presence calmed him. Knowing that did things to her chest. Made her heart feel like it would burst.

"And what are you stealing me away for?" she wagged her eyebrows, unable to hide her grin.

"The war room."

"Oh." Her shoulders fell. "We haven't been flying in ages," she groused.

They still took their evening walks together in the garden almost every night after dinner, as long as there weren't other matters to interfere. But she'd given Talon a good deal of grace. She didn't want to stress him or add to his burdens. She didn't want him to feel like he had to choose between her and his kingdom.

Such was the life of a ruler. She was figuring that out. Even if she hated it.

"I'll make it up to you," he said, pulling her against him, kissing her forehead. "How about flying after dinner?"

Her stomach swooped. "Yes," she breathed. "Deal."

She bid farewell to her ladies and followed him. He held her hand, twining their fingers together. They passed through the main room and she caught sight of Feowen and Jeanine returning. They offered respectful greetings before disappearing down the adjacent stairwell to the lower levels.

She'd given her guards shifts. With eight, she only needed four at a time. They took turns, which allowed them time to explore the city and their own pursuits. They didn't altogether enjoy being enclosed within the tower. They were used to wandering in their forest.

Talon had offered up the queen's garden on the tower's roof as a place of refuge. They were often there, and even tended to the plants. The garden thrived.

Talon led her into his war room, which consisted of a giant table and a map that displayed all of Dragonwall, with little pieces that represented their armies scattered across the kingdom. There were ships, too, representing their navy. "Your Majesties," Koldis drawled. He wasn't the only shield in the room. She also found Bedelth, Dallin, Jovari, and Verath, gazing back at her.

Her eyes snagged on Bedelth. She'd seen a lot more of him lately and knew exactly why. He was avoiding his parents.

Dallin had melded into their ranks seamlessly. On the outside, at least. She wasn't sure what *shield-things* went on behind closed doors. Things she wasn't privy to. Who knew, maybe there were initiations? She almost snorted at the thought. Did he have to hunt the largest grazer? Or get blindfolded and dumped somewhere where he'd have to fight his way free?

"Do tell us, what private joke is so funny?" Jovari chirped.

"Oh." Her cheeks flushed. She blinked and found their intent gazes, including Talon's. He lifted an eyebrow, bunching the scars on his forehead. "Uhm. Nothing."

"Very well," Talon said, calling them to attention. "We thought it was time to tackle the matter of the dragonstones. Taylynn requested we spend some time pinpointing their locations. Claire has dreamt of them in the past. While there's not much else to go on, our hope is that from her dreams, we can glean some idea by using landscape cues to narrow down their locations."

Some of them hummed with interest. "And if we do? Are we to go in search of them?" Verath asked, rubbing his jaw. "That could take weeks. Months, even."

"Indeed. So let's hope we guess correctly."

"Could we not send out others in our stead?" Verath wondered. "Navigators, perhaps? The kingdom's army has plenty of trained cartographers and explorers."

"Possibly," Talon mused.

"Kane used a lot of magic when hiding the stones," Claire pointed out. "No one but a trained mage, or even a sprite, could hope to find and free them."

It was a valid concern, both hers and Verath's, because they didn't have months to spend flying all over the kingdom, and yet, they were the most qualified to free the stones from whatever enchantments Kane had used. These factors created a challenge that needed solving. But they were used to such puzzles.

The remaining hour before dinner was spent pouring over Dragonwall's map. She described each of her dreams in detail—as much as could be recalled. They argued over possible landscape locations, placed pieces around the map, and theorized over how best to reach such places.

By the end of it, she didn't exactly feel hopeful. "Everything will work out," Talon told her, pulling her aside as they left the room for dinner. Her four on-duty guards fell into formation and the others trailed behind, chatting casually.

It often felt like a royal procession.

She asked Talon about his day, listening to him talk about the problems he'd encountered at court and during his council meeting. "I had to try a city official because it was discovered that he severely misused funds set aside for the city's well maintenance. Now the position is vacant, and I've got an entire list of complaints from citizens about unclean drinking water. It's a mess."

"And things like this happen often?" she asked, frowning.

"More often than you would think. If it's not a city official, its merchants caught scamming, or tax fraud, or any number of other financial crises that arise. In a city this size, it's always something. That's just the capital. Each lower council member represents a dragondom, and each dragondom has cities requiring the same level of care, with problems that mirror those in Kastali Dun."

She asked him for more details, especially about the capital city and its funds. She was particularly curious about orphanages and poor houses. He explained that a portion of taxes was supposed to be set aside for both charity to the poor and philanthropy. Those in control of that money weren't always trustworthy.

"But, can't you just check with them to make sure they're using the funds correctly?" she argued as they descended the final grand staircase that led to the dining hall.

"My love," he paid her a patient look. "There are numerous people managing positions like this, seeing to the proper expenditure of taxes. We do. I do. But I am but one person, and some issues aren't visible on the surface. Even with the help of my steward and lower council, we can only do so much before issues arise. Besides, I already don't sleep enough, according to my mate, who reminds me often that sleep is important."

"Oh? Your mate? Who is she? She must be very wise to impart such advice."

"Wise, beautiful, and far too good for the likes of me."

"Talon," she warned, snorting.

They entered the hall and everyone came to their feet. Talon nodded, the signal that they may resume their seats, then led her down the aisle. Once seated, she continued to pepper him for information about his duties. Now that she was forced to sequester herself in her study for hours on end reading over papers, she'd been subjected to a crash course in spriten politics. Those of the drengr weren't all that different.

Their talk turned to less serious matters as she told him about her day and Rosanne's visit. Once he finished eating, he waited for her, draping an arm over the back of her chair, rubbing his thumb over her skin in frustrating patterns. She never tired of his touch.

They went flying just as he'd promised. She saw the path he intended, to Irelia Island. They'd only gone the once. Remembering sent eager chills of anticipation across her skin.

"What can you be thinking?" he teased, knowing exactly where her mind was. Instead of waiting for an answer, he made his own thoughts clear, dreaming up scenarios that involved a moonlit swim like the one they'd enjoyed last time, except this time, there'd be a lot more involved. That was made clear when he imagined exactly how he intended to touch her.

They explored more of Irelia's ruins first. It was a wonder that dragons had once lived here. Seeing the hatching ground a second time reminded her of the mothers that would soon be giving birth to eggs. How long would they warm in the sands before hatching? How large would they be when that happened? As her feet crunched over colorful shell fragments, she imagined picking up a baby dragon the size of a small dog and cuddling it to her.

Warmth that felt a lot like yearning flooded her.

They shed their clothes and waded out into the shallows. Seeing Talon's body was always a wonder, one she never tired of. He didn't display shyness, despite his scars, despite how he felt about them. That he never shied away from sharing this side of himself with her left her breathless. How many had been given such a gift after he'd suffered? A slim few.

"What's that look for?" he asked, wading over after they'd both dunked themselves. The water came to her waist, hiding everything below. Still, she felt shy having her upper half on display. They'd bathed together, seen each other many times, and yet, his attention still left her shivering.

His gaze was possessive as it tracked over her exposed breasts. They puckered beneath his regard. "What look?" she challenged.

"The look you're wearing as you take me in. It looked a lot like wonder, but surely not."

"It was admiration *and* wonder," she clarified, reaching out for him, running her palms over his slick chest, eyeing the droplets that had formed. His chest hair was dark, trailing down to the V-lines of muscle, disappearing beneath the water's surface.

He pressed his hands over hers. "Explain."

"Admiration because you are incredible to behold." Her gaze made a point of raking over him, taking in the deep groves of muscles honed by centuries. They twitched in response. "And *wonder*, because I alone have the privilege of enjoying you like this, enjoying the sight of your saltwater slicked body for my own pleasure."

A growl built in his throat, satisfaction in his eyes. "Such pretty words from such a pretty mouth," he purred, pulling her against him. He captured her lips and then her breath. It was a salty kiss, warm and languid as his tongue stroked hers, like he wanted to taste every corner of her mouth and didn't mind spending an eternity doing so.

An eternity.

The years they had ahead of them certainly felt like it.

She'd only ever expected a human's lifespan. Once they were

bonded, she'd share his. Years and years to deepen their love, to explore each other, to explore the world. To rule. To thrive.

But only if they could create such a world worth thriving in.

Talon's body hardened against hers, his breathing turning ragged. He swept her up. She circled his waist, anchoring herself to him while he walked them deeper into the sea. Their kisses turned hungrier. "Not much longer," he breathed between strokes of his tongue. "I will make you mine."

"Yes," she managed, growing lightheaded. He made her dizzy. What they shared together made her dizzy.

"You'll like that, little mate, won't you? Being mine? Letting me claim you? Letting me worship you? In the many years I have ruled, I have never bowed to another, but I should like to bow to you if you'll let me."

"Yes," she groaned before he captured her mouth again. His hands were dragon-fire hot as they roamed her skin.

A whimper rose in her chest. Her hips were lost to the moment, searching for friction. It was a torturous betrayal that had invisible claws scratching along the base of her spine, curling against the heated flesh of her core.

A gasp fell from her lips when his hand reached behind and below her, until he caressed the one place she needed him. His touch was a red hot brand. It was everything she begged for. It gave and gave and gave while she took and took and took, rocking against him with reckless abandon. Her breath punctuated the crashing waves, mixing and mingling, making music that twined with the rhythm of her body. Talon led her through a song she'd never quite heard—not like *this*. A song she sang soon enough as he dragged sounds from her lips, sounds telling of the pleasure he made her feel.

He added to those sounds, brushing his lips along the shell of her ear, whispering encouragement, begging her to give him exactly what his fingers wished to claim. Begging until she was trembling and collapsing against him. Quivering as wave after wave of bliss crashed over her, harder, more powerfully than those rolling past them.

Then his lips were kissing her forehead, the closed lids of her eyes, the tip of her nose, one cheekbone and then the other. The corner of her mouth, her chin, along her jaw. She breathed, dragging in gulps of air as the world's spinning began to slow. Finally, she opened her eyes and met his. As she stared into the silver gaze waiting for her, she saw that eternity she'd thought of, and something deep in her chest stirred, latching on to it before settling down. And then he smiled.

SWEARING AN OATH

Kastali Dun

Reyr took in the glittering lights of the capital spread before him and felt his chest loosen. Tension fled his weary muscles, though they strained with the fatigue of flight. Weeks had come and gone, days spent rebuilding Fort Squall and helping the people of Squall's End recover after their ordeal. It had been a blessing to spend so much time with his nephew and nephew's mate, but also a strain.

Every moment spent in Fort Squall was a reminder of the brother he'd lost. A place that had once felt like his true home had been sullied. He'd been relieved to leave, though he hated to admit it.

King Talon did not know of his return. None of them did. He wanted to surprise them. Especially after he'd heard the news, rumors carried along by the wind's currents. The joy had been too much to keep him away.

Night shielded him from view because of how he'd timed it. Keeping out of sight, he landed in a deserted courtyard and strode through the keep, doing his best to stay out of sight as he made his way to the king's tower. A few servants spotted him and stared, then quickly bowed and rushed away.

Dinner was long over, and if he wasn't mistaken, the king was probably meeting with his shields right about now. His chest expanded at the thought. It was always difficult, being away.

His steps faltered at the sight of the tower door. Where two guards used to stand, there were four. Still the usual two put in place by the king, but now two additional. His eyes lingered on the sprites, standing at perfect attention beside their human companions.

Interesting.

They all seemed to stand straighter as they spotted his approach. "Lord Reyr," Rahlif Dorvyre greeted. "It is good to see you."

"Indeed, it is good to be back." He nodded a greeting to Elyon Marquin, who was on duty with Rahlif, as well as the two human guards who shared rotations, Ashton and Savas. "They in there?" he added.

"Yes, milord," Ashton said.

"Good." He strode through the door and into the entryway. The voices in the main room fell silent. There was a gasp, and then a squeal of delight. He caught a blur of motion as Claire raced towards him. She flung herself at him and he caught her up, laughing and spinning with her.

The remainder of his tension fled.

"Reyr," she breathed, burying her face in his neck. He buried his in her hair, breathing her in. He was vaguely aware of the others in the room coming to their feet. Of Talon making his way over. There were two other sprites in the room, standing near the far wall.

"You didn't tell us you were back," Claire accused, her words muffled. He cupped the back of her head, keeping her firmly in place. He was protective of his queen, perhaps more so than he was of his king. But Talon wouldn't mind—would prefer it that way.

He chuckled, letting her slide down him, holding her face in his hands. She was exactly as she had been weeks ago, and yet it felt as if it had been ages. His gaze darted between her eyes, over her expression, searching, always searching, to make sure she was well. "You are happy? Healthy? Nothing amiss?"

"No. I mean, yes to both, but nothing amiss." Her grin was brilliant and warm. Exactly what he needed. "I missed you," she breathed.

His chest swelled. "I missed you too."

A throat cleared. "If you are quite done with her, I'd like my turn," came Talon's gruff voice.

Claire's happy smile turned shy. She stepped from his grasp, biting her lower lip. Only to be replaced by Talon, who wrapped him up in a fierce hug. "It's good to have you back. I take it you intended to surprise us?"

"He wanted to make an entrance, obviously." This, from Koldis.

He pushed Talon to arm's length, holding his shoulders and looking him over. His gaze was earnest as he said, "Congratulations on your bonding announcement. I couldn't be happier."

"You should have seen how he quaked in his boots when he announced it," Bedelth said.

Talon tried to shrug. "I might have been a little nervous."

"Oh, he did wonderfully." Claire stepped forward, taking Talon's hand and pulling him from Reyr's grip. The tender look on her face was precious. His eyes darted between them. He wasn't sure he'd been this happy in decades. "Come, let his other brothers have a turn."

He greeted the others with hugs, Bedelth, Jovari, Koldis, then Verath. Only then did he notice Dallin hanging back. He strode to him, covering the distance, and reached for his forearm. They shook, and then he pulled him into an embrace, slapping the young drengr on the back. "They haven't been giving you too much trouble, have they?"

"No, Lord Reyr."

"Just Reyr. You know that."

"Actually," Talon said. "Now that you're back, I've another announcement to make."

Everyone turned to the king.

"Dallin?" Talon stepped towards him. "You've proven yourself and integrated into our group seamlessly. Verath is pleased with your progress—we all are. I had worried you were too young, but my worries were needless. So I will ask you this now. Is becoming my shield truly what you desire?"

"Holy gods," Koldis breathed.

Dallin's throat bobbed. "I... I..."

"He's positively shocked, Talon." Claire pinched her mate's arm. "You shouldn't have sprung this on him."

"It's what I want," Dallin said, straightening his shoulders. "I have considered my options. I have taken your tests and guidance seriously. I am decided. I wish for the honor to be your shield, if you will have me in your ranks, that is." His gaze was fixed on Talon, but at the last moment, he glanced at the rest of them. A true sign that he understood them. Understood that while Talon was the ultimate decision maker, the rest of them had a say.

"All right." Talon nodded, turning to his shields. "Are there any of you who would deny his request?" The room remained silent. "Shall we take a vote then? All in favor?"

"Aye," several said as every hand lifted, even Claire's. Her grin created dimples in her cheeks. "I'm voting for Cyrus," she clarified. "He says he approves."

Reyr's throat thickened, making it hard to swallow. Talon's eyes softened. Everyone gave a tiny reaction of their own, at the mention of Cyrus. It was unconventional that a dead shield would have a vote, but since Cyrus wasn't entirely gone, he deserved a say in the person who replaced him.

Dallin's lips parted, eyes bouncing between everyone's raised hands. "Truly?" he breathed, eyes going glassy. "*Truly?*"

"Looks like it," Talon said, his mouth twitching with a smile. He was the first to step forward, clasping Dallin's shoulder. "We are glad to have you. There's all sorts of oaths you must swear..."

"Don't forget, a chaste maiden to be sacrificed," Jovari reminded them.

"Oh, and a heart to be eaten..." Koldis thew in, catching on.

"He must also slay a demon," Bedelth added, lips twitching.

"And bathe in the blood of our enemies." Verath's voice was the only one that sounded more bored than amused. But at least he played along. Reyr tried not to chuckle.

Dallin's brow furrowed.

"They are jesting," Reyr said, putting him at ease.

"Except for the oaths," Talon clarified, amusement dancing in his features. "Those are real. But we can bother with them tomorrow. Welcome to our inner circle."

Dallin's exhale was one of relief.

Meow.

Reyr jerked his head around. His eyes fell on a little black blur and he said, "What in the gods' holy hell is a cat doing in our tower?"

Nearly everyone in the room laughed.

~

OF ALL THE SHIELDS, Dallin had spent the least amount of time with Reyr. It hadn't been intentional. Things had simply been what they were. He was eager to know the young drengr better.

"Nervous?" he asked. They strode through the keep, down a narrow corridor running parallel to a courtyard. It was bustling with activity, busier than he'd ever seen it. Servants prepared the keep for the upcoming bonding ceremony, rushing about with cleaning supplies and fresh linens for the guests who were traveling from estates outside the city. From the looks of it, they planned to scrub every bit of exposed wall and walkway, going so far as to use brushes to get the mortar in between. The place would be sparkling by the time they were done—metaphorically speaking.

Dallin's eyes darted toward him. His throat bobbed but he managed a nod.

"Don't be," Reyr reassured him. "Swearing the oath is an honor. Mostly, you'll just repeat a bunch of fancy words, get down on one knee, all that."

"It's the meaning of it, not the actual doing of it," Dallin clarified.

"Ah, good answer."

The ceremony was private, to be held in the throne room. Reyr had suggested he and Dallin take a walk until Dallin was summoned. The others were already getting everything ready.

They rounded a corner and he caught sight of several familiar faces. "Mikkin, my good man. It's good to see you," he called in greeting.

Mikkin, Jamie, and Unka were striding down the corridor straight for them. They stopped to exchange pleasantries. "Reyr," Mikkin greeted, grasping forearms.

"Lord Reyr," Jamie greeted, his eyes darting between Reyr and Dallin.

"My lord," Unka said, giving a tiny bow of his head. He was dressed in court clothes. Reyr's eyes nearly bulged at the sight of it. Someone had tailored a squire's attire to fit his tiny frame. His doublet was made from a fine black brocade, and matching black pants. He even had a sword belt to hold the fancy blade he carried.

"Unka, looking sharp," he said, trying to withhold a grin.

He turned to Jamie. "Have you met Dallin?"

"Uh." Jamie blinked rapidly.

"We met," Dallin said. From the corner of his eye, Reyr saw Dallin's shoulders draw back straight, making him appear taller. Interesting.

"At...at camp," Jamie clarified. A tinge of pink crept along his cheekbones. Interesting, indeed.

"Well, good." Reyr filed that away for later and said to Mikkin, "How are you settling in?"

Mikkin shrugged. "As good as can be. Since we've arrived, we have explored the keep in its entirety." Reyr doubted that very much, but said nothing of the secret passages. "We've gone into the city a few times, the famed market. We're headed back there now, as a matter of fact."

"And you haven't had any...issues?" Reyr's eyes darted towards Unka.

Unka seemed to grow a little taller. "Unka take care of him."

"Himself," Mikkin corrected.

Unka's brow furrowed, but he said, "Unka take care of himself."

"Can," Jamie added, lips twitching before his eyes darted straight for Dallin and the smile dropped.

"Can?" Unka looked utterly perplexed now.

Mikkin sighed. "Unka *can* take care of himself."

"Oh!" Unka's face brightened like he'd uncovered some great mystery. "Unka can take care of himself. Thank you, Mikkin."

"All right," said Reyr, trying not to grin, "now that we've established that, well noted. I'll trust that you can. Just make sure you keep these two with you in the city. I don't trust everyone, especially down by the docks. It can be dangerous."

"We've had a few slight...misunderstandings," Mikkin clarified. "Vendors, mostly. But once you show them a bit of coin, they change their tune. Mostly it's been a lot of gaping. Figured it's better for people to see more of him. Reduces the fear. But..."

"There are people who have lost family in the goblin Wars," Jamie explained, sounding more confident in his words than he obviously felt, from his shy expression. Was he showing off? After all, a lad from the north probably didn't know much of southern politics, except for what he'd picked up lately. "Those are the ones we worry about."

"If you..." Dallin stopped himself. Reyr glanced at him. Dallin cleared his throat. "If you would feel safer with a drengr in your company, I would be happy to accompany you into the city when you go."

"Except for right now," Reyr clarified.

"Right." Dallin blinked. "Another time, perhaps."

"Because we have a ceremony to go to."

"I'm swearing my allegiance to King Talon, the oaths that will make me a shield." Dallin lifted his chin.

Reyr almost snorted under his breath, but refrained. Jamie's lips parted in surprise, eyes darting over Dallin.

"*We are ready,*" came Talon's summons, just in time. He must have spoken to both of them because Dallin jerked.

"Time to go," Reyr said, grinning at the others. "Come." He placed a hand on Dallin's shoulder.

"See you around," Dallin said to them.

"Good luck," Jamie called, then winced like he regretted it.

Reyr had just a moment to exchange a loaded glance with Mikkin, understanding passing between them, before they were away. "What was that about?" he asked. They descended a staircase that would take them to the throne room.

"What was *what* about?" Dallin sounded all feigned innocence.

Reyr snorted. "You do realize that in joining our ranks, you will be mercilessly prodded about your love life the same way all of us are." Dallin's muscles tensed. "Think nothing of it," he added, knowing exactly why Dallin had reacted. "Your preferences are no matter to me, nor to the rest of us. Just try not to break the lad's heart, eh?"

Dallin sputtered.

There was no time to say anything else. The doors were before them. He led them through, shutting them behind him and ushering Dallin up the center of the room. The throne room was a magnificent feat of architecture. Giant stained glass windows depicting the drengr monarchy's history, beautiful pillars, flagstone floors. Their footsteps echoed in the silence.

"Sorry for the delay, Your Majesty. We had a bit of flirting to do. You know, bolster his confidence and all that."

Dallin choked, nearly tripping, but Reyr's hand tightened on his shoulder, urging him on. A couple of snickers echoed off the rafters. Everyone was present.

Talon stood on the first step of the dais. Beneath him were his shields. The chairs that were usually there had been removed. They would all stand for this.

Reyr took up his position beside Jovari and Koldis, to one side of Talon. Bedelth and Verath stood to the other. They were all dressed in finery, but none more so than Talon. His deep blue doublet was of the finest silk brocade. The belt that held his sverak was buckled with gold. The dragon head insignia rested above each of their breasts, to symbolize the kingdom they served. It was the crown atop Talon's head that truly shone.

"Dallin," Talon said. "Step forth and draw your sverak."

Dallin did as commanded, falling to one knee, head bowed as he presented his weapon. What followed was a sacred tradition not to be spoken of outside the king's inner circle. A tradition passed from king to heir, generation after generation. A tradition that would soon be modified to allow shields to take mates, if they wished.

As Dallin repeated the sacred words, spoken in the old language, Reyr felt chills snake down his spine. The words were a memory, one he felt deep in his bones that tied them together. Old and worn like a favored cloak, one that each shield had donned earlier in their lives.

It was an exchange, a back and forth, that spoke of intention. Words of fealty and honor, words of protection and promise. Reyr's chest expanded, filling with powerful warmth. Even his eyes prickled. When he glanced to his right, taking in his brothers, they all wore similar expressions. Rigid masks, both serious and unyielding, except for their glittering eyes.

As the final words were spoken, the tension in the room reached new heights and then fractured. Reyr exhaled. Talon took a single step back. His face transformed, a rare smile spreading across his lips. "Rise, drengr fairtheoir. Greet your comrades as brothers. Welcome *officially* to our ranks."

"Welcome," they each echoed. Tears of shock and joy flowed down Dallin's cheeks, as had happened for each shield upon their fateful oath day. It was a heavy moment, one they each understood, the severity of which dug deep into Dallin's heart.

A moment of silence fell, but only just a moment. It was immediately broken by Koldis's whoop. He was the first to surge forward and gather Dallin into a bone crushing hug, clapping him on the back. The rest gave cheers and whoops of their own, hugging him, welcoming him into their little family.

A family that was connected by the ancient magic of those who had come before. A family stronger than their greatest doubts and deepest fears. A family unbreakable, even in death.

CHAPTER 27

A CROSSROADS

Kastali Dun

Saffra barely saw anything through her blur of tears. Jocelyn paused in the doorway to her bathing chamber, a gown draped over her arm. "My lady? Is everything all right. You look like you want to murder your breakfast."

She barked out a laugh, quickly blinking to clear her eyes. "No. I'm fine. No need to fuss."

"Is it the luncheon with Lord Bedelth and his parents?"

She swallowed down her sudden ball of nerves. "No, not that."

"Are you sure? I can always claim you are indisposed."

"And leave him to his parents? No. I'll go."

"Then, what?"

"Bats," Saffra mused.

"What?!" Jocelyn gawked at her.

"I dreamt about them last night and the night before that." There wasn't much to say. The images were blurry at best. She'd always thought bats were sort of cute, but not these.

"Is it something prophetic? Something we should be worried about? Like when you dreamt of the dragon mothers?"

Saffra's eyebrows pulled tighter. "No... Yes... I don't know. That was more of a vision. This isn't."

Jocelyn hummed. "If there is something I've learned, it's that when you have persistent dreams, they mean something."

"Yes, true." As if she didn't also know that.

They didn't discuss it any further. Instead, she made quick work of her breakfast before Jocelyn helped her into her day gown. She spent the next portion of her morning working with Marcel, drafting up notes, or trying to. Eventually, she fled to the royal library.

She immediately felt more relaxed in its domain. Seeing it as a girl had elicited mixed emotions, with its massive collection of books she could barely read. Now, she regarded it with fondness and possibility. An entire hall filled with the knowledge of the world.

She greeted several familiar faces before seeking out her target. "Hello Master Roland," she said, greeting the wizened man behind the librarian's desk. His face brightened. "I'm working on a new project. A research project, of sorts. I'm looking for information on bats."

His brow furrowed. "Bats, you say?"

"Yes. Not traditional bats as we know them. Something...more ominous, perhaps? Or more dangerous? A modification of the species." She didn't want to give too much information away. She could only imagine if someone took her words to heart. There'd be rumors of giant bats swarming the keep and people would lose their minds, thinking what she'd seen was a vision.

Her stomach soured. Gods, she hoped it wasn't some kind of vision. That would be...she shuddered. Awful. Positively awful.

"Hm..." Roland pulled her from her dark thoughts. "It sounds like a task for my apprentices."

She brightened. "Yes, I had hoped so. I will begin my search, but if they find anything, please inform me."

"Of course, dear." He bowed his head and shuffled off. She watched him go for all of a moment before disappearing into the stacks, combing row after row, until she had a small pile of books that looked promising. She took them to a nearby table and began flipping through. Mindful of the time, she stopped just before the meal with Kadeen and Seishi. She put her books on hold and departed.

When she knocked at the door to their guest suite, she was ushered inside by an attendant. She found Bedelth first, his hulking frame with his back to the room, gazing out a window that overlooked the city. A zing raced down her spine. She ignored it. Kadeen and Seishi were engaged in a game of *Origin,* a popular strategy board game. They stopped and stood as she entered.

"Lady Saffra," Seishi was the first to warmly greet her, followed by Kadeen. Bedelth turned from his place at the window, keeping his hands clasped behind his back, and bowed his head. She looked away from him as quickly as possible, but still felt a hint of color rising in her cheeks.

"I hope you weren't waiting too long. I got tied up at the library." She fisted her hands in her skirts.

"There is no need for apologies," Seishi assured her, walking over, keeping her voice warm and eager. "We are simply glad to have you. Come, let's eat." They gravitated towards the dining table, which had been set for four. She caught Bedelth's gaze as he pulled a chair for her before taking his own. Her heart beat a little faster.

They hadn't seen much of each other over the past few days. He'd kept busy for obvious reasons. It hadn't been until yesterday that he'd pulled her aside. "You received my mother's invitation?" he'd inquired. She'd indeed received the note just that morning. "You need not accept," he'd gone on to say. "They will understand if you are too busy."

She had tried to read his expression, but failed. "Will you be there?"

"I will."

"Then I will not leave you to them, not if you would rather I join you." Only then did she notice the small expression of relief, there and gone, as his features betrayed him. They had decided to be a team in his efforts with his parents. Thus, she was here, sitting with him as he braved their company.

The serving attendant stepped back to give them space, to ensure they had all they needed, then departed.

"What work calls you to the library?" Kadeen asked, his voice one of casual curiosity.

"Oh, nothing overly important," she lied. "I'm researching magical creatures." This earned several raised brows. "Bats, in particular."

"Bats?" Seishi asked. "There exists such a thing as magical bats?"

"I cannot say, as of yet. But I will find out."

The woman regarded her, perhaps trying to determine if it was a joke, then shrugged. They began dishing up servings of rice and vegetables. Bedelth was, unsurprisingly, quiet through this exchange. "My mate does not eat meat," Kadeen explained when he noticed her questioning perusal. "I try to respect her wishes when possible."

Saffra was momentarily stunned, but managed to say, "I did not realize." Her eyes darted to Seishi, whose brown skin had flushed.

"As you can imagine, it is not a common dietary preference around the drengr," Seishi explained. "But...when you must watch your mate hunt and slaughter—at least for me—it turns the stomach. Most riders aren't troubled by it. I don't fault my Kadeen. He must consume meat to survive. He is a predator, after all. But that does not mean I must also be."

"Of... Of course not," Saffra managed, throwing a glance in Bedelth's direction. He simply dished up his food with an unreadable expression. Interesting.

They began to eat, exchanging simple conversation, mostly centered around Saffra. They inquired about her home, her parents and family, her adjustment to life in the capital. To them, such a change probably felt like a short span ago. To her, a decade had passed and it felt like a lifetime.

"You must be very honored to be in such a powerful position,"

Seishi commented. "I can only imagine. To have such magic *and* the king's ear. Few will ever be as important."

She squirmed under their obvious worship. "It is an honor," she meekly said. "But not without its sacrifice."

As for *what* that sacrifice was, she did not wish to elaborate.

"Ah, but what is a little sacrifice? Such things are inconsequential when it comes to the kingdom and the greater good of the people," Seishi said. She heartily disagreed, but didn't voice that. Sacrifice was sacrifice, and every sacrifice mattered, even if it was for a good cause—especially if it was for a good cause.

"Indeed. Most of the kingdom would agree," Kadeen added.

She frowned then opened her mouth—

"Mother, Father, how has your visit been, thus far?" Bedelth asked, saving her from a response. She didn't dare look at him. "I apologize that my duties have kept me largely unavailable."

"That is the way of important positions," Kadeen said. "It has been excellent. We have had the opportunity to meet with much of the nobility. Yesterday we took breakfast with Lord Taahir Hash, then toured the gardens with Lord Abdus Morad. They were glad for updates on the fort. Today we have plans to spend the afternoon at the market with Lord Sion Aziz and Lord Finlay Murry."

Lower council members. That much was unsurprising. Bedelth's parents continued on, dropping names like it was some sort of competition. She was happy to eat without giving more than a head nod or a hum of acknowledgement. Bedelth was clearly used to this sort of thing, for he too let them talk and talk.

"So," Kadeen said after a time, "I hear there is a new drengr fairtheoir in the king's ranks."

"Yes, you must tell us," Seishi said, dropping her voice. "Are the rumors true?"

"Indeed. Lord Dallin swore his oaths two days ago," Bedelth confirmed, sounding rather proud.

"We must seek him out and offer our congratulations," Seishi said to her mate, who nodded. "Perhaps he will agree to a luncheon," his mother added. Saffra almost snorted. "Is it also true that he is the youngest drengr in history to swear an oath?"

"Yes, I suppose so," Bedelth said.

"That's what I thought." Seishi nodded to herself. "A whole decade before you, if my memory serves." She drew herself up. "There is something to be admired in that. That he recognized the honor and chased the opportunity before any others beat him to it. All without his parents to push him towards it. Now *that* is a drengr who knows how to recognize an opportunity."

Saffra's stomach twisted into a hard knot.

"Oh?" Bedelth said, leaning back to regard his parents—his mother specifically. "Some would argue that taking the oath at such a young age is careless. He's at his mating age. What will happen if his mate appears, but he's already sworn himself to the king? That is not the struggle one should live with."

Kadeen snorted, waiving a hand in dismissal.

Seishi said, "He will do the honorable thing, obviously. He will choose his duty over his heart, as it should be for someone in his position. As you well know."

"As I well know," Bedelth parroted, a sharp edge creeping into his voice. Saffra risked a glance in his direction. His jaw was clenched, hand gripping his cutlery in a savage hold.

"Oh, please," Seishi said, drawing her shoulders back. "It isn't as if we haven't had the same conversation with you, my son."

"Yes, I well remember," Bedelth ground out. "There is no greater honor than that of becoming a king's shield. Even if it means *sacrificing* my other half to serve my kingdom. Tell me, father, would you have made such a choice, knowing it would condemn your mate—my mother—to a human life? And me? I would not exist."

"I would have taken the honor, had it been available to me," his father said, his voice hardening. Seishi nodded in agreement, as if it were some noble thing to accept the possibility. Saffra's palms grew sweaty. She abandoned the remainder of food on her plate.

How had the conversation deteriorated so quickly? It was made all the more awkward by the fact that she was sitting *right here*. She opened her mouth to change the subject, only to be deprived of the opportunity as a loud pounding sounded at the door.

There was a long hesitation and a frown from Seishi, before she said, "Come in."

As if their conversation had summoned him, Dallin poked his head into the suite. "Forgive me, Kadeen, Seishi, but the king has requested the immediate presence of his prophetess and Lord Bedelth. I'm afraid I must steal them away."

Bedelth rose quickly—too quickly. She was slower to rise, confusion hidden behind a blank expression as she took in Bedelth's parents. Wouldn't the king have just asked Bedelth himself? Mind to mind?

Bedelth's parents were slower on the uptake, oblivious to what was really happening.

Kadeen set his linen napkin on his finished plate before standing, followed by his mate. "Of course," he said. "The king cannot be refused. Thank you, Lady Saffra, for your company. It has been an honor. He bowed his head."

Seishi echoed the same sentiments.

A blink later, Bedelth ushered her from the room, his hand at the base of her spine. It wasn't until the door closed behind them that Dallin said, "Hopefully I didn't wait too long?"

"No, your timing was perfect," Bedelth said, his relief evident.

"Did you two plan that?"

Dallin grinned. "I was told to be on standby."

"Is that the sort of duties new shields are relegated to? To rescue their fellow brothers from certain abominable parents?"

"Just the very thing," Bedelth said, sharing a grin with Dallin. "Thank you."

"You're welcome. Now, if there's nothing else, I have a certain... friend I promised to show about the market this afternoon."

"Go. Enjoy yourself," Bedelth said.

"So, we aren't meeting with the king?"

Dallin gave a high pitched laugh. "King Talon is tied up with his lower council all afternoon. So, no." With that, the young drengr slipped away.

Bedelth continued to lead her through the keep, his hand at her back. She hardly realized when a door opened and he ushered her inside. Until she blinked and took in the interior. "Is...is this your room?"

She'd never been here. It wouldn't have been appropriate. He'd visited her chambers plenty over the years, casually, as a *friend*. But now that they were obviously more, it felt almost dangerous.

She stepped into the middle of the space, immediately curious. A shelving unit displayed a vast, elaborate collection of daggers. She gravitated towards it. "This is..."

"The others like to give me a hard time about it. But, well, we all have our vices."

"And yours is collecting daggers. Not exactly a crime. It's just... how many are there?" These weren't plain weapons. Far from it. They all had unique hilts, gemstones, and beautifully shaped blades. Some curved. Some needle thin. Others broad and short.

"One hundred and twelve." His voice oozed pride.

A small laugh burst from her chest. "I never took you for someone materialistic but..." She glanced around the rest of his suite. It was clean, organized, showing off bookshelves on one end near the sitting area, an ornate table, a finely crafted bed. The more she looked, the more she realized exactly how far Bedelth's taste in fine things went.

Her own room suddenly felt drab in comparison. When she turned towards him, she was surprised to see a flush creeping up his neck. He shrugged. "I like nice things," he said.

"There's nothing wrong with that. I just...always took the drengr race to be a rugged bunch. Almost...utilitarian in nature. But it makes sense. Dragons are hoarders and they are your cousins, after all." She moved back towards the middle of the room and placed her hands at her temple, massaging the building headache. "Your parents are..."

"A lot. I know."

"Not just a lot, Bedelth. They're rather awful!" The words were out before she could stop them. Her hands flew to her mouth, covering it. "I'm sorry," she squeaked.

Bedelth was at a loss. He lifted a shoulder to dismiss her words, moving around his suite like a restless creature. Stopping, then pacing, picking things up only to set them down again. He turned towards her. "I shouldn't have said anything, shouldn't have provoked them when they brought up Dallin. I just..." He sighed.

"No, you absolutely should have. There's nothing wrong with standing up for yourself and your beliefs. To believe Dallin is too young for an oath, despite having accepted him into your ranks, is your own opinion and it's valid, especially considering your own experience. But it wasn't even that. It's the fact that they insinuated he was somehow *better* than you, for not needing his parents to push him towards the position. As if you should have selflessly abandoned everything to swear an oath. It's...it's..."

Bedelth watched her, his eyes slightly widened, his chest rising and falling. As if he was seeing her anew and liked what he saw. That look sent heat licking over her body, zinging straight to her tummy. His arms were at his sides, fists clenched. She had a sudden and overwhelming urge to go to him. Her feet took several steps forward before she could stop them.

"How do you put up with it?" she managed.

"It isn't easy." He exhaled. "They're my parents. Just because they're awful doesn't mean...doesn't mean I don't love them. I think it's *because* I love them that it hurts all the more when they say things like that. I've been forced to earn their love, day after day, year after year, century after century. It's exhausting. Like, if I make the wrong choice, I'm punished for it, but if I make the choice they agree with, I'm suddenly worthy of love. I hate it," he snarled.

Her heart cracked open. She walked towards him, her body moving before her mind caught up. She lifted a hand. He stilled as her fingers brushed over his cheekbone, down along his jaw. "Bedelth," she whispered. The feel of his skin beneath the pads of her fingers sparked something in her belly.

He shuddered beneath her touch.

When she pulled her hand back, he captured it in his, laid it flat against his cheek and leaned into it, closing his eyes. He was seeking comfort. The kind of comfort only a mate could bring. Suddenly, that was the very thing she wanted to give him.

"Bedelth..." she found herself whispering again. It was a question, a plea, an admission, all wrapped in one. His eyes flew open, his warm gaze snaring her.

Before she could talk herself out of it, she went on her tiptoes and kissed him. Blood rushed past her ears, morphing into a roar of nerves. He didn't move, didn't respond as her lips pressed against his. His were soft, warm and lush. She pressed into them, moving over them. He hadn't even closed his eyes, just stared at her with an expression of utter shock and disbelief.

Doubt needled her belly. This was a mistake. She should not have—

Bedelth rapidly blinked. His hands came up, grabbing her before she could back away, as if sensing this moment was fragile and close to fracturing. He groaned, pressing his hand against her lower back, the other against the back of her head, pressing them flush together. His lips were on hers now, hungry and desperate. His mouth moved with an intensity that spoke in more ways than words could.

Despite the hunger, he did not overstep. It was only lips. But even lips could be erotic and delightful.

She sighed, ignoring her doubts, pushing them away to lose herself in the moment. A moment that felt so right. So...perfect.

Her heart drummed against her chest, keeping pace with her mouth. She struggled to breathe. Air was the farthest thing from her mind as she kissed him back, melting against his hard body. Her tongue darted out, traced along the seam of his lips. He allowed her to lead, allowed her to set the pace. It was too slow and too fast all at once. And it left her head spinning in the best way.

She explored him, brushing her tongue against his, hesitant at first. The feel of his blunt teeth, pointed canines, and soft warmth was bliss. Heat surged through her veins, weakening her knees. Bedelth's hand tightened against her back, supporting her as she continued her onslaught, taking what she should have taken from him months ago, when he'd first made his desires clear.

As if sensing her urge to take, the moment changed into something searing.

Their kiss turned savage, tongues and teeth clashing. He

nipped her lower lip and she gasped. No one had *ever* kissed her quite like this. Not even the man she thought she'd spend a lifetime with. No kiss had ever felt so perfect, like it was made exactly for her the way a custom gown was, with all the extra trim and accents she could ever want.

Their breathing was frenzied when at last, she pulled back to avoid fainting. Bedelth's eyes darted between hers, filled with nothing but wonder and disbelief. "Did you...did you mean to do that?" he asked. As if it had all been a dream.

She tried to clear her throat, to take a step back, but his arm didn't move.

She sighed, relaxing against him. The doubt pressing in around her chest was distracting. What had come over her? What had possessed her to do this? Moreover, now that she had, how could she ever go back to the way things were?

This was a crossroads. A moment where two paths collided. She could claim it was a mistake, that she had gotten carried away. Or she could own up to the budding desire he'd awoken in her.

What would his parents do, she wondered, if they discovered what she was to him? If they discovered that they were mates? That she was his, and he was hers?

Possessive heat radiated through her chest. What would it feel like, for him to belong to her? To lay claim to such a male? To hold his heart for safe keeping.

That sudden, rebellious desire grabbed ahold of her with its deadly jaws. Perhaps it was just an excuse, because excuses were easy. Truth was harder. But she knew exactly what she wanted to do.

Resolve settled into her chest. She gave a tiny, breathy giggle of disbelief. "Kiss me again," she whispered, no, *demanded*. There was absolutely no hesitance as his expression turned hungry, as his lips descended. It was easy, she realized, to lose herself in it—in him. So she did exactly that.

CHAPTER 28
ROOFTOP CELEBRATION

Kastali Dun

Claire whirled around at the sound of muffled curses. Moments later, she saw why. Talon was balancing with his arms lifted and his hands full of flowers. He was at risk of toppling off the stepstool and onto one of the tables beside him. He secured the final colorful lantern into place, grumbling, before jumping backwards off the stool. He staggered back several steps, wiped his hands on his pants as if to rid himself from this whole trying experience, then rounded on her. She pressed her lips into a firm line to keep from laughing at his display.

"Remind me again, *my queen*, why people from your world choose to subject themselves to this sort of thing?"

Her hands covered her mouth but a giggle broke free anyway. "It's a bachelorette party, Talon, it's meant to be fun."

Well, *technically*, not quite a bachelorette since they weren't getting married.

"I am speaking of your insistence against magic," he growled, stalking towards her. A huff left her chest. The sight of a massive drengr stalking its prey was frightening. The sight of Talon doing it left her heart pounding. She found herself scampering backwards, away from him until her hips collided with the battlement surrounding the rooftop garden. The tallest garden in all of Kastali Dun. The most beautiful place she could think of to host a party like this.

What a party it would be!

The sight of it stole her breath, seeing the finished product. The garden was already magical. Paired with massive garlands erected on trellises, hanging lanterns in different colors, an archway, and low tables scattered around with giant silken pillows. The place looked like something from a fairytale.

They'd done it entirely themselves. She wanted it to be a surprise for their friends, but she couldn't have done it without Talon's help. Together they'd schemed for days, sneaking in everything they would need. The only other person who knew about it was Tess. She'd recruited the head woman early on to ensure they'd have enough food.

"Magic makes this too easy," she reminded him. This wasn't the first time. He'd hemmed and hawed earlier, too. "I want our friends to know how much they mean to us—how much effort we put into this for *them*. Besides, it's part of the whole experience." She filled her expression with mock sadness. "Aren't you enjoying my company?

"Impossible woman," he huffed, bracing his hands on the battlement behind her, caging her in. The heat of his body, the closeness and familiarity between them, quickened her heartbeat. He dropped his head level with hers. "You know I enjoy every moment with you."

He brought his lips to hers. It was a claiming kiss, pressing their bodies together. Heat seared everywhere he aligned with her. She felt a little moan rise up in her chest before he swallowed it with his mouth.

He pulled back, almost too quickly. "You know, had you allowed magic, we could have finished in half the time, leaving the rest of the afternoon for...other pursuits." He rocked his hips against hers, letting her feel exactly what *pursuits* he meant.

A little gasp fell from her lips as tingles raced up her spine.

It had been punishing, the days leading up to their bonding ceremony, each harder than the last. Not just for how busy they were, for the stolen kisses they were forced to share between moments, but because when they did come together, it took everything to keep from plunging past the point of no return.

Talon had always been adamant that they seal their bond as part of the ceremony. It felt rather old fashioned to her, reminiscent of medieval consummation of marriages. But the drengr tradition was revered, and she respected that. There would be a ceremony in the throne room, a large celebration to follow, and then Talon would whisk her away from the public to the privacy of their bed.

For him, any other way felt cheap, and she respected his wishes.

Still, they had tempted fate several times, especially in the past week. In those late hours before falling asleep, they explored each other, touched each other, kissed and licked. There were many things lovers could do with their hands and mouths, many explorations to chart, that kept them within the bounds of the bonding rules. More often than not, it had become a punishing game.

"We've got a few minutes," she whispered against his lips. "Suddenly, I find myself very interested to know all about these pursuits you speak of."

Heat licked her core, even as she said the words.

Talon's low chuckle vibrated against her chest. He pushed harder against her, pinning her. His strength felt delicious, especially when a muscled thigh pressed between hers. He lifted his hands to cup her jaw, thumbs stroking her cheekbones. Their gazes held for several moments, sparks crackling between them, before he dipped his head. He licked along the seam of her lips and she melted beneath his touch.

They kissed for long minutes beneath the brilliant spring sky, soaking in the afternoon sunshine. The sun was sinking towards the horizon, casting the queen's garden in a golden glow. It looked alive with magic.

She wanted to stay like this forever, trapped in this moment, in

Talon's arms. Dragonwall lay stretched beneath them, but up here, suspended in the sky on the highest point of the keep, she felt removed. Like everything happening in the world didn't exist. It was just the two of them, breaths mingled, tongues warm and curious.

She sighed, pulling her mouth away to nuzzle against him. His arms came around her, wrapping her up and shielding her. This was what true contentment felt like.

Everything she hoped it would be and more.

As the sun disappeared beneath the horizon they gathered their inner circle around them. The only people missing were Byron and Tamara. She felt a pang of disappointment remembering Tamara's letter. The new fort leaders were busier than anticipated, and although they hated to miss it, their responsibilities wouldn't let them travel to Kastali Dun for the ceremony. She understood, she really did. But she would miss them.

Instead of dining in the hall, Tess had arranged everything they would need. It was already waiting in the garden.

"Are you going to tell us what this is about?" Reyr grumbled as she led the charge, ushering everyone from the tower's main room and up the stairs. "I am highly aware that we are missing the evening meal."

"Never come between a drengr and his meal," she heard one of her guards mutter. Probably Feowen or Jeanine.

"Oh, quit your grumbling," she teased.

She was the first to emerge. Despite having seen it only hours earlier, it looked even more magical at night. All the lanterns glowed with life, in shades of pink and blue and orange, hanging from poles and suspended from trellises. Set against the backdrop of the night sky, they took her breath away. She stepped aside so the others could gather behind her. Talon took up the rear before he moved around to stand beside her.

Gasps echoed as everyone beheld their efforts. "What is...?" Reyr's eyes darted in her direction. "Did you do this?"

She didn't answer, waiting for everyone to soak it in before speaking to the entire group. "Talon and I wanted to do something special for all of you. In my world, as part of my culture, the night before a wedding the bride and groom usually host bachelor and bachelorette parties. I've had to abandon so much that I wanted to try and hold on to a piece of that. Normally, these would be separate events. I'll spare you some of the more scandalous details."

Talon chuckled, because she'd already told him plenty.

"We wanted to remind you of how special you are to us, so we've secretly been planning this party for over a week."

"She wouldn't even let us use magic to hang the damn flowers," Talon grumbled.

"Aww. Poor, powerful male," she cooed, giving him a face. "Did I work you too hard?" His eyes darkened. She only grinned before turning back to the others.

"You did all this for us?" Verath asked. He stood beside Desaree. She was thrilled to see them holding hands. It was the first time he'd shown any kind of physical affection towards her in public. It left a warm, satisfied feeling pounding in her chest.

She also noticed that Saffra stood closely to Bedelth. They weren't touching, but considering how much Saffra had tried to avoid the drengr, she could only wonder.

"We did. And as Talon said, we didn't use magic for any of it. We did it all by hand because we wanted you to understand what your loyalty and friendship means to us." She felt Talon's eyes on her, almost like a physical touch. "Nothing about our situation has been normal, but we know we can count on you—all of you."

"Always," Koldis rasped. The others echoed the same sentiment.

"For the first time since Eymar and Isabella's reign, Dragonwall has come back together—drengr, dwargs, and sprites. But unlike the last time, I have no intention of letting that end. This time, I want it to stick—a kingdom united. For too long the sprites and drengr have been at odds. For too long the dwargs have hidden away, content to keep to themselves. When we defeat Kane, because we will—*I will*—things will be different."

She glanced at Talon, who was gazing not at their closest

friends, but entirely at her, his lips parted. She gave him a brief smile.

"It is for that reason," she continued, "that we will usher Dragonwall into its fourth age. An age of peace and prosperity. An age where drengr, dwargs, sprites, and perhaps even goblins work together and thrive."

Her words were met with silence—utter, shocked silence.

"A fourth age," Reyr whispered at last, glancing between them. "Truly?"

"We thought it was time," Talon said. "Every age in Dragonwall's history has been marked by a monumental change. From the time of the Awakening, to the rule of the drengr monarchy. Claire's coming back to our world is no coincidence. What she brings with her, her knowledge, her modern practices, we can all stand to learn a little something from that." He squeezed her hand, casting her a look of such love her heart felt like it would burst.

She could only gape at him as the others broke into speech.

"We are interested to hear your thoughts, but we think it is the right thing to do."

"It is the best idea I've heard in a long time," said a voice, ringing out into the garden.

Everyone froze. Claire gasped. She knew that voice, but how? From behind the group, Princess Taylynn emerged. Claire's eyes went wide and she almost choked at the sight of the princess.

"What... *How*?!" she gasped as everyone moved to get a better look at her. The sprites immediately bowed. While Claire might have been their queen, Taylynn was the princess they had revered for thousands of years.

"I only just arrived. Imagine my shock to see you all having a party and no one thought to invite me?" Her whimsical voice held a hint of amusement.

Claire glanced at Koldis to find him struck dumb, watching his mate from the other side of the group. She almost wanted to laugh at the look on his face. He gave his head a subtle shake, recovering enough to drawl, "Had we known you would feel snubbed, *mate*, I would have hand-delivered the invitation myself."

Claire covered her mouth, to hold in a snicker.

Taylynn turned, ever so slowly, to face her mate. Something told her that Taylynn had been very aware of Koldis standing there the entire time and had purposefully ignored him. Their relationship was a curious one. It only went to show how well suited they were.

"It's no matter, *darling brute*," she said, a wicked smile spreading across her lips. Koldis's gaze raked over her expression, lips twitching. It's like everyone had disappeared around them as they watched each other.

"Oh, for the love of the gods, will the two of you just kiss already so we can get on with it," Reyr growled. His words broke the stillness of the moment. Koldis leapt forward. In front of everyone, he snatched Taylynn by the waist, dragging her against him, then captured her mouth. Taylynn gave a surprised little gasp, then melted into him.

Claire felt her own pulse speed up at the display. Talon's hand tightened in hers. He wasn't unaffected either. Gods, romance was rubbing off on all of them. When she caught Desaree's dreamy expression, and Saffra's bright eyes, she couldn't help but smile.

"Well, now that that's settled," Talon said, "shall we sit down to eat? I intend to enjoy our evening."

"Oh, I very much plan to enjoy mine, too," Koldis grumbled, as if Talon was keeping him from what he really wanted. He kept his forehead pressed to Taylynn's. The princess's eyes were clouded over with lust. Even an ancient being as old and wise as the spriten princess was not immune to Koldis's charm, nor the mate bond that tied them together, even if Koldis hadn't sealed it yet.

Claire should have known that Taylynn would come back for the ceremony.

Everyone began moving about the garden, taking in the decorations, or seating themselves at the low tables. She caught sight of Reyr's hand as it darted out to grab a little dessert. He plopped it into his mouth. They shared a silent look before she copied his actions and snuck one too. Eventually they all settled on the cushions.

Drinks were poured and they served themselves. The sound of conversation filled the air as they talked and laughed. Taylynn gave them a brief update on her activities, seeing the dragon mothers settled in their hatching grounds. One had already laid eggs, which were now hardening in the sand. Claire's heart gave a little tug at that.

Quietly, she said to Talon, "Maybe we can stop there on our honeymoon," because she'd forever regret it if she didn't get to see baby dragons at least once in her life.

"If you wish it," came Talon's response.

The others knew of the honeymoon they planned. Another of her customs she wished to carry over. She'd already explained to everyone how newlyweds would often go off on their own for a few days or even weeks. In her case, they were planning to treat it as an opportunity to hunt the dragonstones. She'd worked with the others to pinpoint a few promising locations. At the end of their journey, she would visit Esterpine again and transfer her crown to Taylynn.

This trip was something she and Talon would do alone.

The others hadn't been happy to hear it, that they'd be left behind. But it was her chance to have some time away with her mate, just the two of them. They'd keep to the skies, flying by day and camping by night. It'd be safe enough, especially given how much her magic had grown.

The thought of visiting the dragon hatching grounds only increased her anticipation.

The evening passed in a blur of excited conversation and speculation. Spirits were high, and only soared higher the more wine they consumed. They ate and laughed and sometimes even cried when the laughter was heavy enough.

She couldn't help but look around at this group of people and feel the choking emotion that rose in her throat. This was her family now, one she'd chosen. She loved them and couldn't wait to spend the rest of her life with them. It hurt, knowing the sacrifices she'd made to be here, the world she'd left behind to do it. But in moments like these, it made everything worth it.

She was just looking around, smiling as she watched their obvious merriment, when a loud cry from Bedelth's lips silenced everyone. She saw why a second later. Saffra had collapsed into his arms. And just like that, a knife was wedged into her stomach, destroying the happy evening she'd worked so hard to create.

A burst of anger rose up, hot and piercing, but she quickly stifled it. It wasn't directed towards Saffra, not really. The seer couldn't help when visions took her. It was just that for once, she would have liked something to go right.

Everyone stared at the seer, limp in her mate's arms. Claire's gaze met Taylynn's. Something in Taylynn's expression, a knowing, made her hiss. "What is it?" she whispered. "What is she seeing?"

"I..." Taylynn's brow furrowed. "I cannot be certain. In truth, it has been hidden from me."

"What has been hidden?" Talon's voice carried a sharp edge. Despite Taylynn being Koldis's mate, Talon still harbored a deep mistrust of her.

Taylynn steeled her spine. "Something is coming, Your Majesty. I can feel it like a storm on the wind. Only, I do not know what."

"But the tree does?" Claire challenged.

Taylynn shook her head. "Not...entirely. A threat. A force. But that is all."

Saffra gasped, her eyes fluttering open. For a moment, she looked dazed, then her eyes darted to Bedelth and her forehead furrowed. She tried to sit up. He helped her, looking almost reluctant about it, as if he wanted to keep her in his arms a few minutes longer.

Everyone was quiet, giving her the time she needed.

Claire felt Talon's tension radiating in waves. He knew better than most that when Saffra had a vision, it wasn't a good sign. Her visions had only brought devastation, and while it wasn't Saffra's fault, it was easy to resent those visions nonetheless.

Saffra's throat bobbed. When she looked up, it was to Claire and not Talon, as if she was too afraid to meet her king's eyes. "What did you see?" Claire whispered, softly, gently.

"We're going to be attacked." There came a collective gasp.

"Soon. I can't say when, exactly. But it felt soon. But…" Saffra's brows drew together. "It was the bats. Swarms of them."

"Bats?" several voices echoed.

"She's been seeing bats in her dreams," Jocelyn offered, not exactly helpfully. Saffra's handmaiden only realized it when Talon's expression morphed.

"You didn't think to tell us sooner?" he harshly demanded.

"*Easy, love,*" Claire silently said to him. She placed her hand on Talon's thigh to calm him. The moment she squeezed, his muscles relaxed and he seemed to shake off his budding anger. Anger she knew emanated from worry. He had a kingdom to protect, and that wasn't easy.

"They were just dreams," Saffra murmured, as if dazed. "Vague and almost impossible to sort out. But I started doing some research and came across a few alarming things about large bats— who knew such a thing existed?—from the north. Still, I hoped it was just… I didn't want to worry anyone, especially with the ceremony being tomorrow."

"We're not postponing the ceremony," Talon growled, adamant.

"I don't think the attack will be tomorrow," Saffra assured him, refusing to meet his eyes, looking completely apologetic.

"No one blames you," Claire urged, hoping to reassure her. Saffra merely bit her lip. Bedelth's arm snaked around her waist, unconsciously done by the look of it. An instinct to calm his mate.

"What did you see, exactly?" Talon asked, his voice gentler this time. He was trying to hide his agitation. Claire stroked her hand up and down his leg, noticing the way several gazes tracked the movement. She and Talon didn't often display affection in front of others. A kiss here and there. When they did, everyone noticed.

"They swarmed Kastali Dun in droves. Clusters, moving in formations like…like birds often do. It was organized. And…we were there to meet them, our drengr. But fire would not touch them. Almost like with dragons. I do not understand…how could they be immune to fire?"

"How many were there?" Verath asked, already calculating.

"Too many to count. Far more than our own force of drengr."

Reyr swore. "We need to prepare. Your visions are meant as warnings. We would do well to heed this one. I know we have the ceremony. But we must do everything we can despite that, to be ready for an attack like this, at any moment."

Talon's Shields weren't mere guards or warriors. They were skilled tacticians. If anyone could prepare the city for an attack like this, it would be them. Still, it didn't stop the feelings of unease from squirming like worms in her stomach.

A loud sigh broke the tension. Talon said, "There will be time enough to worry. Let us enjoy the remainder of our evening and focus on tomorrow. My mate has put a great deal of effort into this gathering for us to enjoy. After that, we will do whatever is necessary. Reyr, when you leave here tonight, ensure we have extra patrols set, and call additional city guards to their posts."

"It will be done, Your Majesty."

She blew out a breath. She'd half expected Talon to call an early end to things. To escape into his study to brood—which was what he did best. Instead, he wrapped an arm around her waist and tugged her closer. "I wish to enjoy my mate's company before all hell breaks loose," he added, giving her a small smile. It looked forced, but at least he was trying.

Despite feeling the acute reminder of what it was to be a ruler, she pushed it away.

They did what he said, basking in the magical setting of the rooftop garden surrounded by glowing, twinkling lights. They pushed the dread of a potential attack out of mind. They lived in the moment, soaking in each other's company, enjoying it for as long as they could. Who knew better than they, how quickly a moment could be destroyed, how quickly they could be ripped apart and taken from one another.

CHAPTER 29
THE BONDING CEREMONY

Kastali Dun

Claire blinked at her reflection. For a few moments, the chaos surrounding her faded away. Gone were her fussing handmaidens with Desaree to oversee them and Madame Rosanne to make the final adjustments. *Her gown*! It was all she could see in the mirror. Her eyes blurred with tears. One slipped down her cheek. There came additional gasps and fussing as everyone noticed, but she was numb.

To *describe* Rosanne's creation was almost a travesty, for it was unlike anything she could have imagined. Even the sketches hadn't come close to capturing the sight of it on her body. It was something seared into her mind, something she would remember for the rest of her life.

This, like her ballgown, was strapless, putting her bare chest on display. The bodice was styled similar to a corset, but without ties. Little buttons spanned the back. It had taken nearly twenty minutes for her ladies to do them up, pressing her breasts to full attention.

The gown's fabric was plain black silk of good quality. It was meant to accentuate the careful beadwork—if one could call them

293

beads. They were miniature iridescent scales sewn into the shape of a dragon's head that wrapped around her left side, pointing downward, its maw open breathing flames. Even the dragon's eye was done with careful thought, a silver gem to match Talon's.

The flames were made of fine gold and orange beads, tongues of fire expelled from its mouth, flowing over her hip and downwards, all the way to the bottom of her heavy skirts. When she moved, the flames danced with her. She loved the way Rosanne had incorporated so much into the piece.

It was a gown intended to make a bold statement. It told a story about who she was, what she was, and what her bond would mean. Everything had been thought through with care. Golden flames, because women in Dragonwall wore golden gowns for their weddings, not white. Black because of the drengr she was bonding to. A dragon to symbolize him breathing fire. Even the flames were symbolic, to signify her uprising, from an outsider to a queen.

The back of the gown was entirely plain. That was intentionally done, to accentuate her cape. She almost loved the cape more than the gown. It was a nod to her spriten heritage. It, too, had scales on a portion of it, much larger than those used for the beads. They linked together like plates of armor. It started as a choker, encasing her entire neck, then winged out over her shoulders, curving into upward points. The rest of the cape was translucent black. Over it, swirls of sprite markings were embroidered with the help of her spriten handmaidens. They mirrored her own in shimmering thread the same color as hers. They were a stark message against the black fabric. And then there were the dragon scale cuffs encasing her wrists, something she'd purposefully requested.

She looked like a vengeful warrior goddess ready to do battle.

When she next blinked, Rosanne had disappeared, dismissed to find her way to the ceremony. Only her handmaidens and guards remained. They, too, were dressed spectacularly. Her Queen's Guard had donned golden capes over their starlight silver armor, because gold was the color of her escort party. Her handmaidens wore gowns of gold in the spriten fashion, and Desaree wore one in the more popular fashion of Dragonwall.

"Frelikah javkain lerah ormahi, Ayas Drollaya," Selphie whispered, her eyes round, almost glazed. *Too beautiful for words, Your Majesty.*

"Shalaya," she managed, almost croaking.

Her hair was already piled into a beautiful mass atop her head, topped with a plain spriten tiara that Desaree had found within the queen's closet where the other jewels were kept. They'd brushed her cheeks with blush, lined her eyes with kohl. All that was left were her shoes, which she stepped into before they assembled.

Their little side conversations died down until silence fell. It was a heavy moment, no longer filled with excited chatter. A moment that would carve its own place in history. They all felt the immensity of it in their hearts.

She'd stayed up late into the night with her handmaidens, Desaree, Jocelyn, Saffra, and the rest of her queen's guard, including Feowen, holed up within the confines of her portion of the tower. She and Talon had not shared a bed. He'd informed her of the tradition, which aligned with one she was already familiar with. They'd kept vigil, staying up until nearly dawn, speaking in hushed whispers, sharing stories of love and adventure. It had been worth every minute, but she was eager to lay eyes on her mate, eager to get through this.

She didn't allow herself to think about the potential incoming attack.

"I'm ready," she said, squaring her shoulders. A messenger had already arrived letting them know the king was waiting. She was nearly trembling with nerves, hands clenched at her sides. "You have the stone?" she asked, looking at Desaree. Desaree nodded, showing her the cloth bundle in her hands.

The stone, one of black seledonix, was something she'd requested from the queen's treasury within the heart of Esterpine. Her handmaidens had given her the idea when they'd surprised her with a tiara made of the same stone. She'd sent a messenger to the forest after arriving in Kastali Dun, knowing that the ceremony would require a stone for Talon's sverak.

As a procession, they departed the king's tower. She took the lead walking alone, followed by her lady in waiting and handmaidens. Her queen's guard, decked out in their regalia, formed ranks around them.

Her feet were heavy but eager. Each step brought her closer to a change that was a long time in coming. *Did you ever think this would be my fate?* she couldn't help but ask, deep within her mind.

A draconic chuckle that belonged to Cyrus, responded. *I often wondered, but no. There was never this much certainty. I wish that I could claim credit. In truth, you have carved this path all on your own, through your bravery, determination, and resilience.* There was a hesitation and then, *I am so proud of the woman you have become, Claire. I saw it then, but even more now.*

An ache built in her throat. His words steeled her spine, keeping her upright, keeping her chin proud. *I don't think I could have done it without you,* she admitted.

You would have done just fine, Your Majesty.

The use of the title sent chills racing down her spine. She felt the confidence of his answer, wanted to argue with him about it, but decided to accept the praise he offered.

Thank you, she managed at last.

All too soon, she found herself descending into the lowest levels of the keep. It had been eerily empty up until now, and she saw why. The entire population of servants had lined the way leading to the throne room. They threw petals beneath her feet as she passed them. There were so many faces she recognized, people she had worked with after first coming here. She couldn't help but offer them small smiles, which they devoured wholeheartedly, grinning and nodding in return. Their expressions were open and eager.

Had Talon known all those months ago that forcing her into servitude would win them over? That she would make allies out of each and every one of them? She wasn't some far off queen, stepping in to rule them. She had *been* one of them, and that created a kinship that was more precious than gold.

She reached the doors, which were closed. A memory flashed before her vision, of a time that felt so long ago, when she'd faced these doors trembling with dread. She'd been so frightened then. It was Cyrus who'd given her the courage she needed.

She felt his chuckle again in the back of her mind, and despite his lack of words, she knew what he'd say. That it was never him. That she'd had that courage all along, deep inside of her, and had only needed a reminder of it.

Now she was facing the same king.

"Thevas amah mik nekahlla." *Gods give me strength,* she managed to utter. Her knees felt like jello. They all but collapsed facing the closed doors.

"Aya kunyn outah barihon, Ayas Drollaya." *You are our queen, Your Majesty.* It was Feowen's murmur, speaking for all of them. "Verah kunyn leh aya."

We are with you, they chanted, echoing his words.

"And I am with you," she repeated in the common tongue. She looked at the guards flanking the doors and said, "Let me though, I have a king to mate."

Someone huffed, but it was quickly swallowed up by the rapping of a spear against wood. The sound was loud and reverberated deep in her bones. The doors swung inwards, punctuating the silence as they slid over the floor. The throne room was revealed to her.

She sucked in a breath.

It had been *transformed.* Giant pots held massive trees and vines, turning it into a veritable forest. She shot a quick glance at the spriten prince who looked far too smug with himself. So, she hadn't been the *only* one planning surprises around this ceremony. Only a sprite could grow such a thing in the span of a day. Her queen's guard must have been busy last night, likely helped by Taylynn after she'd arrived.

"You did all of this for me? For us?" she whispered.

"We are with you," they echoed again, in the spriten tongue. She blinked back the blur of tears, lifting her chin an inch higher.

"Shalaya," she said, softly thanking them.

Taking a deep breath, she strode calmly into the room. People were packed into every available space, dressed in their finest attire. A quick glance brought surprise. They weren't *all* nobility. There were commoners, some so poor their nicest clothing was thread worn and tattered. Someone had granted even the lowest of birth access to witness this moment. Later, she would reflect on that and realize that Talon had taken her words to heart, that a person's birth and blood wasn't grounds for exclusion. But for now, she hardly noticed them; she was too distracted by something else.

Her eyes went directly to the dais, her breath hitching. Dressed entirely in black stood Dragonwall's king. His powerful figure swallowed the space around him. He stood proudly, one hand braced on his sverak, the other hanging calmly at his side. At this distance, his expression was unreadable. She couldn't make out the scars covering his face, but she could see them in her mind's eye, memorized as if they were her own.

For a moment, she couldn't breathe, *couldn't think*, as everything else faded away. Her vision tunneled. The sight of him swelled her chest, filling it with a heady mix of emotion. She wanted him, longed for him, loved him. She understood him better than anyone else in the world, a privilege so immense she was drunk on it.

For an instant, just a pinprick of time, she saw their entire lives flash before her eyes. Years upon years together, the adventures they'd have, the child they'd raise, the kingdom they'd rule. It nearly bowled her over. He was everything, and he was *hers*.

"*You look...*" Talon's voice set the present back in motion. "*Claire, you are so beautiful.*"

Swallowing, she forced her feet to move, each step easier than the last. Nearly a year ago, she would have done anything to flee in the opposite direction. Now, it was all she could do to keep from running straight for him, from throwing herself into his arms.

As she closed the distance, she finally noticed his shields

standing beside him for support, and Reyr, who stood several steps up on the dais to preside over their ceremony. She also noticed the whispers and gasps, words of awe that echoed in her wake as everyone present took in her dress. Her gaze stayed locked on Talon, on his face, until his scars were visible and his expression readable. He looked at her with parted lips and wide eyes. A look of utter adoration. His expression made her knees weak, but she kept her steps steady.

"Talon..." was all she could croak as she came to a stop facing him.

He wore a simple gold crown atop his head, the band had only a single point in the middle holding a black stone. His hair looked tamer than usual; she couldn't wait to run her fingers through it and mess it all up. The stray thought made her skin heat, but the sight of him set her on fire.

They both simply stood, gazing at each other, sparks crackling between them. Perhaps time stopped, or perhaps they managed to convey everything they felt for each other in an instant. A loud throat cleared. She finally managed to blink, pulling herself from Talon's spell. He seemed to do the same. His throat bobbed and he glanced towards Reyr.

"Let us begin," Reyr said, lifting his hands to quiet the audience.

Her pulse roared in her ears, filling the ensuing silence. Talon reached forward, taking her hands in his. Her eyes widened because—he was *trembling*. She looked him over, taking him in to see that he looked nervous, almost frightened, like he might be sick at any moment. He'd *never* looked quite like this.

"It's all right," she whispered for his ears only, giving his hands a gentle squeeze. He managed a tiny nod. His gaze stayed locked on hers, as if looking away for a mere second would be too much. He held her hands more tightly than usual, as if anchoring himself to her.

Her chest swelled. He was nervous, and it was the sweetest thing. She would be his strength, here and now, if he needed it. She would be whatever he needed, everything he needed and more.

I never thought I would have you, his gaze seemed to say. *I never believed you could be mine.*

But I am yours, was the answering look she gave him. *Only yours.*

His expression softened, some of the nervousness fleeing.

"People of Dragonwall," Reyr said, his voice ringing out over the throne room. "Today, you are witnessing a part of history that will be spoken of for thousands of years. The joining of two great races. There has only ever been one such event, and it too changed history. Nearly fifty thousand years ago, our first king and queen came together on this very dais to pledge their lives to one another, to declare their bond and live as mates. King Eymar and Queen Isabella united to form the monarchy that has seen our kingdom through many times. Times of prosperity, times of war, times of decline, and now...times of change."

Her breaths began to slow. Talon looked calmer, too. They continued to gaze at each other while Reyr spoke.

"Today we are here to witness the bonding ceremony of King Talon and Queen Claire, a ceremony that will unite both the drengr and spriten races. A bonding that will bring our kingdom closer together. A year ago, our king believed he would spend the rest of his days alone, mateless. Our queen believed she would only ever live a mundane life, never to know her true heritage and identity. So much can change in a single moment."

Talon squeezed her hands. She swallowed, trying to push back the lump rising in her throat.

"Fate, it seems, had other plans, bringing these two together under painful, but necessary circumstances. While their beginning might have been a little rocky—"

She blew out a breath, partly a nervous laugh. Talon's lips twitched, no doubt remembering exactly how rocky their initial meeting was.

"—but in the end, they ended up exactly where they were meant to be. In each other's hearts. Now, all that is left is to declare their love and speak the words that will bind them together."

Reyr hesitated and the crowd waited with bated breath. The

back of her neck prickled with nerves. She squeezed Talon's hands this time, to reassure herself that they really were standing here. That this was happening. That she wouldn't wake up back on earth, in her bedroom, to discover it was all just a dream.

"King Talon will now present his mate with her bow. Let her fly with him so that she may protect him in her own way."

Talon gave her hands a final squeeze, then dropped them, turning to Verath who handed over a bow she hadn't noticed until now. It was accompanied by a quiver, the arrows of which had black fletching to match his color. But it was the bow she couldn't pull her eyes from. Its recurved limbs were carved and decorated with intricate swirling patterns that reminded her of spriten weapons, of the bow Pelwyn had given her, inlaid with tiny black gems. Talon handed it to her and she took the cool wood, running her fingers over it before smiling up at him.

She saw every bit of love he felt for her echoed in his gaze.

Though she would be queen, this was a symbol of her status as his rider. An age-old tradition that every mated pair engaged in. She would fly with him into battle, and this bow would be her weapon, a symbolic way to protect him as they flew.

A throat cleared, reminding her of the words she was meant to speak. She licked her lips and said, "I thank you for such a fine gift and token of your love."

Talon's throat bobbed. He gave a tiny nod and stepped back into place.

"Queen Claire will now present her mate with a pommel stone, so that his sverak may be complete, so that he may protect her in his own way." She felt a nudge at her back. In her nerves, she'd forgotten to turn. Heat washed her face. She quickly turned to Desaree, who opened the cloth revealing the beautiful stone within.

She removed it and handed it to Talon. He hadn't seen it until now, but he seemed to know exactly how priceless it was. This wasn't like the common black stones that were often used in his crown or other adornments. This had come from the depths of the Gable Forest. It was rare and absolutely priceless. His lips parted as his eyes darted between her and the stone. He recovered and said, "I thank thee for such a fine gift and token of your love."

He removed his sverak, then handed both the weapon and gem to Reyr, who set the stone into the empty place muttering a word of magic, "Asamat," to fuse the stone into place. There came a bluish glow of magic, and then it was done. Reyr handed the sverak back to Talon, who hesitated, looking it over, then looked up at her. It was the same expression of disbelief he often gave when he was thinking that he couldn't believe he'd found her, that he wouldn't be mateless for the remainder of his life. She offered a gentle smile and a tiny nod. He replaced the sverak at his side.

"King Talon, Queen Claire, take each other's hands. It is time to recite the drengr-rider words we all know in the depths of our heart. However, I would like to do something a little differently this time."

Talon's head whipped towards Reyr, his brows drawn.

Reyr's lips twitched. "I would like our audience and all those witnessing this monumental moment to speak the words with you. Together, we will unite you in your bond."

For some reason, Claire's eyes caught on Taylynn's, who stood off to the side. It was then that she noticed Taylynn's look of surprise, and even intrigue, as she watched Reyr make this pronouncement. She looked back at Talon. His expression seemed to ask, *Are you ready?*

She nodded, then opened her mouth to speak. He joined her, and after a single word, so too did the voices of hundreds, wrapping around them, surrounding them, and somehow deepening the magic that flowed through the throne room that day.

Rejoice!
A bond is discovered—
A lifetime destined by fate.
A commitment unbreakable,
Until Daudagher takes us.
A tender comfort to ease the hardship,

The other's labor has brought.
A love that takes root,
Encouraged by caring hands and gentle kisses.
A promise is made;
A promise is sealed.
A single mind from two combined:
A drengr and his rider.

She felt the shiver that raced through her, and felt Talon's all the way through his hands. Their eyes widened on each other. Then they both smiled, sighing with relief.

"And so it is said, so it shall be," Reyr shouted, lifting his voice. Throughout the throne room, other voices echoed the same thing before turning into cheers and stomping feet. She blinked, then blinked again. A happy laugh burst from her chest. She was just about to turn towards their onlookers when Talon growled, "Isn't your custom to seal it with a kiss?" And before she could stop him, he pulled her into his arms and claimed her mouth with his. Her entire body homed in on the place their lips met, her blood surging. The cries of the audience grew frenzied, hooting and cat calling. When Talon pulled away, she could hardly breathe. His face was lit from within, all but glowing.

"Now," he said, keeping a hand braced against her back, "let's enjoy our celebration."

She could only look at him as he swept her away from the dais and down the central aisle, past the cheering crowd, and out the throne room doors.

CHAPTER 30

BONDING TOGETHER

Kastali Dun

Talon passed from one moment into the next as if in a fever dream. Perhaps he *was* dreaming. His queen in her gown, looking up at him with such love and adoration, filling his arms as they danced—it couldn't be real. Perhaps he was stuck in a cruel reality where everything he wanted was merely a figment of his imagination. Where any minute, he would wake to find his world empty. Lifeless. Cold.

Hadn't that been his reality before she'd come? A drab world where his days bled together, each as cruel and monotonous as the last? She'd broken that vicious cycle, sweeping in, bringing color and warmth. An explosive energy that transformed him. Even his mood swings had dwindled. Gone was his unpredictable temper and in its place, a measure of control he'd never known.

No, a measure of peace.

"I could dance with you all night," Claire breathed, her face close to his, eyes gazing deep into the depths of his soul. Her cheeks were flushed with exertion, her pulse jumping in her neck.

"Oh?" His chuckle was drowned out by the music and merriment surrounding them. "But then I'd never get to unwrap you from that pretty gown. Believe me, I'm already salivating over the taste of you."

"Is that what I am? A present?"

"A gift," he clarified. "One I intend to enjoy thoroughly, over and over." Her lips parted. He spun her in a circle, pulling her back to him, pulling her close and leaning in. Brushing his lips over the shell of her ear, he said, "I can't wait to hear all the delicious little sounds you'll make for me, *my queen.*"

She gasped against him, pulling back wearing a wicked grin. He swept her around again, in a quick motion that left her wide-eyed. The music slowed and came to a stop. Everyone clapped, some dispensing in search of refreshments, others reforming for the next dance.

Reyr appeared beside them, extending a hand. Talon turned and growled. "She's mine tonight."

Reyr barked a laugh and Claire watched the two of them with sparkling eyes. "Come now, Your Majesty. You won't even allow me a single dance?"

"No one touches her but me," he warned. Reyr's lips twitched with amusement. "Go tell her line of admirers to find other partners."

"Talon," Claire scolded. Another song was beginning. "It's only a dan—" Her words died in a squeal as he swept her back into his arms, all but dragging her into the next dance, a faster turn that didn't leave room for talking. She giggled breathlessly.

"*Everyone is going to talk about how stingy you are being,*" she pointed out. His stomach fluttered. He loved when she spoke mind to mind. He couldn't wait to share hers. He half wanted to throw her over his shoulder and carry her out. Or better yet, a darker part of him—the place his beast lived—was ready to strip her down here and now and claim her, audience be damned.

His skin turned molten. "*Gods above, woman. I'm on a short fuse.*"

"*Then why are we still dancing?!*" she demanded, stopping abruptly in the middle of the dance floor. He was forced to stop with her. Couples scattered around them. A mischievous gleam lit her eyes.

"Why indeed?" he said aloud, eyeing her, bracing himself for whatever trouble she was about to cause.

She spun towards the front of the hall and held up her hands, signaling to the minstrels. Their playing immediately ceased. Silence swept through the room like a wave, starting on the dance floor and moving out towards the perimeter where tables were occupied, laden with food and drink. She threw him a bold glare before addressing their audience. "It has come to my attention," she announced, "that my mate is rather impatient to get on with things, if you catch my meaning."

Rambunctious whoops broke the silence.

He swore under his breath, scrubbing a hand over his face, over the familiar scars. The crowd only had eyes for her. It was a beautiful thing, to bask in her shadow. After centuries of unwanted attention, she was taking it from him. And *gods above*, it was a relief. There were days he almost forgot what he looked like, days she *made* him forget, days he hated himself less.

"What do you think?" she cried. "Is it time to seal our bond? Should I put our king out of his misery?"

Her words were met with pounding feet and bawdy cries. He didn't see a single face in the giant hall—only hers—because he couldn't look anywhere *but* her. She smiled, eyes darting over her rapt audience. She was enjoying this—enjoying the attention. Gods, she was a natural.

He took a step towards her, as if pulled by an invisible force right into her orbit. "You vexing woman," he growled under his breath, only loud enough for her.

She spun to face him, her face bright and open. "There you have it, Talon, our subjects have spoken."

He reached for her. There was a brief flash of delighted surprise as he scooped her up, an arm going under her knees as the other wrapped around her shoulders. It was like lifting a giant, black cloud. Her gown puffed around them, making her almost impossible to carry. But he'd be damned if he let that stop him.

"Very well," he called to the crowd, lifting his chin. "I have a queen to bed."

Raucous cheers met his declaration, more bawdy innuendos, some of which he recognized from his own shields. Claire giggled, throwing her arms around his neck before she said against his ear, "Take me to bed, my fierce drengr king. I'm ready to forget my own name."

Liquid dragonfire exploded in his center. All that heat slid down and pooled in one place, making the seams of his pants feel far too tight. Thank the gods her gown hid him from view. He spared a final glance for his shields, their faces glowing with satisfaction—satisfaction for their king and queen—before he swept from the hall.

Claire nuzzled against his neck laying kisses along his skin, kisses that drove him wild with need. "I feel like a treasure you've just discovered in the wilds. Now you're taking me back to your secret trove to do debauched, naughty things to me. You are, aren't you? Going to do naughty things to me?" He growled, growing harder by the moment. Civilized thoughts morphed into beastly incoherence. Something deep inside him, an instinct as old as an age, opened its maw, breathing flame and bathing him in it.

"Vexing woman," he muttered again, completely lost in her.

He could barely put one foot in front of the other, so close to taking his queen right here in the corridor. She deserved better—at least for their first time. He couldn't promise anything for their future, couldn't promise to suppress his urges regardless of their whereabouts. But for now, he carried her to their tower.

It was empty, the guards and staff long gone. He wouldn't stand for eavesdroppers tonight. He wanted every bit of her to himself—wouldn't share the sounds she made with anyone else.

Greedy. He was so godsdamned greedy.

He exhaled his relief when they were safely tucked within his tower, when he set her on her feet and stepped back to look upon her. As it had that first moment, the sight of her nearly knocked him off his feet. A heavy silence descended, amplifying the severity of the moment. All their teasing and joking faded away, peeled back like fruit rinds to reveal the delicacy within. He paced around her, his muscles straining beneath his clothing.

His restraint was close, *so close* to snapping, but he wouldn't give in. Not yet. He would take his time to savor her.

"Talon," she whispered. A question.

"I'm going to peel you out of that dress," he managed, keeping his voice low, circling her like a caged beast with dripping fangs. "I'm going to peel you out of it, then lick every measure of your skin until you're covered in my scent. I'm going to taste you, devour you, claim you, and I will not hold back." It was a warning. She needed to know what would happen. A shiver raced through her, a subtle tremble, until her hands balled into fists. "Tell me now, one final time, Claire. Is this what you want? Am *I* what you want?"

Gods, please don't let her change her mind, he couldn't help but beg. Once they did this, there was no going back. Every day of his existence had brought him to this moment right here.

He stopped in front of her, in time to see her chin rise. "I have never wanted anything so badly in all my life." Those words made his knees weak. He braced his legs, tightening his muscles to keep from falling at her feet. But...hadn't he already fallen at her feet in more ways than one?

He looked down at her gown, at the fire-breathing dragon that was his symbol. Everything she wore was a message of who and what she was to him. Did she realize how bold those unspoken words were? The declaration she made?

Suddenly, he needed to know—was desperate to know—what she thought of it.

"Before I rip it off, tell me about your gown," he managed, his voice rough. He reached forward and trailed his fingers over the dragon's head, over the beaded scales.

She hesitated, then said, "The cape symbolizes what I am, my bloodline, both sprite and drengr. The abundance of markings down the back symbolizes my power, the magic I have conquered. The scales—*your* scales—encasing my neck are to protect my throat as you will always protect me when I have need of it."

His chest exploded with love. He didn't miss her wording. *When I have need of it.* Because she had proven time and again that she could take care of herself. She didn't need a cage. She needed his support. She needed him when she needed him, and didn't need him when she could manage on her own.

He wanted to see her spread her wings and fly. He would never keep them pinned. Never hamper the glow with which she was meant to shine.

"The gown symbolizes you. Your fire, your flame, transforming me into your queen. Dragonfire hot enough to melt away everything I was before, so that I may rise from the ashes more powerful than ever. The color black, obviously, because it is tradition to match your scales." She pulled her bottom lip between her teeth, thoughtful.

"And the dragon scale cuffs on your wrists?" He'd never seen such a thing worn. But he knew they weren't meaningless pieces of jewelry.

She lifted her wrists, rotating them as her eyes traced the wide cuffs encasing her delicate bones. Then she froze and looked up at him. "I do not belong to myself anymore, but to you and to my people—our people. These symbolize my submission—" Her throat bobbed. "My submission to *you*, Talon."

Pride, hot and fierce, blew through him.

"Claire..." he breathed, sinking to his knees before her. He had never kneeled for anyone, never planned to, but here he was doing exactly that. For this woman, and this woman alone. "It is *I* who submit to *you*, my queen. I never wish for you to feel anything less than my equal. In all matters of ruling, in all matters of matehood, you are mine to stand beside me, and I am yours. You do not submit to me." Her eyes widened slightly, darting between his. Had she truly believed she would be inferior to him? That she would sit in his shadow, bend to him when he required it? That he would *allow* her to?

"I will never force your submission." A small smile tugged at his lips. "Except in the bedroom, in which case, I expect you fully at my mercy."

She sucked in a breath, then reached out and removed his crown. There was fire in her eyes, as she tossed it away. He listened to it thud on the rug. She ran her fingers through his hair, messing it up. Then her hand became a fist, clenching his locks, sending a small measure of pain shooting over his scalp—delicious pain that made him shiver with draconic delight. She moved his head, to angle his face upwards so that she could look upon him.

He'd never felt so vulnerable on his knees, his facial scars on full display to a woman who looked like a goddess. A woman who had the power to lift him up or break him. Perhaps both. She could shatter him into a thousand pieces and he'd let her. There was something so freeing, putting himself at her mercy.

Hot coals stoked between them.

Her fingers relaxed, then fell away. "Rise, my king." Her mouth smugly twitched. "For if we are equals, then the only time I want you on your knees is when you're between my legs."

He blinked, momentarily stunned, then stood and leaned in close. "I will gladly worship on my knees whenever my queen desires."

The green of her irises were swallowed up by her pupils, blowing wide. His throat bobbed, thickening until it was almost impossible to swallow. He lifted a hand, hesitant at first, to unclasp the collar about her neck. His fingers trembled as he undid the fastening and watched the cape fall away. Her neck was bared to him, her shoulders exposed. He exhaled, his breath rough. She watched him, those green eyes all but making him squirm with nerves and a desperate need to bury himself inside her, to crawl into her skin and make a home within the temple of her body. He was ready to rip out his own heart, to hand it over, to bury it in her chest beside her own.

She held perfectly still as his fingers traced down the front of her shoulder, to her heaving chest. "So soft," he murmured, eyes darting between his fingers and her face.

"That's not the only place I'm soft."

He groaned because he *knew*. So he leaned in and tasted the divot at the base of her neck, then flattened his tongue and licked up the column of her throat. A tiny gasp escaped her lips, followed by a flush that crept over her skin in wake of the trail he made. He hadn't been lying when he said he wanted to lick every measure of her.

She lifted her chin, better exposing herself. If only she knew how that gesture unhinged him. Letting his teeth elongate, only his teeth, keeping the rest of his dragon suppressed, he opened his mouth and bracketed her throat in his jaws. Gentle, so, so gentle. For an enemy, all he need do was bite down and he'd rip out their entire throat. The points of his sharpened teeth pressed into her delicate skin. A soft moan fell from her lips. He pressed harder, but not hard enough to break the skin, only hard enough to show her who he'd be in their bed—*what* he would be.

Her knees buckled. He wrapped his arms around her, holding her to him, keeping her upright. Gods, she was so perfect against him. Even in her gown, she fit his every curve, soft against his hard body.

His teeth shrank and he pulled his mouth away to find her panting and flushed.

He helped her find her feet, then walked around behind her and began slowly, *achingly slowly*, unfastening each button along her back. More and more of her skin revealed itself. Beautiful swirls of spriten luminescence. "I want to trace every one of these with my tongue," he murmured, then leaned in and followed the pattern of a particularly beautiful marking. She shivered beneath the touch of his mouth.

After the last button, her gown slipped to the ground in a heap. She stood in the center of it, entirely naked. He'd seen her body many times before but he would never get enough. The sight of her smooth skin, now lined with glowing marks, was a beautiful work of art.

His eyes dipped to her bare breasts, then lower, taking in the sight of her womanhood. His pants grew unbearably tight, painfully so. When his gaze lifted, a knowing gleam lit her eyes. She slipped her hand into his, so much smaller, and stepped forward over the heap of fabric. He couldn't wait another moment to feel her against him, to taste her. When he kissed her, he lifted her, pressing their bodies together, only to growl at the barrier between them, at his clothing that separated them.

"I get to undress *you* now," she murmured against his lips, pulling away from his mouth as he set her down. "Hold still."

He huffed, but complied.

She reached for his belt first. It had been ceremonial. He'd forgone his bandolier and daggers for today's occasion. She let the leather and sheathed sverak drop to the floor. His breathing grew heavier, made all the worse by the sight of her body. She dropped to her knees and fussed with his boots. He managed to keep his balance as he lifted each foot, allowing her to slip one off, then the other.

The sight of her there on her knees...

"I have made a grave error," he rasped. She came to her feet.

"Oh?" She arched a perfect eyebrow, mischief dancing in her gaze. She reached for his tunic next, loosening the ties down the sides, then taking the hem. His arms lifted and she slipped the silken brocade fabric over his head.

"I should have addressed my attire *first*, before undressing you."

She pouted, reaching for the ties of his pants, then hesitating. "*Poor beast*. Now you must wait while I parade around naked. It must be absolute torture." She began slowly untying his pants; he was forced to suppress a groan. "Don't you like the sight of me?" She pressed her biceps inward against her breasts, making them perk up while keeping her fingers in motion. He all but lost it.

"Gods above." He couldn't stop staring. He nearly bent forward and took a dusty rose colored nipple between his lips. Already, his mouth was salivating.

She pulled his pants open and he could have wept with relief as he sprang free. He lifted his hands to hasten the process, to remove the damned pants. She froze, then tsked. "Ah, ah, ah, my king. It is only fair that I do this for you. Now, hold still."

His warning growl was enough to scare away even the bravest. She merely paid him a scolding glare. "You really think that will work on me?"

"Careful, my queen."

"Or *what*?" She slid his pants down, and he felt the brush of fabric over his skin, making every nerve ending in his body come alive. She crouched so that he could step free, then stood.

"Or *this*." He lunged, scooping her up by her full hips, forcing her legs to circle his waist. The feel of her wrapped around him, their hips nestled together, cemented itself in his memory forever. He was across the room, her back pressed against the wall before she could suck in a full breath. He took her delicate wrists and pinned her arms above her head. Her back arched into him, nipples rubbing against his chest.

Divine—it felt so godsdamned devine, the friction of her skin against his.

He groaned, looking at the sight of her, at the way she responded to him. He couldn't help but lean back, keeping her hips firmly pinned, to see where their bodies met, to see the length of him pressed between their bodies.

Her breathy laugh tightened every muscle in him. "Am I your prisoner, Talon?"

He expelled a ragged breath. "You are mine—is what you are. At my mercy, to do with as I please."

She rocked her hips, the friction sending shivers shooting down his legs. The movement was a taunt to end all taunts, effectively silencing their words. The heat of her core against him snapped his lingering restraint. His carefully laid plans fractured and scattered, leaving behind single-minded need. There would be no more gentle caresses.

He claimed her mouth, sliding his tongue between the seam of her lips, probing her with the same rhythm now taken up by his hips, by the relentless rocking he needed to create such delicious friction between them. She met his movements, squirming against him. He found her jaw, laying kisses along it until he reached her ear. He traced the lobe of it with his tongue, listened to the little mewing sounds she made as he ground against her.

"Talon, please," she whimpered as he nipped the tip of her earlobe. Her plea was a drug, one he was desperate for. He felt her words all the way to his center. The way his name rolled off her tongue made his abdomen tighten.

He dropped her wrists and gripped her hips, wrapping his fingers beneath her. "If I were a gentleman, I would lay you across the bed and bury my face between your thighs. I'd take my time, finishing you on my tongue first before—"

"But you're not a gentleman!" she cried, impatience riding her voice. "You're a beast. Start acting like one. Don't make me wait a moment longer."

He snarled, unhinged.

She reached between them. He gave her the space, holding tight to her hips. Her fingers wrapped around him, and *gods*, the feel of her warm palm on him drove him into a frenzy. Scales began rippling along his skin, desperate to break free, the thing within him writhing like a caged beast. A cry escaped his lips, betraying his delight. He forced his dragon into submission.

She guided the hardness of him against her, placing him at her entrance, then she wrapped her hands around his neck. His body acted on instinct. Locking his gaze with hers, he offered up a silent question. She gave a brief, desperate nod, her eyes glazed over with lust. It was all he could give, that single, brief question, before he was sinking into her, sinking into oblivion. His hips rolled, the movements gentle at first, working himself in, little by little, until he was entirely sheathed. Then he froze—they froze, staring at one another.

For the span of a single breath, every thought in his mind wiped clean. He wasn't a king. He wasn't a drengr. He certainly wasn't a scarred, broken creature. He was only this, flesh and blood, desire and yearning, hunger and need. And *she* was the only thing that would save him.

His thoughts returned, and with them, the desperate need to move. He rocked his hips, claiming her, letting the sounds from her lips guide him. Her chest heaved against him, her hips meeting his, matching him stroke for stroke.

"You are so very precious to me," he breathed, all but trembling inside her. "There is nothing I wouldn't do for you."

"Talon," she begged, desperation edging her voice. "More. I need...*more!*"

He huffed, abandoning the tethers between them, setting a relentless pace until their voices and breaths mingled. Until he wasn't sure where he ended and she began. Her body tightened around him, the blunt ends of her nails digging into his shoulders. His own fingers pressed into her soft hips, as if he could hold on to her very soul within the grasp of his hands.

Everything in him tightened, coiled and ready to spring. He caught her mouth again, teeth and tongues clashing. He wasn't gentle.

Light, beautiful light, filled his vision. Her markings glowed until she shone like a star. She brightened as his body slipped into that place on the brink—at the edge of pleasure and pain. "You're perfect, Talon," she breathed. "Exactly as you are. *You're perfect.*"

Shivers raced over his skin.

He hadn't realized how badly he needed to hear those words. Release blasted through him, and then through her as she clenched herself around him. Her light exploded, blinding him as he uttered her name, crying out as if she were the only divinity he would ever need.

His mind expanded, swelling. A sudden barrage of heightened emotions slammed against his thoughts, almost sweeping him off his feet. He tightened his hold on her and slowed his movements, claiming every last bit of pleasure, riding it out, giving her exactly what she needed. They came down together, breaths labored, eyes locked, thoughts flowing freely between them.

The sight of her undone before him would haunt him for the rest of his days. Her eyes widened. She sucked in a breath that made him twitch inside her. He groaned, still overly sensitive to her every touch. "You...we...it *worked!*" Her elated words mingled with her thoughts—thoughts that now belonged to *him*.

"Of course it worked, *mih cralla.*"

"My heart," she translated. A soft, tender smile spread across her lips, cracking his chest wide open. "We can converse in *Ednuar* now."

"We can."

"Good. That's...good." He heard her relief—felt it, too. "We are one now," she said. "Never again will you walk this world alone. I will walk it beside you, and cherish every moment for the rest of our lives."

Her declaration made his throat ache. He swallowed. This woman was his undoing.

He shifted, sliding free of her, but only so long as it took him to carry her to their bed. "You will never be rid of me now, *mih barihon*. Rihal." *Never.*

Her only answer was a happy sigh as he surged over her, ravaging her with his mouth and teeth, until she was squirming beneath him with need. They sank into each other over and over, just as he'd promised. Until every need was known and realized and every moment was joined with both mind and body. Forevermore.

CHAPTER 31

REACHING THE CAPITAL

Kastali Dun

Bennett watched the familiar sight materialize in the darkness. A city glowing with light, a fortress jutting up towards the sky at the top of a hill. Kastali Dun. They'd made excellent time, due in part to his careful plotting. He'd consulted multiple charts to ensure they took the fastest route.

But it was Cat who'd made the difference.

She had surprised him, using some of her magic to create a fake wind that filled their sails and propelled them forward. It drained her often, and yet, each time she rested she insisted on starting all over again. When they'd set out from Oshea, it had been with a two day lead. Cat's magic had gained them an additional two days, perhaps more. Dragonwall would need every extra moment to prepare.

"Make ready to drop anchor!" Jonah shouted as the crew prepared for their entry into the bay.

He glanced at the woman standing beside him and did a double take. He still wasn't used to her shorn hair, but he had to admit she looked even more beautiful, with her accentuated cheekbones and strong jaw, and her long, feminine neck.

"You're sure you do not wish to join me?" He tried to make it sound like a taunt, but it came out as a soft question. That was happening more and more around her. The taunting jibes they used to share had all but disappeared. She spoke to him in hushed tones, and the fire that had once crackled in her gaze had been replaced with something softer but no less potent.

Truthfully, he didn't know what to make of it. Too often, it got his thoughts into trouble.

"I do not wish to leave this ship, as I already said."

"Very well. Did you have anything else you wanted to add to your list?" he asked, eyes roving her side profile.

"No. It's all there."

She'd drafted a list of items, mostly for her magery. Things she needed to concoct brews for the crew. He'd gone through the list, estimated the cost of everything, and noticed that she hadn't been extravagant or overly needless with any of the items.

Lady Faith came to a standstill as the anchor did its job. There wasn't a moment to spare as the rowboat was readied. He took a small group, including Jonah, who would meet with the dock master and provide the needed paperwork to allow them to remain anchored within the bay.

He bid goodbye to Cat, taking in her features in the darkness a final time before stepping into the boat. When they reached the docks, he was met with the familiar sounds of a night in full swing. Taverns glowed, music spilling from open doors. Revelers staggered up and down the street, some carrying tankards that sloshed onto the dirt road, others with arms around women earning their evening pay.

They split up, and he began the trek to the keep. "Seems a bit... off tonight, don't you think?" he mused, glancing about. Tris and Emmon merely grunted, too busy looking at the people they passed on the streets. He tried to catch snatches of conversation, most of which centered around the keep.

"Something's happening up at the king's castle," Tris finally said.

"Well, we'd better hope whatever it is doesn't cause us any issues," he grumbled.

It was a twenty minute walk through the city, taking the fastest route. His legs were barking by the time they reached the gates. Everything glowed bright with torches, people coming and going from beneath the main gates. Guards watched, arms crossed, eyeing everyone that passed.

"Them gates supposed to be thrown wide open like that?" Emmon asked.

"Must be a party," Tris added.

"You there!" A guard reached out and grabbed his arm. He wore armor like all the rest, but had a large black mustache. "What business have you?"

"Looks like a party tonight. Thought we'd join."

"Don't look dressed for a party." Mustache drawled. "Were you one of the invited guests?"

"No, we have other business, actually. We're here to speak with the king."

One of the guards beside Mustache let out a bark of laughter. "Ain't no one speaking with the king tonight."

"Then I'll speak with one of his shields. It's imperative." He considered telling them why, but realized it would be prudent to break the news to the king's shields first before inciting any sort of panic among the general populace.

"Please, I am captain of the *Lady Faith*, and we've just made a voyage at the greatest haste from Oshea on Lord Bedelth's orders. It is imperative that I speak with Lord Bedelth, or any of the shields. I'll pay you handsomely if you escort me." He pulled a gold dragon from his pocket.

Mustache's eyes widened. "Fine. I'll escort you inside—just you, not your friends. I can't promise any of the shields will agree to talk to you. I'll take that dragon now, for my efforts." Mustache reached out and plucked the coin from Bennett's fingers.

"Thank you. Tris, Emmon, wait for me here." Mustache led him through the partygoers, carving a path forward. "What's going on here, anyway?"

"You really don't know?" the guard harrumphed.

"Been at sea."

"King's bonding ceremony."

"Tonight?" He was taken aback.

"Obviously," Mustache drawled, taking them down a corridor and into a beautiful entry hall that spilled them into a massive dining hall. He glanced around, briefly forgetting why he was here. It was staggering. Music played, couples danced, party goers gorged themselves on food.

Mustache pushed through the crowd towards the front of the room, then came to a stop and said, "Forgive me for the intrusion, but this...sailor—"

"Captain," he corrected.

"—said it was imperative he speak with one of you."

He stepped around Mustache to get a better view. Three large drengr lounged in chairs. He recognized the golden haired one— remembered meeting with his twin brother many months ago. "Lord Reyr, I must speak with you immediately."

Reyr's eyes narrowed. "Captain Bennett?"

"Aye."

Reyr must have read something in his face because his eyes darted towards the other shields, giving them a brief nod before he stood. "Very well, follow me."

The guard almost looked surprised. But at last, he gave a small bow and departed. Reyr was silent, tense, as he led him and the other two through a small side door that brought them into a narrow corridor. From there he ushered Bennett into a sitting room.

"Please, have a seat. The others will be here momentarily."

Bennett glanced at the fine furniture, guessing the castle probably had many rooms like this, meant for entertaining small parties. He found a seat, then rubbed his hands on his pants. Compared to what the others wore, he felt positively unfit for their company. He should have bathed before coming here.

The door opened and closed several more times until others filled the room. He took in their faces. "Captain Bennett," Bedelth said, striding over and extending his arm. Bennett stood to greet him. "I didn't expect to see you back in the capital so quickly. But I can only guess whatever news you carry isn't good to bring you back so soon."

He grasped the shield's forearm and managed a nod. Seats were taken, and silence fell, every expectant face turned towards him. "Who are they?" He indicated the women in attendance. His eyes snagged on one, whose particular beauty almost made him too nervous to speak. Her knowing eyes left him squirming, never mind her bone white hair and delicate face. She was a forest sprite. He hadn't realized they existed—thought them a thing of stories.

"Our confidantes," Bedelth answered, his eyes darting towards a female of darker skin. She sat proud, back straight with her hands in her lap, wearing an unreadable expression.

Did any of them know Cat? Had any of them played a role in sentencing her? How would they react if they knew she was on his ship? If they knew she'd helped him get this information, and what she'd sacrificed for it?

He pushed her from his thoughts and cleared his throat. "All right. Well, there's no real way to say this delicately, milords..." He pulled at a stray thread on the cuff of his coat. They waited, the silence almost too much. "I took my ship to Oshea just as you asked, Lord Bedelth. Did some investigating at the port. You see, you were definitely right about the whispers. When we arrived, there was already a navy mustered and ready to set sail for Dragonwall."

A breath hissed. Feminine. From one of the ladies present.

He launched into a detailed explanation, telling them exactly what they'd discovered, how many ships, the number of soldiers on those ships, and the bats they carried. He expected shock at the revelation. Instead, they simply shared knowing looks, many of them turning towards the darker skinned lady beside Bedelth.

"None of this is new to you?" His brow furrowed.

"Some of it, but not everything," Bedelth admitted. "Our seer," he motioned towards the woman at his side, "saw a battle with bats. We simply didn't know when such a thing would occur."

"Well, I hope you're ready for it now, because the Oshean navy will be here in a matter of days." His words were met with absolute silence. "You *did* hear me, aye?"

Bedelth exhaled. "We should tell the king," he managed, looking at Lord Reyr.

"Over my dead body," Reyr growled. "Unless that army is battering down our gates at this very moment, I will let nothing, and I mean nothing, disturb him this night. He and Claire deserve this—this one night for themselves."

The others in the little parlor nodded, looking almost relieved.

"A single night for our king isn't going to make a difference," Lord Reyr continued. "In fact, it's better that he does not know yet. He'll need this night of peace before chaos breaks loose."

"There's plenty we can do in the meantime," one of the shields said.

"We should document as many details as Captain Bennett remembers, then send him on his way." Bedelth looked at him. "You are surely tired from your journey?"

"Aye, very. I came straight here as soon as we dropped anchor. But I am happy to help."

For the sake of thoroughness, they left the parlor and moved through the castle. The sounds of revelry died down the farther up they climbed, until he found himself led down a beautiful carpeted hallway filled with paintings of drengr kings and their queens. "The *Hall of Kings*," said a woman's musical voice beside him. He glanced down and tensed. How in the name of the gods had she snuck up on him? "I am Princess Taylynn."

His steps faltered. "A...a princess?"

"Why, yes. Of the sprites."

"You really are... You... You're...?"

"A sprite, yes." The grin she gave him set the hairs on the back of his neck on end. They had fallen back to the tail of the group. Everyone filed through a door, but she placed a hand on his arm and held him in place. In a single blink, they were alone. "A woman travels with you, yes?" His muscles tensed. Cat—she was referring to Cat. His hackles raised. "The others do not know. They have not seen it. Keep her with you. She still has a role to play in all of this."

His brow furrowed. "Ain't never met a sprite. They all this cryptic?"

A surprised laugh broke the tension. "I like you, Captain Bennett. It's refreshing to find another who doesn't walk on eggshells around me."

"Oh, I can assure you, I'm crunching all over 'em."

She only grinned and said, "Come, I am sure there is much more to be discussed."

IT WAS NEARING DAWN when Bennett's feet found relief on the deck of his ship. *Lady Faith* rocked in the current as it ebbed and flowed past her hull. It was a mercy to be away from the noise of the city, the almost irritating merriment of celebration. He usually enjoyed his time on land, but this was a little too much.

That's the argument he made, anyway. Deep down, he knew what had pulled him back. Why he was here and not in one of the taverns searching for a wench. In fact, he couldn't remember the last time he'd sought one. Certainly not since Cat had come aboard.

The deck was quiet, but it wasn't empty. The crew on night shift milled about, keeping to their tasks.

"You're back?"

He whirled toward the voice, only relaxing once he had cataloged Cat from head to toe. As if anything might have befallen her while on board. "No trouble while I was away?" he asked. "No one came aboard?"

She lifted a brow, staring at him. "Afraid someone might learn that I'm here? Whisk me off to a trial long overdue? Slit my pretty throat for my crimes? I would deserve it, you know. As I've told you before."

He closed the distance between them until the tips of his boots touched hers. Looking down at her, he said with a quiet voice that surprised him, "Do not speak like that."

She frowned. He took her chin in his fingers, tilting her face up so that he could see the pull of her lips in better light. Her eyes betrayed her, falling to his mouth, lingering for a moment. Something swelled in his chest—satisfaction.

"I was successful, by the way. Thanks for asking."

She reared back, staggering as the spell that wrapped around them shattered. She blinked. "You... You spoke to the king?"

"No, actually. His shields. King was tied up, matter of fact."

"Tied up?"

His lips twitched at the pun. "Yes, bonding ceremony. He was too busy bedding his mate to meet with me."

She made a choking sound. Her hand went to her neck, rubbing the muscles there. Was she thinking of how close she'd come to losing her head? A sudden stab of fear mixed with anger turned his flesh hot. Once more, he closed the distance between them. "No one will touch you," he growled, looking at the emotions that flowed across her face.

"I..." She scoffed. "I thought I'd marry him one day."

"I know." And then, because he couldn't stand to see this side of her, he said, "Aren't you glad you ended up with me instead?"

It was meant as a joke—to pull her out of her mood.

It had the opposite effect he'd expected.

She lifted her chin, holding his gaze. "Yes, actually. I am. For the first time in my life, I feel meaningful. Everything I do is because I want to, to serve a purpose that isn't my own. Or, maybe it is a little selfish to want to feel useful. But it's also fulfilling, to carve my own path. To earn merit for what I do, rather than my name. To start fresh."

His eyes locked on her mouth. Gods above. He needed to leave this deck—now. He needed to get as far away from her as possible. If he didn't—

"Aren't you going to kiss me?" she breathed.

The string of curses that fell from his lips made her smirk. His heart accelerated, jumping forward like a ship whose sails caught a gale. He lifted a hand, taking hold of the back of her neck, pulling her against him, then dipped his head and brushed his lips over hers. A little gasp broke the silence between them. He moved slowly, chastely, sucking her bottom lip and then her top between his own. Tasting them—tasting *her*.

What felt like hot lead dropped into his belly, bottoming out. Gods, he could taste her forever and never grow tired of it. In fact, he wanted to, but thought better of it. This wasn't like his other conquests; she was part of his crew.

She was part of his crew!

Alarm bells started ringing. He pulled back slightly. "Cat..."

"Don't you dare," she hissed, as if sensing his withdrawal.

"If we do this, if it goes wrong—"

"Then we handle it like the mature adults that we are. Besides I hate you, remember? So I can hate you now, and enjoy you while I do. And if things go wrong, I'll still hate you. Nothing to lose," she managed, saying all this with her lips still grazing his. Every point of friction had heat dropping pooling low.

"You don't hate me."

"No? Are you sure? Because I would very much like you to take me below deck, to that godsdamned window cabin you're always boasting about, so that I can show you just how much."

"Gods, woman, but you light me on fire."

"I certainly hope not. I'd hate to see your precious ship burn," she cooed.

"Won't be the ship that's burning," he muttered before tightening his grip and kissing her again.

He was only vaguely aware that the rest of the crew on duty had stopped moving. He could feel their eyes upon him. He didn't give a single damn. He felt a lot of things at that moment. Lust, namely, and relief that Cat was allowing him to touch her like this. He also felt something deeper that scared the salt out of him, something he was in no place to acknowledge—at least, not tonight. But he also felt a little pride, knowing he was the only one on this ship holding her body against him.

"So?" Cat pulled away, running her hands over his chest,

looking at the way his muscles twitched beneath her touch, as if she was only noticing his build for the first time. Suddenly he wanted to rip his shirt off like a barbarian and show her exactly what he was made of—salt and storm and rugged waves.

"Let's go," he growled, already feeling the strain of his pants. Taking her hand, he ignored the expressions on his crew. Some gaped with surprise, others snickered with smug knowing—as if they'd been waiting for this to happen. He didn't care what they thought.

The only thing he cared about was getting this woman in his arms, in the quiet of his cabin, and forgetting the rest of the world while they still had the chance. He'd done what he'd set out to do—he'd warned the king of the impending attack. Now he'd take what remained of this night for himself, for Cat, and he'd do it knowing the king wasn't the only one, up in his fancy castle, enjoying the lips of a coveted woman.

CHAPTER 32

THE MORNING AFTER

Kastali Dun

Claire settled deeper against the warmth at her back. Her limbs felt heavy, muscles tight. She was thoroughly sated, well used, satisfied beyond her wildest imaginings in a way she'd never felt before. A low, drowsy grumble vibrated against her ribcage making her blink. Her gaze blurred then came into focus as events of the previous night came rushing back, accompanied by a deep sense of satisfaction that...*wasn't hers*? Well, yes, *she* was satisfied. But this? This was pure *male* satisfaction—male pride. It was entirely Talon's.

A small grin spread across her lips. She could tell exactly how he felt. Nothing made her more smug.

"You're smirking," the male in question rasped against her ear, nuzzling the sensitive flesh behind her lobe.

"So what if I am?" she managed, a breathless whisper.

Talon's arm tightened around her waist, his mind flooding hers with intention. All sorts of lurid thoughts of what he wanted to do to her, exactly how he wanted to do it. It left her speechless. Her belly heated, liquifying into molten lava. Talon wasn't merely a skilled lover, he was an exceptional one. She once worried that his

327

abundance of experience with women—though long ago—would bother her. She hadn't exactly come to him a virgin, either. Instead, she realized that it was all to her benefit. Knowing that he was capable of pleasing her beyond her wildest dreams was utterly reassuring.

He'd proven it, over and over.

"I'd be happy to prove it again," he murmured, placing open-mouthed kisses along her shoulder, up the back of her neck. Goosebumps spread across her skin as an ache formed between her legs.

He knew exactly what she was thinking and vice versa; their minds were melded. It had happened the moment their bond sealed. Her entire body had shattered apart in a single breath, and when she'd pieced herself back together, it was to find his presence there. She'd been glowing, her spriten markings casting a brilliant light around them—a physical response to what she'd felt.

Talon liked that very much. He had made a game of it the rest of the night, getting her markings to flare every time he made love to her. Smugly satisfied when they did. Hence, his male pride.

"I'll show you male pride," he rasped, pressing himself against her backside, letting her know exactly how ready he was.

His hand splayed over her bare stomach before caressing her naked skin, sinking lower, going in the direction she needed him. A shiver raced over her in anticipation. Yes—she wanted him again, so badly she *ached*. His breath was hot against her ear as he said, "Waking up next to you is my new favorite thing—"

"Forgive me, Your Majesty."

She yelped. Talon cursed. For a moment, she just blinked with surprise, then realization dawned.

She had intentionally kept her mind closed, but here with Talon's mind linked to hers, there was no avoiding when someone chose to speak with him. This time, that someone was Reyr. And right now, she was all but ready to skewer him for the interruption.

"I really didn't want to interrupt your morning—pleasant as I am sure it must be." There was a sense of smugness to Reyr's words that made her roll her eyes.

"I am enjoying my mate, Reyr, as you well know. Whatever it is can wait."

"Actually, it cannot—"

A barrage of images and emotions flooded Talon's mind. She gasped, as if caught in a whirlpool, spinning and spinning, with nothing to grasp on to. Her heart began to race. Only seconds passed, but in those seconds, she and Talon fully understood why Reyr had interrupted them.

A sense of dread settled into the pit of her stomach, destroying any arousal she had felt. With that dread came all the other things she hated. Fear, worry, and the sense that what was happening was more than she could handle. More than she was ready to handle.

"We refused to disturb you last night," Reyr said, unaware of the growing turmoil within her mind, even if Talon wasn't. *"But, this cannot wait any longer."*

"No, it cannot," Talon said, finding and holding her gaze, an apology written deep in his eyes. Last night had been perfect, and she'd never wanted it to end, but it must. Sooner than she would have liked. Duty was duty, and she had better get used to it. That didn't mean she had to like it.

"Godsdamn it," she hissed, staring at Talon for a single long moment that stretched. Then they simultaneously scrambled into action, emerging from their bed. Later, she'd register the state of it, ripped sheets, pillows flung all over the floor, the comforter hanging off the foot. For now, she raced into Talon's bathing chamber, hot on his heels, and submerged herself in his bath—they both needed it after last night.

They efficiently set about their morning ablutions. Talon's mind was chaotic, frenzied even, as Reyr continued to batter him with details. She followed along but stayed quiet, absorbing everything until her stomach ached with anxiety. When she emerged from the bathing chamber, she found a discarded sheet, still whole enough to cover herself, took in the mess, kissed Talon on the cheek, then padded from their bed chamber to her queen's quarters.

Like soldiers at the ready, her handmaidens were waiting for her.

In the back of her mind, she was aware of Talon as he doled out telepathic orders. He wanted everyone to meet in his war room as soon as possible. It was strange, so very strange, to be in his head listening to him give commands. She hardly spared a shred of awareness for Miera and Selphie as they dressed her. Desaree had spent the night with Verath and would be along shortly.

They each felt the impending danger and remained quiet. She was too worried to be angry, even knowing it wasn't supposed to be this way. She should have been wrapped up in Talon's sheets, or getting peppered with questions from her handmaidens about last night. Gossiping. Blushing. Whispering. Instead, they were stuck in their own heads, going through the motions.

Completely numb with shock.

It was a testament to their years and years of experience that her spriten handmaidens knew exactly what to dress her in. This gown was a deep midnight blue and free of adornments. An impending battle created an atmosphere of seriousness and they'd dressed her to look serious.

"Come, we must gather in the war room," she said when they'd finished. Her voice was low, as if speaking too loud would hasten the army sooner to their doorstep. They looked surprised, but didn't question her.

When they climbed the stairs and crossed the main tower room, there was already a bustle of activity. Everyone had been permitted to reenter the tower after having been kept away. She caught a glimpse through the doors to their bed chamber. Her cheeks flushed. Servants scurried around within, tidying the space, stripping the mattress, placing fresh linens. No doubt there would be plenty of gossip despite the circumstances, about what had transpired on their bonding ceremony night. But certainly no question about consummation.

The war room was already crowded with everyone she cared about. They greeted her with subdued smiles that made her feel cheated. This was supposed to be a happy time—a time they all celebrated. Instead, it was stolen away from them.

The next several hours passed in a numb blur only interrupted when servants brought food and refreshment. Very little was eaten —no one had the stomach for it. Discussions over numbers, army allocation, city guards, the bats—of which they knew very little about—and the safety of the city's inhabitants circled around and around. They weren't certain about a siege, but prepared for one nonetheless.

Stuffed for hours within the same space, the room felt hot and stuffy. Their inner circle made the space feel small. Add in everyone else, and there was barely room to breathe. Even Taylynn was in attendance.

By the end of it, a plan of preparation was in place. Saffra was off to the library with Desaree and Jocelyn to research more about the bats. She'd already begun the process days ago, but now there was even more reason to. The shields split up, some going to the fort to oversee preparations while others would meet with the city guards or king's army. Her own queen's guard also took on respon-sibilities, setting out to assess the city walls.

Claire soon found herself alone with Talon. It should have been a relief. It felt nothing of the sort.

He studied her, so much flashing between them in a single look. Her anxiety was mirrored in his expression. There was indeci-sion too, deep indecision radiating from him. Enough to make her say, "I know what you're about to suggest, Talon, and you already know it would be a waste of breath."

"We're not ready to fly together like this."

There. The words were out. Knowing they would come didn't make hearing them any easier.

"Claire... It is not my duty as your king to hide the truth, nor to soften it. Most truths are hard, as you well know."

Despite his careful wording, she read between the lines. As her king, he was a hard male who didn't soften his blows. As her mate, he wanted to soften everything. It was a fine line to walk, that of ruler and mate, putting them in such a precarious position.

She blew out a breath.

"Even if we spend the next few days rushing through the training curriculum, it wouldn't be enough to prepare you for aerial battle, *mih cralla*. Meeting an enemy in the sky is far different than meeting them on the ground."

His thoughts betrayed him. For a brief moment, she caught glimpses of the battle he'd taken part in centuries ago. Caught sight of the harrowing ice giants pitted against the drengr. The anguish of his loss. The fear still surrounding it.

She clenched her jaw, pulling her shoulders back. "Well, then. We will do the best we can in the time we have. I know you want to spend every waking moment micromanaging preparations, but you need to trust your shields to manage them for you so that you and I may prepare as best we can."

Usually when a bond was sealed, a drengr-rider pair began training together, a curriculum that took months, even years to learn. Pairs learned to fly under harsh circumstances, training with flight maneuvers in various battle formations and beyond. It started with trust falls and progressed once those were mastered. She hadn't known much about this until today, until her mind was joined with Talon's. It was his knowledge, and now hers, too.

That knowledge sat heavy in her belly, creating even more doubt than what already plagued her.

He feared putting her in dangerous situations—he always had. It was the same shortcoming he'd grappled with time and again, to put her in harm's way, even knowing she always managed to take care of herself...usually.

"We are mated," she said at last. "Talon, I made a promise, as did you. We exchanged more than vows. I will fly with you when our enemy strikes. You know this. You see it in my mind—that my mind is made up on the matter. The only option left before us is to prepare as best we can."

"Stubborn, headstrong woman," he breathed, closing the distance between them, taking her in his arms. They stared at each other, the will of a drengr king matched against the will of a spriten hybrid queen. Equals.

At last, he dipped and kissed her and said, "As if I could ever deny you a single thing."

~

THE SUN WAS MORE than halfway across the sky by the time she found herself with Talon, soaring over the city. She was nearly trembling with nerves. The worst part? She felt stupid for it. Stupid for letting something so small scare her. She'd faced many dangers. She'd even faced Kane. Here she was, fearing the idea of falling.

"*Mih cralla,*" Talon's gentle murmur warmed her chest. "*There is nothing to feel stupid about. Nerves are perfectly normal.*"

She scoffed. Nerves were for people who *weren't* queens. She had a kingdom to rule.

Speaking of kingdom...

Far below, people swarmed the streets as siege preparations were made. They had perhaps four days until the fleet from Oshea was upon them. For a brief moment, everything fell away as a single thought blossomed. This world was vast, so much vaster than the kingdom of Dragonwall. There were other countries, and so much of it was unknown. She'd never taken the time to revel over how wondrous it was. Had the people in *her* world felt like this before the entire globe was mapped?

"*Mih cralla...*" Talon's voice forced her to focus. She loved that he'd plucked the endearment from her knowledge of the spriten language. "*The most important thing to learn before flying into battle is how to recover after a fall. It's the first requirement of all newly mated pairs.*"

She saw the requirement clearly enough in his mind. She even recalled Tamara telling her something similar, about her own experience when she'd first begun flying with Byron. Once more, she glanced down, trying to calm the butterflies in her stomach.

"*So, just to be clear, I just let myself fall and you'll catch me?*"

"*I will always catch you.*"

Something about the way he said it...he was talking about more than just today, more than just this exercise. Gods, she loved him so much it hurt.

"*And I love you. Now, will you please, for the love of the gods, focus?*" She stifled a giggle, hands covering her mouth. "*There are a number of ways to accomplish this exercise, and we will practice all of them. I can catch you and toss you back onto my back, or sweep up beneath you. Or, if you're feeling particularly brave, you could catch yourself by grabbing onto me, my tail perhaps, and climbing up.*"

That sounded awfully terrifying.

"*I want to be well prepared.*"

"Isn't the whole point of a harness to keep me from falling in the first place?"

A patient snort sent plumes of smoke into the sky.

"*Harnesses are not a guarantee. If the straps break, if you get ripped from my back…*"

She swallowed. How bad could it be, anyway? It would be like skydiving but without a parachute. Her stomach lifted into her throat. Oh, gods, who was she kidding—nothing about this put her nerves at ease.

"*I'll be your parachute,*" Talon rumbled. Because, of course, he knew what one of those was now. He would catch her, she knew it deep in her heart. But catching her now, when the sky was calm, was different from catching her in the midst of battle. When they met the looming threat in the skies over Kastali Dun, it would be utter chaos.

"*And that is why we must practice until it is second nature.*"

"Okay," she muttered aloud. "I can do this. I have faced plenty worse than voluntarily jumping off the back of a dragon."

Talon's mental chuckle reverberated through her body.

She unbuckled the clasps of the harness, slipping her legs free. They had circled out over the water, the sea sparkling far below them. That would do little to break her fall if she smacked into it from this height. She forced the thought of her body going splat on the surface of the glassy ocean far from her mind.

"*It is called a trust fall for a reason,*" Talon reminded her. His wings were stretched wide, allowing him to glide through the sky, drifting on the sea breeze. She swallowed down the nerves bunching in her throat, then glanced down, between the open space that gave her a clear view of their elevation.

"Okay, do it now, before I lose my nerve."

"Are you sure?"

"I'm sure—damn it." Talon hesitated a beat, then tucked his wings and rolled. She was tossed from his back, the way she might be tossed in battle.

Her stomach lifted into her throat as a moment of weightlessness overcame her. Then she was plummeting. The wind roared, whistling past her ears. At first, all she felt was abject panic, but then it abated. She did as Talon had coached her, letting her arms and legs spread to slow her fall. A flash of black was followed by a rumble of approval. Talon dove past her, then aligned himself, his wings flaring to come up beneath her. She braced for impact, making sure to keep her face from smashing into his body.

She slammed against him and scrambled with her hands to find purchase. "Oof," she moaned, wincing against the jarring impact of his body. There'd be bruises afterward. They would heal quickly, even if it hurt now.

"Well done," he said, amusement coloring his voice. *"It was sloppy, but I didn't have to snatch you from the sky."*

She huffed, trying to calm her raging adrenaline. *"What can I say, I learn quickly."*

"Ready to go again?"

She exhaled. It really hadn't been half as bad as she'd made it out to be. *"I'm ready,"* she said.

They repeated the exercise, again and again, with variations. The first few times she thought she might throw up, but with each passing success, she got more comfortable. Soon, Talon was tossing her off when she least expected it, to simulate what a real surprise it would be.

"How long must we keep this up?" she managed, when he'd decided to catch her in his clutches and toss her behind him. She was breathless with exhilaration.

"Until it no longer frightens you."

"I'm not afraid anymore," she demanded. But he knew better; he was in her mind, after all.

So they spent another hour doing the exercise until she truly no longer feared it. What had started as terrifying had become fun and satisfying. She hadn't realized how badly she needed this little success, or how much better it would make her feel about herself.

When Talon touched down at the fort instead of the keep, she hadn't thought to look inside his mind to see why. It was only when he transformed and led her into the fort's dining hall, only when a roar of cheers split the air wide open, that she realized what was happening.

"Every first trust fall exercise is celebrated between a newly mated pair," he told her. And she realized in his mind that it was true. That trust fall exercises were a jumping off point, a milestone for new mates. She caught the sight of Talon's shields, grinning smugly. Somehow Talon had snuck this past her. She'd been so caught up all afternoon that he'd managed to organize it in the depths of his mind without her noticing.

She'd been worried, admittedly, that sharing minds would take all the surprise out of life. How wrong she was. Only a day in and he'd already caught her off guard.

She grinned until her cheeks hurt while drengr and riders—many of whom she now recognized—came up and clapped them on the back. They offered congratulations, asking questions about how it went. "We will dine here tonight," Talon told her, even though he didn't have to. She already knew that from his thoughts, but she appreciated that they didn't completely change their behaviors just because they shared their minds now.

It was to this small victory that they sat down around those who were like them—most of whom had also completed the same exercise at some point in their lives—to bask in their accomplishment. Talon's coming here was two-fold. To celebrate, yes, but also to plan. He intended to spend the time after dinner working with the fort's wing leaders and wing seconds. So she made the most of these simple moments, and then they got to work.

This would be his stage—the place to showcase his efforts.

He walked about, getting a feel for the place, moving about the rocky formations. Rocks tall enough to tower over him like giant walls. Some even formed corridors.

Dragonwall would fight its battle within the capital city. His would be right here. This place he'd carefully chosen, where it would all end. This was his failsafe. No matter what outcome the Oshean navy achieved, he would achieve one of his own.

He memorized the formations, made notes in his mind, then carried out a rehearsal of his plans right here, adjusting and readjusting the location until he was satisfied. The more intimately acquainted he was with the landscape, the easier and more foolproof his plan would be.

For a time, he simply stared at the key to it all. How strange it was, that something so old had stood the test of time. Marked with glyphs, its magic remained intact. It was fitting. The thing that had inadvertently thwarted him would now offer the simplest solution to his problems.

At last, he turned away and opened the vial of water he carried, splashing it on a nearby rock face. It shimmered and then revealed the room that twinned to it, the deepest cavern within his fortress. He gave his surroundings a final glance, knowing that when he was next here, everything would change, then he walked through and was swallowed up by the darkness.

CHAPTER 34
NO REGRETS

Kastali Dun

Jeanine found the hilt of her sword as she spun on her heel, confronting the darkness beyond...and the shadow that had been tailing her. Her eyes narrowed. She sighed, relaxing her grip. "You're following me," she said. Not a question—not really. She should *not* have been surprised, after all.

The shadow shifted, moving into the light. Prince Feowen, still in his armor, moved closer, turning to lean casually against the wall. "Was I that obvious?" He almost sounded bored, but she knew better. Even when they were alone, he often hid his emotions behind casual, playful words.

"You aren't unintentional, Feowen." Like all sprites, he was a master of stealth when he wanted to be. He'd made his actions obvious on purpose. He'd wanted her to know that he was here.

She willed her shoulders to relax, willed her stomach to untie itself. That didn't happen. She'd been tied up, twisted tight, since the news of the impending attack had come. What should have been a beautiful time, the celebration of a king and queen coming together, a celebration of love and the welcome of a new age, was tarnished, marred by impending danger.

She felt that danger like claws digging into her skin, gripping her tight.

"You've been sneaking out of the castle," Feowen pointed out. "At first, I thought nothing of it. Curiosity got the better of me." He shrugged.

"You could have asked," she muttered. Truthfully, she'd hoped he wouldn't notice.

"Ah, but where is the fun in that?"

"If you must know, I'm looking for Jahl."

"Oh, I know."

She hesitated, then frowned. "Well, then." She turned on her heel, carrying on down the street towards the edge of the city. She'd been searching guardhouses around the city since arriving in Kastali Dun. She didn't want to ask outright. The gods only knew it would have saved her time. Time she rarely got to herself, especially now.

"You are going in the wrong direction," came Feowen's deep, lyrical voice.

She stopped and let out a sigh, staring straight ahead as she said, "You know where he is, don't you?"

The sound of his footsteps squelching in the mud signaled his approach. He stopped beside her, mirroring her stance, then smirked that infuriatingly smug smile of his—that she secretly loved so much—as he glanced sidelong at her. "This is the part where you reward me with a kiss for being so thoughtful."

"A kiss?" She tutted. "Just for that, you're never getting one you stubborn prince. Where is he?"

"You truly wish to reconnect with him? After the way things ended?"

"Careful, you sound a little jealous." She lifted an eyebrow. It was easier to tease and play when danger loomed. It helped disguise the churning in her gut.

Feowen snorted. "Jealous? Of a—?" He wisely stopped himself. "Oh, *all right*. He's been stationed at the east gate, sector two."

A needling thought crossed her mind. Her eyes narrowed. "You haven't spoken to him, have you?"

"Upon my honor." He placed a hand over his chest, bowing slightly. "Haven't even made my presence known."

"Good." She hesitated, then set off. Feowen kept pace beside her. Despite the late hour, the city was a flurry of activity. People rushed to complete last-minute tasks. Estimations put Oshea's forces at a mere two days away. Since the alarm had sounded, she'd hardly had a moment to breathe; she and the others had been occupied carrying out all manner of tasks delegated to them by their rulers. It helped with the nerves, but only just. Never mind trying to sleep when an army loomed on your doorstep.

But they'd done all they could, assessing food stores, instructing the general populace on how best to take shelter, adjusting guard rotations, soldier regiments, stockpiling weapons, bracing the walls for a siege, and all other manner of precautions. She'd been sent scrambling from one side of the city to the other.

For long minutes, she walked in silence with Feowen beside her. She had too many thoughts like flurries in her mind. If she let herself think too much, her stomach threatened to upheave itself. She almost snorted. That's all she needed, to spew vomit all over the street in the sight of the city's inhabitants.

"We'll be all right, you know." Feowen reached for her hand, lacing their fingers together. She glanced down at the connection and swallowed. Would they?

How could he promise such things? His sister wasn't even certain. She was the one who could often predict the future.

"*Jeanine*." He stopped, using her hand to turn her until she faced him. "The capital city has never fallen. There have been attempts throughout history, a few more serious than others. Kastali Dun has always and will always stand proud against our enemies. This isn't the first time the Osheans have made a move against the monarchy." She didn't answer. His grip on her hand tightened. Normally, her chest would have fluttered with the contact, with the feel of him. Instead, all she felt was discomfort. "I won't let anything happen to you—you know this."

Her jaw tensed. She hardened her features, feigning more

strength than she felt, and said, "Your queen—*our* queen—should be your first priority. Not me."

"Such bravery," he tsked. "You've the heart of a lion. *My* lion." Feowen's eyes danced. "How, might I ask, do you propose I protect our queen while she's flying up in the sky with her king. Hmm? Shall we ask Talon to hitch a ride?"

She ignored the whole lion thing and snorted.

"There now, see? It will all be okay."

"No. No it won't." Perhaps he couldn't see it the way she did. She was human. All it took was a single lethal blow, and that would be the end of her. Feowen could take blow after blow and he'd survive. For him to promise that she'd be okay felt laughable. She had no intention of hiding. She'd face their enemies head on. That came with a certain level of danger, and no promises for the future.

Not for the first time, her doubts about what she and Feowen were to one another roared to the surface. This was why their being together was careless, dangerous.

A rare flash of concern crossed Feowen's features, as if he could read her thoughts. There in the streets, regardless of those who scrambled past them in the midst of preparations, he reached out and cupped her cheek. "Jeanine. You are scared and you are granting that fear power over you. We are going to get through this —you and I. And we will have many happy years together. The rest, we will worry about another time."

She blew out a breath. "I have this feeling, this dread, that something awful is going to happen. Not...not to me, I don't think." Feowen's head tilted. The gesture was so normal for him. She'd seen it a thousand times when he was curious, or thoughtful, or contemplative. "Maybe it's...it's nothing. Just the eve of battle."

The last time she'd faced dire circumstances, it was to lead her village to safety. There'd been no warning. Maybe it was better that way. All this waiting, preparing for the worst, was agonizing.

How was it possible to have too much time, and not enough, all at once? Not enough time to prepare, but too much time to worry. That worry was eating her alive.

Feowen's hand wrapped around the back of her neck, pulling her against his armored chest. Hers had been left in her room. She was off duty, and while she loved the regalia, she hadn't wanted to wear it meeting Jahl, assuming she found him.

Feowen kissed her forehead, letting his lips rest there. The familiar comfort of his touch spread through her. "I watched you face an army of goblins—fearless. I know you are afraid now, but when the time comes, it will be that same courage and bravery you had then, rising to the surface."

She exhaled. Standing there beneath a dark sky as the drengr swooped overhead, she allowed Feowen to hold her for just a moment more while she collected herself. Then she squared her shoulders and stepped away.

～

Jahl was exactly where Feowen had promised. She caught sight of him from the shadows, standing with a group of guards before the eastern gate. City watch patrols had quadrupled. More shifts, and more guards on shift.

For a few minutes, she simply stood there with Feowen beside her, watching her childhood friend. Memories flashed before her eyes. Moments they'd spent together, sparring and hunting. So many happy moments, despite the circumstances, despite her bitterness towards Kaljah and her parents for taking her from the life she'd grown comfortable with.

She'd felt less and less of that emotion since discovering the sprites and finding a new place. But sometimes things triggered it, and it resurfaced. She'd hated her mother and father's decision to remain in a backwater village after she'd experienced such a vibrant life in Lincastle. Jahl was, perhaps, one of the best things to come of her time in Kaljah. Then he'd abandoned her, going off to chase his dream. She didn't blame him, not entirely. Still, it hurt. That he'd left her so easily.

"I can return to the keep if you'd rather talk to him alone?" Feowen's voice pulled her from her thoughts.

"Oh." She considered. "No, I'd... I'd like you to stay."

She strode forward, navigating the people who crowded the area, even at this late hour.

News of an impending attack had sent the city's inhabitants into a panic. The time before a siege was always dangerous. Looting and crime increased as people tried to take whatever they could before barricading themselves within their homes. Many residents tried to flee the city in a chaotic mass, requiring extra guards at the city's gates. The capital, under the protection of the king with its massive walls, was the safest place to be during the invasion. It was too unsafe for unarmed, unprotected citizens to escape out into the surrounding countryside with an unpredictable enemy on their doorstep.

The Oshean soldiers, when they arrived upon Dragonwall's shores, would sweep through the surrounding lands, burning and pillaging. Any village within a day or two's march from the city was especially vulnerable. Hence, many of the king's drengr had been evacuating villagers and bringing them into the capital. They'd set up makeshift shelters, tents mostly, crowding courtyards like the one Jeanine now passed through as she made her way to Jahl.

They could not predict exactly where the Oshean ships would land, so they took as many precautions as possible. That included pulling soldier regiments from surrounding areas. Which meant the city was also playing host to an increase in troops.

The distance between her and Jahl disappeared. He was in conversation with a couple of guards beside him, a concerned expression pulling his brows together. He didn't notice her approach until two of the guards stopped speaking mid-sentence, then gaped at her—no, at Feowen beside her—and elbowed him. His head swung in her direction. She caught a brief moment of surprise, before his expression softened. He mastered himself quickly, schooling his features, hardening them.

Her stomach dropped. This...this had been a bad idea. They'd parted on bad terms.

Yet seeing him in front of her, for just a moment, everything that had happened between them disappeared. It was just the two of them. She didn't hesitate then, bridging the gap between them to throw her arms around his neck, despite his armor. "Jahl," she breathed, hugging him.

They'd been best friends for more than a decade. That sort of bond didn't just disappear after one bad conversation. Beneath her arms, Jahl was rigid. Then, ever so slowly, his arms came up and around her, holding her. He gave her a quick squeeze, then dropped his arms and stepped from her embrace.

It wasn't the greeting she would have preferred, but it was better than cold indifference.

"I heard you were in the city," he murmured, looking her up and down, as if searching for the telltale armor worn by the queen's guard. Armor she'd left behind to avoid drawing too much attention, which hardly mattered now with Feowen at her back.

"I... Yes." A sinking sensation filled her stomach. "When did you find out?"

"Not long after you arrived." Something flashed in his eyes. Regret? Shame?

"You didn't..." She glanced at his companions, still gaping at her and Feowen.

"All right, you lot. Clear off. Give them some privacy," Feowen growled before doing the same. She sighed with relief.

Now alone, she said, "You didn't come and find me?"

A needle of hurt pierced her chest.

Jahl's throat bobbed. Closer, she could see how much he'd changed even in a couple of months. He was broader, more muscular. He filled his armor nicely. "I did not think you would wish to see me."

She failed to hide her surprise.

"You're a queen's guard now, Jeanine. A godsdamned queen's guard. I wasn't exactly..." He rubbed the back of his neck. "Wasn't exactly tactful when I took my leave."

"I've been searching for you for weeks," she hissed. "And you knew..." She blew out a breath. There was no point in getting angry. "Is it... You're well? They are taking care of you? You're happy?"

He hesitated, as if reluctant to abandon their previous topic. "Yes. Happy. Well. I'm... I'm seeing someone." His eyes darted over towards Feowen, who stood far enough away to give the illusion of privacy with his hands behind his back, gazing up at the sky as if it held the most interesting sights. Jeanine knew well enough Feowen's spriten ears would pick up the entire conversation.

"You are?" she blurted, surprised, shocked even, but...happy.

Jahl sighed. "I shouldn't have left the way I did. I was... Jeanine, you were my best friend." Her chest cinched tight at the use of *were*. "But I felt things for you beyond what a best friend ought to feel when such feelings aren't returned, and it wasn't fair to you. I— part of me thinks it was because you were there, we were close, it was convenient. When I saw you with...with him,"—his eyes darted towards Feowen again—"I got jealous."

"I know," she managed, the words coming out a whisper.

"Leaving was necessary, to clear my head, to figure myself out, to get my life in a place I wanted it. It made me realize that even though I believed myself in love with you, it wasn't the kind of love that lovers share."

She gaped at him, mouth dropping open at the *L* word. She regained her composure and said, "I'll always love you as a best friend, even a brother."

"The feeling is mutual."

A whoosh of breath left her lungs. "Then we can still be friends? I don't...I don't want to lose that—our friendship I mean."

The corner of his lips twitched, but his expression held firm. It made her realize how much he'd changed. How much more of a soldier he was now. "Still friends, if you will have me. I promise to conduct myself better in the future."

A weight lifted from her chest, one she hadn't felt the immensity of until it dissipated. She'd been carrying it subconsciously since his departure. "I want to be angry with you still," she blurted. "For abandoning me, for keeping your distance despite knowing I've been here weeks, but..."

He eyed her cautiously.

"But," she continued, "we have a battle on the horizon, and that puts a lot of things into perspective."

"If you are here to clear the air because you think something might happen to me—" He lifted a brow, and she recognized the sarcasm for what it was.

"It's no joking matter," she managed.

"I'll be careful, I promise. I'm more worried about you. Fighting for the queen? Had to go and out do me, as always." This time, his eyes danced.

She huffed. "Will I get to meet this lady friend of yours? Once this is all over?"

"Deal." They eyed each other before he stepped forward, this time taking the initiative to hug her. "I'm glad you came and found me," he said into her hair.

"Me too," she managed, forcing her eyes to remain clear of tears. She stepped back. "If I don't see you before the battle, stay safe, all right?"

"You as well."

Their gazes held a moment longer, then she turned and walked towards Feowen. He wasn't secretive about their relationship as he held out his arm for her. She didn't balk, walking into it, letting him wrap it around her shoulders and lead her away.

"That went better than you expected, I take it?"

"Gods," she swore. "Are all sprites as nosy as you, Prince?"

He only chuckled, then dragged her beneath a dark awning to kiss her. When he pulled away, her body was humming. "Impending battle has a way of clearing the air. I am proud of you. Finding him, making peace. It is good to live life with as few regrets as possible, for the future is uncertain."

She lifted a hand, running her fingers down the side of his cheek, along his jaw. His eyes drifted closed. "Do you have any regrets?"

His eyes popped open. He hesitated, his expression darkening, then said, "A few." He didn't elaborate. Part of her wanted to push him, but he'd open up if and when he was ready. His expression cleared, softening. "Now, shall we return to the keep, my lion? Clearing the air isn't the only good practice on the eve of battle."

"Oh? What other practice am I missing?"

"I can think of one in particular. No regrets," he reiterated, eyes heating as his gaze swept over her. Her core clenched.

"No regrets," she whispered. The words came out breathless. The implication was obvious. She considered it, for just a moment, before her mind was made up. She'd been putting this moment off between them. Partly because she was uncertain if she was ready, but also because once they crossed this line, there would be no going back.

But Feowen was right. If battle came and something happened to them, leaving this thing undone between them would haunt her for the rest of her days—assuming she lived. She'd be left wondering what it would have been like. Wondering how it might have changed her.

"I've...I've never been with..." The words failed on her lips.

Feowen pressed his forehead against hers. "I'll teach you all you need to know, if you will allow me?"

"Like when we are sparring?" she teased, unable to help herself.

A surprised laugh burst from his lips. "Yes, only this will be much, much better than that sort of sparring." She felt the hardness of his body, of his arousal pressed against her belly.

A moan threatened to break free of her lips. "Then I accept your offer—but, Feowen?"

"Hmm...?" His eyes were glazed over with lust, his breaths coming faster and faster. Sprites were perfectly composed beings. To see him so unhinged made her insides drip with heat. They'd forgotten their surroundings, that they were still in the slums near the eastern gate, hiding in the shadows, the din of noise around them all but drowned out by their own breathing.

"I don't want you to think that I'm only doing this because of... circumstances." She didn't want to cheapen what was between them. "I'm doing it because I *want* to, because I've wanted to for a long while. With you."

There was a brief hesitation, then his hungry lips found hers, his tongue sweeping in across her mouth. He showed her what he felt, that he understood. Then he stepped away, taking her hand and leading her back to the keep.

CHAPTER 35

CAVE SCREAMERS

Kastali Dun

Bedelth found his mate exactly where he'd expected to. It was quiet this morning, with dawn not quite upon them, a muted light casting everything in shades of blue and gray. For a moment he stood back, watching as Saffra fired arrows toward the distant target. Her form was perfect. Not for the first time, he thought of what an excellent rider she would make.

It was too dangerous a hope, and yet he indulged repeatedly.

They hadn't gotten so far as to discuss it, to discuss what came next. They'd kissed, yes—much to his shock and delight. She'd launched herself at him, catching him completely off guard; he'd been too shocked to do much else beyond follow the drive of his body. When she'd left him that day, after the luncheon with his parents, he'd chalked it up to a one-off thing. Argued that she was simply reacting to the tension with his parents.

But she'd kissed him again when they'd been alone after Claire and Talon's intimate party, after her vision. Or rather, *he'd* kissed *her*. It had been softer that time, because of what had happened with her vision. He'd let the kiss stretch onward, trying to reassure her with his mouth that despite what she'd seen, they would be all right.

But would they? There was no guarantee of it. He certainly couldn't promise it. Not now.

He strode towards her. "I see this is how you've chosen to spend your final hours before battle."

She hesitated mid-draw, then let an arrow fly. "I'm clearing my mind."

"Aye. I gathered as much." The knots of tension in his chest loosened as he came to a stop beside her. Simply being in her presence relaxed him. He fell quiet, letting her nock and fire several more arrows.

A ball of nerves unfurled in his belly. It was rare for him to fear, to worry, but he did now, even if he couldn't quite guess as to why. He had an idea though, which drove him to say, "You should be flying with me today."

She sighed. "We went over this yesterday and my answer remains the same."

Went over it was one way to put it. He'd asked and she said no. There hadn't been a discussion. There hadn't been time for one. He'd been called away almost immediately. Over the past three days, they'd seen nothing but bare glimpses of each other.

Since the news of the impending attack, a million thoughts had churned in his mind. The idea of flying together. The desire to seal their bond so that they might be connected in case anything happened. He hated knowing they would be separated. So much could go wrong. She wasn't like Claire, couldn't reach out to him if something went amiss. They could only speak when they flew together, skin touching scale.

Perhaps *that* was the reason for his worry. For the first time in his life, he had someone who meant something to him. Something so deep, he ached at the thought of losing her.

She wasn't even his—not technically.

"Is there a reason you refuse?" he couldn't help but ask.

"Yes. For the same reason you should know better than to ask. We are untrained, Bedelth. I cannot have you distracted while flying with the king who, mind you, almost refused to allow *his* mate to fly with him for the same reason. *We. Are. Untrained.*" At these last words, she whirled to face him, accentuating each one.

"But I *will* be distracted. I'll worry *more* knowing that you are off somewhere I cannot protect you."

"I don't need protecting." Her jaw clenched.

"No, I suppose you do not." His eyes darted towards her bow. It killed him to say those words. It was in his nature, a desire as strong as an instinct, to want to spread his wings and cocoon her within them. To hide her away for himself, the way dragons of old hoarded treasure.

Something in her expression softened. She lifted a hand to cup his cheek. His eyes fluttered closed, cheek leaning into her touch. "I will not go off in search of danger, Bedelth. I promise."

His eyes opened to regard her. She was so small beside him. Sometimes he forgot just how small. But a small stature didn't mean small everything else.

She could fill a room with her larger-than-life presence. It was the way of a king's prophetess, he supposed, to exude power and regality with a fierce presence of mind and strength to go with it. Yet, when he let those things slip away and saw only her body, he was reminded of the fact that her head came only to his chest, that he was nearly twice as broad as she, all muscle to her soft, feminine curves.

She'd been a skinny little thing as a child, and yet she'd grown into a woman's body, especially over the past couple of years. He'd all but blinked and here she was, a goddess incarnate with beautiful brown skin and lush lips, eyes he could lose himself in, dainty hands that still held enough strength to draw a bow. Hands he wanted all over his body.

Gods.

"I want you, Saffra, more than I can even put into words." The admission slipped free before he could stop himself. Her pupils expanded, darkening her eyes. "Why do we fight it? What is the point? An army arrives today, and I cannot promise what the future holds. What if...?"

He couldn't finish the sentence. Yet, she seemed to understand. "What if something happens to one of us and we never took the time to truly know one another?" He could only nod. "There will be time enough after the battle for that."

He frowned. Would there? How could she be certain?

She sighed, almost exasperated. "You will live, Bedelth. If for no other reason than because I command it of you—your *mate* commands it of you."

A pressure expanded within his chest, a beast that roared to life, all heat and flame and hunger, eager to devour.

"Then you will...you will accept me?" He could only gape and blink, not quite believing it to be true.

"Let us get through the next few days and we will...explore the idea."

His knees nearly buckled. The irony wasn't lost on him, that he was one of the most powerful drengr in the world and she'd reduced him to a nervous mess, a creature who could barely hold himself erect in her presence. Yet, for all the weakness he felt, there was still strength. Strength she gave him—a will to survive, if only to have her as his prize.

"You have just ensured that I will live through this thing."

Her lips twitched, satisfied, because that had been her intent all along. "Good."

"And you? You will stay with Desaree and Jocelyn?"

"Yes. Miera and Selphie too. They are sprites, Bedelth. There will be the keep's guards, too. I won't be unprotected."

Her words should have reassured him, but they failed. The unease in his gut remained. The thought of her in the keep, as if it would not be safe when in reality, it would be far safer than the battle taking place in the sky. So...why? Why did he feel like this?

He swallowed.

It was just his mate bond talking, nothing more. She would be fine. She was the king's prophetess, after all. She had to be fine.

Before he could think better of it, he reached for Saffra's waist, pulling her to him. Her face was framed with stray tendrils of hair that had come free of her bun. He smoothed them back, relishing in the way her eyelids fluttered at his touch.

He hesitated, then lowered his head, brushing his lips against hers—

"*We've got a problem.*" He reeled backwards as King Talon's voice filled his mind.

Saffra frowned up at him, at his sudden and unexpected retreat.

"The king," he quickly explained. "*What problem?*" he simultaneously asked.

"*My tower. Bring Saffra.*"

Bedelth eyed his mate. "Something's happened. Gather your things—quickly."

To her credit, she acted without question, retrieving her arrows and gathering her things. She slung her bow over her shoulder and he took her hand, leading her through the keep. Servants were beginning to stir, some delivering breakfast, others getting an early start on the day. They stopped to curtsy or bow as he and Saffra rushed past.

"Did he say why we are needed?" Saffra asked.

"No."

The tower's sitting room was already full, everyone in varying stages of dress, or rather, undress. He and Saffra were the last to arrive, understandable since they'd been out on the practice fields. Claire had nothing more than a robe wrapped about her. She didn't exhibit a shred of shyness over the fact that she was completely unclothed beneath, which might *not* have been telling, had her mate not been in the same state. Talon in a bathrobe. Now, *that* was a sight. The king either didn't realize how it appeared or didn't care.

"What is it?" Bedelth demanded, looking among them. Claire's guard, those on duty at this early hour, were lined along the far wall, standing motionless, while those not on duty were calmly sitting. "Is it the patrol we sent?"

"They did not return." King Talon's jaw was rigid, tense.

"Perhaps they got—"

"No. They are dead."

"What?!" He all but choked out. The others didn't react as he did, which meant they already knew. "How?" he managed in a choked whisper.

"Claire. She...her barrier was down. Their distress call, which was sent to the fort, was also intercepted by her—me—just before I called you all here."

"We knew it was a risk sending scouts," Verath mused. "We have only a vague idea what the Oshean navy is capable of, not to mention the bats."

Beside Bedelth, Saffra shivered. Her hand was still grasped in his. He didn't care. He squeezed, glancing at her.

"They were seen." This, from Claire. "They only had seconds to warn us before the bats were upon them."

Bedelth's blood turned cold.

"Lady Saffra," King Talon turned towards her. "Have you discovered anything new?"

"Nothing beyond...beyond what I have already relayed." Saffra appeared dazed. While they'd spent day after day preparing, she'd organized the library staff into a massive search of the royal stacks to weed out whatever information possible about bats.

The king eyed her a moment longer before he nodded, turning back to the rest of them. "Our enemy is half a day out. When they reach our shores, it will be chaos. The projections Claire and I received just before—" Talon's hand balled into a fist. He shook it out, flexed it, then continued. "The sight of their navy... I have never seen such a vast fleet of ships. Captain Bennett was correct in the numbers."

"You caught a glimpse of the bats?" Bedelth stepped forward.

Claire winced. "In their projections, yes."

"And?" Bedelth kept a firm hold on Saffra's hand.

"They moved like...like a swarm of...well...bats. But it was the way they hunted our drengr. A whole wing, decimated in a manner of minutes."

"How?!" Dallin croaked. The rest of them seemed too stunned to speak.

"I... I don't know," Claire admitted. "They sort of swarmed about the wing of drengr and...and everyone caught in the swarm, drengr and rider alike, just...just...froze. The noise—the sound almost hurt my ears. Their minds were sending projections but their bodies stopped working and they plummeted, caught up in the swarm the whole time. Giant wings, bats half their size but twice as many, three times as many."

"Cave Screamers..." Saffra whispered.

Bedelth whipped around to stare at her. "Cave...what?"

"I saw mention of them—just once. But it wasn't...it was so brief that I disregarded it. It didn't even say it was a bat. Just a winged creature that..." Saffra's throat bobbed. "I'm sorry, Your Majesty. It was nothing, just an aside, a brief mention that I glided right over because it only spoke of the paralyzing, high pitched scream of cave creatures in the north that capture their prey in such a way. I had no idea it could—*would* be bats."

"It's all right," Bedelth said, moving close enough that her shoulder was pressed to his chest. "You are not at fault."

"The other information," Verath said, standing up to pace, "how does this fit in?"

"Bats use echo-location," Claire reminded them. She'd pointed it out previously and they'd been completely befuddled by such an idea. She'd explained that it was something scientists in her world had discovered. "They can emit signals, essentially, to determine where they are with regard to what's around them. What if this screaming ability is similar to that. A sound they emit that creates paralysis?"

"Then we're all dead," Koldis muttered. Taylynn was beside him on the sofa, sitting erect, as if the chair might burn her.

She'd been quiet up until now. She turned to Koldis, placed her hand on his leg. "Not dead. No. You must shield your ears—"

"But then how will we—"

"You all speak to each other in your minds. What use have you for ears?" Claire tsked, looking at Koldis like it should have been obvious.

"It cannot be that simple," Talon mused.

"Maybe it is," Claire said. "Earplugs for the drengr and their riders."

Jovari snorted. "Yes, right. Plugging up a drengr's ear holes. So simple."

"Lots of people use wax ear plugs," Claire countered.

"Except that wax will melt when exposed to a drengr's internal temperature," Verath countered, deep in thought.

"Right, I hadn't considered that," Claire said.

Taylynn stood and everyone fell quiet. "If you're all quite done now. Truly, you forget who you have in your company—and I am not simply referring to myself." Koldis snorted, rolling his eyes. She motioned towards the queen's guard, all of whom were spriten besides Jeanine.

Claire's eyes widened before she smacked her forehead. "I feel so dumb," she muttered. Whatever her realization, it was obvious to Bedelth that they'd all gotten so wrapped up in worry and shock that they weren't thinking clearly—a bad situation when lives were on the line. Talon's head swiveled in Claire's direction and a look of understanding passed between them.

Talon's frown deepened. "It is too much to ask of them, too much risk."

"It's all we've got, Talon."

Taylynn snorted—actually snorted—in a most undignified way. She turned to the rest of them. "While they *argue* in their heads. Claire has clearly put the pieces together. Spriten magic— and I tell you *dragons* this in confidence—falls into elemental cate- gories. One of those elements is air. The best way to destroy sound is to eliminate the air through which it travels. We are masters of such manipulations. So, what she is very likely suggesting to her king is that her guards, who were to be positioned on the tower's rooftop, will now focus on keeping your wings safe by shielding them from sound during confrontations with the bats."

Voices burst into speech all at once. Questions of how such a thing was possible, how the magic could be steadily maintained, how they would avoid slips and disasters. Bedelth had questions of his own, but instead, he glanced down at Saffra, at their joined hands. She must have felt his gaze because she looked up, offering a weak smile.

He whispered against her ear. "Your revelation may have saved our lives." Her eyes widened. He allowed his lips to linger, allowed them to brush against the shell of her ear and felt her shiver.

Gods! When this was over, he planned to lock her in his room for a week, just to have her alone—

"Enough!" Talon's voice rang over the others and immediate silence fell. "I am in agreement with Reyr. Our sprites will have far too much to focus on by keeping the city safe while maintaining magic to protect the drengr."

A snort from across the room—Feowen.

"Have you something to say, Prince?" Talon's eyes narrowed in challenge. He was losing his patience. It was always obvious when his temper began to rise.

"It couldn't possibly be your drengr bias speaking, could it, Your Majesty? Sprites protecting the drengr? Unheard of!"

A muscle in Talon's jaw twitched.

"Talon..." Claire reached out, wrapping her fingers around his wrist. A flash of something crossed his features. The transformation was immediate. Bedelth watched in fascination as the queen calmed her king. "It's the only thing we've got."

Everyone remained quiet.

"I do not like it," the king said at last, holding her gaze.

"The bats hunt in swarms. Our sprites need only keep track of each swarm. When they swarm a wing of drengr, spriten magic will protect that wing by manipulating the air around them to ensure that the sound does not penetrate."

Talon stepped back, away from Claire's touch. He turned his back on everyone and paced away, walking across the room as he ran a hand through his hair. He stopped, then turned and walked back. Bedelth witnessed the sight, more amused than he had right to be. If circumstances had been any less dire, Koldis would have made some sort of joke that Talon was finally forced to share authority with an equal. That he could no longer boss them about.

The king sighed, then turned to his queen.

"I trust them with my life, Talon," she said.

He scrubbed a hand over his face, over his scars. "I am aware." His eyes darted over the sprites in attendance, landing on Taylynn. The princess stood motionless. "You will be with them, Princess?"

"I will, Your Majesty."

"And can you guarantee the safety of my drengr?"

"I cannot, Your Majesty. War is war. But I can promise to do everything in my power to protect them."

Talon held her gaze a beat longer, then turned back to Claire. "You are certain this is how you wish to proceed, *mih cralla?*"

"*Neem.*"

Bedelth knew very little of the spriten language, but he knew she'd said *yes*.

"If that is settled, then we must not waste another moment," Reyr said, taking control of the situation. "We have mere hours to make our final preparations. The army is on our doorstep, and they will be here before nightfall."

They all knew what they needed to do. As a single unit, they broke apart, scattering to dress, collect themselves and make ready. Bedelth spared his friends and family one last look, then pulled on Saffra's hand and led her from the tower.

CHAPTER 36
THE FINAL MOMENTS

Kastali Dun

Saffra struggled to breathe, struggled to keep pace with Bedelth's long strides as he all but dragged her down the *Hall of Kings*. She was hardly aware of the door opening, then closing behind them, her body being pushed against it, his lips capturing hers. She groaned, the touch of him breaking the spell of shock surrounding her, pulling her from her fear and replacing it with frenzied desire.

For a brief minute, the roaring panic abated. There was only the bulk of a male before her, pressed against her, his lips roving over hers. She gasped against his mouth, letting her tongue explore his. Her hands grabbed at him, fisting his tunic, the leather of his baldric. She ignored the press of daggers against her chest where they met.

"Time," he breathed, separating their lips briefly. "I wish we had more time."

She swallowed against the thickness building in her throat. Time...

A flash of guilt had her eyes darting anywhere but his face.

They would have had more of it, had she not fought this thing between them.

His expression turned from hungry to soft—to understanding. "Saffra, my gem, my star, do not go there." He ran his fingers over her cheeks, soothing her. She exhaled. "You needed time to process, to come to terms with what we are. There is nothing we can do to change the past."

These minutes were the final minutes they might get together before chaos ensued. This was their goodbye...for now. "We will have our time," she told him, summoning her courage. "When this is all over, I will give you that time I refused to give you before."

Bedelth's expression crumbled into pure yearning. His lips were on hers again, his breaths jagged. He smelled like smoke and earth. The scent reminded her of her childhood, of late nights watching the sun set before an outdoor bonfire.

She tried to memorize this moment, cementing it into her mind. The feel of him pressed against her, heat passing between them. The ache building in her abdomen. The taste of his lips. The press of his hands against her face, gentle, cradling her—hands strong enough to break bones, but never hers.

He pressed his forehead to hers. "I... I must go. Reyr is summoning me."

"I know," she breathed. "I know."

She, too, needed to go where she was expected, down in the lowest floors of the keep where she'd be working with Desaree and Jocelyn until this was all over. They shared a final kiss, a thing wrapped in hunger, desperation, and so many unspoken promises. Then they broke apart and went their separate ways. She refused to believe this was the last time she'd see him.

Saffra worked until her feet ached, then she worked some more. The entry and dining hall had been set up as an infirmary in anticipation of what was to come. The city's healers had been assembled. Together, with Desaree, Jocelyn, and Claire's spriten handmaidens, they'd set up designated areas to reduce the chaos that would ensue. Piles of fresh linens, bandages, and healers supplies sat in heaps in several locations. Massive amounts of water and bath salts for cleaning wounds had been stored in barrels. Rows and rows of pallets sat empty.

"Surely we would never..." Desaree's voice faded, gazing out over the sea of beds. There were two hundred between both halls.

Saffra reached out and grabbed her hand, squeezing. "I hope it won't come to that."

"My lady," a male servant appeared. Besides the healers who helped oversee the set-up, the entire keep's serving staff had been enlisted. "An additional reserve of pallets was located."

"Thank the gods," Saffra breathed.

"We have them stacked neatly in the corridor just outside the throne room, as you said."

She swallowed the hard lump forming in her throat. Would it come to that? Would there be so many injured people that they'd need to fill King Talon's sacred seat of rule with bloodied bodies? She ignored the queasy feeling in her stomach and said, "Good, thank you, Arman." His face turned red when she used his name. He bowed twice before he scurried away.

A large group of people filed in, mostly men. They looked almost lost, glancing around with wary eyes. She looked at Desaree. "Would you like to do the honors, or shall I?" Des shook her head and took a step backwards. Saffra sighed. "Fine. Follow me."

Most of the organizational work had been completed. She strode to a nearby intake station, grabbed the stool, and climbed atop it. "May I have your attention!" she called. Her voice barely lifted over the murmurs and discussions taking place. She repeated the command, this time shouting until her voice cracked.

Silence fell.

"Thank you. If you will gather around." She waited until everyone was clustered together before handing out formal instructions. The healers would remain within the halls, treating new patients. The servants would be on hand to carry water, bandages, and run other necessary errands. They would also assist with various mundane tasks like cleaning wounds and calming patients. If they had complaints about their change in duties, they didn't voice them.

The other volunteers would be runners and messengers. They would help bring the injured through the city and into the castle. A long debate was held when they'd first discussed the location of their injury ward. They'd looked at various warehouses throughout the city. It was decided that the injured would be safest within the keep, behind the extra walls. Sick bays in the city could still be a major target if the enemy discovered the location. There were people aplenty to help bring the wounded in. They were given gurneys for those who might not be able to walk.

"If there are no other questions, then we will break up." Saffra hesitated, waiting for someone to speak up. Her words were met with silent acceptance. "Good, then get whatever rest you can find, and meet back here when—"

The rest of her words were replaced with a loud bell. Just a single bell, at first. It let off a handful of rings before another, and then another, and another sounded. In less than a minute, the entire city was echoing with the sound of warning.

Saffra and Desaree shared a look. Jocelyn came speeding into the entry hall from the main staircase, out of breath. She glanced around, then rushed for them. "They've been sighted—come."

Saffra hesitated, then turned back towards the gathered crowd. "Do not forget your duty," she reminded them, hoping they wouldn't panic. "Remember your instructions and do not stray far."

She jumped from the chair.

It took mere minutes, racing after Jocelyn with Desaree, Miera, and Selphie on their heels. They rushed to a terrace on the second floor. Her blood ran cold.

A military fleet. Ships upon ships, filling the horizon. They were still dots, the size of her thumbnail.

"Gods above," she whispered. Knowing what was coming had been one thing. Seeing it was another. Her hand pressed against her stomach. This was what their armies would face. This was what Bedelth would face.

The sound of vomiting had her spinning. Desaree was hunched over a nearby planter with a statue in the middle. Her body heaved several times, then she stood and wiped her mouth, her face pale as a ghost's, eyes wide. They all shared fearful glances.

"We must be strong," Saffra said.

"Our queen will protect us," Selphie agreed, nodding. Out of their small group, only Miera and Selphie looked composed. She'd never seen them particularly emotional over anything, really. How old were they? Had they ever lived through a battle like this, sequestered in their protected forest? Were they so immortal that they had no fear of dying?

Saffra reached out and took Desaree's hand in hers, and then Jocelyn's. Soon, all of them were gathered, hand in hand, just breathing, mustering the strength they would need to carry on. Saffra felt every ringing bong of the bells as each one reverberated through her body. She closed her eyes to simply breathe. Her mind flashed to Bedelth. He'd be flying with the king's wing. Claire would be at the pinnacle. Surely no harm would come to them.

Her mind immediately betrayed her, thoughts of the cave screamers swarming them, immobilizing them, bringing them down. Her eyes flew open. "We must set to work. Waiting will only leave us vulnerable to our thoughts. Let us busy ourselves as best we can."

The others nodded.

If she thought there would be a moment to rest, to muster her strength before the onslaught, she'd been wrong. Resting would only leave her prey to her thoughts. With a final glance at the horizon, at the fleet of ships racing towards Kastali Dun, and the smaller naval fleet that would meet them in open water, she turned and led the others away.

❧

Saffra was relieved when Claire made an appearance, sweeping into the entry hall with all eight of her queen's guard in formation around her. Everyone froze, then dropped to one knee. Saffra followed, but did not lower her gaze—couldn't lower her gaze. She couldn't take her eyes off the woman standing before them.

Claire looked as she never had before.

Saffra threw a glance at Miera and Selphie, knowing they were responsible for how the queen looked today. And it wasn't just how she was dressed, but the battle-ready expression on her face, as if having King Talon in her mind had turned her into *him*. A warrior.

She wore similar armor to that of her queen's guard, but not as many plates. Instead of a gown, she was in a black tunic and pants. She had a spriten short sword strapped to her hip and upon her back, her Rider's bow and quiver of arrows. These arrows had fiery red-orange feathers and Saffra knew which arrows these were. She'd heard of Claire's time in the forest, of the phoenix arrows she'd been gifted. In her hand, Claire carried her spriten quarter-staff, which she quickly handed to Prince Feowen.

"Rise, please," Claire said. Saffra stood and Caire made a beeline straight for her. She took Saffra's hands in hers. "You've transformed this place."

"We did what we could with the time we had."

Claire's eyes darted around, taking everything in, holding tight to Saffra's hands. Their friends shuffled closer. Claire's eyes returned to Saffra's.

"I came..." Claire's throat bobbed. "I came to say goodbye—for now. We're taking to the skies in a few minutes. But—"

"No." Saffra knew where this was going. "Don't even think about it."

"Saffra, if anything happens to me, I'm counting on you to be strong for the rest of us. Our kingdom is relying on you—*needs* you. Not just for your gifts, but for your strength of will, for your spirit, for your heart. If I should fall,"—Saffra's heart briefly stopped—"then I'm counting on you to take care of everyone in my stead. Our little group has grown. You must be the glue that holds it together."

"Why are you talking like this?!" Saffra managed, failing to hide her fear, accompanied by a seed of anger taking root. How dare Claire add fear to an already frightening situation?!

Claire's throat bobbed, her expression softening. Something flashed in her gaze, there and gone. Saffra's blood chilled at the sight.

"Just... Please, Saffra. I promise to stay safe, to stay alive, but our victory is not certain. Even Taylynn, when I questioned her this morning, didn't know the outcome. She's being...strange. I have this awful feeling."

"You're scaring me," Saffra managed.

"I'm scaring myself." Claire's eyes went unfocused, then, "Talon says it is time. I must go. Promise me, Saff. Promise me you will be our glue, if anything should happen. That you will be the strong one. I cannot have you...you know?"

Saffra blinked. "You cannot have me fall apart like I did with Daxton."

"Yes."

Saffra squared her shoulders. "I give you my word, my queen. Should anything happen—and it will not, because you and our king are meant to rule together—I will make sure that we remain strong and steadfast in our fight against Kane."

"You will keep a level head."

"I will keep a level head," Saffra repeated, as if swearing a formal oath, "even if the others do not."

A look of immense relief spread across Claire's features. "Thank you. I just... I needed to make sure."

Claire dropped her hands and pulled her into a hug. It was brief —too brief. Saffra found herself holding the queen tightly, afraid that this could be the last time, afraid that something could go wrong and the queen that Dragonwall had needed for centuries would be snatched away from them just as quickly as she'd come. No. She couldn't think like that—couldn't afford to.

Claire turned towards the others, giving Desaree a long embrace, whispering something to her that had tears pooling in Desaree's eyes, had her swiping at her cheeks. Then Claire turned to her handmaidens and began speaking in rapid spriten. Saffra was too worried to be annoyed. Whatever Claire relayed to them, they lifted their chins, eyes darting about the room, then nodded and gave some sort of assent in the same language. Instructions, probably, similar to those Claire had given her. Claire turned to Jocelyn and said, "You've always kept a level head, Joce. They'll need it."

"Of course, my queen." Jocelyn stepped forward and pulled Claire into a hug. It was brief, but as they pulled away, they held each other's gazes, something passing between them.

Claire turned to the crowd and lifted her voice, "Our injured will be in good hands—I am certain of it. I am trusting you with their lives. Today, your strength will be tested. You may not be on the front lines of the battle, but your mind and body will fight all the same, a different kind of fight, but one just as important. Our people will rely on you in a way they haven't before. You will make Dragonwall proud. I thank you for your service to your kingdom."

And then Claire did something that made her people gasp. She bowed. Everyone in the room gaped, their eyes widening. A moment later, the queen rose and strode from the hall, her guard tightly packed around her.

CHAPTER 37

THE BATTLE BEGINS

Kastali Dun

Claire shielded her gaze, looking out beyond the bay to the fleet of ships dotting the horizon. So, *so* many ships. She swallowed down the ball of nausea turning her mouth sour. The view was unparalleled atop the king's tower, amidst the garden. To think, less than a week ago they'd gathered here to celebrate. Now they gathered for an entirely different reason.

Somehow, they'd all managed to squeeze into the space. Talon and his shields with her queen's guard, all standing near the battlements. Her guards formed a line, their posture rigid. Summer was upon them; the humidity made it harder to breathe—or was that simply her nerves?

"Deep breaths, love." Talon's comforting voice should have been soothing. Unfortunately, nothing would fix the impending doom churning in her stomach.

She spun away from the approaching ships, lest she be sick all over the stones at her feet. Her gaze landed on her mate, speaking with Dallin. "I know you wanted to fly with us," he said, "but I need someone I can trust. It must be you." Talon had a hand on

Dallin's shoulder. The young drengr frowned, an expression of indecision playing out on his face. He teetered between argument and acceptance. "It's the only way to ensure reliable communication between our wings and Claire's guards."

Dallin's shoulders dropped. He gave a curt nod—good enough for Talon, who strode away to speak with Verath. Reyr stepped into the space that Talon vacated. His voice was low as he said, "I know you had your heart set on this."

"I should be flying with you, Reyr. With my brothers. Not standing here doing something any drengr could manage."

"I understand." Reyr sighed. "Please know this isn't a ploy to get you out of the way or protect you. You're young, yes. You've never seen battle, true. But those aren't valid reasons for you to remain here."

Dallin blew out a breath, nodding.

"Our king trusts you over the fort's drengr. Claire's spriten guards have the most important job of all. Without them, we will all be dead. If something goes wrong with their magic, your warning will be the difference between life and death. That is a heavy responsibility, one the king wouldn't put on just anyone. It must be one of us."

"I am the logical choice," Dallin concluded, his expression clearing and his shoulders straightening.

"All right, listen up." Talon spoke, garnering everyone's attention. "The fort's wings are in position. We will fly out to meet them. The farther from land the better. Stick to the plan. We keep the bats distracted, and sink as many ships as possible. Once they catch on, there's no telling what will happen."

They'd found records of past battles with Oshea, one in particular. Sinking an Oshean vessel was no easy feat. They'd be protected from dragon fire, but there were other ways. Records from the past had pointed out unique solutions, such as dropping heavy boulders that ripped into the ships and broke them apart.

Claire had used her own creativity over the past few days to formulate a plan; she only hoped it would work.

"Feowen?" Talon said, turning. He'd stopped using the prince's title recently, not out of disrespect, but familiarity. They were technically family now.

"*Ayas Drollaya.*" Feowen stepped out of formation, placing a hand upon his heart.

"Aya cathalla nih brikah." *You must not fail.*

"They will do as you have commanded." Taylynn's musical voice sounded as she emerged from the garden's entrance. Or perhaps had been standing there the whole time. "As with all matters of war, there is always risk."

The princess's words were clear enough. The sprites would try their best, but there was no guarantee they'd keep everyone alive. So much could go wrong.

"Thank you," Talon said. "That is all I ask."

The ships were closer now. Too soon, bats would be swarming and screaming in the sky. Claire palmed her stomach, willing herself to calm down. Was she the only one close to crumbling?

Talon certainly wasn't. His expression was composed. His thoughts, too. Each one was a precise string of logic. These wings would fly here. Those wings would fly there. This wing would focus on the bats. That wing would fly backup. These guards would hold their position at the city's gates while those soldiers would maintain their infantry positions near the shore to confront whatever enemy landed on Dragonwall's soil.

Strategy upon strategy. Layers of planning. His focus was an iron fist.

She glanced at Reyr, who briefly met her gaze and nodded. Like the others, he gave nothing away. A frown pulled at her lips. How were they not falling apart? How did they manage to stay so calm?

It wasn't a difficult answer to find. They were centuries old. They had experience with this sort of thing.

"*Assembled and awaiting your orders, my king.*" Fort Kastali's leader.

A breath exploded from her lungs.

"It is time," Talon said.

She turned to address her guards. "I cannot put into words my gratitude for what you will do here today, so a simple thank you must suffice." She glanced between each of them, holding Feowen's gaze the longest.

Her heart tugged with a desperate wish, to be here with them, to weave her magic with theirs as they had done in Squall's End, to protect the wings of drengr. But she was needed elsewhere for different reasons.

"You are in charge here, Cousin," she told Feowen. To the others, "His orders are to be followed as if they were my own."

"Ayas beyah, outah skapah." *Your will, our command.*

The words were spoken in unison. As one, they turned towards the oncoming enemy, even closer than before. Taylynn stepped up beside Feowen. The princess brushed her fingers against the back of her brother's hand, a tiny gesture of reassurance.

Claire moved to Talon's side—her rock, her strength. His shields gathered close, falling deathly silent. "I suppose this is the part where I make some flowery speech about honor and courage and bravery."

Koldis snorted. "How about simply telling us what is in your heart?"

Talon nodded. His hand had reached for hers, their fingers twining together. Talon's gaze circled their group, holding each person's eyes. She could feel the weight that passed between them, as if it were her own, and in a way it was, as were the emotions surging up and outwards from him.

"This will be our first battle together as brothers. As a family." Many of them had fought together as young drengr during the war with the Kalds. This was different. "Each of you came to me under different circumstances, for different reasons, pledging your life to your kingdom—to your king. Sacrifice is no stranger to any of us. What we share, our bond, runs in our blood, tying our very souls together.

"I would not be the king I am today without you. As king, I must ask you to make yet another sacrifice, to put your safety aside to serve me, our kingdom, our cause." Talon's thumb stroked over the back of her palm. "When we last fought, we were fighting for a different world, one far bleaker and less promising. Now we fight for something far greater—a new future, one we ourselves have forged with our own fires. Will you fly with me, brothers? Fly to protect the world we have only just begun to know?"

"Wouldn't dream of anything else," Reyr said, as the others echoed similar sentiments.

Claire's eyes blurred. She blinked back the threat of tears before they could form. Talon's warm hand squeezed hers. "*Mih cralla?* Would you like to add a few words?"

Her cheeks heated but she managed a nod. "I'd rather give each of you a big hug and tell you how much you mean to me—"

"We have time enough for that, I think," Reyr said, grinning.

"But," she lifted her eyebrows at his teasing interruption. "I suppose I would like to tell you that each of you is precious to me. That I love you very much—yes, even you Koldis," she added, glaring at him when his face twisted into a feigned grimace to hide his sudden embarrassment over her sentiments. "I would rather do a thousand other things than fly into battle today, but since we must, I cannot think of better males to be with. I trust each of you with my life, with Talon's life. And if any of you goes and gets killed, I will find a way to hunt you down in the afterlife and rip you to shreds for being so careless."

Several snorts.

"All joking aside, I have only just come to know you, to love you. Please, please don't die on me. Please don't... I already lost one of you. I cannot—*will not*—lose any more of you. Understand?"

Those words made them immediately sober. "Yes, my queen," they echoed. Their faces said enough. They were all thinking of Cyrus in this moment. The brother who would not be flying into battle with them.

"*Now* do we get our hugs?" Jovari asked, a small grin tugging at his lips. His words shattered the somber moment.

"Yes," she breathed, throwing herself at him first, wrapping her arms around his neck, before he passed her off to the others.

"It is time, my queen," Talon whispered against her ear, when it was his turn. He pulled her away from the others for a moment of privacy. She gazed up into his silver eyes, letting the world around them fall away. They could stare at each other like this, sink into their shared minds together, and find themselves in a completely different world. A landscape that resembled—as it usually did—volcanic lava fields.

"Have I told you today how very much I love you?" Talon murmured against her lips, his forehead and nose pressed against hers. He didn't need to tell her. She knew it the same way she knew her own name. His love was a deep part of her now, the essence of it flowing through the very marrow in her bones.

"We will fly fierce and strong," he said, whispering the words for her ears only. It wasn't a goodbye. She couldn't bear for it to be. "We will show them no mercy. No one comes into our kingdom with ill intent."

"We will make them regret the day they thought it wise to attack," she breathed against his mouth.

"Yes, my queen." He hesitated, holding her hands in his, sandwiched between their chests. "You are quite good with a bow, are you not?"

"Excellent, as a matter of fact," she teased right back.

A gleam lit his eyes, the eager edge complementing his wild gaze. As a drengr, Talon and his kind were not so different from dragons. Dragons lusted for battle and bloodshed. The drengr were simply better at leashing themselves.

Today, they needed to abandon their leashes.

"You will let it out," she told him. "You will do whatever it takes to protect our people."

"Yes, my queen."

"You will not hesitate. You will strike true. You will strike hard."

"Yes, my queen."

"You will be the king you were always meant to be."

"Yes, my queen."

"And when this is all over, you will take me away somewhere where we can be alone, where I can show you the king you are to *me*."

"*Yes*, my queen." With each affirmation, his gaze darkened.

She swallowed, then nodded, her forehead still pressed to his. "Then let us get this over with."

He took a step back, their hands still clasped. "Yes, my queen."

His eyes held so much meaning, so much trust, love, devotion, determination.

She dropped his hands at last, backing up to give him space. Already, his shields were jumping into the sky. A quick glance towards the fort showed jeweled forms rising into the air, like gems stranded together into jewelry.

Talon transformed, the action taking mere seconds. She reached behind her, to feel the rider's bow at her back. Talon had given her a fine weapon, one she cherished beyond measure. Beside it, Pelwyn's quiver and phoenix arrows waited. She'd strapped her spriten blade to her hip. It was shorter and wouldn't get in her way. Not like Cyrus's Sverak. It had been a difficult decision, to leave it behind, but she couldn't carry that many weapons upon her person while flying. It felt...not wrong, per se, but not right, either. As if she were excluding him.

A mental snort dashed that thought immediately. *I don't need a material object to be here in your head, you know.*

Her mouth twitched but her insides swelled with love. Talon's emotions swelled, too, betraying how he felt at hearing Cyrus speak. It was new for him, and while it chafed at old wounds, it also brought him peace.

I am glad to have you with me, my friend, she said, knowing full well that his battle experience would come in handy. But there was no more time for sentiment. The Oshean fleet was closer than ever. Close enough that she could begin counting the ships. She spotted the smudges of color that made up their flags.

She took off running. A battle cry fell from her lips as she vaulted onto Talon's back. She made quick work of the buckles around her legs. Her spriten quarterstaff was already buckled into place, just in case.

Talon waited for her signal, then unleashed a roar. It was quickly swallowed up by hundreds of similar battle cries. He lunged, springing into the air, clearing the battlements and sweeping downward before catching an updraft into the sky. She turned back towards the keep. Giving Dallin one final look, she said, "*We are only a thought away. Be safe,*" to which he returned a similar sentiment.

She confronted the sight before her.

They looked like insects at first, locusts, perhaps, their dark bodies lifting from the ships. Their enemy took flight, swarming and splitting and reforming. Her stomach dropped, plummeting at the sight. A fresh wave of fear washed over her. "*Breathe, love. Acknowledge your fear and move past it.*"

The swarm of bats writhed and twisted high into the air like a tornado, then split into several different formations coming straight for them, leaving the ships behind to catch up. Behind the king's wing, the drengr fanned out into an apex with their king at the forefront. Challenging roars split the sky wide open. She joined her voice with theirs, listening to it mix with the voices of other riders.

Bow at the ready, she nocked an arrow, waiting. Seconds ticked past, the bats growing larger and larger. When they were close enough to see their true size, she pulled her bowstring taut, remembering everything Pelwynn had taught her. It was as if he'd trained her for this moment. The fear she felt vanished, replaced by fierce concentration. She located the closest formation, partitioning her mind, then fired. The arrow hit its mark, disrupting the swarming formation. A bat plummeted towards the sea.

Drengr voices lifted in triumph. Their queen had landed the first shot. Pride welled through her chest—Talon's pride.

Silence swept over her, encircling her wing within an eerily quiet bubble. Spriten magic. Her heart beat once, twice, creating heavy pounding sensations against her chest. There was a moment of clarity as the writhing formation of bats churned in front of her. Talon's claws were outstretched, ready to draw blood. She braced herself. Talon burst through the enemy formation, scattering it. They were swept into the churning mass of furry bodies and leathery wings. He rolled to avoid a nearby bat and the world heaved, her stomach lifting into her throat. Then they were upright again.

"*And so it begins,*" Talon said.

Her ears filled with her raging pulse. It beat beneath her skin, pounding like battle drums. Projections began flooding her mate's mind. She separated herself enough to concentrate. Fiery pain erupted against the back of her neck. Talon roared, the sound mixing with her own pained scream. She felt a bat's claws digging in before disappearing as he rolled away to safety. She clenched her teeth, ignoring the gush of hot blood trickling down her skin.

"*You're all right,*" Talon encouraged, feeling the pain as if it were his own. "*Just a scratch. It will heal.*" She pushed the painful sensation from her mind, ignoring it as more bats swarmed, reaching with their claws. The sound of them against her metal armor made her shiver.

Another arrow was already in hand, her bow nocked. She fired, turning in her harness to get an eye on her intended target. Other riders were doing the same. Arrows flew at the swarming formations. There were six. Her spriten guards had split their magic to protect all those who interacted with the swarms.

Talon tumbled in the air, caught off course as bodies churned about them, knocking them around. Each time he got his bearings, another flutter of wings, another furry body, slammed into him. Too many to fight off, like being swept up in a current.

She gasped, as if drowning. Each breath was a struggle. Her hands worked of their own accord. She fired arrows in rapid succession, forcing the swarm to regroup. Talon's wing of drengr burst free. For a brief moment, sound returned to the world, loud screams of frustration from the bats as they realized their attempts to paralyze had failed.

They circled around just as the swarm rushed for them, swallowing them up again.

Additional wings moved in, creeping past them along the perimeter, heading towards the ships. She prayed they would go unnoticed, that they would hit their mark. Until then, they had to keep the bats distracted.

Each of her arrows struck its target, staying lodged long enough to inflict damage, before disappearing and reappearing in her quiver. If she ever saw Pelwynn again, she would fall on her knees and thank him for such a gift. Other riders would eventually need to return to the fort to refill their quivers.

A deep pain pierced her chest, stealing her very breath. She gasped, curling inward on herself. The first death. She felt the lethal dragon lance, accompanied by its projection. Felt the light leave the drengr's mind as he died. The last sound was his rider's pained scream before plummeting towards the sea below. There was no time to look out towards the ships. She saw enough to know the weaponry they carried. A cry lodged in her throat, paired with the deep sense of gut-wrenching loss. Riders didn't live long without their drengr.

"Stay focused." Talon's command was unyielding.

She inhaled, gathering her strength. She drew another arrow, nocked, then moved around for a clear shot. Bats swarmed Talon's wing. His mind was chaos, and somehow he juggled it perfectly, separating projections and giving updated orders. He played the role of commander and warrior simultaneously. Flawlessly.

Another sharp pain filled her, and then another. Two more deaths. The other wings were nearly upon the ships, dodging a sky filled with lances as the fleet fired upon them. She pushed the painful sensations away, counting down the seconds. Just a few moments more, and they would make it. Her arms began to shake, sweat beading along her temples. How much time had passed? Each minute felt like an eternity.

Bats dropped towards the sea, but not nearly quickly enough. Just enough to remain distracted, and then—

"They made it!" Talon turned on his wing tip, circling them around. His shields broke from the swarm following their king. She caught sight of the approaching fleet, just in time to see a projection. One of their riders dropped the first jar.

Her hearing returned.

She watched, transfixed, as the jar plummeted, its insides dancing with a faint green glow. It smashed against the deck below. Her sprite fire exploded outward, swarming over the surface of the ship like a rapidly growing infestation.

A concussion of air and its accompanying boom hit her a moment later, rustling the hair around her face, stealing the breath from her lungs. The entire ship went up in flames and the world paused in shock. Then a lance drove straight into the heart of the drengr who'd made it possible. He dropped from the sky. Seconds later, his glittering blue scales were swallowed up by the sea, both drengr and rider lost. Their sacrifice would never be forgotten.

CHAPTER 38

CLAIRE'S MAGIC

Kastali Dun

Koldis released a snarl of satisfaction, ignoring the gaping wound on the underside of his belly as it knitted itself back together. He wasn't the only one. Every one of his brothers had taken a beating. Even his queen had blood splattered on her beautiful silver armor. She was slower to heal than the rest of them, but still much faster now that she was mated to Talon. Not to mention the sprite blood in her veins. As her magic grew, so too would her healing abilities.

Every one of their injuries was worth it—seeing the first ship burst into green flames. He spared a moment to admire Dragonwall's queen. She looked like vengeance incarnate, her golden hair coming free in strands, a bow in hand, and armor bloodied from battle.

Claire had spent hours preparing her sprite fire jars, putting a drop of her fire magic into each one. Sprite fire was something the fleet hadn't anticipated. But how long would it take their sorcerers to react and recover?

A pang of shock echoed through him as the drengr who'd

landed the first blow plummeted towards the sea, his rider with him. There was no time to mourn. More and more jars were dropped over the ships. One vessel after another burst into flame. For a brief instant, it seemed victory was certain.

Until he took in the expanse of the fleet. There were still so many. How would they conquer such a force?

As a single unit, the bats changed direction, sensing the greater threat. They sped off towards the ships. *"The sprites are reconstructing their shields,"* Dallin's voice filled his mind, relaying messages to the king. *"They will do their best, but it's chaos out there!"*

Chaos was putting it mildly. Lances flew through the air, giant arrowheads promising pain, forcing formations apart and back together. Injured pairs fell from the sky. Bats swarmed.

Talon gave his command to follow the bats. They changed direction. He beat his wings, straining against the budding fatigue in his muscles, straining to regroup with the drengr force above the fleet. A needle of panic pierced his composure. The Oshean navy was too close to the shore. Claire's jars were barely making a dent.

A horn sounded, the call taken up and echoed by more horns. Dragonwall's fleet appeared, right on schedule, cutting through the bay's waters to follow their king. They were the last line of defense against the enemy and would intercept the ships before they could enter the bay.

It would force the ships to change course, force the soldiers to head for the beaches north of the city, protecting the citizens behind the city's outer walls. There, Dragonwall's army would be waiting.

A dragon lance shot through the air, straight for him. He rolled. The tip of the ice metal grazed the underside of his belly. He hissed. Unlike the scratches from bat claws, this was a wound that wouldn't heal quickly. *"Careful, brother,"* came Jovari's warning when he witnessed the injury.

Only a fraction of their drengr wore armor. There hadn't been enough to outfit the entirety of their forces. It had been split between both forts during the battle at Squall's End, much of it remaining behind when they'd departed. He regretted that now, but how could they have anticipated this?

Another lance shot towards their wing. They broke apart, scattering then regrouping. More lances came at them as they reached the ships. It was nearly impossible to hold formation. Koldis fought for third position. Talon was directly in front and to his left. His king growled as the tip of an arrowhead sliced along his forearm. The sound was echoed by Claire, a cry of pain for her mate.

With the spriten shields now protecting those in direct danger of bats, the clash of battle hit him head on. It was an assault to his senses.

Below them, the creak and groan of war machines fired lances into the sky. It was paired with cries of, "*Reload!*" and, "*Fire!*" Green flames sparked and crackled, swallowing up entire vessels, while new explosions went off periodically as drengr wings fought their way towards the back of the fleet. Cries of agony for those caught in the explosions added a harrowing backdrop as soldiers were forced to jump ship.

In the sky, there came a constant whistle and hum of lances cutting through the air. It was paired with the roars of the drengr and the screeching of angry bats. Bat claws against armor. Hissing cries of pain. Flapping wings. Twanging bowstrings from riders.

Each individual sound turned into a maelstrom of noise. The sky was nearly impossible to navigate. This was what war looked like. Death and suffering, with small victories on both sides.

"*They're deploying,*" King Talon warned.

Rowboats dropped into the water heading straight for Dragonwall's shores. Several wings broke away and swooped for them, breathing tongues of red orange flame, attempting to incinerate them. It did nothing. Whatever sorcerer magic protected the ships also protected the soldiers and their small vessels, forcing their wings to take up alternative tactics. They upended boats, dislodging the soldiers, but it didn't stop the Osheans. There were too many; they moved like ants with a single minded focus, swimming for the shore.

"Our sprites are struggling," Dallin shouted in warning. *"The bats are finding too many ways to work around their protections. Keep the formations together!"*

"Hold your formations!" Talon cried, sending the command to every wing. But it was impossible to restore order out of chaos. A nearby contingent of bats let forth a piercing scream, bathing a scattered wing with their paralysis-inducing cries. Koldis watched in horror as the scattered drengr froze. Before anyone could act, they were picked off, ripped to shreds, caught up in a rapid swarm that lasted seconds. Body parts and gore rained down, disappearing into the sea below.

A roar ripped free of his chest.

"We're doing the best we can, Dallin!" Talon bellowed, his words laced with panic and anger.

"It's not enough, Your Majesty. They're...they're burning through their magic!" Dallin sounded panicked, which meant the sprites were also panicked.

Koldis swore, hissing a stream of smoke as he took in the scene before them. Too many, they were losing *too many*. Nearly a third of their forces were injured or dead, missing from the sky. Acidic bile roiled in his stomach, lifting into his throat.

He glanced down.

Less than half the fleet burned green—not nearly enough. Those jars should have been enough to damage the majority. They had failed. A brief sense of hopelessness washed over him as he wondered how they would come out of this in one piece.

"Ignore the soldiers!" Talon cried, issuing new orders to the wings that had split from the main force. *"Our military will deal with them on shore. Focus on the ships!"*

"We need to stop those bats," Koldis growled, getting Talon's attention. *"Otherwise we don't stand a fighting chance."*

"No, we stick to the original plan," Talon countered.

"I can burn them with my sprite fire," Claire suggested, sounding hopeful.

"No, Claire. There is too much risk," Verath countered. A lance flew towards their formation. They were forced apart, rolling and

scattering before regrouping. Their momentum carried them off course, sweeping them out and around the perimeter of the destruction zone. *"The bats are too intermingled with our forces. Burning them would mean catching our own drengr up in your flames. We are not immune to your fire."*

"But..." Claire's gaze was trained on the forces in the sky. Even as they watched, another small contingent was ripped to shreds.

"The only reason the bats are immune to dragon fire is because of their sorcerers," Talon growled. *"We eliminate the sorcerers, we leave the bats unprotected. Our forces will char them to bits. We proceed as planned—we destroy the ships."* Talon's order left no room for debate. There was no time, anyway. Every moment, more of their drengr died. But how many of them would they lose in the time that it took to eliminate the ships? He couldn't bear to think of it.

"Mih cralla?" Talon's voice again, speaking so that his entire wing would hear. *"Are you ready? This is your moment."*

This was why Claire was with them. Yes, she was Talon's mate and rider. But for this battle, she was here to serve one, final purpose. Her mastery of sprite fire went beyond the normal abilities for a sprite. She was their secret weapon.

"I am ready."

"Good. With me, brothers," Talon commanded, immediately turning on his wing tip. They swept around, moving towards the perimeter of the chaos. From afar, it merely looked as if the king was taking up a vantage point on the edge of battle, to better command his forces.

Koldis kept his focus on their queen, knowing Talon was capable of protecting himself. Claire reached for the buckles of her harness and freed her legs. She got into a crouching position, then stood for a better view. It took perfect balance to keep her body upright while Talon glided through the air...and something more. Sprite magic. Without it, she'd have tumbled from his back.

She began to sing, the notes of her voice catching in the wind. He felt the power seeping from her words. Talon swooped, bringing them around the fleet.

He'd never seen anything like this. She was a queen in every sense of the word, standing atop the massive black dragon as she sang forth her wrath. He felt the air shimmer with her power.

The sounds from around him were silenced. It took him a moment to realize why. Claire worked more than one form of magic. Not only was she using a binding force to keep her in place, she had woven a protection bubble about their wing to keep the call of the bats from harming them. Then her words began to change. They turned deeper and darker. He felt her malice, her anger, her drive to punish their enemy.

His gaze flicked across the sky. Only half their aerial forces remained. Gods above. More than one hundred drengr injured or dead. How could they ever come back from such a loss?

Come on, Claire, he urged, listening to the sound of her voice. He knew more about her magic than his brothers did, having been with her as she'd developed it, deep within the forest. He knew that much of it could be done without singing. But for this, she'd chosen to revert to the basest form of magic, to reach deep into herself, to call upon the roots of what it was to be a *spirit singer*.

On his left in second position, Reyr let out a roaring whoop. An entire row of ships burst into green flame. He opened his maw and let forth a bellow of his own. Talon continued to circle, their wing skirting the perimeter as Claire focused her magic on the fleet below. Her gaze remained fixed, arms outstretched as she sang.

If his scales could, he would have erupted into chill bumps at the sight of her. His queen, doing the unthinkable. Another swath of ships burst into flame. It was working. Gods above! It was working!

Just as another swath of vessels burst into flame, the bats changed direction, as if finally realizing who the true threat was. It was too late. Whatever magic Claire had woven, she'd woven it tight. Their wing stayed in motion, and try as they might, the bats could not penetrate the barrier Claire had set in place. It was more than what the sprites had done. It wasn't simply an absence of air, it was an invisible wall that she'd blanketed them with. Bat after bat rammed against her shield, but it held firm as her voice carried.

More and more of the fleet burned.

On the shore, tens of thousands of soldiers had formed ranks. It was less than the one hundred thousand traveling with the fleet, but still significant. It would put a dent in Dragonwall's army. They'd worry about that later.

He was vaguely aware of Dragonwall's navy, forming an unbreakable line. If Claire succeeded, there would be no need to engage them. The bay would remain protected, keeping the bulk of the battle north and west of the city.

Claire's voice faltered and cracked. It began to waiver, to weaken. The sound of her gasping between words tightened his chest with fear. He glanced below. Only a handful of ships remained. She'd done it. She—

"I...can't!" Claire's body went limp.

Koldis bellowed at the same time his king screamed. He watched in horror, time slowing, unfolding, as Claire lost consciousness and tumbled from Talon's back. Without the magical barrier, the bats broke through their cocoon of safety.

His heart stopped.

Talon forgot their formation and plunged, streaking into the swarm after Claire. She toppled, her limp form slamming into the back of one bat, then buffeted by the wings of others. Koldis braced for the paralyzing screams that would kill them—kill his queen. The screams did not come. Somehow, the sprites had been watching their queen, had managed to weave individual protections around her and the rest of the king's wing. He didn't have time for relief.

There was only crippling fear.

They followed their king. Talon fought tooth and claw. He was a mate enraged, breaking through the swarm to follow his queen as she dropped to the sea below. They reformed, keeping a tight pack about their king, diving with him. The sea swept up to meet them. Talon's forearms reached. He snatched his mate's limp body seconds before she struck the surface.

Were it not for her armor, the bats would have destroyed her, broken every bone in her body, bruised every stretch of skin, scratched wounds too deep to heal from. Thank the gods for starlight silver. He'd kiss his spriten mate, kiss her brother, kiss every damned sprite in existence for creating the material that saved his queen.

A roar of relief burst from his chest—from the chests of all his brothers. Their wing swept around and Talon headed straight for the keep. He was vaguely aware of Reyr giving orders to the remaining wings in the sky. The bats followed them towards the king's tower. They were close enough to see the sprites on the battlements—or what remained of them. Only four bodies stood, the rest having fallen unconscious under the strain of magic. A sigh of relief showed Taylynn with her hand tightly clasped in her brother's.

They were singing, their eyes fixed somewhere behind him. A moment later, he felt the heat of sprite fire at his back. He didn't need to look, to know. The remaining bats were destroyed. In diverting them from the battle, they'd separated them from the drengr, allowing Taylynn and Feowen to use what was left of their magic to destroy them.

Beside them, Jeanine stood, an anxious expression on her face. The other guards had been arranged comfortably on the ground in their unconscious state. A couple had bloody noses. They would recover, but they would be no more help for this battle.

Talon swept over the tower, releasing Claire from his grasp. She dropped. Dallin caught her up in his arms, pulling her against his body.

So small. His queen looked so small and frail. His stomach squirmed. Already, Taylynn was rushing to Claire's aid, brushing a hand over the queen's unconscious face. Pride muddled with worry. She would live. She would be okay. She had done something so incredible, the bards would sing of it for thousands of years. She had destroyed what remained of the Oshean fleet, but it had taken its toll on her body.

"*Get her to safety,*" came the king's orders to Dallin. "*Ensure that she is well protected as she recovers.*" Talon's voice was laced with anguish. It went against Talon's nature to leave her, but he was a king, and he had a duty to his kingdom as much as his mate. With reluctance that could be felt to the deepest depths of his core, Koldis followed his king as they turned and departed. They had a battle to win.

CHAPTER 39

THE BATTLEFIELD

Kastali Dun

Bedelth kept close to his king. They flew towards the mass of soldiers forming ranks near the beach. At least fifty thousand had made it to shore. They aligned into tidy formations, split into grids, with spears and swords and shields at the ready. Flags flew, the banners waving in the wind.

Every marching step was done in unison. It was a well trained army. One that intended to claim their city. Thank the gods the ships had been destroyed with their siege weapons.

Their own forces numbered half of what Oshea's did, standing at the ready outside the city's walls. They'd considered withdrawing into the city, but it would have made for cramped quarters and a prolonged siege. Everyone was eager to end this thing sooner rather than later.

Had there been more warning, they could have summoned troops from further away. They were at a disadvantage. A mere twenty five thousand mustered troops, with another two thousand guards inside the city.

"There are sorcerers in their ranks," Reyr warned, not a moment too soon. A plume of shimmering air shot skyward then spread.

392

More columns of shimmering air shot upwards, then spread like mushroom tops, joining together to blanket the soldiers.

"*It's some kind of shield,*" Verath observed.

"*I thought we'd killed them all,*" Koldis muttered. "*Wasn't that the purpose of destroying their ships and risking Claire?*"

"*They snuck some ashore,*" Jovari observed.

"*Let's see what we're up against,*" Talon said, suppressed rage dripping from his tone.

Bedelth roared in answer, following his king as they dove towards the enemy soldiers. Their bodies were met with a solid wall, a shield. The impact jarred his bones, sending pain shooting through him. He roared again in anger, the sound echoed by his brothers. Most of their wings were picking off the few remaining ships Claire had failed to destroy. Talon had ordered three additional wings to flank them. They all met the same barrier.

They tried again and again to get through, battering at the invisible wall with their claws.

"*We'll have to do this the simpler way,*" Reyr announced, spotting the front lines, the empty gap where the Osheans approached Dragonwall's army. "*Who is up for a little swordplay?*" Reyr's question was sent to every drengr in the area.

Challenging, eager roars split the air. The king's wing soared off towards the front lines, followed by their flanking wings. Bedelth braced himself, diving. Dragonwall's soldiers rallied when they saw their king approach, shouting and cheering. They landed on two feet, completing their shifts in midair.

Their flanking wings were slower, letting their riders dismount first. Talon issued orders, spreading them along various parts of their army. He gave additional orders to his shields, forming them into pairs. Jovari and Koldis split away, moving farther down the line. Bedelth and Verath teamed up, taking over another unit of soldiers, placing themselves at the front. Talon kept Reyr beside him, taking the central force.

"Our enemies think they can take our homes," Talon roared, his voice booming over their units of soldiers. "They think they can claim what is ours."

Angry voices lifted in response.

"We will not let them!" Talon roared. "We protect what is ours!" The king hefted his sverak, the challenge obvious. Behind him, rows and rows of soldiers did the same, crying out in unison. "For Dragonwall!" The cry was echoed down the lines as Talon surged forward, soldiers at his back.

His shields mimicked the motion.

Bedelth shot forward, Verath at his side. "Shall we see which of us causes the most destruction?" he said, offering Verath a challenging grin.

"You're on," Verath growled, hefting his sverak. They had just a moment to brace before the enemy lines clashed together. The magical barrier put in place by the sorcerers swept over them, but could do little more. It was meant to protect the Osheans from aerial attacks and would do nothing against the mass of soldiers on the ground.

For a brief moment, Saffra's face swam into Bedelth's mind. He was fighting for so many reasons. But the deepest reason was her.

He let forth a battle cry, then swept his blade around, decapitating the first Oshean that approached him. Before their head rolled, he was already snapping forward with a quick thrust, sending his blade between the seams of armor shielding another soldier's abdomen. The soldier cried out and crumbled. He didn't stop. His feet danced, blade swiping and thrusting.

Minutes ticked by. Soon, he was spattered in blood. Some of it was his own, minor slices and grazes of an enemy blade. In human form, the drengr wore no armor. There was little that could kill them. The enemy might have used ice metal for the arrowheads on their dragon lances, but they hadn't bothered with it for their infantry weapons. They'd planned to pit their foot soldiers against other humans, not drengr.

A normal steel blade wasn't enough to remove a drengr's head. Such blades broke when confronted by a sverak, with a single blow aimed in the right way. It made them look like gods.

"I'm at eighteen already," Verath cried. They fought shoulder to shoulder, as if they'd done this a thousand times.

"Fourteen," Bedelth growled, watching the next soldier topple. Verath was better with a blade. Not as good as Cyrus, but perhaps as good as Reyr. He refused to admit that Verath might best him. No, he'd wait until the battle was done and their counts tallied.

He knew his brothers were engaged in similar contests. Projections were exchanged between them. He caught glimpses of Talon's sverak, newly decorated with its beautiful black stone. Beside him, Reyr fought ruthlessly, careful to guard Talon's back just as much as his own.

Thinking came easier with each stroke of his blade. Something about the movements calmed him. Focused his mind.

He could do it for hours.

A rapid change in the air set the hairs on his arms on end. He had just a moment to blink before a concussion of air rushed past him. He staggered, bracing. Beside him, Verath moved his body into a bracing stance. The soldiers around them weren't as lucky. They toppled backward, losing their footing, stumbling to the ground.

"The sorcerers!" Verath shouted, right as Bedelth made the same realization. "There!" Verath didn't point, because already enemy soldiers swarmed around them. Instead, he shot Bedelth a quick projection. A sorcerer lurked nearby, placed strategically within the Oshean ranks.

There was no time to strategize.

Bedelth hissed as a blade sliced his leg. The deep gash sent him staggering. Verath's grip around his arm got him upright again. He lunged, driving his blade through his attacker's shoulder, ripping it free, then slitting his throat. Blood splashed his hand, leaving it sticky.

Just as soon as one body went down, another filled its place. He and Verath were surrounded. They'd gone from fighting with ease to fighting for their lives.

His breath came in staggered gasps.

He caught projections from the others, stuck in similar circumstances. The kingdom soldiers that had been attacked with magic were slowly getting to their feet, but some weren't fast enough.

Those who were shook off their confusion. Just as soon as they were back in action, another concussion of air sent waves penetrating deep into Dragonwall's ranks.

"If we don't get that sorcerer," Verath growled, "we're dead!"

Together, they redoubled their efforts, fighting dirtier than ever. He kicked out, shattering kneecaps, using every bit of surprise to remove a head from its shoulders, or sever a hand at the wrist. He caught a glimpse of the sorcerer again, backing further into the ranks of the Osheans.

"Cover me," he shouted at Verath. Before his brother could answer, he lunged, ducking and sprinting through a gap in the soldiers. Verath grunted behind him; a quick projection showed he'd taken a blade to the shoulder. It would take a lot worse than that to bring down a drengr, especially a king's shield, *especially* Verath.

With an extra burst of speed, Bedelth lunged, ducking and then rolling, scattering several soldiers. His blade swept around before the sorcerer spotted him, slicing clean through the sorcerer's legs. The man roared, his eyes going wide with shock and disbelief. Bedelth stood. "Your first mistake was marching on Dragonwall," he spat, lifting his blade, looking deep into the sorcerer's eyes. "Your second was crossing a king's shield." He drove his blade into the sorcerer's gut, quick as an adder, before the sorcerer could chant any magic to offer protection. Then he slid it free and removed his head. The body crumbled. He was already moving again, sweeping around to take out several soldiers crowding around Verath.

"I'm counting the sorcerer as two," he shouted, earning a smirk from Verath, whose focus was intent on the soldiers. He looked worse for wear, but he'd survive.

The sorcerer's death allowed this section of Dragonwall's soldiers a reprieve from their magic. At the sight of the dead sorcerer, the soldiers rallied, roaring and banging weapons against their shields. Some of them chanted his name, *"Bedelth! Bedelth! Bedelth!"*

And damn, it felt good. The boost to his ego gave him a burst of added energy. He felled three more opponents.

Slowly, step by step, minute by minute, they made progress, pushing back the lines. He sent quick projections to the others, boasting of his victory against the sorcerer. Soon, they followed up with similar victories of their own. Each sorcerer's death made the enemy soldiers easier to cut down.

They were brothers in all but blood, and each victory felt good, no matter whose it was.

It was that same connection that alerted him to Dallin's approach. The purple drengr gave a quick update to the king, informing him that Claire was resting, sleeping off her exhaustion, before landing at Verath's side. Bedelth gave him a quick nod and said, "I'm already at one-hundred-and-fifty-two. Verath is at…"

"One-hundred-and-seventy-one!"

Bedelth hissed, irritated that he'd fallen behind. Still, he said to Dallin, "You've got some catching up to do."

Dallin took the challenge and jumped into the fray. The three of them, flanked by the kingdom's soldiers, pushed deeper into the Oshean ranks. Years from now, soldiers would tell their families stories of how they'd fight beside Bedelth, Dallin, and Verath. How they'd watched the king's own shields wreak havoc upon the enemy. How they'd taken down soldiers with a single blow of their sveraks. How much honor could be felt in standing with them. Those stories would morph and grow into legends, and he'd be forever immortalized.

For now, he focused on the matter at hand.

Once again, he felt a surge of magic, a tingle against his skin. This time, it came not from the air, but something beneath his feet. A shudder within the earth. It cracked open and split apart, traveling through the ranks, all the way to the city wall, where it slammed against the city's barrier, cracking it open. The giant gash sent soldiers screaming and toppling into the earthen depths. Bedelth, Dallin and Verath had just a moment to jump aside, momentarily separated, before they lost their footing. He stumbled, regaining his balance amidst the quaking earth. Tremor after tremor followed, making it nearly impossible to stand.

"Another sorcerer," he bellowed, pointing with his sword towards their newest enemy. A look came over Dallin's face. He knew before he could shout otherwise that the young shield had taken up this challenge for himself. He shared a single look with Verath across the giant gash in the earth before the three of them took off running. Dallin gained ground, leaping over the gash with inhuman speed. He rolled then came upright, taking off again. Bedelth and Verath covered him, striking aside Oshean soldiers to give Dallin a clear path.

This time, the sorcerer saw him coming. It was only Bedelth's quick thinking, a muttered counter incantation of protection, that drained him but kept the sorcerer from striking Dallin before Dallin's sverak lifted and sliced clean through the barrier of protection around the sorcerer. Sveraks could slice through rock, why not magic too? Talon would be interested in that fact. He sent a quick projection to the others.

The sorcerer had a blade in hand. He shoved it into Dallin's side as the young drengr stole a killing blow, right into the sorcerer's chest. Dallin stumbled back and ripped the blade free, roaring with victory before sliding it into his bandolier as a prize weapon. Verath gave a whoop of surprise, clapping Dallin on the shoulder. Bedelth offered Dallin a nod of approval—all there was time for—before the three of them turned back to back to take on the fresh wave of Osheans surrounding them.

A few projections told him that some of the Osheans had made it to the crack in the city wall and were pouring through, where they were met with the city's guards. It was a narrow gap, and would allow the guards to cut them down more easily. He didn't have time to worry about it. There were still too many Osheans on the battlefield.

The clash of weapons echoed through the air. The sound mixed with the cries of battle, shouted from both sides. Death was usually quiet, but sometimes it could be heard in the form of a final, anguished scream. Then there was the smell. Gods, it was overpowering. Blood, sweat, and loose bowels. Most soldiers at death's door lost control of their faculties.

Only in the stories did a thing like this seem real. He'd never fought in such a battle, on foot, against countless soldiers—not even the goblin ranks had been this organized. Yet, battle was in his blood. He was more than a drengr. He was a warrior.

A flash in his periphery showed King Talon and Reyr fighting back to back. He wished he had a moment to watch his king. Even a brief glimpse told him that Talon was a sight to behold upon the battlefield, his massive frame towering over enemy soldiers.

"I'm at seventy-three!" Dallin proudly announced. Automatically, Bedelth and Verath both shouted their counts, well over four hundred now, but Verath was in the lead. A little while later, he proudly proclaimed the moment he reached five hundred.

Together with their soldiers, they'd carved through half the ranks of the Oshean army.

His focus began to slip. There were times he missed a target or got sloppy. Were he human, he'd be long dead. Two more sorcerers confronted them. Verath finished them off, roaring with victory each time.

The scent of fire began to seep into his nostrils. He had a vague awareness that parts of the city were burning. Enemy soldiers that had broken through. A few sorcerers from other parts of the field had managed to split additional openings into the city's outer wall.

A roar from the sky announced the approach of the remaining wings. He wanted to weep with relief. They had defeated the last of the ships. A quick burst of flame near the back ranks of the Oshean army told him all he needed to know. They'd killed enough of the sorcerers to weaken the enemy significantly.

Night had fallen when at last, they had closed ranks enough to fight beside King Talon again. A mixture of joy and pride burst through him at reuniting. This was what it meant to stand with his king. There was no one in the world he preferred to be with on the battlefield.

When at last, they'd surrounded their enemy, Talon shouted

his offer for surrender. Not a single sorcerer stood. Only, several hundred enemy soldiers remained. Talon offered mercy—though he'd sworn he wouldn't. The soldiers didn't take the offer. With a final roar, Dragonwall's remaining army swallowed up what was left.

It was this final stand that sent a message to the rest of the world. Kastali Dun had never been taken. It would never fall. Neither would Dragonwall. The monarchy was strong, so long as there were those who supported it with willing sacrifice. When the victory cries split the air, Bedelth watched as Talon crumbled to his knees, body bloodied but whole, and wept with relief.

CHAPTER 40
A MESSENGER

Kastali Dun

Saffra wiped her forehead with her sleeve, keeping the beads of sweat from dripping into her eyes. Her breathing was labored, exhaustion pulling at her every muscle. How much longer could it possibly last?

Already, servants were rushing around to light sconces and hauling chandeliers up by ropes and pulleys. The light was fading, night approaching fast. She prayed it wouldn't go on much longer.

In the back of her mind lived the constant fear that Bedelth wouldn't make it. She struggled to keep those thoughts controlled. The chaos helped.

"Over here! There's an empty bed—here!" Desaree's voice rang distantly in her mind. A haze had descended, making things seem far away. She blinked, looking across the hall. Desaree stood, waving another injured soldier over.

The doors to the hall stood wide open, a steady stream of people coming and going. Mostly coming. Mostly injured.

Assistants helped to bring the injured up into the keep. Those that arrived came in varying conditions. Some limped along, others had to be carried. Over the past five hours, she'd seen organs spilling out, minor cuts, head wounds, amputated limbs, and much, much more. She'd vomited a total of six times.

Messengers kept up a steady stream of updates on the battle's status. For the first hour, she'd waited in silence with the rest of the hall, shuddering whenever she heard the harrowing screeches and roars out over the sea, the distant explosions that were proof of Claire's efforts. Then the battle had moved to Dragonwall's shores. Everything had changed. The ships had been destroyed, but the Oshean armies were on their doorstep.

The king's forces were battling for their lives, protecting the city. She had felt the world tremble once, twice, three times as the walls shook and broke. A messenger had told them the news. Sorcerers marched with the Oshean army. Beyond the frustrating aspects, like the ability to protect the Osheans from dragonfire, some of them had the power to split the earth and break holes in the city's walls.

The fighting had moved into the outer portions of Kastali Dun, pressing inward.

"My lady—Saffra." A messenger appeared, fighting to be heard over the cries of pain. "The fighting is nearly at an end."

Her body sagged, all but collapsing onto an empty bed. "You're...you're sure?"

"Yes, my lady. I was just there, came straight here to tell you. It should be over within the hour. The king is there, my lady, with his shields."

"Thank the gods," she breathed, looking over the sea of beds. Hundreds lay injured, attended to by healers and mages alike. She caught the stooped form of Marcel, going from soldier to soldier.

"Tell me," she said. "Did you see an orange drengr flying with the king's ranks?"

"Lord Bedelth, my lady?" She nodded. "Yes! He was there. All the king's shields, even the purple one, Lord Dallin, who came to join the fighting not long after it moved onto shore."

The relief barreling through her stomach made her gasp. "Thank you," she breathed as the messenger rushed off.

Long minutes stretched onward. She rushed about, using what

little of her magic remained, until she was completely drained. The only thing keeping her on her feet was sheer stubbornness and a desire to see Bedelth when he returned. She kept back just enough magic to stay conscious.

Somewhere nearby, Miera and Selphie also worked. She caught snatches of their singing voices as they healed the worst wounds, along with the Magoi. Jocelyn rushed by her, a basket of fresh cloths in hand. Their eyes caught, offering encouragement, before rushing off to tend to more wounded.

They would survive this. They had to. And they'd be stronger for it.

A scream made her wince. She located the injured soldier, newly deposited in the bed behind her. He thrashed, wide eyes gazing up at the hall's rafters. "Help me hold him," she cried to the closest servants. A group rushed to her aid, taking his shoulders as she assessed the damage. Blood poured out of the wound in his leg.

She swore under her breath. Among his most dire afflictions, a blade had nicked his artery. He had mere minutes, if that.

She began shouting orders, binding his leg to cut off the circulation before he bled out. Her hands came away red and sticky. "Find me a healer," she cried to the nearest servant. They rushed away. The other two worked beside her to clean and assess other wounds.

The soldier continued to thrash, seconds ticking by. Every instinct in her screamed to use her magic. When she grew tired of waiting— "Is there no healer?!" she cried to no one in particular, beginning to panic.

"They're all busy, my lady," someone said, rushing by.

"Oh gods," she cried, grabbing the soldier's bloody hand in hers. "What's your name?" she demanded. She had to repeat the question three times, squeezing his fingers to get his attention.

"J-Jett, my-my lady," he managed, finally swinging his gaze to hers.

"Jett," she repeated. "I'm Saffra. We're going to get you all fixed up, yes?"

He licked his lips, eyes still wide, darting over her face. "I... I'm not ready to die. Got...got my wife, my daughter."

"Tell me about your wife and daughter. What are their names?"

He began rambling, but she managed to distract him with questions. At long last, a healer appeared with a bag, fishing for supplies to stabilize the worst of the soldier's wounds. With a prolonged battle like this, most of the mages had exhausted their magic, leaving the healers as a last resort.

She held Jett's hand until the worst of him was taken care of, making sure the healer administered a strong dose of medicine for his pain. Then she moved to the nearest wash basin and cleaned her hands, trying to wash the stain of red from her skin. Heaps of bloodied rags lay nearby.

Closing her eyes, she took a deep, steadying breath. The influx of patients had slowed drastically. If ever she was going to steel herself, this was the moment to do it—

"My lady!" A servant appeared, agitated.

She opened her eyes to regard him. "Yes? What is it?"

"You've been requested—the queen."

"What?" She blinked, glancing around. "Claire?" A sudden worry gnawed at her. As if sensing it, Miera and Selphie appeared beside her, quickly cleaning their hands.

"Is her majesty all right?" Saffra demanded.

"Fine. Fine, milady," the servant assured them, but his expression only made her anxiety mount. "She has need of her ladies."

"Oh." Saffra quickly glanced around. If Claire was requesting her, then she had good reason to. "All her ladies?" She clarified.

"Yes, my lady."

She got Desaree and Jocelyn's attention, motioning them over before giving a few rushed instructions to the nearby servants. The five of them followed the messenger at a rushed pace through the lower corridors and out into a courtyard on the far side of the keep, large enough for a drengr to land. "Did she only just return from the battle?" Saffra asked, confused. She must have remained with Talon during the bulk of the fighting.

"Yes, milady. Just here."

They raced into the middle of the empty courtyard. Saffra blinked, looking around. "Where...? Is she here?"

"She was just here, milady. Not but five minutes ago."

"Perhaps she got called away," Desaree proposed. "Or maybe he brought us to the wrong courtyard?"

"It is the correct courtyard," a low, male voice assured them, stepping from the shadows.

"You!" she hissed, frozen in place. Her blood went from hot to cold in an instant.

The servant backed up, as if to disappear. "Thank you for your services," the cloaked figure said.

It was Kane.

Before she could blink, a blade shot from Kane's hand, sinking into the servant's throat. The servant's mouth opened, a small cough sounded, followed by the gurgle of blood. Shocked, she could do little more than gasp, watching the life drain from the servant's gaze. He crumbled in a heap. Lifeless.

Her mind spun to catch up. She whirled, sliding her dagger free, clutching it for dear life. Miera and Selphie stood shoulder to shoulder arms lifted, already chanting to weave magic.

"I wouldn't do that, were I you," Kane snarled.

"Desaree!" Saffra cried, her body freezing with icy dread. He'd taken advantage of their shock, grabbing Desaree when they'd been too busy watching the servant die. Desaree blinked back tears, whimpering as she squirmed. Kane held her by the hair, a blade to her throat. A bead of blood broke from the skin where the dagger pressed too hard.

"Release her," Saffra hissed.

Kane barked a laugh. From beneath his hood, she caught a flash of his red gaze. "Cease your chanting, *Sprites*, or I will not hesitate to kill her."

Miera and Selphie's words died on their lips. Saffra pushed Jocelyn further behind her. The dagger she clutched in her fingers trembled.

"Very good," Kane said. "Now, you will follow my orders exactly as I give them."

"We won't do anything you say," Desaree cried. Her words were firm despite the obvious fear in her voice. "You'll just have to kill me!"

"Desaree," Saffra breathed. "Quiet."

"Yes, Desaree. *Quiet*," Kane purred, dragging his shadowed nose along the shell of her ear. Des whimpered, flinching, but couldn't move away from his touch. "I give you my word. If you follow my instructions exactly as I lay them out, I will not kill any of you. Fail, and I will not hesitate to end your lives. You can join the servant there." He motioned with his head.

Saffra could only blink. This couldn't be happening. How could this be happening?! How had he gotten here?

But she knew. In the midst of the battle, with everyone distracted, Kane had slipped in. Her stomach dropped. Had this been the true intent all the while? Pretend to take the city so he could instead slip in unnoticed.

Oh, gods. They'd been completely blindsided. How had she not *seen* it?! If ever there was a time to be betrayed by her abilities, it was now. She opened her mouth to scream, to call for help, but Kane anticipated her. His blade pressed harder, earning a shocked gasp from Desaree. The blood on Desaree's neck trickled.

Saffra's stomach churned, acid clawing up her throat.

"Very good. Now, you there. Step forward." Kane looked behind Saffra. To her credit, Jocelyn did as ordered, without making a sound. Her jaw was clenched, but her shoulders were back.

Courage, saffra breathed under her breath.

"What is your name, girl?"

"J-Jocelyn."

"Jocelyn. You know who I am?" Jocelyn nodded. "Good. Then you know I will not tolerate disobedience."

Jocelyn's swallow was audible.

"I have a bottle of liquid over there by the pillar. You're going to move over and pick it up. Nothing more. Don't try to run. You run, and your little Desaree is dead. Understand?"

Jocelyn nodded.

"Good. Then do it. Now."

Snapping to action, Jocelyn rushed over to the pillar where there were two glass bottles. She picked one up, then scurried to Saffra's side.

"Excellent. It seems you can follow instructions. You've officially become the messenger." Saffra placed a hand over her stomach. Her eyes darted to the last messenger. She couldn't lose Jocelyn. She couldn't!

"You will remain here," Kane continued, speaking to Jocelyn. "The rest of us are taking a trip. Once we've left, Jocelyn, you may seek out your queen. I've got a message for her. Are you ready to hear it?"

The only bright spot of relief was that Jocelyn would be safe here. But what of the rest of them? What did Kane have planned?

Jocelyn managed a nod, eyes wide and frightened. Saffra reached for her hand, hoping the movement wouldn't be noticed. Jocelyn's fingers tangled in hers.

"You will tell your queen that I will kill the rest of you unless she comes to find me. She can use the magic water you carry. Splash it on a nearby wall. You'll see soon enough how it works. She must come *alone*, understand? If she brings *anyone* with her, especially her beloved mate, I will know."

"We're not going with you," Desaree hissed. Kane ignored her.

"Repeat your instructions, girl," Kane said. Jocelyn managed to relay everything back to him, keeping her voice steady. Saffra squeezed Jocelyn's hand, a final goodbye, then stepped forward.

"Take me instead," she said. "Leave them. Take me. I will change places with Desaree."

Kane looked ready to deny her request.

"You've wanted to kill me for months," she argued. "Wouldn't you rather your blade at my throat instead of Desaree's? I'm far more valuable."

She didn't necessarily believe that. Claire loved each of them. But this was something Kane would believe—that her seer abilities made her more important than everyone else.

"Saffra, no," Des hissed, knowing full well that Saffra's abilities were irreplaceable should anything happen. She twisted in Kane's grip. Little good it did.

"Hm. Tempting. Once we arrive at our destination, you may switch places. I'm not stupid, girl. And drop that weapon!" His words were accompanied by a flex of his hand that brought her eyes back to Desaree's neck. Any more pressure and Desaree would be dead. Her dagger clattered to the flagstones. "Good. Now go and get the other vial of water."

Bravely, she stepped forward and retrieved the bottle, looking it over.

"Splash it on the wall there—hurry up."

Uncertain, she uncorked it then did as he ordered. The water covered the wall, creating a shimmer. Then the entire wall turned translucent. A door. She gaped in wonder, her fear briefly set aside for confusion, at the sight of the rocky landscape beyond.

"Walk through it," Kane ordered. "You too, *Sprites*. I haven't forgotten about you. Now, Jocelyn, dear, you remain behind for your queen. And don't forget my instructions. She comes alone, or your friends are dead. Understand?"

Jocelyn gave a small whimper, her courage wavering, but she nodded, clutching the glass bottle in her hands.

Saffra glanced at Desaree, considering her options. There had to be another way around this. *Had to be!* But the thought of the blade at Desaree's throat, the blood already beading up around it. One swipe and her friend was dead. There was no other choice.

Steeling her nerves, she walked through the gateway. It tingled, like she'd walked through water. A moment later, she found herself in a rocky landscape, some of the formations towering above her like walls. When she looked back, she saw into the courtyard. Miera and Selphie walked over to the gateway, hand in hand, then slipped through, emerging to join her. Their faces were cold masks. She was certain they could have bested Kane, or at least put him off long enough to escape. But they hadn't. They would never betray their queen by saving themselves and leaving the others to perish.

Kane was the last to follow, hauling a whimpering Desaree at bladepoint.

"Where are we?" Saffra quickly whispered to the spriten hand-maidens. They glanced around, shaking their heads, uncertain. Or perhaps afraid that a single word would result in Desaree's death.

Kane emerged. She watched him step through dragging Desaree. The moment his feet touched the dirt, the gateway behind him began to close. She caught one final look at Jocelyn's frightened expression. Their eyes met, and held. Then the gateway wavered and disappeared, taking all hope of freeing themselves and returning to Kastali Dun with it.

CHAPTER 41

AN UNEXPECTED TWIST

Kastali Dun

Claire was shaken awake. It took long moments for her haze to clear. Longer still for the memories of what had happened to resurface. One moment she'd been destroying the Oshean fleet, the next, she was here. Her magic was depleted. She'd lost consciousness and fallen from Talon's back.

She groped for Talon's presence in her mind and found it. He was there. Steady, but preoccupied. A quick glance through his consciousness told her enough. The battle was nearing its end, the Oshean troops nearly defeated. His confidence over their assured win was the only thing that kept her from panicking on his behalf. She knew better than to distract him at a time like this.

When she blinked again, it was to find Jocelyn's frantic expression. "Joce?"

"They're gone! He took them. I'm to deliver a message, but I don't believe him—he'll just kill them. What are we going to do, Claire? You cannot do what he says! It's a trick. He's going to hurt you. They're gone. I don't..."

"Wait, wait. Slow down." A prickle of dread started at the base of her spine. She hauled herself up, pushing aside the blankets. Someone had settled her into bed.

"I came straight here, to find you."

"All right. Here, sit beside me." She placed her hand on Jocelyn's arm, inviting her to explain everything. The longer Jocelyn talked, the sicker she felt. "And you're sure he'll kill them if I bring anyone with me?"

"That is what he said." Jocelyn swallowed, her gaze distant.

"Then I will go. Hand me that bottle."

"What?!" Jocelyn cried, jumping to her feet and backing away, holding the bottle to her chest. "No. No, you can't. That is what he wants."

"If I do not go, he will kill them, Joce. I know Kane well enough to know it's the truth."

"But...but if you go, he will surely kill *you*."

Claire sighed, thinking through her options. She had the staff, when before she did not. Perhaps she was finally ready to take him on. She blinked, then remembered that the staff was tied to Talon's harness. Her king was still on the battlefield. Unless she waited for him to return with it, the staff wasn't a viable option.

She swore under her breath.

If Talon got wind of this, he'd *never* let her go. She had to act—fast. With Talon distracted, she had to slip away now or risk losing her dearest friends. She knew her mate too well. Talon's love was fierce and possessive and it warred with his upbringing as a king. To him, the lives of Desaree, Saffra, and her spriten handmaidens would not mean as much to him as her own life. As a king, he'd made many sacrifices. Their lives would be another he'd make if it meant keeping his queen safe. It was the logical choice. Even *she* could understand that.

Her stomach turned rock hard. "I cannot begin my rule with their deaths," she said. But it was more than that. Her ladies had become her home. Her life in Dragonwall would never be the same without them. "No matter what happens, if I leave them to their fate, I will regret it until the day I die. I will always wonder if I couldn't have done more. If I choose the safe path, the guilt I live with will turn to poison and it will eat away at me until I go mad and succumb."

"But... He could kill you."

"We do not know that with certainty. But if I do not go, he will surely kill them."

Jocelyn's eyes were wild with fear. "I..." Her throat bobbed.

"Kane has done enough damage, don't you think?" Jocelyn nodded. She glanced around and found her armor. Someone had removed it, along with her weapons, when they'd put her into bed. Jocelyn helped her reattach everything with trembling fingers.

"Do you have a plan?" she whispered, sounding hopeful.

"Yes. When I arrive, Kane will be focused on keeping four women under his thrall. I can imagine that will be difficult. I'm going to focus on protective magic and use that to my advantage. Now is not the time to kill him, not without my staff." She sighed, coming to a distasteful realization. "I'll probably need to bargain with him. Carefully. But bargain nonetheless."

"Desaree and Saffra will never forgive you if you trade our kingdom or your life."

"This, I know. They'd hate me for it. They will probably hate me for coming after them anyway. But..." Her throat began to ache. She swallowed down the ball of emotion rising. There had to be a way around this. She refused to accept this as the end. Refused to abandon the most important women in her life. "Tell me more about the place you saw through the portal."

Jocelyn continued to work on the buckles and clasps, securing each plate of armor as she prattled on about the rocky landscape Claire was soon to confront. Her magic wasn't at its fullest, which put her at a disadvantage, but what other choice did she have? Something about this situation gnawed at her gut. She knew with certainty—she *had* to do this. Perhaps it was intuition, or Dragonwall's gods spurring her on, or even the king tree nudging her, though she couldn't speak with it without the staff.

"If the king returns while you are gone?" Jocelyn asked.

"He will, and soon. We must hurry. When he does, you may tell him everything. I would never ask you to lie to the king, Joce. And he's *not* to get angry at you—I will be cross with him if he does. This is *my* decision, after all." Jocelyn nodded, her eyes glittering with unshed tears. "Come here." She folded Joce into her arms, squeezing her tight.

"Please don't die," Jocelyn murmured.

At this, Claire barked a laugh. "He's tried to kill me so many times, you'd think he would give up already. No. I don't intend to die."

Jocelyn stepped away, drying her eyes. She handed Claire the bottle. It was cold and heavy in her hands. The cork came free and she splashed it against a nearby wall. "You're not to follow me through," Claire warned, seeing the fierce determination giving Jocelyn away. The handmaiden's expression immediately fell. "Saffra would never forgive me if I allowed it," she added. They shared one long look before Claire turned towards the wall. A shimmering portal had appeared. This was not like the gate she'd once traveled through. She could see out to the other side, see the rocky landscape Jocelyn had described.

Taking a deep breath, she stepped through. The king's tower disappeared behind her, replaced with the landscape she had spied through the portal. The moon was not fully risen, and the air held the chill of night. Her magic was already standing at the ready. Her feet moved, silently pulling her towards the shadows cast by rocky formations scattered over the landscape—

"So wonderful of you to join us, *Your Majesty*." A voice stopped her in her tracks. Kane's voice. Shivers raced across her skin.

The enormity of what was happening finally sank in, followed by Talon's angry roar as it filled her mind. Despair, shock, confusion, even a touch of betrayal flooded her senses. Talon had discovered her disappearance. "*Claire?!*" His voice pressed into her mind.

She had no choice but to push him aside with a whispered "*I'm sorry, Talon, but I had to.*"

His distraction could cost lives. It pained her to tamp down on the part of their minds that they shared, but she had no choice. She needed to focus.

He raged against the press of her, as if beating invisible fists against her constructed barrier. It would not completely separate them. That would never happen—was impossible. But it kept the bulk of him suppressed.

She hated it—the feel of suppressing her mate. It felt wrong and awful. The pain of it brought tears to her eyes. But it was only for a little bit, until she could free her friends. Talon would forgive her, eventually.

She looked at Kane. She noticed the haunting flash of his red eyes against the dark night while taking in the scene around her. The sight of her ladies made her stomach drop. Kane had Saffra by the hair, her head wrenched back, a blade at her throat. Even in the darkness, Saffra's expression was a mix of anger and confidence. The seer had courage and she displayed it now.

Desaree was another matter. She wept in the arms of Meira and Selphie. A quick assessment showed blood dripping down her neck. As if Kane's blade had also kissed her skin, perhaps before finding a home against Saffra's. Meira and Selphie looked at Claire with unreadable expressions, but she caught enough to know they disapproved of her coming here.

She didn't care. No one would die for her today. "Let them go," she told Kane, steeling her nerves. "Your fight is with me, not with them."

"My *fight* is with Dragonwall. But as you say, perhaps a trade?"

"No, Claire!" all four women cried at once.

Selphie detangled herself from Desaree and stepped forward, turning her piercing eyes on Kane. "We will gladly die for our queen." Then she turned to Claire. "*Haan nih haan etah, Ayas Drollaya.*"

"But I must," Claire answered, without explaining why. She had nothing more to go on than a gut feeling. She had to do this, even if it seemed reckless. Whatever forces spurred her on wanted her here, in this very moment in time.

Selphie's face shuttered but she gave a nod and turned back towards Kane.

"I will trade my place for theirs, for their freedom," she told Kane. "But my offer is not without its conditions."

Kane looked as if he expected this. A flash of something crossed his gaze, making her second guess his words. As if she were playing into some master plan of his. "Very well. I will hear your conditions."

"I want your word that if I trade my place for theirs, you will release them and send them home. Furthermore, you—nor anyone or anything under your control—will kill me."

"My, my, you are careful with your words," he tsked. She simply stared at him. "And if I agree, you will submit yourself to my mercy? Content to be my...prisoner?"

"Yes. But I want your assurances set in stone. You will make an unbreakable promise to me, and I will pay close attention to how you word it. If it is not to my liking, if I have any reason to suspect your intention to kill me, the deal is off."

Kane looked thoughtful, intrigued even. She tried to pick at his expression, his body language, to see if he intended to double-cross her. All she saw was his growing eagerness. Maybe this had been his plan all along. If so, she needed a way to work around it.

"Hmm..." He pretended to think over her conditions.

Surely he knew about her mate bond with Talon. As his prisoner, it was only a matter of time before Talon came to her rescue, assuming she didn't find a way to free herself before that. Was *that* what Kane wanted—to capture her in hopes of luring Dragonwall's ruler to him?

Within the recesses of her mind, Talon had gone quiet. She could feel him there, observing. He knew her mind—saw the reasons why she'd done this.

"Very well," Kane agreed at last, though he did not release his hold of Saffra. He looked at Selphie. "There is a glass bottle behind that rock there. Go and get it. Yes, good." Selphie held it with both hands, her fingers squeezing the life out of it. "Once I have made my promise, you may splash it on the rocks and depart. It will deposit you just outside the capital."

Selphie quickly disguised her surprise, glancing down at the water stoppered within the glass.

"Just outside?" Claire asked.

Kane chuckled. "Yes, Your Majesty. I'm not that careless. I wouldn't portal them right back into your precious keep. By the time they reach the city, you and I will be long gone from here, and the portal will have dried up. Your beloved king will be unable to follow."

"How do we know you aren't *lying*?" Meira lifted her chin.

Kane sighed. "Very well, splash the water against that rock and see for yourself."

Selphie did as he said. The magical water coated the giant rock, turning to a shimmery doorway. Despite the darkness, she caught sight of a beautiful city glittering with orange light in the distance. Kastali Dun. He was telling the truth. The portal must lead to a hill a few miles from the capital. Just close enough that her ladies could make it home on two feet.

Selphie nodded, as if the portal passed her judgement.

"Your promise, Kane," Claire prompted, turning her attention back to him. The sooner she got this over with, the better.

"*Are you sure about this, my love?*" Talon's voice was distant in her mind, but he'd moved from anger to resignation. She felt his trust, burning bright. If this was her choice, then he would stand behind it. Especially now that she'd made clear she had no desire to die today.

"*I am sure.*"

Kane inhaled, looking right at her. His next words held power. She felt the magic hum around her, skittering over her skin. "I, Kane, the greatest asarlaí to have lived, make the unbreakable promise that I will release your friends and allow them to return home in exchange for you, as a willing prisoner. In return, I promise that I will cause you no harm, nor will anyone at my disposal. This, I vow."

The air shivered, then fell still.

"Does that pass your inspection, *Majesty*?"

She couldn't believe he'd done it. That he was willing to vow not to harm her.

The portal was beginning to shrink, the water drying up. Time was ticking. "Yes. It is done. Release them."

"As you wish." Kane moved and Claire screamed. In a single blink, he dragged his blade across Saffra's throat, blood spraying, before throwing her into Selphie's arms. Saffra made a strangled choking sound, her eyes wide with shock, as her hands went to the gaping wound at her neck, trying to stop the blood. A series of shocked cries muddled together—Desaree's, Meira's, and Selphie's.

"No!" Claire lunged for Saffra, readying her magic to knit her skin back together. Only, her feet didn't move, stuck to the ground. A gale rushed past her, sending all four women tumbling through the portal.

She screamed again, reaching out as it closed. The last thing she saw was Selphie and Meira lowering Saffra's limp body onto the ground. Darkness replaced the harrowing sight, until she was staring at nothing but rock.

She blinked rapidly. Hot tears streamed down her face. Somewhere in the back of her mind, she heard a drengr's anguished bellow. Talon's? Bedelth's? Oh gods! Bedelth!

She pulled at the bonds holding her in place, looking at Kane with more fury than she'd ever felt. Disbelief was a cold wave that crashed against her skin, dragging her under until she couldn't breathe. She felt her magic rising, readying to meet Kane in open battle. "You!" she hissed. But still, she couldn't move. "You broke the terms—"

"I said I'd release them and send them home. I never said I'd spare them. The seer has been problematic since the beginning. After she so graciously agreed to trade places with *sweet* Desaree, how could I resist? Anyway, I left the other three unharmed. I thought that was rather generous of me, don't you?" A thousand awful things were on the tip of her tongue, ready to burst free. "Ah, ah, ah. Don't try anything careless—no magic. Remember, my promise binds *you* as much as it binds *me*, and if you break it, you will die."

What?!

That stopped her dead in her tracks; her magic fell silent. Her chest rose and fell, trying to take in air between her sobbing gasps. *What had she done?!*

"Breathe, love. Deep breaths." Talon's words were a balm to her breaking heart, but they weren't enough. He should have been raging at her. Furious. Filled with blame. Instead, he was merely a steady press of comfort. Comfort she no longer deserved after what she'd just done.

"Come, let us go."

"I'm not going *anywhere* with you," she spat. "Not after what you did."

"But you will, because my promise said *willing* prisoner. Therefore, you must be willing. Use of magic, any act against me while you are my prisoner, makes you *un*willing. You do know how the promise works, don't you?" His grin made her stomach drop. Even in the darkness, the chilling expression turned her bowels watery. She took a deep breath, as Talon had said to do.

"You are Dragonwall's queen," he reminded her. She wanted him to yell at her. She wanted his anger, not his encouragement. Why wasn't he cursing her for doing this? For putting herself in this situation—

"Shall we?" Kane asked, motioning her forward.

She lifted her chin and took a single step. Then another. And another. Each one got easier. Kane led her through the rocky formation as she tried to calculate his next move. Tried to make sense of what had happened. Tried to anticipate a way to free herself. To find a way around the promise. She didn't want to unknowingly kill herself by defying the terms.

"The terms spoke nothing of me," Talon whispered in her mind. *"I can free you without violating them."*

But wasn't that what Kane wanted? To lure Talon to him? To pit them against each other.

She clenched her jaw, keeping her chin held high.

"Keep moving, *Your Majesty*," Kane sneered, falling into place beside her. The proximity of him made her sick. She wanted distance between them, but the path didn't allow it.

"You're taking me back to Shadowkeep," she said at last. It's where he'd tried to take her that day in the forest. To the farthest reaches of Dragonwall. Though, she wondered why he hadn't simply summoned another portal to do so. Instead, he led her onward.

She glanced around at the rocky formations, trying to find—

Two pillars came into view. She stopped short, lips parted. The realization had a split second to form, setting the hairs on the back of her neck on end. She recognized the glyphs on the pillars. She opened her mouth—

The sound of crushed glass breaking just above her head was immediately followed by the wet feeling of liquid sloshing down over her hair, dripping along her scalp. She spun to face Kane as he dropped his arm, flinging away the remnants of glass fragments.

"*Claire, no!*" An anguished voice cried out.

She blinked. A cold, clawing feeling spread through her mind, throwing her into a confused haze. Her blinking turned more rapid, as if trying to clear away a confusing image. Her thoughts faltered. She attempted to piece the next several moments together. "What did you—?"

"Consider your time as my prisoner fulfilled, *Your Majesty*."

Before she could process his words, he placed his palms against her back and gave a huge shove. She stumbled forwards, tripping over a loose rock, flying face first, falling...

The last thing she caught sight of were the pillars at her sides before everything went black. Her stomach lurched, lifting nausea into her throat. Acid burned the back of her tongue—

There was nothing.

Then the ground came up to meet her, blackness replaced with glaring sunlight. She face-planted in a bed of soft grass. She groaned and flopped over, as if waking from a deep and strange dream. She blinked up at the crystalline blue sky, wincing at the brightness. An airplane passed high overhead, its faint contrails lining the path behind it. Her brows pulled together into a scowl.

For long moments, she lay there sprawled in the grass. Her mind tripped and stumbled. Try as she might, she couldn't seem to piece together her thoughts. Perhaps only a few moments passed, or perhaps it was several hours.

Her ears began to ring as a harsh voice shouted something in the distance. She remained motionless. The voice spoke again, growing closer.

She moved to sit on her heels. A rolling green landscape greeted her. Beautiful pastoral hills spread out around her, overlooking a small town. In the far distance she could just make out the outline of a large city. Her frown deepened.

More shouting. She turned. The person coming towards her was a middle-aged man in a floppy hat holding a staff. She blinked at the sight of the staff. Something tugged at the back of her mind, but the thought was there and gone. He marched up the hill towards her.

How...*strange*.

He was dressed in overalls and looked irritated. She shook her head, attempting to straighten her thoughts, listening to his question again. The words meant nothing to her, were unintelligible. Then she realized why. He was speaking French. That's why she hadn't understood him initially.

"I'm sorry, but I... I can't understand you," she managed, scowling.

Where was she?

He came to a stop, looming over her, this time repeating his question in heavily accented English. It took a moment for her to sift through the words.

"Oh. You want to know what I'm doing here?" she repeated, only just now glancing down at herself. Her lips parted. "What the...?" She ran a hand over the metal on her arms. Metal like *armor*.

"*Oui,*" the man said in response to her question.

"I'm sorry, but, where is *here*, exactly?"

His head tilted, like the question was preposterous. And in a way, it was. She, too, didn't really know why she was asking it.

"Ten kilometers outside of Rennes," he answered in accented English.

"Rennes..." Her eyes darted over the landscape again. He continued speaking. This was his property. A *private* property. Trespassers weren't permitted. She would need to leave, or he would be forced to report her to the authorities.

She heard his words but hardly processed them.

Rennes was in France. Hence, the French accent, and the fact he'd been speaking French. But...was this some sort of dream?

She glanced down at herself again, and noticed a tiny bit of blue on her skin, peeping from beneath the sleeves of her shirt. She pulled her sleeves back as far as the metal plated armor permitted, and rubbed at the marking. It didn't disappear.

Had she been drugged? Gotten a tattoo while she was under the influence? Passed out somewhere only to awake without memory of it? Some drugs did that, didn't they? Had someone slipped something into her drink?

"I don't..." She trailed off. Quickly, she catalogued everything she knew here at this moment. She was dressed like she'd dropped right out of a book. There were strange blue markings on her skin. She was sitting in a field in rural France, just outside one of its biggest cities.

But...none of this made any sense.

She wracked her brain, clawing at her memory. Something at the corner of her mind flickered, there and gone as she tried to make sense of this bizarre situation. Why wasn't she at home, watching over the farm for her parents? What would they do when they realized she was not there?

She didn't remember leaving the house. Didn't remember getting on a plane to France. Didn't even remember traipsing out into the middle of this field.

That was the problem. When she dug deep enough, her last memories were of her parents leaving for Florida and her agreement to watch the farm in their absence. Instead she was here, and for the life of her, she couldn't explain why.

CHAPTER 42
A CRAFTY DISGUISE

Kastali Dun

Reyr had never heard a roar quite like Talon's. He hoped to never hear it again. Even now, it echoed in his mind, haunting his memory. His heavy heart was broken in half, though not as badly as Talon's.

He stood near Talon's fireplace, hand braced on the mantle, gazing into the flames. The others sat around the room—everyone but Saffra and Bedelth.

He still couldn't believe what the sprites had done for the seer. What Meira and Selphie had managed in a matter of seconds. They'd acted quickly. The moment they'd fallen through the portal, they'd used their magic, singing healing into her wound, knitting the skin back together as the final dregs of her lifeblood drained away. Saffra wasn't human. If she had been, they'd have failed. Thank the gods for her magic.

No, thank the gods for *the sprites*.

Bedelth had fallen to his knees before them, weeping. He'd promised them a life vow in exchange for saving Saffra's life. Such a thing wasn't done lightly. Now her mate was indebted to them. A small price to pay.

422

Bedelth was with her now, watching over her in her chambers. Her stubborn mate refused to leave her side. No one faulted him for it.

The rest of them were here, recovering from their shock like a lost flock of sheep. The king looked like an empty shell of himself. As if Claire had left their world and taken him with her. His face was blank, his eyes glassy and empty. Resigned.

Talon had tried to go after her in those initial moments. He had transformed and leapt into the sky. It had taken four of them to subdue him, to keep him from rushing off so recklessly.

That was exactly what Kane wanted.

Reyr glanced around the room. Every face was bleak. Many expressions still held fragments of disbelief. It felt like a dream. He half expected Claire to walk through the tower door and ask them why they all looked like someone died.

But she wouldn't. She couldn't. She was...*gone*.

Even little Batty knew something was wrong. He'd crawled into Talon's lap and mewed up at the king with sad eyes. A tiny little thing pleading with a beast of a man. Talon's large palm rested on Batty's small body, absently stroking his fur. It was the only sign that there was still some part of the king lurking within.

Their discussion had come in fits and starts. Broken segments that didn't quite fit together.

When he did speak, Talon continued insisting that he fly halfway across the kingdom to the gate Kane had used in Celenore. It would take nearly two days to get there, leaving the king exposed. And yet, every moment they waited, Claire was at risk. Who knew *what* danger she would find, getting dropped into her old world?

Reyr knew—he'd *been* in that world. "She will do better than you give her credit for," he had argued. "She knows how to navigate her world far better than you, my king."

"What of the gate beneath the keep," Feowen said, finally speaking. He'd been unusually quiet. Likewise, his sister beside him. Even Taylynn looked utterly shocked. This had not been an expected turn of events. It turned out the all knowing sprite princess wasn't entirely...all knowing.

"What of it?" Verath snapped. He, too, had a short temper. Desaree was cradled in his lap. It was a shock to see such a composed drengr who wouldn't normally show affection publicly fawning over the woman he loved. He'd let out a dangerous growl upon seeing the blood marring Desaree's neck. He hadn't calmed down until she'd reassured him that she was unharmed.

"*Well*," Feowen said. "The gate beneath the keep is not a three day flight away."

"It's broken," Reyr reminded him.

"By Isabella, yes. She used some kind of sprite magic to break it. I've heard the story. But...what if it could be...restored?"

Reyr growled. "Don't give him any ideas, *Prince*."

"So, what?" Feowen crossed his arms, his expression turning dangerous. Sometimes it was easy to forget that he was thousands of years old. Immortal. "You're just going to leave my cousin in her world? You heard what the king said. Kane did something to her. Used some kind of potion on her. We need to go to her. *She. Is. Our. Queen.*"

Reyr flinched. As if he needed reminding. How did one balance an entire kingdom's safety against a single woman? Especially a woman who had become that kingdom's beating heart?

"There is no *we*," Talon said, speaking again. Some of the awareness in his gaze returned. "I will go and get *my* queen." The proprietary use of that word was not lost on them. Talon was volatile. He needed to express his possessive nature in whatever way he could, claiming Claire for himself above all.

Everyone broke into protests again. "But, leaving the kingdom is exactly what Kane wants," they argued. "A kingdom without its king is vulnerable. Kane will sweep in and plant himself on the throne—"

"We need a plan." The voice that spoke from the doorway was filled with calm authority. Silence fell. They turned to find Saffra looking worse for wear. Bedelth stood behind her, frowning, as if this was the *last* place he wanted her. He would have to learn what it meant to be wrapped around his mate's finger.

A pang of sadness tightened Reyr's chest. He'd learned that lesson once. Now he would be alone...always alone—

"Saffra!" Desaree squirmed free of Verath's lap. Jocelyn also rushed over, taking Saffra's hand in hers. Their faces brightened.

"I think Claire knew something was going to happen," Saffra said to the room. "Before the battle, she was acting odd. Perhaps she didn't anticipate this, but she did have an inkling, an intuition. I made her a promise, to keep a level head and be the glue that keeps this group together should anything happen. Why do you think she made me promise that, if she thought we'd all be fine?"

Silence filled the room.

"As I said,"—Saffra lifted her chin—"we need a plan."

"The plan," Talon growled, his voice rough and insistent, "is that I'm going to find her."

"That settles it," Feowen announced, as if he'd been waiting for the right moment to back the king. "Talon will go and rescue his mate, and the rest of us will hold the kingdom together in his absence."

"And how do you propose we do that when news breaks that the king is no longer here to protect his kingdom?" Now free to stand, Verath was on his feet, his face flushed.

"It's simple," Taylynn said. "We don't allow the world to find out."

"Talon holds court almost daily," Reyr said, keeping his voice calm. "Not to mention the vast numbers of meetings with prominent court individuals and his lower council. He could be gone for days, months? We don't know. And what do we do in the meantime? You forget, Princess, that there is a kingdom to run."

"No, Lord Reyr, you forget the bounds of spriten magic." Taylynn glared at Reyr. A chuckle sounded behind him. Koldis.

"Fine. What do *you* propose?" His words came out harsher than intended. The result was a low growl, followed by the pressure of a hand as Koldis found his shoulder and squeezed. It was both a warning and a restraint. Reyr sighed, then glanced at his brother. "Forgive me, I am at the end of my tether."

"It is my mate to whom you should seek forgiveness."

"She started it," he grumbled, caring little for how childish the argument sounded. This entire situation had all of them acting out of character. No wonder Claire had made Saffra promise to be the glue holding them together. They were all about to fall apart.

"*You*, Lord Reyr, will act as king in Talon's absence," Taylynn announced. He huffed, ready to shoot down the absurdity of the argument. Taylynn beat him to it. "Our magic will transform your appearance. A guise, if you will. We can place the deception over you like a shroud. No one, not even the drengr, will know otherwise. Well, they might suspect, should you be a poor actor. But surely you are willing to play the part if it means your king will be free to rescue his queen?"

She lifted a challenging eyebrow.

His mouth opened and closed. Speechless. She'd rendered him speechless.

Koldis's hand, which still rested on his shoulder, squeezed then disappeared. Koldis was mates with the women. He knew better than the rest of them how she could be.

"But...but..." Reyr tried to sputter his way through a refusal. "Talon will need a guide in Claire's world. I've already been. I can help him navigate the absurdities there." Two snorts sounded—Jovari's and Koldis's.

"You forget, brother, that we were there, too." Jovari stepped forward. "We know—"

"Jovari will be coming with me." Talon's voice silenced the room. Everyone turned to the king, who was now standing, Batty warming his place in the armchair. "Jovari is mateless and the obvious choice. Koldis, your mate is here. I will not put a world barrier between the two of you. And Reyr, I need you here running my kingdom. You are the one I trust for this."

Koldis and Taylynn shared a glance.

Talon turned towards Jovari. "Are you willing to come with me?"

"Need you even ask?" Jovari blinked at Talon as if he'd grown a second head. "I am your *shield*. I am at your command, my king. I go where you need me."

Talon blew out a breath, his shoulders dropping from their tense position.

"Good, it is settled then." Taylynn's face brightened. "Let us work out the details. My brother, who is skilled at reversing magic, will take a look at the gate beneath the keep. I, in the meantime, will work with the rest of Claire's guards to devise a fitting disguise for Lord Reyr. I am afraid, Your Majesty, we will need you for the process. Think of it like posing for a painting."

Talon snorted. "I don't pose for paintings."

"No? Then you will not be adding your painting to the *Hall of Kings* when your mate returns?" Taylynn knew just the right thing to say. A flush crept up Talon's cheeks. He muttered something that none of them could hear, but gave her a curt nod.

The next several days both crept and flew by. Talon would have left the moment Claire disappeared, if given the choice. Instead, they used the time to enact their plan. Feowen spent most of his days beneath the keep, studying the magic that the first queen of Dragonwall had used to break the gate. In the meantime, Reyr was hidden away with Talon to undergo his transformation. Because the guise was implemented in layers, he could not leave the king's tower. He was forced to remain in the lower levels, Claire's levels, away from the servants. Only their immediate circle could know of this. Otherwise word might get out, ruining all they had worked for.

First his golden hair changed, from orderly locks to messy and dark. Then his frame was enlarged. While all drengr were larger than humans, Talon was one of the largest of their kind. His shoulders were slightly broader than Reyr's. His muscles, slightly bulkier. Then came the most difficult part. Talon's scars. It had taken three days to cover his body in the same, identical markings.

Finally, his voice and eyes. That was the moment he found himself looking in the mirror, gasping at what he saw. There was nothing of Reyr left in his appearance. He was an exact replica of his king.

"While I used my own magic to construct the guise, it will feed from your drengr magic to maintain it," Taylynn explained. "Be careful of how much magic you use. Do not let yourself be weakened. Otherwise, maintaining the guise will become impossible."

It was done.

He didn't need coaching on how to behave or act. He knew all of Talon's tells. But he did spend time practicing, forcing himself to act in a way that wasn't natural for his body.

It wasn't until Feowen appeared, announcing that he had found a way to reverse Isabella's magic, to rebuild the gate and save Talon from flying to Celenore, that the enormity of their plan came crashing down upon him. The realness of it. The pressure.

"How do you do it?" he managed to ask Talon, during one of the rare moments they found themselves alone. They stood side by side on a lower balcony in the darkness, looking out over the sea. Had anyone seen them, they'd have died with fright. Two of King Talon was far more frightening than one.

"I'm almost glad you get to do this," Talon said. He'd been in a better mood since the day of Claire's disappearance. Having a plan and a goal to work towards had instilled a measure of hope in their king. "Now you get to suffer as I do. You get to see exactly what it's like. If I'd have known it was this easy, I'd have begged the sprite princess to do this earlier. Who knows, maybe when I get back, I'll bribe her to keep the disguise in place. Or maybe, I just won't come back. I'll slip into Claire's world—"

"Don't you dare finish that thought," Reyr said, whirling on him. "You are needed here, and I am but a poor substitute."

Talon cracked a small smile, the only one he'd seen in days. Before Claire, his king had never smiled. He'd grown fond of the changes she'd wrought in him. "You are better than you think, Reyr."

Talon's faith meant a great deal.

They stood side by side, soaking up each other's company, knowing this was the last night they'd be together for a while.

The following morning wasn't easy. Feowen managed to repair the gate, but none of them was willing to test it out. Talon insisted he didn't want anyone going through besides himself and Jovari. They'd face whatever world they found together, without the risk of any others. "And don't you dare follow me. Any of you. No matter how long I am gone. You are needed here."

Orders were given, choked goodbyes, promises to keep in the king's absence. None of them wanted to consider what might happen if he never returned. Especially not Reyr, who would be stuck ruling for the remainder of Talon's reign.

The important thing was fooling Kane. The sorcerer needed to believe he'd successfully sent the queen away, and that the king had not followed. It was genius, really, fixing the gate beneath the keep. It was unlikely that Kane knew of it. He'd have the capital watched, and was likely waiting to see the king depart north to find his queen.

The sorcerer would be disappointed on that matter.

Talon spoke to each of them, saving Reyr for last. They'd said all they needed to in the past few days, sitting together, undergoing Reyr's transformation. It didn't stop Reyr's heart from seizing up, fear and worry taking hold. He hated goodbyes. He'd lost so many loved ones. Would he lose Talon, too?

No. He couldn't bear to think of it.

Everyone watched in strange fascination as two identical kings clasped forearms and then hugged. Talon clapped him on the back. "Do not forget—you are me now. Big shoes to fill, yes? But you will do brilliantly. I wouldn't allow this plan otherwise." Reyr's throat closed up. He blinked, then nodded.

Jovari said a similar goodbye to each of them.

Everyone stepped back on the rocky outcropping in the cave that had offered them so much discovery, wonder, and possibility over the past months. They stood together as Talon and Jovari stepped up to the gate. Reyr suppressed a shudder, remembering a time when he'd faced a gate just like this to search for Cyrus. Time, it seemed, loved to come full circle.

He pushed the thought away.

"Shall we?" Talon turned towards Jovari. "How about together?"

Jovari's throat bobbed, but then he nodded. Talon hooked a brotherly arm around Jovari's neck, then guided them forward. Every breath in the cave was held as every eye watched in unison. The king of Dragonwall, paired with one of his trusted shields, walked forward between the two pillars of black stone, then disappeared from Dragonwall completely.

CHAPTER 43
UNCONDITIONAL LOVE

Kastali Dun

Bedelth followed Saffra out of her chambers, stopping short at the sight of his parents. Kadeen and Seishi were striding down the corridor, directly towards him. A muffled curse fell from his lips. Saffra let out a quiet, "*Oh.*"

His heart kicked up as it always did at the sight of his parents, in nervous anticipation.

"We were just coming to find you," his mother said, eyes darting between them and Saffra's door. A suspicious confusion clouded her gaze, there and gone. "You look well—both of you." She gave a differential bow to Saffra and added, "My lady."

His father did the same.

Kadeen and Seishi had been there for the battle, choosing to fight among the fort's auxiliary wings. The kingdom had lost many lives that day; he should have been more grateful that his parents were counted among the living. He hadn't seen much of them in the days following, too preoccupied with Saffra's recovery. The circumstances following the battle, like Claire's disappearance and Saffra's near-death experience, had been kept within their inner circle.

"It's wonderful to see you both," Saffra said, recovering the quickest. "With everything that has happened, it has been hard to find time for simple things, like visiting loved ones. I'm sure you are eager to catch up with your son." Saffra turned to Bedelth. "Shall I go—?"

"No." He stopped her, then swallowed. "Actually, there was something I wanted to tell them. Will you stay with me?" And then, before he thought better of it, he reached for her hand. His mother frowned at the gesture, more of that confused suspicion entering her expression, while his father took a step back.

"Of course." Saffra's features softened. She seemed to realize what he was doing. She could have refused, or changed the topic. They'd only just begun to explore the idea of accepting their mate bond—Saffra, specifically.

"What is going on?" his mother asked, her eyes pinned on their joined hands.

"We're mates." The words landed like a blow. His mother blinked.

His father sucked in a sharp gasp. "Impossible."

"No. I assure you, Father, it is quite possible, and quite true in our case."

"Tell our son that this cannot be," his mother said, looking at Saffra as if she expected the seer to be the sensible one.

Saffra stiffened. "I will do no such thing. Furthermore, I am appalled that your first reaction is denial and refusal when something so monumental should make you happy." Never mind that those had been Saffra's two key emotions when they'd discovered the bond. He'd never in a million years voice *that* observation. She was defending him. It left a mess of warm emotions tangled in his chest. "You are his parents," she continued. "You claim to love him. But now I am left wondering if that's true."

His mother's intake was a shocked hiss. The female rider from Fort Lin would never disrespect someone in Saffra's position. "Of course we love him, my lady. We only want the best for him. As his mate, I would think you would understand this."

"I do, quite well in fact. I want what is best for him." As she said these words, Saffra squeezed his hand and turned her soft brown eyes on him. His chest tightened, a mix of pleasure and pain. The way she looked at him—he'd never wanted her more badly than he did in this very moment. "As far as I'm concerned," Saffra continued, turning back to his parents, "his happiness *is* what's best for him. I can give him that much, at the least."

"Son, this is... This will... This will *ruin* you."

"How so, Father?" He was glad for the quiet authority in his voice. The question was spoken exactly the way his king would ask it.

Kadeen's mouth opened several times before he said, "You are a shield. You cannot take a mate. Your oath is for life. The law—"

"The king has already made plans to amend the law. The announcement has not yet been made. It will be. Soon. We will wait to seal our bond until then. Regardless, this is my choice, and my king has already given his blessing."

His mother and father blinked at him, utter disbelief marring their features. He sighed, disappointed in himself, having hoped that perhaps they might take this in stride, support him in his decision. It wasn't the *only* thing he felt, though. There was pride, too, at what he'd done. All his life he'd feared his parents' judgement, feared disappointing them. Now he cared little for what they thought of him.

This was their problem, not his. Making that realization and coming to terms with it was freeing. A weight lifted from his shoulders. He was lighter than he'd felt in ages.

"The king should not change the law so rashly," Kadeen growled. "They have been in place for tens of thousands of years, since the beginning of this monarchy—"

"Are you questioning our king's decision?" Saffra's voice was harder, colder than Bedelth had ever heard it. Even *he* was tempted to take a step back from her. Her firm hold on his hand kept him from moving.

"No. No, of course not, my lady. We would never do such a

dishonorable thing," his mother amended, saving his father from further disgrace. She shot her mate a look that silenced any more protests over the king's decision. "Our king has the authority to amend laws as he sees fit, with the guidance of his councils. We respect the law, and its outcome."

"Yet, you will not approve of your son taking a mate. Because despite the changing law, you are still for the old ways." Saffra scoffed.

His heart burst wide open. He felt *so much* for this woman. "It's all right," he said, leaning down to murmur in her ear. "Allow them their opinions." His mate gave a subtle nod and let the matter drop. "I suppose you will be taking your leave, then?" he said to his parents, giving them an out. There was no point in lingering over such a tense subject.

His father seemed relieved at the topic change. "Yes, we depart later this afternoon."

"Good. We bid you a safe journey home." It was the stiffest, most emotionless goodbye he'd ever given. All he could do was tug on Saffra's hand and move away from his parents as quickly as possible. He left them sputtering in his wake.

Perhaps later he'd feel bad that it hadn't been more heartfelt. No hugs. No kisses to his mother's cheeks. There was a tiny bit of guilt that this could be the last time he saw them. But, no. He needed to set boundaries.

If they wouldn't support him on this, they could stew on their archaic beliefs. He couldn't force them to accept his mate, accept his decision, but he did not need to keep them close, allowing them to make him feel guilty for his choices. Saffra walked silently beside him all the way to King Talon's tower, then up the winding steps until they emerged on the top of the keep, in the queen's garden.

The fresh air was an immediate balm.

Everyone in their inner circle had taken to using the place for solitude over the past week. It was a place to feel connected to the rulers now missing from their kingdom. A reminder of what they still fought for. But also simply a place of peace.

"Are you all right?" Saffra asked after they'd taken a seat on one of the benches spanning the parapet, looking into the depths of the garden. His hand was still clenched in hers. She pulled both their hands into her lap. He glanced down, noting how small hers was compared to his.

"I am—or, I will be. It feels good. I never thought it would."

"To stand up for yourself?"

"Yes." He grunted in acknowledgment at the absurdity of the matter. That he'd failed to do this for himself before. But standing up for oneself wasn't always easy, especially when it was to those whom you held in high esteem. Those you cared about most. That made him feel all the more victorious.

"I'm glad you did it," Saffra said. "That was brave, Bedelth. I'm proud of you."

His head whipped towards her. "You are?"

"I am." A small smile spread across her lips. "Very proud. And not just of your decision to stand up to your parents, but of *you*, in general. You are truly something." He wanted to freeze this moment—the image of her—in his mind. Forever. She wore a smile that was just for him—offering it to him because of what he'd done.

"You stood up for me too, you know."

"I did, didn't I?" Her smile grew. "I suppose that's what mates do."

Delirious happiness exploded in his chest. Before he could stop himself, he was dragging her into his lap, kissing her. Her lips were soft. She tasted of chamomile, the many cups of tea he'd been insisting she drink to recover from her ordeal. Her tongue brushed his and he groaned. Gods, this woman! This woman was everything to him. How had he ever been selfless—careless?—enough to let her be anything but?

She tugged at his lower lip with her teeth. The muscles in his gut clenched tight. He wanted her—badly. But he would not dishonor his oath. He would not claim their mate bond before the law was amended. She deserved that.

"How did Talon do it?" he breathed against her lips.

"Do what?" She pulled back to look at him, a small frown

pulling her brows together. His face was framed in her hands, cheeks warm beneath her palms. His own hands circled her waist tightly, like he never intended to release her.

"Knowing Claire was his mate, how did he go months without sealing their bond? How did he stay sane?"

"Sane?!" A laugh burst from her lips. They both smiled at that. "If you think Talon is sane…"

"Fair point." He nuzzled her hair. The moment turned serious. Because she was his mate, he voiced his insecurities. But only for her. "I'm worried about him. Do you think he's all right, where he's gone?"

There was a long hesitation. "I hope so. King Talon will do whatever necessary to get his queen—*our* queen—back. Besides, maybe this will be good for him."

"How so?"

"Well, can you imagine what it's going to be like for our king experiencing his mate's world? Oh, gods. I bet he'll have to meet her parents, do you think?" A manic laugh fell from her lips. "He's going to be squirming in his boots, trying to navigate a world where he isn't king. Poor thing. I do feel a little sorry for him. There will be no bossing people around. No barking orders. Except to Jovari."

Bedelth growled, the image of her words forming nebulously in his mind. "Maybe you're right. It's always good for a king to be humbled once in a while."

"I cannot wait to hear of their adventures. They'll be all right, I think. They have to be."

"Have you seen something?" He held his breath, hoping she had. Anything to lessen the needles of anxiety everyone was feeling.

"No, no visions. But think about it. Claire is our chosen one. The king tree shares a special relationship with her. Do you think, in all its infinite wisdom, she would have been selected, brought into our world by the strangest circumstances, a woman of two bloods, who faced Kane multiple times, faced many other trials too, only to go and get killed back in her own world?"

It was a valid point.

"No. I've learned enough to know everything happens for a reason. If she's there, it's because she needs to be there. If our king is there, it's because he also needs to be there. I just wish we could all be there with them on their next, grand adventure."

He sighed, a bit of relief welling up inside him. "You're right. Of course."

"I'm always right." She turned to look at him, eyes dancing. "You'd better get used to it, if you are truly serious about making me your mate."

"Gods, woman. If you accept our mate bond, you can be right about everything for the rest of our lives, even when you're not." His lips twitched and her smile widened. "It's a small price to pay for having you."

His arms tightened. He was suddenly reminded of how close he'd come to losing her. He didn't want to think of what he might have done. How he might have broken.

"Let's go flying," Saffra declared, sensing his mood and knowing exactly how to improve it. "That always makes things better."

"Right on all counts." He chuckled. "There? See? Already I'm telling you how right you are—again."

"Oh, stop." She nuzzled into him, then nipped at his jaw before planting a chaste kiss to his lips and hopping off his lap. He watched her for a moment, this incredible creature that was his, and could only bask in her glow. "Well?"

"All right, all right," he grumbled. "I'm coming."

He transformed, careful not to smash any of the precious flowerbeds. Saffra stepped forward, and for the first time, pressed her bare hand willingly against his scales. A shudder went through him at her touch, as their minds melded. Together, they viewed the rolling hills that bordered their homeland, the deserts of Austar just visible on the horizon.

"*Home*," Saffra whispered in his mind. "*That's what you've always felt like to me*," she admitted.

A fierce pride welled up inside him. *"I am honored to be the place you call home."*

Saffra was grinning as she climbed up to the divot between his neck and wing joints, settling in. Their bodies remained in contact, their minds connected. Shivery excitement raced through him. *"May I?"* he couldn't help but ask.

"Yes."

That single word changed everything between them. He delved into her mind as she did the same. The landscape of their homeland shifted as they sifted through thoughts and memories. He saw her younger years, her family, the small cottage they occupied in the hills south of the Austar Gate. He saw the nerves she carried when first coming to the capital, the pressure of her new position. There was fear, too, so much fear over her visions. But it was mitigated with happy memories as she settled in and learned archery. The memories with Commander Daxton were tinged with sadness. He tried not to look too deeply at those, for fear of the jealousy he'd feel. And then he came to her latest memories. He saw himself the way she saw him, and that only increased his hunger for her.

In a matter of seconds, they'd devoured years, but that was nothing compared to the years of new memories they'd make.

He shifted, and launched into the sky. As he flew, Saffra continued to sift through his thoughts and memories. After all, he had several lifetimes worth. He relished in the closeness of her body and the comfort of her mind.

With the kingdom in chaos, he should have been anxious. Here in this moment, he felt only hope and excitement. Having Saffra made everything less frightening. Whatever they faced, they would face together, leaning on each other. Her love would never be conditional. He'd never need to perform the best, or be the best, to earn it. He could simply be himself, and that would always be enough.

~+~+~+~+~+

The Dragonwall Series continues in book 6: Jovari the Blue

If you enjoyed this book, please consider supporting me by leaving a review or rating on Amazon and Goodreads. These help get my book noticed which is important for indie authors like me.

IF YOU WOULD LIKE to stay up to date with book news, new releases, spoilers, and bonus content, sign up for my newsletter mailing list at https://www.authormelissamitchell.com/newslettersignup

ABOUT THE AUTHOR

Melissa Mitchell is a fantasy romance author and creator of the seven-book *Dragonwall* series. Her love of fantasy began with *The Dragonriders of Pern*, and she now writes stories full of dragons, magic, hidden royalty, and slow-burn romance. She holds a PhD in physics and lives in Atlanta, Georgia with her husband, a husky, and four very spoiled bunnies. When she's not writing, she enjoys baking cookies, bullet journaling, and figure skating—usually while plotting her next book.

Visit her online at: authormelissamitchell.com

Also by Melissa Mitchell

The Arcane Artifacts

Bound by the Blood Ruby

The Dragonwall Series

Talon the Black

Reyr the Gold

Verath the Red

Koldis the Green

Bedelth the Orange

Jovari the Blue

Dallin the Violet

The Lady Witch Series

Wielder's Prize

Wielder's Bond

Wielder's Might

Witch's Ruin

Witch's Heart

Witch's Crown

Royals of Dragonwall Series

For the Crown

Stand Alone Titles

Blood and Ballet